# "Thank ye, lass."

He brought her knuckles to his lips for a kiss that made her belly flip. She'd already gone weak and willing, so when he hauled her into his arms, she didn't protest.

"How is it," he asked heavily against her mouth while he bent her slightly over the crook of his arm, his fingers stroking her temple, her cheek, "that ye're able to banish m' troubles with a wave of yer delicate fingers?"

She shook in his arms, her gaze warm and yielding on his, hungry and eager for his kiss.

They met somewhere between need and desire, touching, molding, each tasting the passion in the other. Fire. He ignited it in her. He held her close and confidently, making her feel safe in his strong arms yet again. He kissed as if he'd been doing it for years, his lips soft and plump. She surrendered her mouth to his, clutching his plaid in both hands as he crushed her in his embrace. She held on while his tongue swept through the deepest corners of her mouth, while his hands moved over her back, her buttocks, drawing her closer.

"The Scottish highlands and a pirate ship provide the colorful setting for this well-written, exciting, and action-packed romance." —*RT Book Reviews*

"Vivid...Quinn's steamy and well-constructed romance will appeal to fans and newcomers alike." —*Publishers Weekly*

## The Seduction of Miss Amelia Bell

"Plenty of passion, romance, and adventure...one of the best books I've read in a long time...a captivating story from beginning to end." —NightOwlReviews.com

"A witty, sensual historical tale that will keep you glued to the pages...This beautifully written, fast-paced tale is a true delight." —RomanceJunkiesReviews.com

## Conquered by a Highlander

"Rich, evocative historical detail and enthralling characters fill the pages of this fast-paced tale." —*Publishers Weekly* (starred review)

"What a conclusion to this fast-paced, adventure-filled story with characters that jump off the page and will capture your heart." —MyBookAddictionReviews.com

## Tamed by a Highlander

"Top Pick! Quinn's talents for weaving history with a sexy and seductive romance are showcased in her latest Highlander series book. This fast-paced tale of political intrigue populated by sensual characters with deeply rooted senses of honor and loyalty is spellbinding...Top-notch Highland romance!" —*RT Book Reviews*

# A Highlander's
# Christmas Kiss

Also by Paula Quinn

# A Highlander's Christmas Kiss

## PAULA QUINN

FOREVER

NEW YORK   BOSTON

Copyright © 2016 by Paula Quinn
Excerpt from the next MacGregors: Highland Heirs novel copyright © 2016 by Paula Quinn

Cover design by Claire Brown
Illustration by Alan Ayers
Cover copyright © 2016 by Hachette Book Group, Inc.

Forever
Hachette Book Group
1290 Avenue of the Americas, New York, NY 10104
forever-romance.com
twitter.com/foreverromance

First Edition: September 2016

Forever is an imprint of Grand Central Publishing. The Forever name and logo are trademarks of Hachette Book Group, Inc.

The publisher is not responsible for websites (or their content) that are not owned by the publisher.

The Hachette Speakers Bureau provides a wide range of authors for speaking events. To find out more, go to www.hachettespeakersbureau.com or call (866) 376-6591.

ISBN 978-1-4555-3530-9 (mass market), 978-1-4555-3528-6 (ebook)

Printed in the United States of America

OPM

10  9  8  7  6  5  4  3  2  1

*For Kim. Fly free with laughter beneath your wings.*

# MacGregor/Grant
## Family Tree

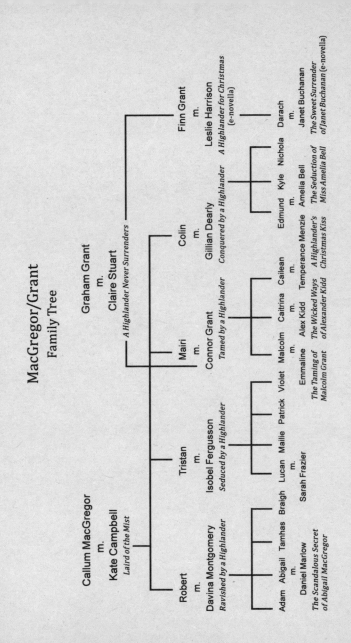

Callum MacGregor
m.
**Kate Campbell**
*Laird of the Mist*

Graham Grant
m.
Claire Stuart
*A Highlander Never Surrenders*

Robert
m.
Davina Montgomery
*Ravished by a Highlander*

Tristan
m.
Isobel Fergusson
*Seduced by a Highlander*

Mairi
m.
Connor Grant
*Tamed by a Highlander*

Colin
m.
Gillian Dearly
*Conquered by a Highlander*

Finn Grant
m.
Leslie Harrison
*A Highlander for Christmas (e-novella)*

Adam  Abigail  Tamhas  Braigh
m.
Daniel Marlow
*The Scandalous Secret of Abigail MacGregor*

Lucan  Mailie  Patrick  Violet
m.
Sarah Frazier

Emmaline  Malcolm  Caitrina  Cailean
m.
Alex Kidd
*The Wicked Ways of Alexander Kidd*
m.
Temperance Menzie
*A Highlander's Christmas Kiss*
*The Taming of Malcolm Grant*

Edmund  Kyle  Nichola
m.
Amelia Bell
*The Seduction of Miss Amelia Bell*

Darach
m.
Janet Buchanan
*The Sweet Surrender of Janet Buchanan (e-novella)*

✣

# Chapter One

"Need a room fer the night, sir? A bed?"

"Nae."

"A warm bath then, mayhap, to shed ye of the dust of travelin'?"

Cailean Grant looked down from his horse and cast a scathing glance at the lad about to reach for his reins. "I said nae."

The boy swallowed and jumped out of the way of the three riders following him. Cailean didn't look back at the child and he didn't seek forgiveness for not caring. It didn't matter what the circumstances were. He kept people out. For his own good, not theirs.

"Ye should take the bath," Patrick MacGregor said, catching up. "It might do ye some good to have the cockles of yer heart warmed."

Cailean didn't acknowledge his cousin's good-natured suggestion but kept his eyes on the icy road before them. He liked his cockles the way they were. Cold. Empty. Safe.

"I think the boy shite his breeches," Erik MacCormack

laughed from his saddle behind them, then kicked another lad out of his way.

"What?" He chuckled again when Patrick glowered at him. "The waifs will likely rob us the moment we remove our purses."

"They'd be disappointed by yours, Erik," said Erik's brother, Dougal, riding at his left.

Patrick moved his horse closer to Cailean's. "These are the men ye chose over yer kin?" He shook his head at him. "Men who kick children oot of their way?"

Cailean glanced over his shoulder at the brothers, who had arrived at Lyon's Ridge a fortnight ago to join Lord Murdoch's band of mercenaries, the Black Riders. "They've been hardened by their pasts," Cailean told him, turning back to the road. "What d'ye expect from them, courtly manners?"

"Ye dinna belong with them, Cailean. Let's go back home."

It was a conversation they'd had often. Cailean didn't want to go home and Patrick wouldn't leave without him. "I do belong with them, Patrick," he said, and turned away to spread his gaze over the packhorses ambling through the market, laden with grain and other wares and led by peasants from the local farms.

He'd come to Kenmore to purchase some fresh vegetables in the hopes of eating something other than the shite served by the cook at Lyon's Ridge Castle. If he had to consume another moldy carrot he was going to kill someone. He missed eating at Camlochlin. He missed home. But he couldn't go back. After Sage...and Alison, he had changed too much to go back.

He didn't mind Patrick's traveling with him to the marketplace. Patrick's easy nature and constant reassuring smiles had a way of making everything seem trivial, save for Cailean's decision to join Lord Edward Murdoch's Riders. Patrick didn't approve of thugs for hire, but Cailean was where he needed to be—with men who didn't care about love or dancing around with their words—or anything else. They left him alone for the most part, save for when Patrick was around. Patrick was well liked by everyone who knew him.

Cailean had been like him once, smiling at life and wreaking havoc on village lasses. But that part was gone.

Living at Lyon's Ridge helped him forget the crushing weight of what he'd lost—what his cousins back home had: bonny wives in their arms and loyal hounds at their feet. He'd wanted the same. He'd lost it, and with it his confidence that no cataclysmic tragedy would ever befall him or his family. Nothing was certain. In fact, it seemed the cards were stacked against him. It had changed him into something harder, emptier, and determined to stop feeling.

He'd been surprised when he saw his reflection in a basin this morning. His physical appearance had changed since Alison died. His hair had grown long and fell down both sides of his face. It created shadows along the gaunt planes and dips of his features. He appeared as dark and hollow as he felt.

"How much do you think *she* costs?" Dougal asked, eyeing a merchant's daughter while she beat a blanket outside a cutlery shop with a painted sign depicting crisscrossed knives.

"To hell with the lass," said Erik, called the Red by the other Riders, due to his red hair and Viking heritage. "My belly grumbles. I want to eat!"

Erik and Dougal MacCormack were two of the twenty Black Riders in Lord Murdoch's employ. Both of them combined couldn't muster up the compassion or courtesy of an angry ogre.

But Cailean didn't mind them, since he was the ogre.

They came to a shop with a barrel on a pole and stopped for a cup of ale.

"Go on inside," Cailean told them, dismounting. "I want to purchase a few things. I'll catch up with ye all later."

He left them to wet their tongues and headed off toward the tightly packed vendors selling everything from onions to surgical procedures.

Pulling his fur cloak tighter around him, he looked up from beneath his hood at the useless sun caught between billowing dark clouds, and grumbled. The sun offered him no warmth, the clouds reminding him of his life, gray and ominous.

He spotted a vendor selling apples and went to have a look. It wasn't unusual that a lass caught his eye. He was still a man, after all, even though he hadn't partaken of the pleasures offered to him by any of the gels at the castle.

This lass, though... this lass parted the clouds.

She strolled out of a nearby fabric shop, dressed in pale layers of soft cream-colored wool. Her face was half-hidden beneath a matching hood, her wrist was looped through the handle of a basket, and a sweetly content smile was on her lips.

What was she so happy about out here in the cold mud and the reeking stench of sewage on the wind? And why did she draw him like a moth to a flame? He moved behind the vendor's tent, his curious eyes fixed on her while she pushed back her hood and bent to feed a piece of bread to a stray dog.

Something in Cailean's chest softened just a little at her gesture.

Eyes painted in vivid hues of blue and wreathed in lush, inky lashes danced across the faces of the folks she greeted when she lifted her head. Hell, the sight of her and the way the sun illuminated a hundred different shades in her flowing mahogany hair buckled his knees a little.

"She's bonny."

Cailean turned to Patrick biting into an apple, his cousin's glimmering green eyes on her. "Let's go greet her."

Cailean stopped him from leaving with a hand on his arm. "Nae, I'm no'—"

"—As devilishly attractive as I am?" Patrick's grin was wide and playful. "Dinna let it get ye doun, Cousin. Few men are."

Cailean cast him a cool glance. "Why are ye no' drownin' yerself in ale with the others?"

He paid for Patrick's apple and bought a bag for himself.

"And listen to their God-awful conversations aboot their lack of basic hygiene? I can only find so much humor in mindless chatter. I'm no' a saint, ye know."

"Farthest thing from it," Cailean agreed, then fastened his eyes on the lass again.

"Who is she?"

Cailean closed his eyes when he heard Dougal's voice behind him next. "Now's there's a rump I'd like to shove my—"

Cailean's fist, crashing against Dougal's jaw, silenced him. He collapsed to his knees but not before Patrick had swiped the drink Dougal carried with him and saved it from falling to the ground with its original owner.

Patrick held up the cup to his cousin. "'Tis good to know ye still possess some decency." He guzzled what remained and then tossed the cup over his shoulder.

Cailean ignored him and the man knocked out cold at his feet, and his frown deepened when he noticed the lass had gone.

After they revived Dougal with a bucket of water, they purchased more winter supplies and then met up with

Erik for a few hours of drinking before heading back to the castle.

They reached the mountain pass above the River Lyon with Patrick's off-key singing to break the wintry silence.

Cailean almost didn't hear the thump of the arrow piercing his cousin's chest.

*This isn't happening*, Cailean told himself as he kicked open the doors of Lyon's Ridge Castle. This wasn't real. Patrick hadn't just been shot by an unseen assailant. Cailean hadn't pulled him unconscious and barely breathing off his horse and onto his own.

Stepping out of the cloud of snow he'd loosened from the stones above the door, he entered and stood with his cousin and best friend hanging limp across his fur-clad shoulders.

Cailean could scarcely see through his misty eyes. "Come quickly!" he shouted through the halls, his call reaching the rest of the Black Riders in the great hall. "Quickly!" he commanded with his heart battering against his chest. He felt sick with horror, filled to the brim with sorrow. *Not him. Dinna take him!* "We must help him!"

They would. They had to. These men fought for a living. They were familiar with wounds and patching them up. They would know what to do.

"What happened?" John Gunns, a mercenary from Caithness, asked, reaching him first. Two more men appeared and carefully removed Patrick from his shoulders.

Briefly free of his cousin's dead weight, Cailean inhaled a breath that stretched his cloak across his chest. Still his heart refused to slow its frantic pace.

He raised his trembling hands to his hood and pushed it back. Dark hair fell over his forehead and hollowed cheeks.

He swiped it away from his eyes. "We were returnin' from the market in Kenmore...."

His mournful gaze fell to the arrow that rose from Patrick's chest while the men carried him to the great hall. Cailean looked away, almost overcome with the basic need to scream, to run...to fall to his knees. *God, please, don't have me watch someone else I love die. I will perish altogether. Is it not enough that hardly any part of who I was still remains?*

"Does he still breathe?" His own breath still came hard, freezing in the chilled castle air and floating before him. He hadn't wanted to ask because he wasn't sure he could accept the answer. But he had to know.

This was his fault. If he'd left his new profession as a mercenary and returned home to Camlochlin as Patrick had wanted him to do, none of this would be happening.

"He breathes," said Cutty Ross of Orkney before he swept his massive arm across the table in the center of the cavernous hall.

They laid Patrick out and began to remove his clothes. The lasses who worked at the castle helped bring the men what they needed to soak up the blood.

Cailean looked at all the blood. He felt it, still warm at the back of his neck.

He stepped back, away from the work of saving Patrick's life. His breath faltered and his hands shook at his sides. He vowed that whoever had done this would die. He would ride through every villiage like a plague no one would ever forget until he found who was responsible.

"Hell," Brodie Garrow of Ayr swore. "It'll be hard to get out."

Cailean's muscles twisted into knots. Part of him was afraid of what he would become if he lost his cousin. Patrick was more than that. He was Cailean's closest and dearest friend, the only one who'd managed to bring a little light back to his life, and with it a wee bit of his old self. He raked his fingers through his hair as that same feeling of helplessness he'd experienced twice before coursed through him. What would he tell Patrick's parents, Tristan and Isobel?

His blood sizzled in his veins. He wanted vengeance now. He flicked his gaze to the only man who had not risen from his chair to help. Duncan Murdoch, son to Lord Edward Murdoch of Glen Lyon.

"Ye know this land and the people on it. Who could have done this?"

Duncan grinned. Cailean wanted to punch his teeth out. The lord's son was a jealous, squeaking twit who'd hated Cailean a day after he'd come here, when his father, Edward, first began praising the Highlander for battle skills superior to his son's. Their dislike for one another had grown after Cailean began visiting the lord's solar for long, quiet games of chess. His son, Murdoch had told him, had never been able to learn the game. Despite Cailean's brooding nature, the lord of Glen Lyon was fond of him. Still, he wouldn't take kindly to Cailean's killing Duncan. Presently Cailean didn't give a damn.

"If ye dinna answer me," he warned, his voice deep and taut, his eyes glimmering behind strands of dark chestnut, "I'll be standin' over yer chair before anyone can stop me, includin' ye, and I'll see to it that ye never speak again."

Cutty may have heard him because he stopped working and turned to look at him, as did Tavish Innes of Roxburgh. What would the other mercenaries do? Cailean wondered. Would Cutty try to kill him if he went after Duncan? Cailean had given his allegiance to Edward Murdoch, not his son. He'd come here to escape the memory of a life filled with expectations. He was paid to fight and protect Murdoch's land. Not to give a damn about the men who fought with him. But today he needed them to help Patrick.

"Where did the shooting occur?" Duncan asked him with an irritated sigh.

"The arrow was fired from the direction of Fortingall. That's all I know."

"The Menzies," Lord Murdoch's son told him, his smile returning, this time with a curl more sinister than mocking.

The Menzies. The lord's tenants in Linavar. Decades-long enemies of the MacGregors and Grants. The closest villagers to the mountain pass.

Immediately Cailean's heart turned hard toward them. "Why would they try to kill innocent men?"

"Because, Grant"—Duncan sneered as if Cailean were too dense to figure it out—"all they know in these parts is us, the Black Riders. They hate us."

"They dinna know who we are," Cailean argued. He wanted to be sure before he took his vengeance. "We were no' wearin' our coverin'. Why would they think we were Black Riders?"

"Do you want to conduct an investigation or do you want justice, Grant?"

Cailean didn't like him. At all.

"I want justice."

Murdoch's smile widened. He liked trouble. He also liked wine and women—one in particular. Cailean had never asked her name. He didn't care what it was. He felt pity for her to have such an admirer. Nothing more.

"When do you want to leave?" Duncan asked.

"As soon as Patrick is stable."

Murdoch laughed at him. "Your sentiments make you weak."

Cailean dipped his head and glared at Duncan from beneath the shadows of his raven lashes. "Come with me to the practice field and let me prove ye incorrect." One corner of his mouth curled in a cold sneer. "Yer faither will likely thank me."

"I'll kill you for that, Grant," Duncan promised. "But not tonight. It'll be dark out soon thanks to these damn short days and I'm drunk," he added, as if his slurred words weren't proof enough. "Tomorrow perhaps."

Cailean shrugged, finished with the useless conversation. Duncan would never touch him. As much as he envied Cailean, he knew his father's admiration was fairly given. Cailean could fight with weapons or without, a dangerous man created in the misty northern mountains.

He went to stand near the table where the men worked on Patrick, but closed his eyes, still unable and unwilling to watch the outcome.

Three times he'd felt life leaving people and a dog that he loved. Two had died in his arms. He prayed Patrick would not be the third.

Sage first, a scrappy hound who had chosen him from among many better men at Camlochlin. Had she known his life would need saving one day, and that she would die for saving it?

Alison. The first lass he'd ever cared for, the one who'd stolen his heart in a brothel. He could still remember her rich russet waves tumbling over her breasts while they made love, he for the first time. Memories of her haunted him. So many things did. It was why he'd given up his passions for cooking and writing, and left Camlochlin five months ago. Why Patrick, who was perfectly content to bed wenches in the Highlands, had followed him all the way to Glen Lyon with the hopes of talking some sense into him about strong-arming defenseless people for pay.

Patrick couldn't die. How could Cailean do anything but live out the rest of his days in dreaded anticipation of the next catastrophe if he did?

"Ye look like ye'd do well to take some comfort in these."

Cailean opened his eyes and looked down at the giant, milky mounds jiggling beneath him. He lifted his gaze to the woman's equally round cheeks dabbed in crimson powder. Madam Maeve herself. The woman in charge of the lasses hired by the widowed Lord Murdoch to serve meals to and satisfy other appetites of his private guard of twenty men, including Cailean and Duncan.

"Ye look tired. Come with me to my bed. I'll help ye ferget all this blood."

Forget? How could he ever forget it? "Not now, Maeve," he practically growled at her.

She pouted her ruby-red lips at him. "Beautiful Cailean," she purred, and moved closer to him. "Whatever 'tis that makes yer eyes smolder like smelted iron and yer jaw tighten like 'tis taking everything in ye not to take yer sword to all of us—whatever that is and wherever it comes from, hold on to it. Share it with me tonight."

"Another time mayhap." His voice was low, as deep as the shadows that plagued his days and nights. He hadn't taken any of her girls before. Why did she think he'd take her now when his cousin was possibly dying ten feet away? A better question was, why did he expect anything more from the people in this damned castle? They were soulless and void of compassion. The kind of people he'd chosen to be with. That kind of man he'd become.

"Have ye met Marion?" Maeve asked, and motioned to a lass who was standing on the other side of the hall, watching what was going on and wringing her hands together.

"She's *new* . . . and free fer ye."

He gave Marion a slow looking-over. She had rich, russet hair like Alison's. That was likely why he decided to help her.

"Is she untouched?" he asked Maeve discreetly. When the madam nodded, Cailean reached into his cloak and pulled out a small pouch. "Let's keep her that way, aye?"

Not knowing that the smile he offered her while he looked into her eyes was as well practiced as his sword arm, Maeve agreed to anything he wanted. Of course the leather pouch filled with coin that he tossed into her hand didn't hurt.

"Dinna offer her to anyone else. In fact, bring her to Perth, to Ravenglade Castle, and after I put m' sword through my cousin's attacker, I'll see to the remainder of yer payment. Now leave me."

The madam curtsied, showing off her ample cleavage once more. "If ye change yer mind about what ye need sooner—"

He wouldn't. He didn't want comfort. He wanted blood.

## Chapter Two

Temperance Menzie looked at her father riding beside her on their way home from Kenmore. He was tall and regal in the saddle, cloaked in wool and wearing the sun as his crown. He hadn't changed much since she was a child save for the featherings of gray at his temples and the creases around his torch-blue eyes. He was still strong and could chop wood faster than any man in the hamlet, including her dearest friend William, who was over a decade younger than he.

Crunching ice and snow beneath them, they rode west over the small packhorse bridge crossing a stream below a waterfall on the southernmost bank of the River Lyon.

"What do you think of a Christmas wedding between you and your betrothed?" Seth Menzie asked, quickening his horse's pace to speak to her.

Temperance issued a long, drawn-out sigh. Did they have to speak of this now, on such a beautiful day? William had asked for her hand just a few short weeks ago. She'd said yes because he'd asked her at the village dance and it was what was expected of her, not so much by her father or Gram, but by everyone else in the hamlet. It wasn't what she wanted, though. She'd hoped to discuss it at length with her father, but she hadn't had the heart to disappoint him. But now he was suggesting a Christmas wedding!

She shook her head and a curl of her chestnut hair brushed over her face beneath her hood. "I don't want to marry William, Papa."

Her father's eyes gleamed in the brisk afternoon when he set them on her. "You've known William since you were a babe. I thought you wanted to marry him."

"'Tis because he's my dearest friend that I don't. He is more like a brother to me."

Her father was silent, pensive for a moment before he nodded. "I always assumed... I want you to be happy—to have what your mother and I had."

She smiled, keeping pace with him. True love, the kind that comes around only once, maybe twice, in a lifetime. She knew he wanted that for her. Temperance wanted it too.

"I know true love is rare, Papa. That's why I would prefer not to marry William."

He stretched his eyes over the snow-draped Munros in the distance. "But I also want you to be safe from Murdoch," he said softly... but sternly. "Someday William will be the leader of Linavar, taking my place. Being his wife is the only way to ensure your safety from Duncan."

She turned in her saddle to look at him. "Would you have me sacrifice never knowing true love for being kept safe? I mean, Papa, there is no guarantee that William or any other *one* man can keep me safe from Murdoch. Why should I bind myself to him?"

"Because I ask it of you. He'll keep peace here and develop good relations with the lord. And that will keep you safe, just as I have done. Now—" He held up his gloved palm to quiet her when she would have pressed on. "I will strike a deal with you, Daughter, aye?"

Her blue eyes glinted at him. "Well, what is it? I mean, if I don't have a choice—"

"I'll agree to the marriage, but only in the event of my death." He grinned at her. "That should be at least twenty years away."

Temperance adored him and she knew he felt the same way about her. She could see it in his eyes when he set them on her. He'd never once blamed her for taking the life of the woman he'd loved so passionately. "Thank you, Papa."

They rode through a stand of beech trees and old pine, with red squirrels and pine martens scurrying out of their way. Temperance loved Glen Lyon and Fortingall, with its glistening streams, quaint farmsteads, and picturesque riverside fields. But there was no place more beautiful than Linavar, situated in a more open part of the glen, a few miles west of the bridge, where the river ran more gently. Wide, still pools were home to whooper swans and goldeneyes as well as an aftrnoon drinking spot for the occasional roe deer.

Almost home, Temperance wrapped her hands around her reins and was about to kick her steed into a full gallop, wanting to get there faster.

"Meet me in the hall after we set down our goods," her father called out. "I wish to have a word with you about something not pertaining to William."

She returned to him. "Something serious?"

He shook his head and smiled, then urged her to go. She promised she'd be there, kicked her horse's flanks, and took off across the snow-covered terrain toward home.

She rode hard with the wind snapping at her face. She didn't want to marry William. She didn't want to be a wife if she didn't have to. She wanted to practice archery and lounge around in the pumpkin patch after the day's work, not hurry home to prepare supper for a husband. She loved life and being outside, riding her horse. She loved digging her hands into the ground and providing food for her family. She loved the majesty of the four three-thousand-foot-high Munros surrounding the tiny hamlet of Linavar, and starry nights often made her pause to give thanks.

She didn't know why her grandmother had named her Temperance. There was nothing temperate about her. She didn't want to spend the rest of her days married to her comfortable old friend.

Her father had given her twenty years. Plenty of time to set her own destiny. She didn't know what her destiny would be, but that wasn't the point, was it?

She reached the house before her father, dismounted, and untied the pouches and her basket from her saddle. Upon turning, she smiled at her grandmother, waiting for her at the doors, and then at their cat, TamLin, purring around Gram's boots.

"I see ye didn't braid yer hair." Gram shook her head at her and pulled on a long curl to examine it through her unpatched eye. "Ye'll be sorry when I'm trying to get the twigs and other sorts of earthly things out of it later."

Temperance laughed, kissed Gram's cheek, and twirled out of her grasp. TamLin followed her into the house, wanting to be picked up and being quite vocal about it.

"I think I saw Duncan Murdoch snooping about earlier," Gram called to her. "Stay close to the house today."

Duncan Murdoch. The only blight on Temperance's near-perfect life. He lived in the castle atop Càrn Gorm with his father, the lord of Glen Lyon, and his accursed mercenaries, the Black Riders. Duncan hated her father because her father kept her from his arms, having promised her to William in order to keep her out of Lyon's Ridge.

Because of her father's good relations with the lord, Duncan had to ask her father for permission to pursue her. Her father always refused such requests.

"I will," Temperance called back.

"Did my finer wool keep ye warm, gel?"

"Like the loving arms of my gram," Temperance called out over her shoulder. She caught sight of her father dismounting in the front yard and returned his smile.

"We found everything on your list, Mum," he told Gram, dragging the old woman's attention to him as he entered the house.

Seeing him had a way of stilling one's heart. "Ye're a good son, Seth," Temperance heard Gram tell him. She agreed.

He would have made a wonderful husband to one of his admirers, but he'd never remarried after he'd lost Sarah. He'd raised Temperance with the help of his mother, and the three of them remained content. Mayhap too content.

Temperance shrugged and continued on her way inside. She loved her grandmother for fretting over her. She was correct about the tangles in Temperance's hair. They were going to be painful to get out. A simple braid would have saved her the torture, but she doubted she'd braid her hair the next time she sped across the braes. It wasn't that she was rebellious. She loved how the wind snapped her waves behind her like a pennant.

And oh, she loved coming home.

The house was quite large and softly lit by great, glowing hearth fires in each room and dozens of candles—more now with the shorter days. The walls were thin but lined with heavy, colorful tapestries sewn by a younger Gram's skillful fingers. Boughs of evergreen and holly were nailed above the entrance to every room. The scents of peat, sweet pine, and blackberry-currant biscuits filled the house and drew her farther inside. A kitchen opened up wide to the right. Inside was a huge stone oven and shelves stacked high with iron pots and bowls forged by her friend William the smith's own hand. A spacious chopping table sat in the center of the warm room. Sacks of vegetables and fruit hung from the rafters and sat upon wooden columns to keep them from rodents, not that they had any with TamLin, Temperance's dangerous cat, on the prowl. Dangerous, that is, to anyone who didn't pick her up quickly enough.

Temperance kissed deep into her fur after exchanging for the cat the pouches of different herbs and spices she'd brought inside. They didn't need to buy fruits or vegetables, since everything was shared inside the hamlet.

"Did you miss me, Tam?"

She kissed her silky, wheaten coat again, then plucked a biscuit from a bowl. She took a bite. The berries were sweet and delicious. Like everything they grew in Linavar. Gram said their crops tasted so good because they were reaped with happy, grateful fingers.

Temperance didn't know if Gram was right, but she hurried back for another biscuit before continuing on to the grand dining hall. Her favorite room in the house was gently bathed in claret and warm gold hues from the deep stone hearth and the polished wooden walls reflecting the light. The chairs and double chairs, crafted of wood and cushioned, had been built for comfort over convenience. Tables made of deep cherrywood were set about, some for drinks, others for games. Books, neatly set upon wooden shelves she'd helped her father make when she was eight, lined two of the walls. The others were arrayed in artwork she'd painted. She loved it here, and today it looked especially beautiful, decorated for the Yuletide season. Garlands of ivy and mountain laurel, along with fresh holly, bedecked every mantel and shelf, and every table as well. Gram loved to cook, and celebrating days no one else had ever heard of gave her a good reason to do it. For the last two nights they had celebrated everything from Mary's Labor to the Dreams of the Wise Men. Gram's own wee countdown to Christmas, outlawed though Christmas celebrations were. After feasting together and sharing laughter, everyone would leave the house and sing beneath the stars.

Her father had built the hall big enough to fit everyone. As the leader of Linavar, he'd wanted a place for the people to gather on cold winter nights for meetings or feasts. As leader he also saw to all dealings with their lord, and kept them safe from him. He made certain everyone received equal shares of the harvest. If there were disputes, he heard and settled them. He was just and fair, and well loved.

Temperance heard Gram's approval of the bolts of fabric her son carried inside. "They are lovely, Seth! I'll make something special fer Temperance," she called out happily, her voice following him while he appeared in the doorway and smiled at his daughter.

"You were right about the patterns," he said to her.

"And you were right about boughs of pine." She set Tam-Lin down and reached for a fresh garland.

He breathed in and nodded, then strode to the hearth fire and stood before the flames. "Tem?"

"Hmm?" she responded, adjusting the mountain laurel.

"There is something I wish to discuss with you."

She looked up. Why did he sound so serious? "So you mentioned earlier."

He turned back to the fire while she went to stand beside him. He began to speak, paused, and then began again.

She smiled at him to ease whatever seemed to be making him uncomfortable. But her own heart began to race. What caused this regal leader's speech to falter?

"'Tis Anne Gilbert."

Temperance kept smiling, not sure what their neighbor five farms down the road had to do with anything.

"I...ehm...I care for her."

Temperance blinked. He cared for her? Since when? She hadn't realized she'd spoken aloud until he answered her.

"I've felt this way about her for over a year now."

While he spoke, Temperance thought of the widow. Mrs. Gilbert was pretty enough, with dark hair and a good figure. But—

"I'd like to ask her to be my wife tonight."

He wanted to marry her? Temperance didn't say anything. Her head was spinning. She hadn't even known Mrs. Gilbert had found favor with him and now he was marrying her? He must love her. Why had he kept it from her?

She knew there were a hundred different things to ask, but she could think of only one. "Does Gram know?"

"She does," he answered reluctantly. "She guessed it first, and when she asked, I didn't deny it."

Her father wanted to take a wife! Temperance tried not to think of how this change in arrangements would affect her. What pricked more was the fact that her father hadn't confided in her. "Why didn't you tell me?"

He turned to look at her and then laughed, restoring her confidence in her future. "'Tis foolish, I know, now that I see you, but I feared you might feel slighted."

All she could do was smile—and shake her head. "I'm fond of Mrs. Gilbert. I'm glad that she's getting such a gallant, thoughtful husband. You deserve to be happy in your life, just like the rest of us."

She caught the sparkle of tears pooling in his eyes as he spoke. "You're so much like your mother, Tem. You and she would have made great friends."

He said something else, but she didn't hear. She rushed into his arms and closed her eyes against his chest, thankful in this holiday season, outlawed or not, for her father.

"What's this about now?" Gram's gravelly voice sprang up from behind her. "Come, gel, we've food to cook before the feast."

Temperance swallowed and broke away from her father. "Gram, if I don't rest from my journey to Kenmore, I'll never make another nine nights of this."

"'Tis the tradition," Gram told her, letting her pass. "And then begins Hogmanay. If ye don't like it, take it up with yer ancestors. They'll tell ye the same thing. Next time don't choose to take such a journey when ye know I'll be needing ye."

Temperance grumbled on her way out that she doubted her ancestors had anything to do with a feast called Caesar's Census. But Gram was right about one thing. Her weariness was her own fault. She'd known she and Gram had much cooking to do. The villagers would bring food with them to put toward the feast. But Gram still insisted on preparing fresh dishes while the harvest was full.

"What"—she turned to look at her grandmother behind her—"would my ancestors tell me of Anne Gilbert, do you suppose?"

Gram eyed her and recognized the playful catch of light in Temp's eyes. The old woman gave her a swipe of her apron across the arse.

Returning to the kitchen, Temperance glanced around and noted something different. William wasn't here. He wasn't on the braes when she rode home. He wasn't in the house. If he'd been in the smithy, he would have seen her and come out to greet her. "What do you think of Papa and Anne Gilbert?"

"I think yer father takes too long to make decisions," Gram said. "Come here. Let me braid that hair of yers before we begin cooking."

When Temperance heard William's voice as he came into the house a moment later, she tried to turn to see him, and Gram pinched her cheek. Temperance covered her face and glared at her grandmother.

"Cooking now. Talking later."

Temperance looked forward to the day when she had her own cottage and there were no rules to break. Until then she loved living with Gram. Her heart warmed just looking at her. How would it be to live with Anne Gilbert too?

They cooked salmon pottage with carrots, parsnips, an array of green, leafy vegetables, and wild garlic. They prepared various bread puddings, and crannachan, made with fresh raspberries, honey, and whisky, also crowdie cheese and oats. More food than they needed.

The village of Linavar was quite small, with thirty-one inhabitants. Thirty-two, Temperance remembered, when Lenore Deware, William's sister, arrived with her husband and their new babe.

More food arrived with Temperance's neighbors, and after more candles were lit and cups were filled on every linen- and holly-adorned table, all the food was brought forward.

Temperance sat with Gram, her father, William, and her soon-to-be stepmother, Anne Gilbert, at the Dewares' table. She'd heard William's voice earlier, when she was heading for the kitchen. She hadn't had a chance to speak to him. Did he truly want to marry her? And so soon? He didn't look at her like a man in love, but sweetly, like a brother who adored her.

"Temp?" he asked, sipping the ale her father had offered. "How was Kenmore?"

She smiled and told him all about the market. She wondered if she was a fool. William was ridiculously handsome, with dark hair and large, luminous, colt-brown eyes that revealed his heart in many matters. He was loyal to her father and steadfast, and had been a good friend to her her entire life. His legs were long and straight, his chest and arms well muscled from banging metal together all day in the smithy. Any one of the gels at Linavar would be happy to take him. But most of them had written him off years ago as being hopelessly in love with Temperance.

But was he?

"Where were ye earlier today, William?" Gram asked him, breaking through Temperance's thoughts. "My granddaughter was worried about ye."

"I was not worried, Gram," Temperance corrected her with a brief smile his way. "William is a grown man. He doesn't have to check in." She eyed her best friend and then furrowed her brow. "But you do look a bit pale, Will. Are you feeling unwell?"

"I'm fine—better now that I'm here. 'Twas a long trip to Aberfeldy and back."

"Och, I had forgotten you'd gone there to trade," Temperance said. "Forgive me, Will."

He smiled at her and held up his hands. "There's nothing to forgive."

She was grateful for William's gracious heart and that he said nothing about a Christmas wedding.

Gram always told her tomorrow had its own worries. Tonight Temperance wanted to enjoy the feast she'd prepared all day and enjoy the people of Linavar. They drank and told tales and laughed until the late hours of the night.

When everyone followed the piper, Angus MacDavies, into the fields behind the house to sing in celebration of the Child's birth and give thanks for a fruitful harvest, Temperance stayed behind in the house with William. It was time she told him the truth. She didn't want to marry him, and her father would allow it only after his death in twenty years, hopefully longer.

None of them heard the sound of horses thundering down the glen.

❈

# Chapter Three

The ride down Càrn Gorm into the vale wasn't long. A crisp chill in the air produced puffs of white from the horses' noses as they descended the mountain. Other than that it was a clear night. As they rode, Cailean and the other Black Riders tied black kerchiefs around their faces and pulled up their hoods. To prevent what had happened today to Patrick from happening more often, they didn't let anyone know who they were behind their masks. Hired mercenaries were not well liked. Who had recognized them? Why had Patrick been shot? He wasn't even a damned Black Rider.

From here Cailean could see a procession of lights moving in the darkness. Where were the people of the hamlet going? His cousin Patrick was fighting for his life because of one of these Menzies and they were parading about the vale late at night.

Cailean was tired of waiting. He wanted recompense and was glad they were finally on their way to get it.

When they reached the bottom of the glen, he looked

around. There was nothing to see but darkness and the small cluster of fires and lanterns to the west. He hadn't been here before, having arrived at Lyon's Ridge Castle a sennight after the harvest, but he believed the people were in the fields.

The Black Riders proceeded with more caution as they entered the hamlet, unseen, like a curse on the midnight gales.

The first thing to rake across Cailean's ears was the laughter. It filled the air like shrill taunts about what he'd let go when he left home. He pushed thoughts of his kin away.

When the Menzies lifted their voices in song, he realized they were celebrating—Christmas, most likely. He surveyed them in the shadows, ignoring their joy and looking for weapons. One of them had tried to kill Patrick, and still might succeed.

His gaze flicked over the inhabitants, looking for any sign of aggression.

"Seth Menzie!" Duncan called out.

Duncan had told him about the leader of Linavar before they'd left. Menzie had a passion for defying the lord he'd sworn fealty to, and a daughter Duncan planned on taking as his wife one day.

Cailean didn't care about one man's defiance or about the future bride of a heartless overlord.

A few of the women gasped and cried when the deadly cloaked mercenaries came closer to the fires and into view. Cailean looked around at the fear in their faces. Good, they should be afraid.

"Duncan Murdoch," the tall man called back, stepping forward, "welcome to—"

"I don't need your welcome upon land owned by my father. And don't speak my name."

"Of course," Menzie agreed.

So, Cailean thought, Menzie knew who Duncan was beneath his covering. If Cailean removed his mask, would the village leader also recognize him as one of the men who had ridden back to Lyon's Ridge today? Did Seth Menzie know the identity of all the Black Riders? Instantly Cailean's heart hardened toward him.

"I meant no disrespect," Menzie continued, sounding repentant but not looking away or lowering his gaze. "What can I do for you? Is everything well with your father?"

"To begin," Duncan sneered from atop his mount, "don't bring up my father to me. If you tell him I was here I'll come back—and I won't be so lenient. Next you can tell me what you're celebrating tonight."

Cailean knew perfectly well what they were celebrating. The same thing his own kin were likely to begin celebrating any day now. So what? Murdoch didn't enforce the law on Christmas. They'd come here to find out who'd shot Patrick and avenge him. He slid a warning glare at Duncan and vowed to himself that if he made this personal, instead of keeping it about Patrick, Cailean would take him to the lists and beat him senseless.

"Caesar's Census!" An old woman with one patched eye blurted her confession. "As ye know perfectly well, Duncan Murdoch! The same days we've been celebrating fer years!"

"Silence, old woman!" Duncan shouted at her, then glared at Menzie again. "Why are you celebrating Caesar when my father is lord here?" he called out, proving to the small crowd watching what a fool he was.

"'Tis one of the events that preceded the birth of our Lord," the leader stated, his feet firmly planted in the land he worked.

"You mean Christmas?"

When the leader nodded, Duncan trembled with fury.

"Then you're breaking the law, yet again. Year after year you defy the laws of the land, Menzie."

"Who gives a damn aboot that, Murdoch?" Cailean kept his voice low but deadly so that only the men closest to him could hear.

Duncan ignored him.

"What do you want, Duncan?" Menzie called out.

"I see it in your eyes," Duncan said, setting his merciless smile on the leader. "What you want to do to me is quite clear. You want to shoot me, just like you shot one of my men today. You're a murdering—"

"I was in Kenmore," Menzie cut him off, his voice seemingly calm but more raspy. He looked around the firelight for someone he evidently didn't find.

"Did you use the mountain pass upon your return?" Duncan asked him. Cailean waited, breath held, for his reply.

"I did," the leader said, lifting his chin like a proud stallion.

Duncan motioned for Cutty to dismount and take hold of the leader, then turned his victorious grin on Cailean. "Did I not tell you it was the Menzies?"

The Menzies. For years they had warred with the Mac-Gregors. They hadn't changed, always seeking trouble. Now they'd found it.

Cailean nodded at Cutty.

The assassin's dagger glinted in the moonlight.

"No!" the old woman cried out, slapping uselessly at Cutty's arm as more villagers began to scream. "Let go of my son!"

Cailean watched in horror. Revenge was one thing. Killing someone's son before her eyes was another.

"Papa!" someone screamed, running toward them from the large manor house. "Don't hurt him! Papa!"

It was the lass from the marketplace, the one Cailean had admired! His heart pumped loudly in his ears, his stomach roiled within, and he knew in that moment exactly what he'd become. The man about to die was her father.

"Please, don't do this!" She looked straight at Cailean when she screamed. A man was with her, his face white as a cloud. His eyes on Menzie.

Cailean looked back at Cutty and called out, "Wait!"

He didn't want this. Not this.

But it was too late. Cutty stepped behind the leader and swiped his blade across Menzie's throat just as his daughter and her companion reached them.

It was so quick Cailean's mind hadn't finished taking it in when the leader began to fall. He landed at the feet of his small family.

The hamlet erupted in screams. The sound reverberated in Cailean's head until he felt his heart begin to rumble from somewhere deep within. But it was the leader's daughter's soul-wrenching wail that he feared he'd never forget. For it rose up toward the heavens, then came down like an arrow straight into Cailean's chest. Whatever shards were left of his heart were completely shattered. Time slowed as he watched her fall to her knees and drag her father into her arms, where he drew his last breath.

Cailean couldn't breathe. He'd wanted to avenge his cousin. He'd been thirsty for blood. But seeing the lass sobbing with her father in her arms, the same way Sage and Alison had died in his, shook him to his core. He knew the pain that contorted her face and made her shriek from someplace so deep, even she seemed not to recognize the sound coming from her.

"No! No!" she cried. "Please, Papa, no!"

Cailean had wanted blood and he'd gotten it.

He felt ill.

Time sped up again and he moved to block Duncan's path to the family. "We need to go. Now."

"He was likely the one who shot your cousin," Duncan reminded him coolly while the woman's weeping filled the air.

*Likely.* They didn't even know for certain. Cailean suspected that for Duncan, this had nothing to do with Patrick. "We'll never know now, will we?"

"They know," Duncan said with a snarl and a gleam in his eyes. He was hungry for more blood. He was hungry for the lass. Cailean knew it before he opened his mouth.

"She'll confess if I take her."

Cailean held up his palm. Duncan would no doubt destroy her, if Cailean hadn't already. He'd tear away at whatever remained of her joyful heart until there was nothing left but misery. She would end up like everyone else at Lyon's Ridge. Her glorious eyes would no longer...Was he mad? Was he about to let his heart rule him on the night he most needed his heart to remain detached?

"Let us leave here now." He had to go. He had to get away from the screams, the wailing of a daughter who cradled her father's limp body.

"We'll leave when I say," Duncan Murdoch snarled at him.

Cailean's cool blue-gray stare made him shrink back.

"Move yer damned horse, Murdoch, or I'll put ye on yer arse in front of all these people."

Duncan blinked, and, knowing Cailean could do it, called to the men that they were leaving.

Cailean lingered in the shadows, watching the three women who had fallen over Menzie's body. The rest of the villagers either wept or tried to help. Nobody could.

His gaze remained on the women...on the carefree lass from the market. He understood how she felt. This was her father, and the other one's son, and likely the third's husband. Cailean had wanted to avenge Patrick, but he hadn't considered the cost of his decision.

He kept watch on Patrick that night and paced before his bed the entire time. He was unable to sleep. Guilt gnawed away at him, breathed life into the dark beast he'd let loose. "Patrick," he said beside his unconscious cousin's bed. "What have I done? I went to Linavar to kill, never suspectin' that anything could be worse than m' own loss. But I was wrong."

*Och, I was wrong. Inflicting that pain on someone else is worse. It's hell.*

And Cailean needed atonement.

He also needed to know that Seth Menzie hadn't died for nothing. Had he been the one who'd shot Patrick? If he had then justice, no matter how cruel, or how much Cailean regretted it now, had been served. But if he hadn't...Cailean needed to know.

After assurances that Patrick would live, Cailean traded his fur cloak for his plaid and changed his boots for the hide boots he'd arrived in. He set out early in the morning. He swore to his unconscious cousin that he would return in a few hours and that when Patrick was well enough to travel, they were leaving Glen Lyon. But there were things he had to see to first.

He reined in his horse and stood on the crest of Càrn Gorm. The mist was thick around his calves this morning and he could barely make out the row of lights moving toward a field in the distance. He realized it was a procession of mourners. Last night they had celebrated and now they were on their way to bury Seth Menzie.

What if Menzie was the wrong man? So what if he'd recognized Duncan in his mask? He'd known the lord's son well
enough, according to Duncan. What atonement did Cailean
expect they'd give him? They'd likely try to kill him. But
he'd been covered. No one had seen his face. Logic told him
to return to the castle and sit with Patrick. But he argued
with himself that he'd be gone only a few hours.

And something had drawn him back here. A need to find
the truth . . . and more than that, a need to make things right.
But how could he? He put his boots to his horse's flanks anyway and raced down the steep braes. He dismounted when
he reached the hamlet and tied his horse to a tree. His heart
pounded while he proceeded on foot.

It wasn't too late to turn back. He didn't want to have a
part in any more sorrow. He didn't want to see any of the villagers, or speak to them. What if *she* saw him? What could
he say to her? He had no reason to be here, but he remained
and stayed out of sight when he saw her arrive with her family. He was a fool to stay when they began giving their dead
loved one tribute. Och, what had he become that he could
cause a family, nae, an entire village so much pain? He was a
monster, too dark for logic.

Temperance clutched TamLin to her chest and watched William and some of the other villagers lower her father's box
into the ground.

She wouldn't cry. She couldn't. She had nothing left.

The morning was overcast and the dirt was hard from
the early frost. It had taken four hours to dig a big-enough
hole. It was as if the ground didn't want her father. Temperance didn't want to let him go. She wanted to break open
that hated box and take him back from death's grip. She
wanted to curse William for being so damned determined

to conquer the frozen ground, and oh . . . she cursed the Black Riders.

*William's heart is lost to you. What do you intend to do about it, Tem?* Her father stood before her, tall and strong, his dark hair blown by the wind of a brisk October day not too long ago. His smile was wide and handsome, and happy. He was always happy and he'd taught her to be the same. That was over now.

*Forgive me, Tem.* His last words, spoken on a strangled whisper before his life left him. Forgive him for what? For dying? Oh, but it wasn't his fault! Duncan Murdoch and his cohort were responsible.

How would she go on when it felt as if her heart had been ripped out of her body?

She lifted her gaze to her childhood friend now. His shoulders heaved from exhaustion but his face showed only sorrow. William loved her father. He understood her pain and the harshness of the truth that, like her, he hadn't been there to stop it.

Twenty years had gone by in a single night. She'd have to marry William now. She and Gram needed the protection of a man. Who better than the one her father had trained as his successor should anything ever happen to him? Something had happened. Her father, her sweet, wonderful father, was dead—and she'd watched it happen. She'd seen that Black Rider nod his approval before his fiendish friend cut her father's throat right in front of her poor gram and Anne Gilbert. She'd never get her father's blood out of her cloak. She'd never forget his last breath, his last words, while he looked up at her. She didn't want to forget. She began to cry again, but her tears were blown away by the wind. She would never hear his voice again, or see him bent to the soil in their fields. She'd never see his smile again, cast over all who greeted him, and soft and indulgent on her.

Temperance listened while Gram said something pretty about her son. There were many things to choose from. Gram spoke about his fairness and thoughtfulness and many of the villagers agreed while they wiped their eyes. Temperance bit her lip and battled herself to keep from crying with them when Gram recounted his steadfast loyalty and devotion, and spoke of how she was going to miss him.

It was Temperance's turn to speak. What was she to say? There was more than just sorrow's weight upon her. There was anger. There was guilt for not having been there to stop Duncan from killing her father.

There would be no more laughter, no more jesting with him and Gram and the others while they worked the land. No more late-night talks with him about politics and life. They had taken it all from her.

She lowered her gaze to the box, now set in place. It took her a moment to gather her strength to speak without a sob. But finally she did. "I'm going to kill them, Papa. I'm going to kill them all."

She sniffed and started to turn to Gram so she could leave. She'd had enough. She couldn't bear another instant.

William's speaking his turn stopped her.

"I vow not to let Temperance fulfill her most recent promise to you, my friend."

What? She turned on him. She didn't care if William was her best friend and her betrothed. Who in damnation did he think he was to promise her father that he'd make her break her oath?

"William."

He knew her well enough to know the chill in her voice, the spark of challenge in her eyes. It didn't matter if Gram gave her a hard tug and pulled her away. She didn't need to say anything more. William knew she was furious. She'd finish this later. It was time to go. There was much to be done in preparation for the celebration tonight. It was customary to celebrate the life of anyone they buried in Linavar. Tonight they would celebrate Seth Menzie. After that they wouldn't celebrate anything else until Christmas and Hogmanay.

Temperance was still fuming when Gram scrutinized her through her good eye while they walked together back to the house.

Temperance let go of the cat and watched her run ahead. "Please, Gram," she argued, though Gram hadn't said a word, "don't come at me with how I must start behaving like a lady and stop defending myself."

"Who said anything about that, gel? Ye'll never hear me spit such nonsense. But there's a place fer pouring out yer passions, and 'tis not at yer father's burial."

Aye! Aye, Gram was right. This day wasn't about her and William. It was about her father. She apologized to her grandmother and continued toward home.

"Temperance?" Gram called out behind her, stopping her. "Keeping busy and celebrating his life tonight and in the days to come will heal ye," she promised.

Temperance nodded and kept going. What if she didn't heal? The thought frightened her. She wanted to kill, not cook. She'd never killed anyone before and she couldn't just ride into Lyon's Ridge Castle and start shooting her arrows at Black Riders and expect to live. No. She had to devise a way to kill the mercenaries and their leader and ensure victory. She'd do it. Her father's life would cost them theirs.

She reached the house before Gram did, but she didn't enter. She turned at the sound of the wailing wind sweeping over the frost-covered glen. She pulled her dark woolen mantle tighter around her shoulders and looked up at Murdoch's castle in the distance, swathed in gossamer fog. She hated it and everyone in it. The people of her hamlet, her friends, weren't safe anymore. They never had been. If the lord's mercenaries could kill the leader of Linavar, what was to stop them from killing everyone else? And what about her? The life she'd hoped for was impossible now unless she did something. If she didn't kill Duncan, she'd never be safe from his desires. She would have to marry William to keep herself and Gram safe.

Something drew her anxious heart—and her cat—away from the castle and into the misty fields.

"TamLin!" she called out.

The cat kept going until she disappeared in the fog. Temperance was about to call her in again when Gram reached her and continued toward the door.

"She'll come in her own time," the old woman said.

Temperance nodded and tried to ignore the hair standing straight on her nape. She hurried inside and forgot all about it as she began chopping onions and an assortment of other vegetables for tonight's celebration.

As was usual for Gram, she turned out to be correct— TamLin did return home. And keeping busy did help Temperance keep her mind off her father and the men who'd killed him. For a little while, at least. She and Gram cooked all day, preparing for the feast. An old cow was slaughtered and fresh meat dishes abounded. The food the villagers had made for the next night's celebration was brought and shared at the feast as well.

Finally Temperance had to rest. The kitchen was hot and she came outside for fresh, cool air. She thought of last night's events. The Black Riders moving out of the shadows like demons from hell. Fear overwhelmed her, urgent and crippling. She wouldn't sleep tonight, just as she hadn't slept last night. She'd never felt anything like it before. This fear. They weren't safe.

"Oh, Papa," she cried, looking toward the pewter sky. "What am I to do now? What will become of us—of me if I don't marry?"

She heard a sound in the twilight, to the right, toward the barn.

"You're to let more than a day pass before you decide that all is hopeless," said a man to her left.

She turned and looked up at William, his dark eyes warm on her, like his smile. Damn it, but she did love him. She'd grown up with him. He, being a few years older, had taken on the role of her protector when she was six and Rodney Menzie had taunted her one too many times. William had knocked two of Rodney's teeth out and hadn't denied his guilt when he stood before her father, and he'd been punished for it. After that they'd grown very close and enjoyed the terrible things they did together. Like moving beehives into their neighbors' cabbage, onion, and pumpkin patches, and letting frogs and other little terrors into people's houses through their open windows. They got away with most of it and grew up laughing about it. They'd spent every day together, save for the two years he'd spent in Edward Murdoch's dungeon. How could she not love him? She was still angry with him, though. She'd been so busy that she hadn't had a chance to speak to him. "Isn't it, William?"

"Nae. Your father wouldn't have wanted it to be hopeless."

"He doesn't have a say anymore. He's dead! He's left us!" It began with the lump in her throat. She should have known right then to calm herself. But she didn't want to be calm. She wanted to cry and shout oaths she didn't know how she'd fulfill. She wanted to fall apart for a moment, just a moment, and miss her father.

"He would want you to remain strong, just as I intend to be." William moved to take her in his arms.

She let him, just because she wanted to be held in a strong embrace. But she kept silent.

## Chapter Four

Temperance woke early the next day and left the house with TamLin. She was careful not to wake Gram.

This was her favorite time of day, when the rest of the world was still asleep, save for a river hawk crying intermittently in the steel-gray dawn. She didn't mind the cold. It helped numb everything, and she loved how spectacular the earth looked drenched in glistening white.

But this morning she didn't see the beauty.

Her life had changed so much in a pair of days. *She* had changed. She felt it in her belly: a void gnawing at her, mercilessly eating its way through the rest of her. She felt alarmingly still, as if she had died with her father. She wasn't hungry and she couldn't sleep.

Despite all the lack, though, one emotion lingered inside her, making her defiant of the cold dew on her ankles that quickened her pace. She hurried to her father's grave and spoke to him for a time before being distracted by a giant hare. With TamLin at her ankles, she chased the hare for about a hundred yards, thinking it would feed her and Gram for at least a month.

It hit her, as it had several times since the day her father left her, that it was just she and her grandmother now. How would they live? And poor Anne Gilbert was alone as well, weeping into Temperance's arisaid until the wool could be wrung out.

She didn't see the horse in front of her. She didn't know how, but she completely missed it. Had it even been there a moment ago? Had it just stepped out of the fog? She ran straight into the poor beast, startling it, and herself even more, before she bounced off the horse's massive shoulder and fell back on her arse.

The rider leaped to the ground after her and helped her to her feet. "Are ye hurt?" he asked, sounding quite concerned.

She rubbed her head. "Where did you come from?"

"I'm...eh...on m' way to Kenmore."

A traveler, then? They didn't get many travelers through Linavar. She tried to have a better look at him, but the morning was still dark and everything above his nose was cast in the shadow of a woolen plaid over his head. A Highlander. She could see his jaw, though, square and classically strong, his chin, set with an alluring dimple that added to the pouty curve of his full lower lip. "'Tis that way." She swallowed.

"Are ye stable enough that I can let ye go?" His warm breath fell against her face. Deeply smooth, his voice resonated off her bones like the sound of a powerful instrument, tempting her to close her eyes and sigh with delight.

She realized then that he was still holding her hands. No. No, she wasn't stable enough at all.

"Aye." She pulled her hands free and held her fingers to her temples. "I cannot believe I ran into yer horse!" She laughed for the first time in two days. "I don't usually miss such large objects."

"Good thing." The slight tilt of his upper lip made her

want to lift her fingers and run them over his rough jaw. "Else these mountains would have doon ye in by now."

His voice swept over her like wind dancing over the mountains. She liked the sound of it.

"Was that yer kin's funeral march I saw yesterday?"

"Aye," she said, quieting down, forgetting his mysterious appearance as her sadness returned, "for my father."

He bowed his head, casting the rest of his face in shadow. "Please." He paused, then, "Accept my deepest sympathies. M' heart aches at yer loss."

She wasn't sure if it was the sincerity in his voice or the tenderness in it that burned her throat and made her cry.

She gathered hold of herself quickly and laughed again while she wiped her burning eyes. She reassured him that she wasn't injured, just daft.

He shook his head in disagreement, but said nothing else.

She wanted to make him smile, but something about the way his mouth was crafted, as if it was fashioned for brooding and melancholy, convinced her that he didn't give his smiles easily.

William called her name and she turned to look back at the house in the distance. "You should go." When she turned back to the stranger, he was already in his saddle and turning to leave.

She didn't see him until two hours later, when she and TamLin found him facedown and unconscious or dead, and bleeding where her cabbages would grow next spring.

She hoped he wasn't dead.

Warily she bent down and made sure he was still breathing. After determining that he was still alive, she hiked her skirts over her ankles and bolted toward home.

Ten minutes later she returned with William and Gram at her side, and a dozen others behind her, with more coming.

She didn't tell them that she'd spoken to him earlier and what a pleasant man he was. They would get angry that she'd stopped to speak to a stranger. Even if he'd helped her after she'd crashed into his horse.

"He's been stabbed twice in the back," Gram informed them, checking him over with her hands and her single eye.

"Who would stab a man in the back?" Temperance asked, and they looked up the braes to Lyon's Ridge. Duncan Murdoch would. But why this man? How did he know Murdoch?

"He needs our help," Gram told the small crowd. "Who volunteers to help him back to the house, step forward."

"What if he's a Black Rider?" William stepped forward, but hesitated, holding up his palm to stop any other advance. "Do we want to help him?"

Temperance certainly didn't, but how were they to know who he was until he woke up and told them? In order for him to open his eyes, he needed to recover.

Besides, she didn't believe he was a Black Rider. He was too kind, his touch too tender.

"What does it matter if we want this or not, William?" Gram asked him, proving she was more forgiving than the rest of them, stepping in front of Temperance to block his gaze. "We do what's right."

Aye, they did what was right. That's what Temperance's father had taught her. Life taught her different, though. Doing right didn't save your life.

"What about Marion? Did we do right for her?" he asked Gram boldly. "She's a member of this village. They took her."

"We don't know if the Black Riders are responsible for Marion's disappearance," Gram retorted in a calm voice. "And be reminded of Seth's warning to make decisions with yer logic and not yer heart."

"How can I deny my heart," William answered, "when it seeks to keep the people of Linavar safe?"

*Aye*, Temperance thought, listening to him. They needed him.

"A steady temper and intelligence will see us through, William."

Dismissing him, Gram ordered the stranger be brought back to the house. Temperance followed and caught the spark in William's eyes as she passed him. Was he so serious about taking Seth's place as leader? She hoped so. He was the only one who'd stepped up to the task. Could he do it? Could he keep the people safe from Murdoch and his mercenaries by keeping good relations with the lord? He'd been furious when Marion disappeared a few weeks ago. Some suspected she'd run off with a man from Fortingall or Kenmore, but William seemed so certain Duncan and his men had kidnapped her. Would he take matters into his own hands now that Seth was gone?

"Ye'll aid me in his recovery," the elder told her granddaughter, pulling her thoughts back to the present.

"Of course, Gram."

Gram offered William a smile when he helped carry the stranger back. Would it be fair to marry her friend? She wasn't in love with him. What did fairness matter? They did what needed to be done. She needed to marry him, and she would. It was, after all, what her father had wanted.

When they finally reached the house, William sent the neighbors back to their homes, promising them a report as soon as he had one. Temperance prepared clean rags, clean water, a bottle of their strongest whisky, a needle, some thread, and her seasoned oak bowl.

They brought him to Temperance's room since it was the closest to the kitchen and whatever herbs Gram needed.

Temperance didn't mind sleeping with her grandmother

for a sennight or two. Neither one of them wanted to sleep in Seth's room.

As soon as they set him down in her bed, staining its coverings with his blood, it hit Temperance that he could very well die in that spot. She didn't want him to. There was nothing she could have done for her father. This stranger offered her a chance to heal at least a small part of herself. She took it.

He'd helped her to her feet. She'd help him live.

"What more do you need from me?" she asked while her grandmother removed his sheathed claymore first, then his plaid and the clothes beneath. After that she covered him from his feet to his waist with Temperance's blanket. She had him turned onto his belly since he'd been stabbed in the back. Blood covered the expanse of his shoulders, pouring from two deep tears in his flesh.

Temperance recoiled. The blood reminded her of her father. She doubted they could save this man.

"Gram..."

"Fetch me my herbs, dove. Bring me basil, clove, coriander, hyssop, lavender, mint, and sage. I need my mortar and pestle. Are you listening, Temperance?"

"Aye, Gram." Temperance severed her gaze from his wounds and repeated the list.

"Bring me also some lettuce juice, bryony, henbane, hemlock juice, vinegar, and some wine, in case he wakes up."

Temperance hurried away, too busy repeating Gram's lists in her head to think about all the blood. Once she returned to the room, she waited while Gram chose the precise amounts of everything she needed and then had Temperance put the ingredients into her hardwood bowl and cook the poultice over the candle flames. Soon the scent of mint permeated the air and gave the room a cozier feel—the way the holiday season should have felt, but didn't.

Dear God, how would any of them celebrate Christmas and Hogmanay without her father? This should have been a time for joy and love shared around decorated tables and gifts of spices, new tools, and leather goods. Homes should have been filled with the delicious aromas of Christmas cakes and puddings, mince pies and shortbread, not tears.

Temperance put away her thoughts of merriment and somberly watched Gram work at cleaning the stranger's wounds, then accept the red-hot iron William handed her. She finally looked away when Gram lowered the iron and the stranger's flesh crackled in her ears.

"Temperance." Gram motioned to her when she was done. "Come here and apply the poultice. My fingers and wrists ache. I'm going to take a quick nap."

"Me?"

"Aye, or has some malady befallen ye also, that prevents ye from using yer hands?" Without waiting for an answer, Gram shoved the bowl at her. "Come now, ye're wasting his precious time. Get to the task and keep him from infection. I'll check in later. Och, and rub some of my oils into his skin and have his drink ready if he wakes up."

It was no hardship. In fact, Temperance enjoyed touching him. She kept her feelings concealed behind stoic features while she moved her fingers around his wounds. She stretched down his back slowly, carefully applying the concoction, cursing the soul who'd tried to take his life. Imagine killing this work of art. Goodness, but he was carved as a clay idol would be by the fingers of a skilled master sculptor. Why, when she'd met him she hadn't been able to help but notice that even his trews fit him to perfection. She looked down at his profile set against her pillow. Unadorned by a wool hood or shadows, his restful face mesmerized her. His full, decadent mouth still pouted, even in his slumber.

Temperance felt sorry for him. He had been stabbed in the back. A coward had done it. The worst coward she knew was Duncan Murdoch. But why would he want this man dead, unless he knew him?

William watched her by the door. She cleared her throat and appeared more diligent in her work. He didn't like her having to tend the handsome stranger, but he couldn't stop her from doing it.

"He could be one of them," he said when they were alone, knowing her well enough to know the right things to say to make her not enjoy her duty. That the stranger was possibly a Black Rider was one of them.

"And he might not be. My father would want me to help him until I'm certain who the stranger is." If he was one of Murdoch's mercenaries, she'd kill him.

After she healed him.

"Temp," her friend said softly. When she looked up, he averted his gaze. "We should talk about our wedding."

Her heart stopped. Now? He wanted to talk now? Of course she would go along with it for her father's and Gram's sakes. But she didn't want to discuss it now. Oddly enough, he didn't seem as if he wanted to either.

"Can it wait just a little while longer, Will?"

"Of course, we can do it after Hogmanay."

She smiled at him. She'd only meant their talk about it, but postponing the wedding was good.

"I need to get back to the smithy," he said, and then left without another word.

Alone with the stranger, she let her gaze rove over him, then dipped her fingers in the oil jar and reached for his shoulder. She'd never seen a naked man before, and never one with such lithe, sculpted muscles. Now that William was gone, she couldn't help but bask in this stranger's corded back, the broad flare of his shoulders, narrowing to his waist. Och, but he was glorious.

She touched her fingers to his skin and rubbed gently. He was hard and majestic like the mountains outside her window. She inhaled deeply and began again. The oil was melting from his body heat, or hers. She didn't know which. She rubbed her palms over the expanse of his shoulders and down his long, sculpted arms, massaging the healing oil in. He felt strong and capable, and for a fleeting moment she wondered how his arms would feel around her. She came to his wrist, his hand and fingers. Was it wrong of her to take such delight in the calluses covering his palm, in the simple elegance of his fingers? Touching him stirred something in her that William had never roused.

She spread her curious palms over his back, careful not to touch his wounds, and then down to his waist and the soft upward curve of the top of his buttocks. Twice she had to wipe her brow and she even said a silent prayer that he wouldn't wake up and catch her admiring him with her hands.

He had many scars—including two that looked recent, and a bullet hole say six to nine months old. His claymore and plaid identified him as a Highlander, and only the good Lord knew all the trouble Highlanders fell into. What was his name? What was he doing in Linavar? Where was his horse now? Had he been robbed for his beautiful stallion? Why had he been stabbed in the back and not in the chest? What had he been doing in her cabbage patch? All questions she hoped he would live to answer.

A little while later, William returned with Anne, who offered to help. Had Will fetched her because he wanted Temperance away from the handsome stranger? Was he jealous? He never had been before.

Temperance accepted the help, deciding it was best to stay away from the man. The last thing she needed was a distraction from her plans to kill Duncan and his men.

"Coming, Temp?"

She nodded and followed William out. The moment they were alone, William turned to her. "I don't like that you might be aiding a Black Rider."

"He's not a—"

"You don't know that. And the way your eyes go soft when you look at him, Temp." He shook his head at her as if he didn't know her at all.

"You're not jealous, are you, William?" she asked curiously. "If I were your wife, which I'm not just yet, you'd have a right to feel as you do, but I'd still hate it."

"I'm not jealous, Temp. But you are to be my wife, according to your father's wishes," he reminded her. He was trying to keep his voice steady and calm, but he was failing. "You're my betrothed and I would prefer it if you didn't fawn over a man who could possibly be part of the vile group of raiding bastards up in that castle."

Fawn? She would deny it, of course! And damn it, she didn't believe the poor man lying in her bed was part of Duncan's group. If he needed help, she would give it. Despite William's orders. "I tell you he isn't a Black Rider. What you saw is plaid. He's a Highlander, not a mercenary."

He looked down at her with his beautiful brown eyes and she saw his heart there, the familiar. He wanted to keep her safe. "What if he is?"

She cut him a playful glance from beneath the sprays of her lush lashes. "If he is, then you can help me kill him."

# ❊

# *Chapter Five*

$S$he hadn't promised William that she would stay away from the stranger, so finding herself alone with him in her room once again didn't make her feel guilty.

This time she stared at him from a chair a few feet away. Someone had turned him on his side while she was away, exposing—in its full glory—the most beguilingly handsome face she'd ever come across, here or in Kenmore. The list of his pleasing attributes would take too long to consider at once. She let her sleepy gaze linger on the parts of him she hadn't appreciated before, the weight of his brow, the alluring bridge of his nose, the lush black lashes that cast shadows over his cheeks.

What color were his eyes? she wondered while hers closed. She fell asleep watching him breathe, wondering who he was and why in damnation he had remained here long enough to get stabbed. She dreamed he was the prince of some faraway land traveling to Linavar for a wife. But soon her dreams of her handsome stranger changed into something else.

A man sat upon a fine stallion that didn't so much as twitch beneath its rider's strong thighs.

He wore a fur cloak and fine leather boots paid for by his master, Lord Murdoch. He looked deadly and moved with grace and authority that had been bred into him, rather than learned. His face was draped in black linen, like those of the rest of the killers around him. Were his eyes silver or was it just the moonlight glinting off them?

He nodded his regal head, like an emperor giving the order to kill. To kill her father.

He called out a word, over and over, but her father still died.

*"Wait!"*

*Papa, wait!*

She opened her eyes, her heart beating like a battering ram, a cry on her lips. She felt a hand on her shoulder.

"There, dove," Gram comforted softly as Temperance woke from her fitful dream, "all will be well."

How could she ever say such a thing after her only son had been killed? No, Temperance decided. It would never be well again. Never.

"Our patient's fever seems to have broken," Gram informed her, then shooed TamLin out of the bed and her granddaughter out of her chair. "He's been moving. I suspect he'll be waking up soon."

"Gram?" Temperance said while she went to him. "Did you see the Black Rider who gave his approval for Father's death? Was it Lord Murdoch?"

"'Twas dark." Gram shook her head. "But even with the bonfires burning, I didn't recognize him."

Temperance nodded. It didn't matter. She'd find out who he was eventually, and then she'd kill him. Right now, though, the man in her bed needed help. She stood over their patient, now lying on his wounded back. He'd need to be turned over again.

He felt cooler to the touch. Her gaze skidded over his mouth and she wanted to curse aloud at the fullness of it, even in deep rest. She'd kissed a few lads here and there. If she had to marry someone, he had to kiss well.

A decadent thought of kissing him, touching more of him, as by running her fingers down the muscles that defined his belly, made her feel flushed, and somewhat traitorous since she didn't know him...and he was unconscious.

"Have you and William set a date yet?" Gram's voice and her question dragged Temperance's attention off the full view of the stranger's face.

She turned her back to Gram and reached for his ointments.

"Temperance?" Gram asked from the chair.

"After Hogmanay."

"Ye still don't wish to marry him?" Gram asked, obviously hearing the hopelessness in her granddaughter's voice.

Temperance shrugged her shoulders. There would be much talk of her wedding in the coming days. Somehow she would get through it.

She hadn't spoken to Gram about her plans of revenge. Her grandmother would try to talk her out of it and forbid it. But there was still a chance of not having to marry a man she wasn't in love with. If she failed she would marry William to keep Gram safe. "My days of wishing are over," she told her grandmother, turning back to her. "I'll do what I must do."

"Good. We need a man around here to help with the work."

"I know." Temperance picked up one of Gram's containers and proceeded to apply ointment to the stranger's wounds. Better to just agree for now. "'Tis just that I feel like a prize horse on display. Men, some of them mere boys"—she cast the older woman a scathing glance that she had never truly mastered—"come here to eat and see what kind of wife I'll make. I..."

"Ye are no prize, dear." Her grandmother said with a light chuckle.

Temperance tossed her a sour smirk. "I know that, Gram. I only meant..."

"Alric of Ayr was ten and seven. Old enough to marry. Ye had refused to marry William because ye didn't love him and the threat of the lord's son wasn't as serious as it has become. I thought to help ye find a man ye love."

"He is two years younger than me, Gram. You—"

Gram held up her palm, stopping her. "Just because ye're fair of face, do not think everyone wants only ye."

"I never said—"

The elder cut off her words yet again. "Men are not lined up outside this door. I practically had to beg William to sup with us. Ye are a delight to me but ye may end up alone with that sharp tongue and stubborn will of yers."

"And what is so wrong with that?" Temperance asked her.

"Child"—Gram eyed her lovingly—"ferget safety. Ferget everything else. Do ye truly want to be alone fer the rest of your life? Ye know yer grandfather, my beloved John, died and left me a young widow to raise yer father alone. 'Twas a difficult life. I don't want that fer ye. Ye're ten and nine, ye know. Ye're not getting any younger."

"I know, Gram," Temperance told her quietly. "But I want to love passionately when I wed. Is that so wrong?"

"Nay, dove, it's not wrong at all. But we live in a harsh world. Yer father protected ye as best he could from Duncan Murdoch, but Seth is gone and we must continue to watch over each other."

Because Temperance loved Gram more than she wanted her own way, she put stubborn defiance aside and managed a smile.

"When has William agreed to come?"

"Any moment now," Gram informed her.

"What?" Temperance turned to the window. "'Tis suppertime? How long have I been asleep?"

"Who's counting hours?" Gram asked her. "Ye're having a trying time and rest is good fer ye."

"And for you," Temperance replied, realizing that Gram had cooked supper alone. "You'll go straight to bed when supper ends and William leaves. I'll tend this poor soul while you rest."

Gram narrowed her eye on her. Temperance was tempted to turn away again, familiar with the power of Gram's scrutiny.

"After ye sit for a time with William at the table."

Temperance nodded, knowing what she needed to do. "I'll make you proud of me, Gram. I will be irresistible."

"Temp," her grandmother said, rising to leave the room, "ye have enough pride in yerself fer both of us. Irresistible!" She laughed, and behind her Temperance smiled.

She knew Gram was teasing her. Gram's mind was still as sharp as a well-loved sword. And she enjoyed keeping it honed on her granddaughter. She'd obviously noted Temperance's blushing over the man a moment ago and she clearly intended to put an end to any foolish fancies Temperance might be dreaming up.

"We know William," she called out, reminding her granddaughter over her shoulder before she left. "We don't know this man. Give William yer attention, aye?"

"Aye," Temperance called back in a soft voice. William was her dearest friend and aye, she might have believed she

was in love with him once, a long time ago, when all the
girls began to notice the extraordinary depth and beauty of
his dark eyes. But the playful banter and the—almost kissing, but not, made her love for him change to the purely
unphysical. There was no all-consuming heat scorching the
air between them. There never had been. William knew it,
that's why he'd never tried to kiss her. She loved him, but the
thought of marrying him made her feel ill.

"Patrick!"

The stranger's voice startled her. She put aside her ointments and comforted him. "There now. There," she whispered while TamLin curled up in the crook of the stranger's
side.

He didn't wake up, but she had quieted him down. Her
soothing voice slowed his breath and his heart.

Who was Patrick? His brother? The man who'd stabbed
him? She hadn't noticed anyone else with him when she'd
run into his horse. He'd been alone. But if Patrick was the
stabber, it would mean the stranger had to know him.

When he grew agitated again, she whispered into the
dark hair falling over his ear. This time he didn't grow
calmer. She tried applying more ointment and singing an
old Christmas hymn to him. She sang of the strong, sturdy
hands of the master builder, then looked down to find that
she was holding the stranger's hand, gently rubbing ointment
into each of his broad fingers and into his palm.

At the same instant she became aware of her boldness
she also felt his eyes on her. He'd awakened and was staring
at her in silence while she sang. TamLin purred at the ends
of his fingers, which slowly stroked her.

"You're awake," Temperance said softly, happy that he
was. The eyes she'd wondered about were huge and wide set,
the color of an icy sea. She smiled, completely beguiled by

his gaze. Poor man. Who was he? Who had stabbed him in the back? She didn't want to question him now. He needed rest.

He didn't speak, nor did he return her smile. He just stared at her, looking confused and pained by more than his wounds.

"You're safe now," she promised. "All will be well with you."

He looked away from her, as if he didn't believe it, or he didn't want to. He closed his eyes and went to sleep once again.

William Deware arrived as expected. Gram made Temperance open the door and invite him in. She felt foolish. William had been to the manor house more times than either of them could count. He looked especially handsome tonight, dressed in black breeches and a cream-colored shirt, belted at the waist and flared at his hips. She knew she should be grateful that a man like William would consider her as a wife when he had so many others to choose from. He held out a bunch of purple winter irises. She was grateful for him.

But her heart accelerated because of someone else. God help her, she was betrothed and she couldn't get an unconscious stranger out of her head. As big and fit as the Highlander was, there was something about him that tore at her heart, especially when he'd set his eyes on her, as if he'd been through something very difficult. It made her feel a certain kinship with him. Did he have a family he was missing, a wife who'd claimed his heart and all that chiseled body? And why in blazes was she hoping he didn't? She was attracted to him, both physically and emotionally. William would likely hate her if he knew her thoughts.

"I know you like heather," her dearest friend offered,

stepping inside with her, "since you're always prancing around in it." He laughed shortly. "But winter heather is dry and when I tried to pick it, it fell apart in my hands."

Prancing? He did see her as a horse then, prize or not. "Aye, William," she said, her smile as bright as the bouquet she held to her nose. "It takes a certain kind of man to handle heather. Mayhap you'll learn one day."

Gram pinched her side and Temperance yelped. William laughed, and all was back to normal. Except it wasn't.

There was a man in her bed who'd stilled her heart for just a moment, though William hadn't claimed it entirely.

What was his name? She wanted to hear how it sounded, how it felt coming off her lips.

She remembered crashing into his horse and how quickly he'd leaped from the saddle to aid her. She remembered his plump, pouty mouth and his strong dimpled chin. His warm breath against her face and the depth and silky cadence of his voice when he'd spoken to her had melted her bones.

*M' heart aches at yer loss.*

His sympathy had been so genuine it had almost brought her to the point of crying hysterically all over again.

She ate Gram's delicious roasted-quail-and-squash soup served with fresh bread and honey, with wine to wash it down, and did her best to keep the brawny Highlander out of her thoughts.

She hated herself for having let her and William's relationship go sour. He was a good friend and he deserved more than her sitting here wishing she were back in her room with someone else.

"'Tis nice to spend time with you again, William," she told him. "I feel like we—"

A shout erupted from her room. She looked toward it and took off without a word to Gram or William.

She reached the bed first. "He's burning up, Gram!" she called out, loudly, so that wherever Gram was she'd hear and reply.

"Rags soaked in my bark oils!"

Temperance hurried to fetch what she needed while Gram called out more instructions. William watched from the doorway for a moment, then, knowing what was right and doing it, helped Temperance in her tasks.

The terrible heat inside their patient lasted hours, with him coming to and falling away again. Once or twice he opened his eyes, and Temperance found herself soothing him, softly and with tenderness. Finally, after much moaning and cries of delusion, the fever peaked. It took the three of them, Temperance, Gram, and William, and all the strength they could muster to roll him enough to change his bedding. He couldn't lie soaked in his own sweat and risk getting another fever.

They tended him until the next morning, while he slept and fought the demons in his dreams.

$\maltese$

# Chapter Six

Cailean was in hell.

His body was consumed by flames. They came from within and without, scouring his blood, searing his thoughts and his mind.

He didn't remember how he'd arrived where he was, but he knew who had probably put him here. Duncan Murdoch. The lord's jealous child had finally grown some bollocks and had killed him. Cailean knew Duncan wanted him dead. And Duncan had proven with Seth Menzie the power he gave to his hatred. Now he'd proven it with Cailean as well.

He was dead.

But the fires of hell? He didn't want to believe it. He knew he hadn't lived an exemplary life, but had he done anything deserving eternal damnation?

The heat drove him mad, but the real torture was that every once in a while he was dredged up out of the burning pit and allowed to refresh himself in the presence of an angel. She sang to him and carried him out of the dark pit. Instinct made him reach for her, a dark and dusty part of his heart wanted to go to her, stay with her while she soothed his roiling soul. No. He didn't want anyone else in his life. He wouldn't allow himself to let anyone else in. Never again. But who was she? Was she real?

Someone strong pinned down his wrists. He didn't fight but saved his strength for the next time he came up. He dreamed of her again and again, listening to her crying out in the night for guidance from a man for whose death he was responsible. Watching her in the morning fog, clutching a cat to her chest and vowing to her father to avenge him. He dreamed of another man holding her and in his sleep Cailean felt the sting of anger. Finally he fully remembered her. She was Seth Menzie's daughter. The one whose heart-breaking wail had ripped him from the dark and jarred him awake from one nightmare and cast him into another. The one who had run straight into his horse and brought a smile to his face.

What was she doing here with him, in this fiery place, so close her warm breath nearly burned him to embers? Surely this dark-haired angel had done nothing to earn a place here. No, he had to be alive. This wasn't hell. Her presence gave him hope. He hadn't died. But he remembered the killing he'd instigated. He remembered nodding, giving his consent for Cutty to kill, and he remembered the shadows of his dwelling for the past two years since Sage died. The fires licked his soul, a shattered place no foul-smelling ointment could heal, where he kept the ones he'd loved and lost. A place he didn't want Patrick near.

He had to get his cousin out of here before Duncan, or whoever had tried to kill him, attempted it again.

Why hadn't he strapped Patrick to his horse and taken him home to Camlochlin? Why had he remained and returned to Linavar for atonement?

He finally came to for the last time the next morning. If he wasn't dead, he refused to behave as if he were.

He was in a bed, a quite soft bed at that. Pain burned his back, making him feel a bit ill. The sunlight streaming in blinded him. He longed for a cool breeze. Just a cool breeze.

Something soft and silky moved through his fingers. A feather? A quill, mayhap? His heart accelerated. He missed writing, poems, odes, anything his heart could produce. His uncle Finn was a bard of Camlochlin, his cousin Darach also. It ran in Cailean's blood.

He opened his eyes and looked down at the huge yellow feline beneath his hand, regal and mildly interested in him. He'd seen the cat before. He knew its name.

TamLin.

"You mustn't sit up yet," a soft voice to his right informed him.

He turned to see Seth Menzie's daughter rising from a seat beside the hearth, facing the bed. She hadn't been a dream. Her singing to him had been real. Her tender voice and the sensation of her small soft fingers rubbing his—it had all been real.

He didn't want to be here with her. He turned his face from her to hide who he'd become. The memory of her screaming and covered in her father's blood would not let him forget.

"I know I'm no' forgiven—"

"Forgiven for what?" she asked softly.

She didn't know who he was, then.

They were alone, save for the cat nudging him to pet her soft head. He pushed her away, the way he had when she'd followed him into the fog.

"How do you feel?"

Her voice was soft, with a fragile edge and a note of

compassion. He didn't deserve it. She came toward the bed like something out of a dream his fevered mind had conjured up. What the hell was he doing here? With her? Why her? Perhaps he *was* in hell and her memory was here to haunt him forever.

He nearly cringed when she reached out to feel him for fever. He didn't want to be here. Not with *her*.

"Rest easy, Highlander." Her whisper led him to her and he turned his head to look up into her eyes. "You're safe here."

Her eyes were large and as blue as the heavens, as deep as a thousand oceans. "Where's here?" he asked.

"Linavar." She smiled and he cursed himself for looking at her in the first place. "In my father's house."

He resumed trying to sit up. No. It was possible that an innocent man was dead because of his desire for vengeance. But if Seth Menzie wasn't innocent, then she knew it. She'd been in Kenmore with her father.

Cailean wanted answers. He needed them. But what would he do when he discovered the truth?

He was alarmed to find his breath so short and his pulse so quick, and even more so because she had something to do with it. Just looking at her did. It wasn't the slight curve of her freckled nose, or the extraordinary depth in her eyes. It was instead the red puffiness of them, and the remnants of sorrow, the kind he was all too familiar with.

"Who are you?" she asked him.

He'd come here to tell her things. Things he was involved with. About her father's death. But when he tried to think of what to say, his heart raced and his mind went blank. She'd been through much. If she realized she'd nursed a Black Rider back to health a few days after her father was murdered, it would likely end with her stabbing him, finishing what Duncan had not, and sending him forth to his scorching destination.

Coming here had been a mistake. Every second that she tended him made telling her the truth more difficult.

He didn't want to look at her. Looking at her made it hard to lie. He instead dipped his eyes to the cat who'd returned to his side, his gaze shrouded in strands of dark hair. "I'm Cailean Grant."

"Cailean."

He looked at her from beneath the soot of his lashes when she didn't say anything else. He thought it odd and a bit ruthless of her to simply speak his name on a wee whispered sigh.

"Who attacked me?" he demanded, guarding himself against the softness of her breath and the delicacy of her fingers when she held them against his face. Hell, but her mouth was bonny. He found himself wondering if a kiss from her would taste as sweet.

"I was hoping you could tell me. I found you already in poor condition. Whoever did it fled. You're still a bit warm."

Of course they had. Cowards who stabbed men in the back always ran after the deed was done. "Where is m' sword?"

"You will get it back before you leave," a man said, coming to stand in the doorway. He crossed his arms and his ankles. "We don't know if you're friend or foe."

Cailean remembered seeing him running from the house with the lass the night the Black Riders had come here.

Did he know Cailean was one of them?

Did he live here? With her?

"What are you doing here in Linavar, Mr. Grant?" he asked. "Our clans are enemies. Perhaps you're one of Murdoch's henchmen?"

Cailean gave him a brief looking-over. The man looked fit and ready to fight, more so than Cailean did presently. He couldn't tell them the truth, not while he was still unable to protect himself. "Duncan Murdoch is m' enemy." It wasn't untrue.

"You know him, then?" the man asked suspiciously, and glanced at Menzie's daughter.

Aye, he knew Duncan well, but he wouldn't tell them how well. "I was a guest of Lord Murdoch—"

"Why would you be a guest of his?" Menzie's daughter interrupted him, letting him see and hear her contempt for the Murdochs.

Why? Aye, that was a good question. He needed a better answer than the truth—that he worked for Murdoch. "I came to Glen Lyon to do some tradin' with Murdoch—"

He stopped when she turned away, understandably hating the Murdochs and the mention of their names.

"Mr. Grant," the man said, pulling Cailean's attention back to him. "I'm William Deware." He stepped forward, his shoulders squared, his chin raised slightly higher with the pride and confidence of a born leader. "Let me push aside pretense and get right to it. Do you have any intention of doing us harm? Because if you do, I promise, I will kill you first."

One corner of Cailean's mouth tilted upward. He liked courage in other people. He shook his head, reassuring Deware about his intentions. "Nae." His gaze found hers and he tossed aside his good sense by basking in the fathoms of her eyes, the resolute curve of her jaw. "None whatsoever."

He slipped his gaze back to Deware. If someone in Linavar had shot Patrick, mayhap that same person had tried to kill him. Mayhap his attacker wasn't Duncan, bastard that he was. "How aboot ye? D'ye know fer certain that m' assailant didna come from Linavar?"

"Not yet, but I'll do my best to find out who is responsible," Deware promised.

Cailean didn't particularly want Deware to go snooping about, looking for answers. What if he found them?

"Why?" he asked. "I'm extremely appreciative of yer concern. But why put yerself through trouble fer me? We hardly know each other."

"'Tis not for you."

Cailean knew it wasn't. Deware didn't want to bring the Grants and MacGregors down upon him. He was glad Deware didn't try to deny it. It made Cailean relax. It didn't mean Cailean liked him. It simply meant Deware wasn't afraid to tell the truth and Cailean admired it.

"And lastly, Mr. Grant—" Deware moved around the bed.

"Call me Cailean."

"Cailean, while you were Lord Murdoch's guest did you happen to see a lass inside the castle who appeared to be there against her will?"

Cailean thought about it and shook his head. "Nae, all the gels in the castle appear to want to be there."

Deware looked as if Cailean had just kicked him in the guts. What was that about? What did Cailean care? He turned back to the lass, who was gracing him with a slight smile while he stroked her cat. He muttered an oath, wondering why the cat had chosen him to latch on to, and what a full-on smile from her mistress would do to him.

"Do you remember what happened to you?" she asked in her sorceress's voice.

"Nae." He pushed TamLin away. She came right back.

"You were stabbed," she told him, reaching for him. He

stopped breathing when she began poking and prodding him with gentle fingers. It took most of his fortitude not to let his thoughts linger on the fresh, citrusy scent of her hair while she examined him, or the pull of her breath when his muscles tensed under her ministrations.

"Neither puncture wound hit anything vital in you," she continued, letting her smooth voice seduce his already muddled thoughts. "But whoever did it wanted to kill you, and almost succeeded."

"If not fer the constant attention of my granddaughter, ye would indeed be dead." A woman slightly bent from her many years of toiling entered the room last and strode directly to the side of the bed. She wore a patch over one eye, reminding Cailean of a pirate he'd once seen on the deck of his brother-in-law's brig.

He'd seen this woman the night of the killing. He assumed she was Menzie's mother.

This was going to be torture. He needed to recover quickly and leave. Telling them wasn't going to help anything. Who needed atonement anyway?

"Then I owe her my life." He turned slowly to find her again.

"Ye most certainly do." The old woman managed to keep her tone friendly while she kept her voice stern. "Ye'll remember yer debt in the days to come, aye?"

"Of course." He darkened his expression, feeling slightly insulted. "A Highlander never fergets what's been done to him, or fer him."

"Good," the elder said. "We've recently suffered a great loss and we just want peace now."

"Aye." He looked away and pushed his hair out of his eyes and closed them. "Ye lost yer son. I'm verra sorry fer yer loss."

"Mr. Grant, how do you know Gram lost her son?" Deware asked.

"Miss Menzie told me the first time we met."

"The first time?" Deware turned a puzzled look on her.

Obviously she hadn't told him about running into Cailean's horse. Damn! His horse. Duncan had either taken it back with him, claiming to have found it riderless, no doubt, or someone in Linavar had the beast.

"We met before he was attacked," the lass explained, tossing Cailean a brief glance of annoyance.

"Temperance, why didn't you tell me?"

*Temperance?* Cailean thought. Odd name. He said it silently in his head. Twice. What kind of people called their daughter a virtue?

"I didn't tell you, William, because you would just worry over me."

"With good reason!" he shouted.

Was she Deware's wife? What did it matter to him?

"You're constantly going off by yourself—" William continued, to which Temperance responded with less restraint than her name implied.

The elder woman must have been watching him watching her granddaughter while she argued with Deware. She leaned in closer to him on the bed and said in a low voice meant only for his ears, "She's beguiling, aye?"

He nodded and didn't bother trying to deny it. "Aye," he agreed, his voice as quiet as hers, "she is that."

And she was…oh so beguiling, wide-eyed and somber. Even when she was angry, there was nothing malicious in her gaze. When she glanced his way and caught him staring, she looked away before he did. Veiling herself beneath lush, black lashes, she drew his eyes downward, over the slight curve of her nose, which indicated a break at some point in her life. He'd like to hear the tale of it. *Braw lass*, he thought, then basked briefly in the fullness of her lips, the well-defined curves of her jaw and chin.

Grandma stepped around his bed and stood in front of him, blocking his view of Temperance. He blinked and looked her in the eye.

"She is betrothed to William," the old woman informed him a bit louder, pulling the lass's attention away from her betrothed and back to them. "We were attacked by Lord Murdoch's men and lost our leader. Without one, without William, we will crumble beneath the weight of our liege. William is strong and she will be well protected."

Crumble beneath the weight? What the hell had Duncan been putting them through all these years?

"Gram"—her granddaughter's voice sounded stiff and mortified—"why are you concerning Mr. Grant with my life—or with Linavar, for that matter? He is passing through. Do not burden him with our troubles. He has enough to think on. Like who wants him dead, and why."

Cailean suspected he knew who wanted him dead. But what if he was wrong? What if it was someone from Linavar? He couldn't fight back in his condition if he was attacked again. He eyed Deware, who was watching him intently.

"I'll be on m' way tonight," he promised Gram. He'd had enough blood and revenge. He wanted to take Patrick home.

Gram cast him a quizzical look, then what was possibly a smile. "Oh?" she asked. "Have ye found someone who's agreed to carry ye away?"

He almost smiled back. Cailean liked Gram's feisty spirit. He knew many like her and already felt comfortable around her. He wanted to tell her that he didn't need to be carried. But hell, he was sure that if he flung his legs over the side of the bed and tried to stand on his own two feet, he would plummet to the floor.

"You're in no condition to move," Temperance scolded him gently, coming closer until her tresses feathered over his arm. "You're just barely sitting up. Really, Gram, why would you discuss his leaving so soon?"

"Because," Gram replied, "his eyes fall upon ye like a man who doesn't give a damn who William is."

Deware looked as if he didn't give a damn who he was to her either. If she were *Cailean's*, he wouldn't ignore the threat of another man.

He had to admit that Gram was partially right. He couldn't take his eyes off her granddaughter—and he tried. But every time she offered him her compassionate smile, his belly knotted with some long-forgotten, unwanted feeling. Desire. And not just a desire to touch her, kiss her, but a desire to know her, to allow himself to get closer to her in an even more intimate way. He fought it and buried it deep.

"I'm no' a cad to try to steal a man's woman," he assured them all. "Yer betrothed is safe from me," he told Deware, keeping his voice bland, his expression stoic. "I dinna want her." He didn't want anyone. He preferred to remain unattached and unaffected by the tragedies life brought. "In fact"—he flicked his gaze back to Temperance in time to see her blue eyes blazing at his harsh declaration— "I'll be gone from here and all the rest of ye as soon as I'm able."

"Mr. Grant?" Temperance countered stiffly, and stepped away from the bed. "I'd be happy to end yer treatment and lend you our best horse." Her cool disregard and flashing eyes only fired his blood. "You can leave now."

Cailean was tempted to apologize, to take everything back that had happened in the last two days.

Gone was that carefree, humming lass he'd seen in Kenmore.

The lass he'd destroyed.

*≭*

# Chapter Seven

Damnation, but Mr. Grant was a stubborn arse!

How many times did Temperance have to tell him not to try to leave the bed? How many times to stop swinging an invisible sword while lying down? And how many times had she come into the room and caught him doing one or the other? How were his wounds supposed to heal?

He'd explained that his constant horizontal "practicing" helped him regain his strength, but he looked more exhausted than ever.

When she'd told him so, he'd regarded her with a frosty look in his blue-gray eyes. "Someone wants me dead. I need to be able to fight."

Her helpless stranger had turned out to be a stubborn oaf. He was a Highlander for certain. The plaid that had been draped about his hard body—and she knew from tending him just how hard he was—attested to it. There was more to it than that, though. He also clothed himself in pride and arrogance, with an extra coat of stubbornness.

He didn't look like any trader she'd ever seen. He was

long-haired and wind-tossed. The dark shadow growing denser on his face by the hour concealed his lusciously sweet dimpled chin and made him look more feral and dangerous. It was his eyes, though, the color of them, the sulky almond shape of them, and the combination of innocence and darkness in them, that captured her heart most.

That and watching him slowly warming up to TamLin.

"Stay in yer bed or I will ask William to tie you down, Mr. Grant," she warned one afternoon while he swung his leg over the side of the bed.

"If ye want yer future husband to have any teeth in his mouth, ye willna make such a request." He sounded indifferent, but when he looked up at her his eyes flashed like lightning within rings of sooty lashes.

Temperance held her position. She didn't know why she cared how tired and wounded he was. He'd made it clear that he wanted to leave first chance he got. He didn't like her, had no interest in her at all. And why should he? He didn't even know her. And that was the hook that pierced so sharply. He didn't want to get to know her. He'd barely spoken to her since the day Gram had told him she was betrothed.

"Hell." He squinted, then held his hand up over his eyes. "Does the sun always fill every corner of this damned room?"

"This is my room," she informed him a bit woodenly while she moved toward Gram's jars. "Tell me," she said after a moment without an apology from him, "how you will fight him when you cannot even stand up?"

He swung the other leg off the bed and set his feet on the floor. He stood upright for a moment, giving her time to take in the sight of him, barefoot and bare-chested, the height and breadth of him balancing on unsteady legs.

Temperance watched him go down on his knees and

walked right past him. "Your wounds are barely healed," she pointed out mildly while she reached for a jar she needed. "William is strong. He has forged many things in his smith, including swords. Don't assume that because he comes from a small village he cannot fight." She paused on her way to him to look him in the eye. "I give you my word, he can."

"I dinna know ye, lass." He ground his teeth at her and pulled himself back to the bed. He moved his feet away when TamLin licked his toes. "So unfortunately yer word means verra little to me."

She almost smiled at his arrogance, but she could tell he was in pain and hurried back to him, dipping her fingers into one of Gram's oils as she went. When she stood before him, he looked away.

"Where does it hurt?"

It might have been his pride that made him pause before answering. But finally he gave in and confessed in a throaty whisper, "Everywhere."

"Your body is sore from the heat." She rubbed the oil into her palms and handed him the jar. "This will soothe you." She massaged his shoulders and worked her fingers down each arm. Goodness, but he was tightly wound. She liked the feel of him, the strength of him. She had to keep her wits about her. Her future depended on it.

"As for words," she said, trying to keep her head clear, "I don't trust yours either."

He straightened his spine. She looked at him to find his face close and his eyes scouring her while he sat on the bed—*her* bed, with *her* cat. Sensuality that was slightly menacing and entirely vulnerable oozed from every pore.

"I'll make certain not to make ye any promises then." His words cut the air between them and sparked a small ember in her belly, at her core. This man had fire despite the frost encasing him. She liked fire. William didn't posses any, at least not for her.

She dropped her hands to her sides and kept her voice even and low when she spoke. "Then let me thank you now for saving us the trouble of being cordial until you leave, which shouldn't be long now according to you. You have my gratitude for that, Mr. Grant."

He sat there while TamLin purred in his lap, staring at her without saying a word. His eyes were shadowed by his heavy brow and strands of his hair. Despite the haunted radiance of his gaze, he looked like something more wild than docile. "Miss Menzie, ye misunderstand me."

She needed to remain steady against the power of his regard. He wasn't about to apologize, as his tender tone suggested.

"I see." She raised a skeptical brow and the edges of her lips rose with it. "So, then, you're not brooding because I didn't help you to yer feet?"

He immediately stopped and traded his frown for a cool upward curl of his mouth that was so slight she almost missed it. "Dinna be a fool, lass. I got up just fine withoot yer help."

"Aye, well, you did manage not to faint."

"Faint?" Laughter danced across the cool gray surfaces of his eyes, sending a tingle of fire down her back. "Dinna be ridiculous, lass. Grants dinna faint."

She smiled indulgently. Stubborn arse. "Of course they don't. Now lie down on your belly so that I can apply this to your back." She waited while he did as she asked and barely moved when he set his icy gaze on her before his head touched the pillow and he closed his eyes.

She spilled oil down the length of his spine to the low edge of his breeches. His flesh was warm and his muscles twitched while she spread the oil over the hills and valleys of his back.

"Hell, that feels good."

She was warm, a little light-headed from the feel of him, the deep, raspy sound of him. She wiped her brow with her oily hand and muttered a slight oath.

"What if next time you fall and crack open that pig-headed skull of yours?" she asked, pushing her fingers deep into his muscles. "Do you know how long it takes to clean up blood?"

She was certain she just saw him smile. Half of him, at least. The other was half-buried in feathers.

"Is that all m' death would mean to ye, cleanin' up m' blood?"

She didn't want him to die. That's why she'd saved his life. The handsome ogre hadn't even thanked her. "There's more," she admitted, doing her best not to sigh over all his rock-hard angles. "Who wants a bed someone died in?" She felt her mouth tilt into a deeper smile when he feigned surprise at her pretended insult. "Of course I don't want you to perish."

"That's kind—"

"Your death would lead to folks looking for you. Once your kin discovered you were in Menzie care and died, they'd kill us all."

He propped himself up on one elbow, then gritted his teeth at the pain in his back and sat up again, almost knocking into her. "Ye're likely correct."

She wished he wouldn't look at her...or that he'd never stop. He didn't look angry. Even the indifferent veneer across his eyes had fallen away like a curtain. But, oh, what was his detachment compared to his scantest smile?

Goodness, but he was distracting. She had plans to make,

things to see to for her future. She had men to kill and a path to choose. She would choose it herself, or try to. The only way to accomplish her goal was to kill the threat that would force her to marry Will. She had no doubts she could do it, as long as she didn't let go of her hatred. Cailean was making it difficult, though. Sparring with him made it difficult to think of anything but his sharp tongue and how it might feel along her skin. Touching him . . . She should ask Gram to finish looking after him. Or Anne Gilbert . . . or anyone else.

"When are ye goin' to marry Deware?" he asked, as if reading her thoughts, or mayhap he could read her miserable expression.

"After Hogmanay," she told him, moving to sit in the chair by the bed. "What were you doing in my cabbage patch when you were attacked?" she asked, hoping to sway the topic off her upcoming nuptials. Her glance found him covertly admiring her form.

"I was hoping to see ye again. To make certain ye were no' injured by m' horse after ye ran into him. After that, I'd intended to return to Lyon's Ridge fer m' cousin and then head home."

His concern made her blush and think about his face instead of the face of her enemy. He was a stranger with no place in her life. So what if he'd been concerned about her? Or if his gaze made her feel a bit light-headed and warm? Arrangements would soon be under way for her wedding with William, and if Cailean Grant kept distracting her from her plans, she'd be attending.

"You said you intended on returning to the castle for your cousin."

"Aye, Patrick. That's correct."

Patrick—the name he'd called out in his slumber.

"Why did you plan to go to Kenmore without him?"

"Pardon me?"

"When we first met," she clarified, "you told me you were on yer way to Kenmore. Do you remember?"

He nodded but said nothing.

"Why did you leave him at Lyon's Ridge?"

He looked as if he wanted to say something...something different from what came out of his mouth. "He was...hungover from one of his wild nights and had nae interest in purchasin' fresh vegetables."

"And you do?" she asked, working hard to conceal her slight smile. Her father used to love to cook with Gram.

"Aye, I'm a master in the kitchen."

"Are you?" He certainly lacked no vanity, she thought. "Pity you're in a rush to leave. I'd like to sample yer plates and see if you're just full of air."

He chuckled—a short, throaty blend of humor and arrogance. "I'd enjoy takin' ye up, but I must get back to the castle."

"For Patrick?" Temperance supplied. When he nodded, she forged ahead. "Why? Is he in danger from Murdoch?"

"He could be. He's a MacGregor, and MacGregor heads are held at high value."

Aye, the proscription against the MacGregors. She'd heard of the Highland persecution, but didn't know too much about it.

"He traveled with me, though against m' wishes," the Highlander continued. "And now, as circumstances would have it, and as I feared, he is alone in the castle of a greedy murderer."

Temperance nodded. Aye, he had Duncan Murdoch right. He was a greedy murderer. But how did Mr. Grant know? He said he was the lord's guest. Did that mean...?

"Did he tell you about it?" she asked him, her voice

becoming more somber. "You were his guest. Did Duncan Murdoch tell you that he had my father killed?"

He could have sensed her dread and said anything, but his gaze told her the truth. She wanted to look away from it, but she didn't. She couldn't. She wanted to know.

"Were you there?"

He looked away first. "Nae, Murdoch boasted of it."

He'd boasted. Temperance wrung her hands together. How could life—her father's life—mean so little? "He's a monster."

"Aye."

"I aim to kill him, and also the one who nodded just before that murdering whoreson"—she paused to swipe a tear or two away from her cheek—"killed my father."

He met her gaze again, briefly. Was her pain so tangible that he felt it? He did look a bit heartsick, as if he understood. Mayhap he didn't know how to comfort her, and that was why he always dropped his eyes to the floor.

She sighed inwardly, expecting him to, like William, try to talk her out of revenge. Well, he'd be wasting his time. Murdoch had boasted. Now more than ever Temperance knew what she had to do. No one was going to stop her.

When he lifted his gaze to her once again, she tried to keep from falling into the endless fathoms of his eyes.

"How?"

She shrugged her shoulders. "I could shoot them full of arrows. My aim is good. Ask William."

She thought she saw his gaze darken, or was it just the shadows his hair cast over his eyes?

"Have ye ever shot a man before? 'Tisn't as easy as ye think."

"'Twas easy for the man holding his blade to my father's throat," she countered, trying to keep the burning at the backs of her eyes from spilling forward. Why was she so tempted to cry on his shoulder? He didn't offer it, but something in his eyes invited her in. He had suffered a loss as she had. He would understand her need to weep properly for her father. "Nay, I've never shot a man, but I would if I had to."

He nodded and the shadows passed. "I believe ye."

She smiled slightly. Just like that? He believed her? Wasn't he curious about who would help her? What if she told him she didn't need any help to kill the men who'd killed her father? Would he laugh in her face? Was he trying not to do it right now?

"He has guardians," he pointed out.

"I know," she told him. "His Black Riders."

He nodded again. "I've met some of them. They willna go doun easily."

He'd met them. This could be useful. "What are they like? Tell me everything about them as payment for saving yer life."

"Nothin' I tell ye is goin' to bring ye a victory against them."

He didn't know what she was capable of doing. She was no fool, believing she could fight sword to sword against a beefy mercenary. He'd slice her up like a cut of mutton. But there were other ways to kill a man. Gram had taught her which herbs could do the task for her.

"Your veiled insult of me being incompetent are words I shall particularly enjoy watching you eat."

One side of his mouth curled upward. "There willna be time enough fer ye to enjoy a fourth, possibly a third breath before they cut ye doun."

She wanted to toss back her head and laugh. Arguing with him felt a bit exhilarating. Even the urge to slap him for his continued insults thrilled her.

She rose from her chair and moved closer to him, until they almost shared breath. She looked him straight in the eyes and trembled at the force behind them. "Then help me, Mr. Grant."

He closed his eyes, giving her a reprieve. Was he considering it? Oh, with his aid...

"Ye'll bring war here, Miss Menzie," he told her in a quiet voice. "I willna help ye do that."

Of course. She should have guessed it. She sounded mad, or at the least foolish. But she didn't care. "They killed my father, Mr. Grant. He'd done nothing to deserve death—and in front of all the people who loved him."

"I know," he said, his voice going soft and heavy, as if he'd been there with her to watch.

"What would *you* do?" she asked him, catching her breath with poignant sorrow. "What would you do if someone you loved were taken from you? If they died in your arms? Would you let their killer go unpunished?"

He didn't answer her right away. He simply stared into her eyes and then shook his head.

"Nae," he whispered, grinding his teeth. "I wouldna let them go."

# Chapter Eight

Cailean sat up. He needed to get out of this damn bed.

He needed to save his cousin and somehow get him back to Camlochlin, and he had to get away from Temperance Menzie and all her talk about killing the men responsible for her father's death.

He was one of those men. She'd seen him nod. She'd seen him in the cold darkness of his despair and she still smiled at him, fought with him, and tempted him to fight back, but not too hard.

When he'd first opened his eyes, he'd wanted her to know the truth: that he was indeed a Black Rider but Patrick wasn't, and someone from her village had almost killed him. But with each moment that passed between them, it became more difficult to confess.

He didn't want to care if she hated him. He never should have come here. He should have just tried to forget. But he was the cause of all her pain, the kind he understood too well. He wasn't certain he could live with that. Damn Murdoch for stabbing him and setting him here, helpless but to watch what became of the family he'd destroyed. It was his penance for his bloodlust.

Hell. He doubled over at the thought of Patrick's death. Cailean knew it had been his own choice to take residence at the castle as a hired strong-armer, despite Patrick's urging that they return to the Highlands, that had put Patrick in his sickbed. Cailean had to save him.

He had to leave Linavar and Seth Menzie's house and get the hell away from his victim's daughter before he ended up helping her do the impossible—and likely getting them both killed.

It wasn't that she affected him to the point that he would let her talk him into helping her kill Duncan Murdoch. He'd wanted to do it himself a day after he'd arrived at Lyon's Ridge. And long before that, after Alison died, he'd promised himself never to lay down the shield he held up around his heart and accept anyone inside. Life was filled with the unexpected. Nothing was certain. No one was assured happiness. He preferred to remain detached, untouched, and pragmatic.

But he wasn't dead.

Temperance Menzie possessed fire that attracted him. He liked the confidence she exuded when she went head-to-head with him. She was braw and bonny, and broken. The last was his doing and because of the circumstances, he wanted to mend her. She made him stare, and she made him care when she spoke about her father. But what frightened him the most were the words he wanted to pen about her, and the fact that he wanted to write anything at all. It had been so long since anything or anyone had moved him enough for him to take up quill and ink. He had begun to fall in love with Alison, but even then he hadn't been tempted to write of her. It had been too soon after losing Sage.

But since coming here, waking in this spirited lass's care, a dozen times already he'd had to clench his jaw against asking her for a quill and parchment. He wasn't ready to let a woman fire up his passions. There were days when it felt as if his nerves were raw and even the weight of someone's breath on him was unbearable. He didn't know how to release everything that haunted him. He didn't know if he wanted to. He was safe here in his solitude.

He wouldn't let Seth Menzie's daughter spark anything in him. And hell, she was betrothed. Was it his pitiful imagination that told him she didn't seem happy about marrying Deware? He didn't care. He wouldn't allow himself to. He wouldn't write, or cook, or love. He was determined to guard himself against caring again, afraid to lose it all. He needed to keep people out in order to remain callous. That's why mercenaries were the best company. No one really gave a rat's arse about anyone else. In their company was a perfect place for him to hide.

But his demons had found him the night Seth Menzie died in his daughter's arms. He was sorry he'd brought that pain upon her. He didn't know how to tell her. He didn't want to.

He swung his legs over the bed and set his feet on the floor.

Miss Menzie hadn't yet been in to see him this morn, but her cat hadn't left.

*Cats*, he thought while this one curled herself around his ankles. They were peculiar creatures. There were many of them in Camlochlin but they tended to find more interest in hunting than in forming any sort of bond with anything or anyone else. But TamLin seemed to have taken a liking to Cailean since the morning they'd put Seth Menzie into the ground and the cat had broken through the fog and found him hiding behind a hill.

Cailean had had dogs his whole life. He didn't know what to do with a cat—a purring one at that.

He left the bed and cringed a little at the pain in his back, but it wasn't unbearable. He took a slow, tentative step, ignoring the dizziness in his head.

"Dinna give me that look," he said, eyeing the feline resting on the bed. "I dinna care what she said aboot gettin' oot of bed. She's yer mistress, no' mine."

TamLin meowed.

How the hell was that sound ever supposed to warn one of danger, the way a large dog's bark would? Cailean almost smiled at the foolishness of it and took another step.

"Mr. Grant!"

Her sharp voice rattled him just a bit and he grasped the wall to keep from tipping over. He turned to cast her a scowl, which she ignored.

"Get back in bed! I may not be yer mistress but I helped save yer life. The least you could do is follow my instructions for a day or two!"

She was angry. Her eyes blazed a most vivid shade of sapphire blue when she was angry. She was also correct. He owed her that much. But Patrick...he had to regain his strength and get Patrick out of Lyon's Ridge. He'd never intended to be gone this long. "Miss Menzie," he said, turning on his ankle. Damnation, he wouldn't mind looking at her for a few more hours. She wore a simple white shift beneath thin woolen skirts of deep emerald. She had plaited two slender braids at her temples and circled them around her head like a crown. Woven through it were tiny flowers as blue as her eyes. The rest of her hair fell in loose messy waves down her back.

She belonged to Deware.

Cailean pushed down the lump in his throat and continued.

Before Alison he'd been a wee bit shy around lasses. He was nothing like his brother Malcolm or some of his cousins, who had such an easy way with the fairer side. He'd always found more interest in fighting, and writing, and cooking. He'd never been with a lass before Alison, and there had been none after her. No more.

"I'm grateful fer what ye've done fer me, Miss Menzie, but—"

"You need more time to heal."

He knew he did, but if Duncan had tried to kill him, what would stop him from trying to kill Patrick as well? No matter how his body felt, Cailean couldn't let his cousin die. He prayed he wasn't too late.

He didn't tell Temperance that there was another reason he wanted to get the hell out of Linavar. It wasn't right that she was helping him recover.

"I need to go."

She glared at him for a moment, looking as if she wanted to call him the biggest fool to ever live—thanks to her.

Cailean wanted to thank her for everything she had done. But it was just as well he let her go without a word. He didn't need to let the strength in her jaw, or the alluring shape and pink hue of her lips, not to mention her sharp tongue behind them, interest him. Most dangerous, though, were her sad, soulful eyes, veiled behind her lashes. He wanted to help her heal, but he was still raw himself.

"You don't need to go," she tried again. "William already went."

He stopped trying to right himself and stared at her, the blood draining from his face. "Where did he go?"

"To Lyon's Ridge to—"

"Why the hell would he go there?" Cailean's heart boomed in his ears. If Duncan didn't kill him first, Deware would find out everything—all Cailean's secrets. Were they secrets? Aye, hell, they were. Cailean wasn't ready for Temperance to find out he was a Black Rider. *The* Black Rider. He didn't stop to ponder why he cared if she knew the truth or not.

"There's no need to raise your voice, Mr. Grant. William has been to the castle many times. He's Linavar's smith and he trades his wares there a few times a year. He—"

Cailean wasn't listening. He should tell her the truth before she found out from her betrothed. He opened his mouth but found he didn't have the courage to tell her.

"Yer betrothed is a fool, Miss Menzie," he said instead. A fool who would likely try to kill Cailean upon his return to Linavar.

"He'll bring your cousin back."

"If Murdoch doesna kill him first." He reached for his shirt and pulled it over his head and shoulders.

"You're not still going?" She came forward, arms folded across her chest, ready to go head-to-head with him. "He's gone to help you and Patrick. Why are you so stubborn?"

When his shirt cleared his vision, she was there to fill it again. For a moment their eyes met in a battle of wills—hers that he stay, his that he go as fast as he could.

"Ye're just as stubborn as I am." He scowled down at her, trying not to let the thick black fringes of her lashes or the tilt of her chin affect him.

"Because I'm right."

"I'm no' arguin' with ye over that, lass," he told her, bending his head a little to level their gazes. "But I have to save m' cousin, and likely yer betrothed as well."

She clenched her jaw as if to hold back the rest of her words. He dipped his gaze to her mouth, sorry to have silenced her.

"Are ye leaving us, Mr. Grant?" Thankfully, Gram's voice at the door pulled him from his thoughts.

"I am, Gram." He straightened and stepped away from Temperance. "Thank ye fer yer care, and thank ye, Miss Menzie." He didn't look at her again when Gram held her hand out to him. He lent her his arm and left the room and Temperance Menzie behind.

The house spun on his way out and his legs felt like warm pudding, but he didn't turn back.

He looked around the spacious house as Gram walked him to the door, appreciating, as his father had taught him to, the masterful workmanship. Had Seth Menzie built it? Connor Grant, Cailean's father, would be impressed. As Camlochlin's master builder, he had built many awe-inspiring houses. He would tip his bonnet to this one if he saw it.

A large hall was built off to the right, and as Cailean passed it, he spread his gaze over the holly and mountain laurel decorating the wooden archways. It felt and smelled like the Christmas season. But the laurel was drying, and the absence of the master of the house could be felt like a December chill seeping through the walls.

Cailean tried to remember the joy of the holidays amid the webs cluttering his head. He swallowed air that felt as thick as pond scum. Suddenly his back felt as if it were on fire. The flames were radiating down his arms, down to his waist.

"I didn't think the Grants raised fools."

He managed to hold on and even smiled, knowing where Temperance's fire came from. "Every family has a few."

She agreed and bid him farewell at the door.

He turned to leave and crumpled to the floor.

•  •  •

Riding toward the fortress swathed in pewter clouds, William paused on his mount and shook away the fear that covered him. He could see shadows of guardsmen patrolling the gray battlements of Lyon's Ridge. There was nothing warm or inviting about his lord's holding. He prayed Marion wasn't inside, or, worse, in the dungeon.

He made it unhindered to the outer wall—and that was where he remained for the night. Only a dozen tradesmen were allowed entry each day. When his turn finally came, he displayed the goods he'd forged in his smith with a swish of a crimson blanket and was let into the inner gate. He quickly blended into the small crowd of merchants, keeping his eyes peeled for any sign of Marion or anyone who looked as if they might be useful in leading him to her.

Four hours, six daggers, and a masterfully forged cooking pot later, he met a scullery maid named Annie and paid her the coin he'd made from selling his wares. In return she gave him information from inside the fortress.

"I know of a gel called Marion," Annie told him while stuffing her payment down between her cleavage. "One of Maeve's new gels, I heard."

"Maeve?"

"Aye, she's the madam inside."

"Madam?"

"Aye, ye know—"

He held up his hand to stop her. He knew what a madam was. But Marion—one of her gels?

William wanted to tear at his hair. He'd been here looking for her before. He should have looked harder. She was here, being forced to... "I have to find her!" He moved to push past Annie but she stopped him. "She's gone."

"Gone where?" His heart throbbed within.

"Well"—Annie adjusted her bodice—"according to

kitchen gossip Maeve was paid a sum of coin to bring her to Perth, to a holding called Ravenglade."

"Paid by who?" he asked, hoping some wealthy nobleman hadn't requested her. "A nobleman?"

Annie shook her head. "Nae, she was paid fer by one of Lord Murdoch's men."

It couldn't get any worse.

"A Black Rider?" he asked, sickened. He'd kill any one of them who touched her. To hell with starting a war.

"'Twas Patrick's cousin, I believe. Patrick MacGregor." She blushed saying his name. William barely noticed.

No. No. It couldn't be. His breath shortened and his heart pounded even faster.

"Cailean Grant?" He had to be certain. Had he been correct all along? He prayed he was wrong.

"Aye, Cailean," Annie the scullery maid confirmed. "So different from his cousin that one is. He's morose and unfriendly. I've heard the men talk about how he sits alone at the table and—"

"Cailean Grant is a Black Rider?" And he'd left Temp and Gram alone with him?

"Aye. One of the most merciless of the twenty, I'm told."

William's blood drained and left him pale and terrified. He had to get home and save her. Temperance was his responsibility. She always would be. Panic filled him. Grant couldn't have fooled them all that easily. And to what purpose?

"You say he's merciless?" William's voice quavered.

"I'm told to his enemies, aye. Around here he's kind enough, but quiet— Oh, there's one of Maeve's gels now! She'll know more about yer Marion." She pointed the lass out to him. "'Twill be difficult to get inside, so if ye want her, ye best go get her now."

He turned to watch the girl stroll to another set of doors. He had to make a decision, the hardest of his life. And he had to hurry.

William dropped his wares at Annie's feet and took off running.

# Chapter Nine

"Och, nae, what the hell am I doin' still here?"

On her way out of her room, Temperance paused and frowned at the frustration in Mr. Grant's voice. She was relieved that he'd awakened from fever for the second time now, but damn it, was being here with her so terrible? The fool was going to end up killing himself, insisting on leaving his sickbed.

"You're about to thank me for saving your life again." She waited a moment, tilting her ear toward the sound of him.

"All right," he finally agreed. "Thank ye fer savin' m' life again."

The full, rich resonance of him snatched the breath from her body even while her logic reminded her that he was nothing more than a stranger. A foolish, stubborn stranger.

She turned back to him, awake now, his belly crunching as he tried to sit up. He groaned and squinted against the blinding sun. Seeing him tossed her logic to the four winds. She couldn't help but let her gaze linger on his whipcord-tight body. She'd felt it. Much of it, anyway, throughout the night and much of the next day. The last twelve hours had been critical, but he'd survived.

"The more you fight it, the longer you'll be here."

His resolve to continue faltered and he leaned down on his elbows. "What am I doin' back here?"

"You collapsed at the door."

"Ridiculous." He groaned again and managed to sit upright. He rubbed his head, as if trying to remember. "Deware...he went to Lyon's Ridge."

Aye, William had gone and she and Gram were worried about him, but they hadn't alerted the rest of the villagers just yet. No need to incite panic if it was unnecessary. She prayed Duncan hadn't killed him for trying to get Patrick MacGregor out. But William was no fool. He knew some of the Black Riders and had traded at the castle before. He would use caution.

Cailean Grant, on the other hand, would not.

"Has he returned?"

He didn't know anything. She could use it to her, or rather his, advantage. She wanted this Highlander to live just so she could think on him, rough and ready, some nights while she lay alone in her bed. She didn't want him to die in her bed—or anywhere else. He needed at least a few more days, perhaps until Hogmanay, after she'd had time to kill at least the three men responsible for killing her father. Duncan, the Rider who'd nodded, and the one who'd held the dagger.

"He returned but has left again," she told him, only mildly repentant about deceiving him. If he died, he wouldn't do his cousin any good. "But he asked me to relay to you that he was able to get inside the fortress and your cousin is alive."

William would pardon her deceit if he knew why she'd done it. To keep Mr. Grant in bed for just a little longer, mostly for his sake, partially for hers. She must admit that she enjoyed tending him, rubbing him down with Gram's oils, feeling the strength and the length of his solid muscles.

She knew he wanted to leave. He'd be gone from her life as soon as he could, and she would either marry William or live her life as a killer. There were no other options.

"You're fortunate to be alive," she told him. "Your fever was verra high, like the first one, and most likely cooked even more parts of you." She lifted her eyes less than an inch and gave his forehead a slight smirk.

His gloriously large eyes and his reluctant smile revealed that he knew she was insulting him, and he didn't care.

"Tell me more aboot Patrick."

More? She didn't know any more. Only that Cailean was afraid Duncan Murdoch would try to kill him for being a MacGregor now that Cailean wasn't there to protect him.

It had to be enough. One dead Highlander would be bad enough. Two and the MacGregors and Grants would seek even worse revenge. "Well, I only know what William told me. And that is that he met your cousin and Patrick is alive and well."

"He met Patrick?" he asked, looking a bit apprehensive.

Did he not believe her? "Aye," she confirmed. Good thing she was well versed in the art of deception, having practiced often as a child after she and William got caught breaking this rule or that.

"Mayhap William will have more to tell you when he returns. You just rest now. I'll make you some tea." She turned to go.

"Did he go back for Marion?"

She stopped and rounded on him. "What do you know of Marion?"

"Only what William's eyes revealed when I told him I didn't know her. I was mistaken."

What was he saying and did she need to sit down for it? She decided she did and sat next to him on the bed. "Are you telling me that Marion is in Lyon's Ridge?"

"Aye, I think so. I hadn't recalled her the first time Deware queried aboot her. But I remembered her in a dream. There was a lass in the castle called Marion."

So William had been correct about Murdoch's kidnapping her all along.

"And William cares for her?"

He turned to look at her. "I believe he does."

Why was he telling her? She looked into the fathoms of his eyes and then glanced briefly away. What would she do if William loved another? She wouldn't marry him, of course. That would leave her open to Duncan, unless she killed him first. What if Cailean Grant rescued his cousin and then stayed? What would it be like to kiss that melancholy mouth? To be the one who made him smile?

"Ye look relieved."

She couldn't help it. She was. "If you're correct then I'll be happy for him. He is my dearest friend."

"But ye dinna love him."

Was it so obvious? She shook her head. "Not the way I want to love a man."

His voice was low, his eyes aflame. "How d'ye want to love a man, then?"

She smiled and thought about it for a moment. "The way my father loved my mother. When she died giving birth to me, he suffered temporary madness. He didn't visit me for the first six months of my life. And then one day he did, and he fell in love all over again."

Cailean looked down, veiling his haunted gaze beneath his thick lashes. "Ye deserve more than a man who loves another."

"It isn't for me to say what I deserve, Mr. Grant."

"Then let me try," he said, and she noticed his hand was close enough to hers on the bed for him to move his pinkie over hers. "Ye deserve a man whose passions overflow fer ye and ye alone, who values your honesty and offers his in return."

Aye, that was what she wanted, but she didn't have time to wait for such a man.

"I don't blame William for not telling me," she defended her friend. "He was following my father's wishes that I should marry him upon my father's death."

He looked down at TamLin snuggled beside him. "If I could…" He paused and then began again, finally lifting his gaze to hers. "If I could go back and change what happened that night, I would do it."

Temperance thought that was the kindest thing anyone had said to her about her father's death. She smiled at him. He didn't smile back, but she was certain she noted a slight change in his expression. He wasn't displeased.

He didn't remain awake too long after that. She was gentle when she covered him. Her tales about Patrick had worked, giving Cailean a bit of reassurance that his cousin was all right and he didn't need to go chasing after him.

But what if Patrick MacGregor was dead? What if William was too? Where the hell was he? Just when she was about to ask Gram to send her two biggest, toughest cousins, Charlie and Jack, to Lyon's Ridge to find him, William pushed open the front door and stepped inside, bringing flurries of snow in with him.

Overjoyed to see him, Temperance ran to him and jumped into his arms. "Where have you been? You had us worried about you."

"Is Grant still here?" he asked her, and squeezed her to him hard enough to halt her breath. "Where's Gram?"

Temperance disengaged from him and stepped back to have a good look at him. He looked well enough, save that his clothes were dirty, along with his face, and his eyes were set on her bedroom door.

"William, what in blazes happened? Where have you been?"

He didn't answer but broke away and started for her room.

She followed him, but he warned her not to come inside. She didn't take too well to warnings and entered the room right behind him.

Cailean was asleep, looking like a peaceful angel, but this was no time to pause to admire him. His appearance didn't stop William from moving toward the bed. "Grant!" he shouted, waking him.

"William." Temperance tugged on his arm.

He ignored her and stared down at Cailean, waking up.

"I've just returned from Lyon's Ridge. I met a young scullery maid named Annie. Know her?"

Cailean blinked his sleepy eyes, then shook his head.

"She told me that your cousin Patrick was ill but was recovering well."

Cailean scratched his jaw and slid his gaze to her. "Ye didna meet him, then?"

Temperance swore under her breath. Now Cailean knew she'd lied. Whatever would he think of her? She felt so foolish she could barely look at him, but she did. And she was glad she had, else she would have missed the slightest curl of his smile, a hint of amusement in his eyes rather than melancholy.

"Nay." William made half a turn and set his hard, knowing gaze on her, apparently suspecting she'd lied. "I didn't meet him."

Temperance took a deep breath and faced whatever was coming from them. She tilted her chin ever so slightly and let the truth fly, setting her eyes on William. "I was trying to save his life. If I would have told him the truth he would have left this sickbed and likely died." She turned to Cailean next. "You should be thanking me."

He acquiesced without a word, bowing his head slightly to her. "You have my heartfelt thanks, yet again, Miss Menzie."

Her heart slowed almost instantly and she wondered how he'd managed to soothe her nerves within the space of a breath. She wanted to thank him for easing her mortification, and for making her smile in the midst of missing her father. Each time she did, she found herself able to breathe a little easier.

"Annie told me much about you," William continued woodenly, dragging Cailean's gaze back to him.

Both men were quiet for a moment while something passed between them. Had William's fingers just moved closer to the hilt of his sword? Had Cailean's eyes just slipped to her? Temperance watched the men's silent interaction. What the hell was going on?

"I was rushing back here to see to your...welfare," William continued, "when I ran into Kate, one of Maeve's gels."

Cailean blinked at him. It wasn't much of a reaction, but it was something, in Temperance's estimation. He recognized the name. Who was Maeve, she wondered?

"Maeve is a madam," William said, turning to look at her as if he'd heard her thoughts. "Marion was going to be forced to be one of her whores."

"Was?" Temperance asked with a shaky voice. She prayed it wasn't too late for Marion. Poor William, if what Cailean suspected was true. "Is she dead?"

William shook his head. "No. She lives, still untouched because of Mr. Grant here."

Temperance slowly turned to look at Cailean, who was sitting up, grimacing as he stretched. Because of him? "What did he do?" she asked quietly, watching him and the way the sunlight fell over his jaw.

"Kate told me that you paid Maeve handsomely to keep Marion away from other men by sending her off to Perth, to a castle called Ravenglade. Why?" William asked him in a deeper, more menacing voice. "Why Ravenglade? Who is there?"

"M' brother and his wife," Cailean replied. "When they hear that 'twas me who sent her, they'll keep her safe."

Temperance didn't move. Why would he do such a thing? Marion was untouched and alive because of Cailean. She wanted to smile at him, lean down and kiss him. So there was a man beneath all that ogre?

"Why did you protect her from others?" William demanded softly. "Do you have intentions toward her?"

Cailean had been correct, then. William cared for Marion. Temperance had thought she was settling, when William was settling too. All his fire and determination to find Marion was from more than just a desire to keep Linavar safe. It was also for Marion. Poor William; what he must be going through. She pitied both herself and him for being forced into lives they didn't want in order to keep peace with their overlord. There would never be peace if Temperance killed the lord's son. Unless...

A way to do it without blame falling on her hatched in her mind, and she smiled at her dear friend.

She loved William, but she wasn't going to marry him. She couldn't. She didn't want an extraordinary life, just a life worthy of the one her mother had died to give her.

"I have no interest in Marion," Cailean told William. "She was offered to me and I refused her. She reminded me of someone I once knew and she looked terrified, so I offered m' aid. I remembered her in a dream but ye were no' here to tell ye."

William remained quiet for a time, letting what the Highlander had told him sink in. When it did he exhaled as if he hadn't done so in weeks. "You have my thanks," he told Cailean. "I owe you much."

Grant shook his head, then continued. "M' brother is the Earl of Huntley and lord of Ravenglade. Marion is safe."

"William." Temperance touched his arm. "You should have told me about your feelings for Marion."

"Why?" He set his rich, dark eyes on her and shrugged his shoulders. "Nothing would have changed as long as I never found her."

"And now that you have found her?"

He turned to look at Mr. Grant and shook his head. "Nothing changes still."

"Nay, Will. We spoke about this the night my father was killed. I told you what Father had said."

"Aye, Temp, but he didn't get twenty years. And I too spoke to him earlier that day. I promised him that I'd see to you."

She didn't care about promises she hadn't been a party to.

She didn't want to argue now. Now she wanted to leave the room so she could ponder what was so special about this "someone" Cailean had once known, whose mere likeness to Marion had compelled him to save Marion from being assaulted by the men of Lyon's Ridge.

She also wanted to escape the haunting splendor of Cailean Grant's eyes. They fell upon her often, hooded and lackadaisical, seeming disinterested for the most part. But they kept returning to her, proving otherwise.

She turned for the door and caught Cailean's eyes on her yet again. Their gazes met and she thought she might have seen his nostrils flare a little, a glint of something warm in his stone-cold eyes. He smiled at her. The smile was soft, subtle, coming from somewhere deep and genuine. It gave her hope that she could find happiness again. With him.

Hell, she didn't want to marry William.

If she had to marry, she'd prefer someone like—she let her gaze linger over Cailean's face—him.

# Chapter Ten

*A*lone with Deware, Cailean watched him pace before his bed. The smith looked pale. Beads of sweat glistened along his temples. Cailean felt a little ill himself. Annie had obviously told Deware that he was a Black Rider. He was caught, his true identity revealed. He wasn't sure if he was prepared for the accusations having to do with Seth Menzie's death. But none of them came.

Deware's dark eyes settled on him and for a moment Cailean thought he was going to have to fight for his life. "You can imagine what went through my mind when Annie told me." Deware stopped pacing and stared at him. "You lied to all of us. You're a Black Rider and I brought you back."

"Ye saved m' life," Cailean corrected him.

"I should kill you now. But for what you did for Marion…"

Even recovering from a dangerous infection, Cailean knew William wouldn't stand a chance against him. The smith hadn't been raised by Grants and MacGregors to be a warrior. He did wonder, though, why Deware didn't tell Temperance what he'd discovered.

"I knew ye would either try to kill me or just let me die if ye knew the truth," Cailean admitted. "I know what happened to her faither and I decided to leave Lyon's Ridge and the Murdochs. I wanted to come here first to offer m' aid but someone stabbed me. I ask that ye dinna tell Miss Menzie."

Deware blinked at him, then stepped closer. The seriousness of his expression compelled Cailean to prepare to spring from the bed.

"I will not be the one to tell her, Grant. You will. For saving Marion I will grant you time. But know this, I will gut you while you sleep if you harm Temperance in any way."

"I have no intentions on harmin' anyone. I just wish to recover and go."

"When do you think you will be ready to leave here?"

"I'm afraid," Cailean began, "this time might take a wee bit longer than the last. There'll be a long way to travel to get home and I dinna want to fall ill again in the middle of nowhere."

"Of course," Deware agreed. "When you're ready, I would ask you to travel to Perth and bring Marion back. Please," he added when Cailean was about to refuse. "As repayment for saving your life and bringing you back here. I cannot leave the village without showing them that their lives come second to Marion's. I must stay and protect them."

Cailean admired such dedication to his people. His cousin, the MacGregor clan chief Rob MacGregor, had devoted his life to his people, as any great leader should. He'd do it. He'd bring Marion back. She was in Perth. It wouldn't be difficult.

"I'll bring her back."

"And then," Deware finished steadily, "you will leave Linavar and not return."

Cailean eyed the soon-to-be leader of Linavar. "So ye could marry Marion without losin' Temperance to me."

"I'm not going to let Temperance lose her heart to a Black Rider, if that's what you mean," Deware assured him. "I'm going to marry her to keep her and the others safe from all of you."

Deware obviously wasn't aware of Temperance's plans to kill Murdoch—or Cailean. Cailean looked toward the door. As soon as he was well enough, he'd fetch Marion, bring her back, and then be gone from here. Good. He didn't want Temperance to lose her heart and he certainly didn't want to lose his. He wasn't prepared to endure the loss of anyone else in his life. Life took away. He knew it well enough.

"As ye wish," he conceded. "I should be fit to leave by Christmas."

"Ye'll stay as long as ye need," Gram said, entering the room with a tray of food.

Cailean cut her an affectionate look. He liked the old woman. Even though she believed him to be dangerous for Linavar, she took careful care of him. "If ye keep spoilin' me with yer delicious cookin', I'll never want to leave. Might I suggest servin' me last week's milk?"

Her weathered skin creased and puckered when she smiled, setting down the tray. "I should chase ye out of here with my broom on yer tail, before Murdoch comes looking fer ye and accuses us of yer condition. But in truth, I'm tired of giving a damn about Mr. Murdoch or his father. I won't cast a helpless man out into the snow. Our compliance doesn't stop them from doing vile things—them and their hell-spawn mercenaries. They've already proven that."

Cailean couldn't keep his eyes from moving to Deware. Would he tell Gram?

Cailean had come here to tell them the truth. But the shame it brought with it made that more difficult than he could ever have imagined, so he said nothing.

He sure as hell didn't want someone else telling them. The sooner he left and paid his debt to Deware, the better the chances they'd never find out. "Christmas. I'll leave on Christmas. 'Tis what?" He turned back to Deware for confirmation. "Three or four days from now? If that's agreeable?"

Deware nodded, but his eyes were already turning for the door. Cailean's followed and beheld Miss Menzie standing beneath the archway. He sat up straight and, for a moment, let the sight of her fully affect him. He knew he shouldn't, but he couldn't look away. Judging from the woolen mantle draped around her shoulders, and her rich pink cheeks, she'd been working outside.

"'Tis too soon." Her voice… or her gaze, finding and settling on his, stilled his breath and muddled his thoughts. What was the secret he was trying to keep from her? "You don't want to leave too soon again, do you, Mr. Grant?"

"Nae," Cailean said. As long as Patrick was safe and recovering, Cailean didn't need to rush to his side. "But I really should be getting—"

"You cannot leave on Christmas," she went on. "Christmas is a somber-enough time. Don't make it worse by leaving."

She'd be sad he was leaving?

He quirked his mouth at her just a bit and hoped she didn't notice. "The day after, then."

She shook her head. "Leave after Hogmanay." She came to him in a rush of sweet-scented air, like honeysuckle, or streams and pine. "'Tis just a little while longer, and at least you will be here to celebrate with us. For now, though, you need your strength and you can begin by eating."

He could do that, especially if it was Gram's duck-and-parsnip stew. He decided the fever had done damage to his head, for he didn't mind staying here a wee bit longer.

"Perhaps William"—she turned to her friend—"can excuse us for the night. Stress to your thoughts can sometimes be as dangerous as stress and strain on your body."

Cailean couldn't read her. Was she truly concerned about him? Deware looked as if he didn't know either, but left the room without saying anything else.

When she turned to smile at Gram, the elder shook her head at her. "I'm staying."

"Of course."

Cailean admired Temperance for maintaining grace despite the disappointment that glazed her eyes while she motioned for him to turn over on his belly. Did she want to be alone with him? Why did the thought of it thrill him and make him want to run...leap from the window?

But then she dipped her chin and veiled her gaze beneath her lashes. She looked as if the weight of the entire kingdom fell on her shoulders.

He was responsible.

He handed his bowl to her, and when she reached for it, he let his fingers brush across hers.

"Thank ye fer yer care, lass," he said, keeping his voice low, though Gram looked as if she might be about to take a nap in her chair. "I dinna deserve it."

Temperance lifted her gaze to his, a quizzical tilt of her mouth making him want to shake his head, as if she weren't real and he needed to prove it by scattering her to the four winds.

"Should I have refused to let you convalesce in my bed?"

He wanted to look away from the depths of her eyes. He felt as if he were drowning in them. "Aye, ye should have."

"Why?" she asked.

"Because I dinna want to bring more trouble to ye."

Her smile brightened into something glorious, but he missed most of it when she poked him in the shoulder to get him to turn onto his stomach.

This time he obeyed and let her tend his wounds.

"If for nothing else"—her breath warmed his ear when she bent to it—"you saved Marion and that alone earns my care." She straightened and waited for him to carefully turn back over. "'Twas verra kind of you to do it." She pushed him forward gently and fluffed his pillow. "You mentioned that she reminded you of someone you once knew."

Cailean's heart stalled. He'd mentioned that?

"Someone you loved, mayhap?"

He didn't want to speak of Alison. He didn't want to remember. But hell, he did remember every day. He wanted peace and he looked to an angel to get it. He didn't know why she made him want to tell her all, why he thought he could find solace in her arms.

"I—ehm—" Gram snored and his gaze softened on her. Did he want to let go of the stale, bitter shadows of the past? Mayhap. "I was coming to love her." It was more difficult than he'd imagined. He forced a smile, hoping it would be enough to end the topic of their discussion.

It wasn't.

"What became of her?" Temperance asked as she sat at the edge of the bed. Her eyes wide, her fist under her chin. Cailean liked seeing her sitting there, comfortable and ready to enjoy her night with him. But he hadn't mentioned Alison to anyone. Even Patrick barely knew anything about her. He sat up and rested his elbows between his bent knees. No one in Camlochlin had wanted to bring up Sage after she died, and that had been fine with him. Not talking about things kept them away and that's where he wanted to keep all those raw emotions.

But they were destroying him.

"She was shot on her way into m' arms, where she..." He paused, unprepared for speaking of her. "Where she died, telling me she was sorry."

"Oh," his bonny nurse whispered, lifting her fingers to her mouth. Her eyes were wide and vivid. They drew him to peer closer, to mayhap even fall into their azure depths. Cailean looked away. He didn't want to fall again.

"I didn't mean to...," she began, then paused and tried to begin again. "Forgive me for..."

He held up his hands. He didn't want her to feel sorry about anything. "There's nothin' to fergive. M' sister-in-law tells me to speak of it, else 'twill eat me from the inside. Turns oot she's correct."

She nodded and light shimmered in her misty gaze. "Aye," she agreed in the barest of whispers. "I can see it in your eyes."

"What?" he asked, just as softly. "What d'ye see?"

She searched his gaze and he was tempted to bare his soul to her.

"I see sadness and anger. I would—"

He dipped his head and leaned forward when she looked away. "Ye would what?"

"I would like to make you smile."

He wanted to smile. Aye, she made him want to do more than that. It surprised him how easily she chased his demons away, how she tempted him to cast away his fears and let her in. He knew he was a fool but he leaned down a bit farther and brushed his mouth along hers. It was a brief, tantalizing touch that sent waves of desire coursing through him. He'd thought he could never feel such need again. She proved him wrong. He moved away before he could press his mouth to hers and let himself fall completely under the spell she was weaving over him. Anyway, Gram could wake up at any moment and smash him over the head with one of her jars.

"Did losing her create the armor you hold around your heart?"

Aye. He wanted to tell her she had it right.

"Tell me of her. What was her name?"

"Alison," he found himself saying. "We met in a brothel. The last place I'd think to look for love."

He watched a slight brush of scarlet streak across her cheeks. He wanted to smile. Hell, he was telling her about Alison and he wanted to smile.

"She was a...lady of pleasure?" Temperance asked, cutting a glance to Gram to see if she still slept.

"Aye, m' brother had brought me to Fortune's Smile to buy m' first..." He looked at her and she quirked her mouth at him, understanding what he didn't say. "...time with a woman," he supplied anyway.

He told her about how determined Alison had been to see him get well after he'd been shot and stabbed by the Winthers of Newcastle. According to his brother Malcolm, Cailean's wounds had been very serious but Alison had never left his side. She was the reason he was alive.

"She was in love with you," Temperance guessed out loud. "Who shot her?"

He told her, at first with reluctance. But then, as he opened up more, it became easier to tell her the whole story.

"My father died in my arms too," she told him softly when he'd finished. She dipped her gaze to hide her eyes from him. He reached out before he could stop himself and touched his fingers to her chin.

"Dinna be ashamed of yer pain, else 'twill burrow deeper and deeper until it becomes a part of ye."

"Mayhap I want it to become a part of me."

He shook his head. "Nae, 'twill turn ye into me."

The tips of her lips turned up into a guileless smile that left him feeling as if he'd just run up Blà Bheinn in Camlochlin.

"I don't see the consequence in that, Mr. Grant."

*I'm the reason yer father is dead.* He wanted to tell her. He wanted to tell her and then . . . climb into a hole and never come out.

"Ye dinna see the consequence of bein' empty and guarded?"

He watched her shaking her head. He watched every nuance of the breath she inhaled, the slightest quirk of her brow. He'd found her beautiful already, but bathed in the candlelight she made him want to pen ten verses.

But she didn't know him, or the things he'd done since becoming a Black Rider. If she knew, she would hate him.

Wasn't that what he wanted? It would make ignoring her effect on him easier. He opened his mouth, mayhap to finally tell her the truth. But she spoke and cut him off before he confessed.

"Being empty," she told him, "just means something must be filled. We can fill it with either stone and mortar, or new dreams and a hope for happiness. Stone and mortar will soon grow too heavy to keep with you."

Cailean nodded slightly. It grew heavier each day. But she was wrong about the void. Stone and mortar couldn't fill it.

"Which will ye choose?" he asked her. He didn't want her to become like him.

"I haven't yet decided. I'm still too angry to know anything else."

"D'ye ride?" he asked.

"Aye. Why do you ask?"

"Ridin' hard and fast helps with the anger. It must be a strong beast to be able to withstand all you've got to give."

He realized what he'd said and how it must have sounded to her ears when a crimson streak stole across her cheeks. He hadn't meant to—well, in truth, he did think about her in his bed.

"I'm afraid all our mounts are old and slow," she told him. "The anger I carry requires a stallion."

His thoughts were already heading that way, so he let them take their own path. Images filled his head of her thighs coiled around his waist and her head tossed back while she rode him until she was spent. He wanted to put his arms around her and draw her into his embrace. He wanted to look in her eyes and lose himself in her smile, kiss her and ask her to take him from the dark. He wanted to take her hand and let her lead him, and then he wanted to free her from the sorrow he'd caused.

"Mayhap"—his smile couldn't help but linger when he spoke—"I could help."

# Chapter Eleven

*H*e lost the woman he loved, Gram," Temperance told her grandmother the next day when she stepped back inside the kitchen carrying a bucket of water. She poured some into a large metal pot, then helped Gram set the pot over the flames of the large open oven. "She perished in his arms, shot dead by a man with a pistol. Isn't that the saddest story you've ever heard?"

Gram began chopping carrots and paused to give Temperance a good looking-over with her unpatched eye. "Aye, verra sad indeed."

"I think my father would have liked him."

"Mr. Grant is a verra likable fellow."

"Aye," Temperance agreed, "he is."

"And he's quite handsome as well."

"Oh?" Temperance picked up a stalk of ginger and began grating it with a knife. "I hadn't noticed." She left the table and tossed the ginger into the pot, and watched Gram do the same with her carrots.

"So then." Gram walked back to the chopping table

and started on the onions next. "I'm to believe ye've gone blind?"

"No, of course not, Gram, but I've been busy tending him. I haven't had time to admire him."

"Good, then I don't have to be concerned about his sad stories or his beguiling smiles stealing your heart."

Temperance stopped cutting herbs and looked at her grandmother across the table. Gram would understand, wouldn't she? She loved Temperance as much as any one person could love another. "My heart has to belong to someone in order for it to be stolen. And in case you don't know, William's heart is lost to Marion."

"I do know," Gram surprised her by saying. "Truly, gel, d'ye think I let William leave this house without telling me? I'm disappointed in him for not telling us. My concern is fer ye, my little dove. I don't want ye to wed a man who loves another."

"I don't want that either, Gram," Temperance admitted quietly. Wasn't Gram the one who often told her that her mother had died giving her life and that Temperance was to make certain she lived a life worthy of it?

"There is no fire between us, Gram. But William still wants to go through with it. For the safety of the village."

"Aye, I know that too."

Temperance couldn't help but smile despite the prospect of her future. Gram might be old, one-eyed, and slightly bent over, but she knew everything that went on in Linavar and in her own household. She'd even known about her son Seth's upcoming nuptials with the widow Anne Gilbert. She was wise and strong-spirited and well loved by everyone in the hamlet.

"I will speak to him about it."

Temperance dropped her knife and ran around the

table to gather her grandmother into her arms. "Thank you, Gram," she whispered lovingly into her gray hair. "I love you."

Gram nodded and sniffed, pretending that the onions had affected her.

"Did you also know," Temperance asked, a playful glint returning to her eyes as she returned to her chopping, "that Mr. Grant has pledged his aid in bringing Marion back to us?"

"I didn't know that," Gram confessed, pricking up her ears while she pushed aside her onions and reached for the skinned and quartered remains of a roasted hare.

"His brother is the Earl of Huntley and Cailean... Mr. Grant assured William that he would enlist his brother's aid."

"And why would Cailean... Mr. Grant lend such aid?"

Temperance ignored Gram's knowing query. She opened her mouth to give an answer but realized she didn't have one.

"Might it be because Mr. Grant wishes to remove William from yer future?" Gram asked. "If William's heart is lost to Marion then bringing her back would ensure no marriage."

Temperance followed her to the oven with the tray of meat. "Why would he care what William is to me?"

Gram cast her an incredulous look as if Temperance should know the answer. She bent to the pot and added the meat to their stew. "He likes ye, gel. 'Tis clear to see."

Was it? "He's very guarded, Gram. I don't think he wants to care for anyone."

"Well, if anyone can change that, 'tis ye, love," Gram said gently. "But I cannot help but think that if not for Marion, ye would find happiness with William. And ye'd be safe. That's what yer father wanted."

Temperance smiled, remembering her conversation with her father the morning they returned from Kenmore. "He knew my heart, and remember, 'twas he who told me that love doesn't come around often. When it does, he always said, 'tis worth whatever it costs."

Gram's gaze on her softened. "Tie yer hair back, child. Lest ye set yerself ablaze." Tender hands, aged and wrinkled and swollen at the joints, smoothed over Temperance's thick curls, lifting the heavy tresses off her shoulders.

"I miss him, Gram."

"So do I." Gram brushed her knuckles across her granddaughter's cheek, swiping away a tear.

Temperance leaned in and kissed her face, then looked up at Cailean standing in the doorway. She hadn't heard him leaving her room or coming into the kitchen.

"What are you doing out of bed?" Temperance straightened and took in the sight of him on his feet. Damnation, but he looked fit and healthy standing there with his shirt and plaid stretched across his broad shoulders, his legs long and straight in his woolen trews and boots.

"I feel restless. I canna remain in bed..." He stepped into the kitchen, then paused when Temperance wiped her eyes. "Is everything all right?"

"All is well," Gram assured him.

He nodded, looking relieved, but as he stepped closer to Temperance, his relief faded into concern. "Ye were cryin'?"

"Just a wee bit," she confessed, moving toward him. She stopped only when she came toe to toe with him. She reached up to rest her palm against his forehead. No fever. But when she searched for the cool detachment in his steady gaze, she could find only warmth. She didn't want to look away. She wanted to delve deeper, even at the risk of drowning. "My father," she explained. After losing Alison, he would understand how she felt. "I was just telling Gram how I miss him."

He severed their gaze and looked away for a moment. When he returned his attention to her, he wore the bleak cloak of winter frost over him once again.

"Someone recently told me," she said as he stepped away from her and moved toward the nearest exit, "'twill eat me from the inside if I don't speak of it from time to time."

He stopped at the back doors and turned to look at her, some kind of battle being fought behind the deceptive winter of those eyes. "They were correct."

He opened the doors and looked toward the castle for a moment, and then he stepped outside.

Temperance made a move to go after him but paused to look over her shoulder at Gram. She wasn't looking for approval. She just wanted her grandmother to know she was going. No protest came as Temperance hurried out the door. What was wrong with him? Had her mentioning her father brought back memories of his Alison? She wanted to ask him if he thought he'd ever love again, but she didn't. In fact, she didn't say a word to him. She just trekked behind him, keeping a short distance away.

"Are ye goin' to follow me all the way to Lyon's Ridge?" he called out to her without turning.

"Is that where you're going, unarmed?"

"Ye think me a fool?"

She remained quiet and he finally stopped and turned to cast her a hard look. "Ye insult me."

"It likely won't be the last time."

Damnation, but he was completely beautiful when he looked incredulous, most assuredly in league with angels. With his large slanted eyes and wide pouting lips, he seemed almost the epitome of innocence. But no angel possessed such a jaw chiseled from granite. Purity and virility in the same dark, cold man. She understood exactly what a woman like Alison would find most attractive about him. It would be difficult for any woman to keep from falling for him. The question was, how did he remain pure in a castle filled with prostitutes?

He didn't move out of her path until she almost stepped into him. She felt him bend to inhale the scent of her hair as she passed him.

"Well?" She turned to him. "Where are we going?"

Back to brooding, he spread his arms out before him and presented the snow-dusted glen to her. "Seems like a good place to clear one's head."

It was. It was a vast hollow where heartbeats echoed off the braes and cries disappeared on the wind.

Instead of looking around at the vast beauty surrounding her, she kept her gaze on him. He was a lot like the land around her, hard and frozen, danger dressed in brutal magnificence. She wondered if he'd always been so somber. Had losing Alison changed him or had he always been serious and thoughtful? What would bring another smile to his lips? What made him laugh?

She watched him while he came to stand next to her. Close, so close that the heat from his body covered her and titillated her senses. How was it possible that she felt safer standing beside him than she had ever felt before? She traced his chiseled profile with her eyes while he spread his gaze over the four Munros. He inhaled the fresh, cold air and closed his eyes.

"Yer wounds are healing nicely. Any pain?"

"Nae."

"Did I say something to make you pout?"

He opened his eyes and turned to face her fully. She tried to concentrate on the topic at hand, but for a moment or two, all she could do was take in the rugged brilliance of his face. She thought it might be better if she kept her mouth shut, for the flash of his gaze was like lightning through a storm.

"I can assure ye, I dinna pout."

She rolled her eyes when he turned away again.

"Do you know," she pressed on, "that some people live out the whole of their lives without finding true love?"

"So?"

"So instead of being sad over what you've lost, consider being thankful for what you had."

His eyes swept over her like a rushing wave, but within the storm, a speck of light danced across the surface. The wind beat against his hair, snapping it across his face like war paint.

She hadn't meant to be insulting. She was just trying to help. Hell, she knew what she suggested was difficult, mayhap the most difficult thing a human heart could ever do. How does one even begin to turn grief into gratitude?

"I must do it as well," she confessed. "I don't know how, but I will."

She expected him to warn her, walk away from her, accuse her of not understanding.

Instead he untied his plaid from around his shoulder and offered her a place beneath it.

"Ye shouldna have followed me oot," he said against her ear when she stepped into his sheltering embrace. "The day is too brisk."

He was probably right, and she most definitely shouldn't have accepted his offer. His body against hers was warm, lean, and unyielding. Her blood raced through her veins like liquid fire, leaving her a bit light-headed.

She wondered if he could feel her heart thumping between them. What in blazes had come over her? She never felt anything like this with William.

"I'm not unfamiliar with the climate," she said, trying to keep her tone steady. He'd be leaving Linavar soon. There was no point in her taking an interest in him. "We have a bit of time before we freeze to death."

Was that a soft chuckle she heard above her, or the wind over the braes? The sound of it brought a smile to her face as she tilted her head to look up at him. She found him gazing at her already, his eyes warm and his smile...oh, Gram was right about his smile. It beguiled the breath right out of her.

"In truth, I wouldna mind it so much," he told her with every trace of frost and all his weighty thoughts gone from his expression—for now, at least. What remained were his shallow breath, an indelible smile that exposed a slightly crooked and wholly endearing front tooth, and eyes that drank her in and searched her soul until she would have promised him anything. "—If these were m' last moments on this earth."

She wanted to ask him why. Did it have to do with her? Was Gram correct? Did he like her after all? But her courage failed her. She felt anxious suddenly, not in control of herself or her emotions. She wanted to fall into his arms and kiss his mouth that had just confessed the most romantic declaration her ears had ever heard. Every brush of his fingers along her shoulder, her neck, tempted her to do the opposite of what everyone else expected. For a terrifying moment she considered living with him...or leaving with him. How far would she follow him? Why him? Why now, when her father was gone and she couldn't hear his thoughts on the man she thought she could find real love with, given the chance?

"Well, I already found you half-dead twice now." She took a step away, separating from him. She needed to. He made her lose her head, and if she wanted to survive the Murdochs, she needed to keep it. They'd already taken Marion. It was only a matter of time before they took her too. "I'd prefer not to have to drag you back to the house by myself. I'd be too exhausted to run if a group of Black Riders appeared over the hill. So let us head back."

"I've decided to stay in Linavar fer a while longer. If that's all right with ye."

His words made her belly flip.

"I'll bring Patrick here to protect the hamlet with me." His voice grew closer. "I'll return Marion to Deware's arms, and then…mayhap we can get to know each other better."

If the deafening beat of her heart was any indication, she wasn't going to survive this. She mustn't have cared very much, because she turned around to look at him. She exhaled the breath she'd pulled in at the sight of him directly behind her. So close, in fact, that she almost stepped right into him.

He lifted his broad fingers to a strand of her hair that had fallen over her cheek. His touch warmed her insides, her heart. She gazed up into his eyes and he smiled at her as if she was more than just a lass who'd helped him recover from his physical wounds. She wanted to tend more than that. She wanted to heal his heart.

For a breathtaking moment, she thought he was going to take her in his arms on the windswept moor and kiss her the way a woman should be kissed: slowly, masterfully, and with passion.

Oh, how she wanted to be kissed as if she was cherished, treasured... by him.

Instead he pushed her out of the way and stood in the path of the lone rider descending the Munro from Lyon's Ridge Castle.

# Chapter Twelve

*J* dinna believe m' eyes! Cailean, ye whoreson, is that ye?"

Patrick.

Patrick! What was he doing here? Hell, 'twas good to see him. Cailean told him so as his cousin carefully left his saddle. He'd healed well at the castle, but by his slow movements it was easy to see that he hadn't completely recovered.

"How d'ye fare?" Cailean asked him. His cousin was the man he had come here to avenge. He hoped Patrick wouldn't say too much. He'd have a talk with him about it later. Right now he was entirely grateful that his cousin and closest friend lived.

"I'm well," Patrick said. "Though obviously no' as well as ye, I see." He turned his most dashing grin, one that had provided him with more female company than he knew what to do with, on Temperance, and reached for her hand.

Cailean cast the heavens a fleeting glance and then introduced Temperance to his ridiculously attractive cousin.

"I've a feeling I've seen ye before." Patrick glanced

Cailean's way and smiled. He recognized her from the marketplace in Kenmore.

Were Temperance's cheeks so red from the cold, or from Patrick? Usually Cailean didn't care whom Patrick took to his bed. This time was different, though. His muscles tensed and hardened at the thought of her with anyone else. Hell, he was letting it happen. She was becoming important to him and he didn't want her to be. But he feared it might already be too late. He'd almost kissed her. He'd wanted to hold her and kiss her for the next century. It was the fevers. He'd gone mad and every time he was near her the madness worsened.

"I've heard much about you," Temperance told him. "And I'd love to hear more. Come, let's go down to the house where 'tis warm. Fortunate for you, Mr. MacGregor, you're just in time for Gram's hot wild rabbit stew."

Cailean stared at her. Was she flirting with Patrick? It wouldn't surprise him if she was. With his carefree laughter, charming wit, and eyes that could change from emerald to topaz, most lasses found Patrick to their liking.

"I thought ye were dead," Patrick told Cailean, leading his horse and following Temperance to the house. "Duncan came back with yer horse and told us that there was nothin' else around the beast but a pool of blood."

Cailean's smile was as cold as the frosted air. He was certain it was Duncan who'd attacked him.

"I didna believe ye could be taken doun so easily," Patrick went on, "but there was nothin' I could do until I recovered. Then one of the scullery maids told m' nurse that a man had arrived from Linavar askin' aboot me. I knew it had to be ye."

"'Twas William," Temperance corrected over her shoulder, with yet another smile.

"William Deware," Cailean explained when his cousin set those damned bewitching eyes on him. "Her betrothed."

She turned while she walked and cast him a look of disappointment and confusion.

"For now," she corrected.

Would it matter that she didn't want to marry her childhood friend? Or that her betrothed loved another? Why should it? He and Patrick wouldn't be here overlong.

Cailean understood why marriages were arranged. It happened often in the Highlands. His own cousin Adam MacGregor was bound by duty to wed Yla MacLeod of the Clan MacLeod of Skye. Adam was not pleased. Marriages were a means of attaining peace, acquiring land, strengthening an alliance, or keeping safe. If it was best for Temperance to marry Deware, then mayhap he shouldn't bring Marion back.

"Pity," Patrick said in a low voice when she returned her attention to the house, and then dipped his gaze to her backside.

"Patrick," Cailean growled.

His cousin flicked his eyes back to Cailean and made quick amends. "Fer ye, I mean. Pity fer ye." He smiled, and Cailean knew that soon every lass in Linavar would be knocking at Gram's door.

What if the person who'd tried to kill Patrick was here? Was it safe for him to even stay in Linavar? With each day that passed, Cailean became less certain that Patrick's would-be assassin was from the hamlet. No one here knew him or his cousin. Why would someone shoot arrows at them? Besides, it had been Duncan's suggestion. What if Duncan had hired someone to do it? Mayhap the arrow that had hit Patrick had been meant for Cailean, and the only thing Linavar had to do with it was that it supplied Duncan with someone to take the blame.

They reached the house and Temperance went on toward the small stable. Cailean stopped Patrick from following her. "She doesna know I'm a Black Rider, Patrick. Ye must no' mention it. Have ye heard aboot the killin' here the night ye were shot?"

"A few whispers here and there. The leader of Linavar was killed?"

Cailean nodded and looked around to make sure they were alone. "Her faither. Duncan accused him of shootin' ye and had Cutty cut his throat . . . in front of her."

Patrick's expression fell. "Och, hell. Poor lass. Were ye there?"

"Aye, I was."

His cousin examined him for a moment, knowing him better than anyone else. "Ye blame yerself."

"Aye," Cailean told him. "And rightfully so. I gave the order to Cutty."

His cousin looked away. "I told ye this way of life would find ye guilty of what ye hate sooner or later. I hope now ye're ready to listen to me and get back to Camlochlin."

Cailean shook his head. "No' yet. I canna leave them defenseless against Murdoch."

"What d'ye intend to do, Cailean?"

Cailean looked toward the stable and watched Temperance Menzie exit it. He'd teach her and Deware and everyone else in Linavar how to fight, and then he'd help Temperance kill Duncan Murdoch.

"I'm goin' to help her."

"Cousin." Patrick put his hand on Cailean's shoulder and gave it a squeeze. "Dinna get caught up in this. I dinna know what happened in that brothel that made ye so angry, but—"

"A lass I was fallin' in love with died," Cailean finally told him. Whenever Patrick had asked in the past, Cailean always grumbled that he didn't want to discuss it. He'd wanted to forget it. But he hadn't forgotten. And now, thanks to Temperance, talking about it wasn't as bad as he'd thought it would be.

"I'm sorry, Cousin," Patrick said, sounding genuinely heartsick over it.

"Is everything all right?" Temperance asked, reaching them and staring at each of them in turn.

Cailean nodded and moved out of the path to the house. "I was just tellin' Patrick aboot Alison."

Temperance turned to his cousin, surprised. "You didn't know?"

Patrick shook his head, just as surprised. "Ye did?"

They both looked at Cailean. Temperance looked as if she might want to smile at him, but she didn't.

Patrick, on the other hand, raised a dark-auburn brow at him and hooked his mouth into a knowing grin.

Cailean shoved him forward the instant Temperance turned away.

They entered the house and were met by a mewling Tam-Lin and the delicious aroma of Gram's cooking.

"Do I smell ginger?" Cailean lifted the cat in his arms and his nose to the air and inhaled. It was indeed ginger, one of his favorite spices. There were others wafting through the house: thyme, sage, coriander, basil, and parsley.

"Aye, we put some in the stew and Gram is making us ginger mead to wash supper down."

. The men followed her to the kitchen, where Temperance introduced Patrick to Gram. The two got along right away.

"How did ye know to look fer Cailean here in Linavar?" Gram asked him after she'd settled him into a chair opposite Cailean at the table.

Patrick explained how his nurse had carried the kitchen gossip at Lyon's Ridge to his room. "Once I knew someone from Linavar had asked fer me, I figured 'twas m' cousin, who Murdoch claimed was dead."

"He's a real devil, that one," Gram muttered, joining Temperance in serving.

"Here." Cailean rose from his seat. "We can get our own."

"Nonsense!" Gram scolded. "Ye and yer cousin are our guests. Now sit!"

They spoke about everything while they ate, with Temperance and Gram quite inquisitive about Camlochlin and their kin. Cailean understood their curiosity. For most of the folks in the kingdom, the MacGregors and their staunchest allies, the Grants, were a mystery. No more than tales whispered around campfires and at the bedsides of willful children, tales of cloaked wraiths that rode out of the mists to exact vengeance upon the wicked.

Patrick answered most of their questions with his natural good temperament, seeming to mesmerize both women. He made them laugh over ginger mead and tales of pirates and a certain October hunt on the braes of Sgurr na Stri when his cousin Adam had shot his own brother in the backside. Poor Tamhas hadn't been able to sit for a month.

Aye, Cailean remembered that night. He smiled and then he too laughed. Making hearts feel light was Patrick's gift and, for the last four months, that gift had been Cailean's annoyance. He hadn't come to Glen Lyon to be merry. He'd come because he was done with the world and the way it worked. He'd become a mercenary because cutting himself off from everyone and everything he loved was the only way forward for him.

But something in him had changed. He was enjoying this night. Being here made him feel good again.

"And yer grandfather, the devil MacGregor." Gram's smile faded softly. "Why does he hate the Menzies?"

"'Twas long ago," Patrick told her, sobering. "The Menzies were the Campbells' hired henchmen."

Cailean had forgotten that part of his kin's history. He'd heard it many times when his grandfather's strong voice filled the great hall of Camlochlin, retelling how the Menzies had branded the face of Rhona MacGregor during the first proscription.

"Well, we are no longer those kinds of Menzies," Gram said, looking a wee bit indignant.

"And we," Patrick answered with the return of his guileless—or was it?—smile, "are nae longer those kinds of MacGregors, though I mean nae dishonor to m' kin who bled to keep our name alive. Any ridin' we do below the Grampians now is to pillage a lass or two, no' to fight."

Cailean was lifting his spoon to his lips when he felt Temperance's eyes on him. He looked up at her from beneath his dark brow. In the past Cailean had never minded being lumped together with Patrick as a rogue, though nothing could be further from the truth.

Tonight he minded.

"No' me," he corrected, sounding more like a bear than a man, and then returned to his stew.

"No' him," Patrick echoed. "Nothin' comes before perfectin' the swing of his blade, coverin' his fingers with ink, or the quest fer the perfect ingredients for blueberry crepes and crème brûlée."

Cailean blinked when Patrick grinned at him. Was his cousin now the bard of Camlochlin, retelling details he'd prefer to tell on his own? Cailean wasn't against hitting him to shut him up. He'd grown up with a dozen cousins. Fists had sometimes been exchanged. But they were kin and forgiveness came with the next round of laughter.

"Ye know how to make crème brûlée?" Gram asked him, pulling his attention back to her.

"Aye," he told her, "my brother has a French cook. When I was last at Ravenglade, she showed me how to make it." He felt Temperance's eyes on him. When he slipped his gaze to her, he found her smiling.

"Tell me, Mr. Grant," she said, capturing his attention again with the delicacy of her voice and the beguiling arch of her brow. "If you didn't come below the mountains to win the favor of lasses, why did you come?"

He stared at her face, her eyes, wondering how she made him want to tell her all. He wanted to tell her that he'd come to Glen Lyon to do what he did best—fight. Fighting helped him forget and it fed the beast of anger inside him. "Fer solitude," he confessed. It wasn't untrue. "And to nurse m' wounds."

"Alison," she breathed.

"Sage." Patrick nodded at the same time.

"Who is Sage?" Temperance set her huge, lovely eyes on Cailean.

Patrick answered for him. "His dog." He turned to Cailean and aimed an easy smile at him. "Read to her from one of those parchments ye carry aroond."

"Parchments?" Temperance asked.

"We can speak of it another time," Cailean interrupted. He'd had enough of their speaking about him. Patrick's misdeeds were much more entertaining. "Tell the ladies aboot yer faither and yer elder brother, Lucan. I think Temperance and Gram would enjoy hearin' aboot their noble beliefs."

He realized just how naturally clever Patrick was when his cousin sat back in his seat and aimed his most radiant smile at them. "Honor, dear lasses. M' faither aspires to live a life worthy of a Thomas Malory tale. Like the heroes in

Malory's writin's, he is the imperfect knight, reformed by the love of his lady."

"And yer brother?" Temperance asked, enjoying the tale.

"Ah, Lucan," Patrick sighed wistfully. "He is the genuine knight. 'Tis all quite dull if ye ask me." He yawned and stretched as if just speaking about honor tired him. Cailean knew the topic's effect on Patrick. It quieted him one way or another. "I'm afraid I'm no' yet m'self. Is there somewhere I could rest m' head, dear Gram?"

"Why of course, Mr. MacGregor. Come." Gram stood from her chair. "I'll show ye to Temperance's room, where yer cousin is staying. Ye can share the bed with him."

"Ye'll sleep on the floor, Patrick," Cailean called out, then reached for his cup.

Beside him Temperance giggled.

Cailean eyed her from above the rim of his cup. She liked Patrick. "He's verra charmin'."

"Aye, he is," she agreed. She smiled at his deep scowl and rested her chin on her fist. "But not nearly as appealing as you."

# Chapter Thirteen

He looked especially handsome against the backdrop of twilight and mountains. His dark hair whipped across his face, eclipsing his steel-blue eyes.

Temperance couldn't take her eyes off him while they walked along a small path leading to the well, each carrying a bucket of plates and pots and with TamLin at their ankles. After Gram and Patrick had retired, she'd accepted Cailean's offer to help her clean up. She was glad she had. She liked walking beside him. Of course she liked tending him while he lay on his back or his belly. But when he was on his feet, his strength and virility warmed the blood coursing through her veins. It was the oddest thing, but being near him, with him, made her feel feminine...like a woman. She liked it. She liked too much about him. She tried to stop it, but it was no use. She liked his being here. She didn't want him to leave.

"Will you tell me of your dog, Sage?" she asked him as they came upon the well.

He set down his buckets and she did the same. "If ye

truly want to know." He released the rope and dropped the well bucket into the deep.

She smiled, watching him gather water. "Mayhap 'tisn't a good idea. The look on your face suggests you'd rather fall down the well than speak of it."

He glanced at her and then unleashed a smile on her that snatched the breath right out of her. It was a good thing it didn't occur often or she'd likely faint at his feet and hate herself for the next year.

"She reached m' waist," he began, "and was the color of the sky before a storm. Others might argue, but I dinna give a damn what they say; Sage was the bonniest of her sisters."

He hauled the first bucket of water over the edge of the well and poured its contents into her bucket. Then began again.

She wanted to tell him not to lift too much, but he looked perfectly able to lift her and carry her over a mountain if he wanted to.

"Sage used to look at me like she knew every part of me, what I was thinkin', what mood I was in. She knew me better than anyone else. But I didna want a dog hoverin' aboot m' ankles or m' horse's hooves. Sage had other plans."

"She won you," Temperance breathed, unable to hold in her breath any longer.

He paused and slanted his gaze on TamLin sitting at Temperance's feet. "Aye, she won me," he confessed on a whisper that lay his empty heart open to her. "And she humbled me thinkin' how I had almost rejected her. I took her fer granted, though, never lettin' it cross m' mind that she would be gone soon."

"What happened?" she asked, washing supper plates in the clean water.

He filled his bucket and started washing the pots. "I went

on a foolish adventure in Nairn with a pair of m' cousins to reunite with three sisters we'd met in Sleat. We got caught in the house with the gels. Their faither bound us and whipped us quite thoroughly. I dinna think he had intentions of lettin' us go alive. Sage had been with me, waitin' ootside while I stole m' first kiss from Colleen Rose inside. After we were captured, Sage returned to Skye, somehow bravin' the rain and hail of the season. She led m' faither and m' uncles to us and saved me and m' cousins."

Temperance noted the drop in his tone, his cadence slow and weighted down with deep guilt and regret.

"She grew sick not long after we returned home," he continued, stopping his work and severing his gaze from hers. "Fer a while m' aunt's herbs seemed to help her. But she declined rapidly and... finally left me while I held her."

Temperance watched him through tear-filled eyes when he returned to his task. "I havena spoken of her since she died."

She nodded, understanding and feeling honored that he'd shared his dog's story with her. He carried a lot of weight on his shoulders and she wanted to help him throw it off.

Oh, if only she'd met Cailean before her father died—when she was happy. How could she help him when she was grieving her own loss?

They remained at the well cleaning plates and pots and without many words between them. The silence wasn't awkward but comforting.

It wasn't until they headed back to the house that Temperance spoke up again. "You believe Sage's death was your fault."

"'Twas," he told her, turning to look at her. "'Twas m' fault."

Temperance smiled and took his hand. She understood

that losing his loyal dog and then the woman he cared for, both of them leaving the world in his arms, had left deep scars in the flesh beneath his armor. She suspected he held the armor close to remain untouched by anything or anyone again.

"Not all of us," she said thoughtfully, "are so fortunate to have a friend who would give up his or her life for us. You are counted as blessed. It might not make it easier, but it should be comforting to know that such a noble animal found you worthy of her loyalty and her life."

Cailean stared into her eyes, a wistful smile tugging at his lips. "That's a nice way to look at it, a way I hadna thought of m'self."

"I would like to think of it like this," she told him, picking up her steps again and traipsing by his side. "Our kin have to love us. 'Tis their sacred duty. As a woman, I understand perfectly well how Alison would pledge her love and loyalty to you. But Sage was a dog, better proof of a man's character, and, I believe, a better judge of good and bad than most people. Her life and death speak highly for you."

His smile softened on her. Her knees went soft. "Thank ye, lass." He brought her knuckles to his lips for a kiss that made her belly flip. She'd already gone weak and willing, so when he hauled her into his arms, she didn't protest.

"How is it," he asked heavily against her mouth while he bent her slightly over the crook of his arm, his fingers stroking her temple, her cheek, "that ye're able to banish m' troubles and heal m' wounds with a wave of yer delicate fingers?"

She shook in his arms, her gaze warm and yielding on his, hungry and eager for his kiss.

They met somewhere between need and desire, touching,

molding, each tasting the passion in the other. Fire. He
ignited it in her. He held her close and confidently, making her feel safe in his strong arms yet again. He kissed
as if he'd been doing it for years, his lips soft and plump.
She surrendered her mouth to his, clutching his plaid in
both hands as he crushed her in his embrace. She held on
while his tongue swept through the deepest corners of her
mouth, while his hands moved over her back, her buttocks,
drawing her closer. She was certain the wind wailing around
her was about to lift her and Cailean off their feet and set
them adrift over the frosty vale. But she wasn't cold. His
warmth washed over her, his breath filled her. His body
enveloped her like a thousand whispers, telling her things
she'd always thought she should hear from Will, but never
had. She felt desired, cherished. She wanted never to leave
his arms.

She didn't think anything could be better than his kiss,
but she was wrong. Watching the effects of her kiss on him
when he withdrew was better—his eyes beginning to open,
his sulky lips parted in the aftermath, his breath quick and
shallow, as if he was as surprised by the wonderment of their
intimacy as she was.

Watching him clench his jaw and gather his senses only
convinced her of the mastery he had over his body—and
how she wanted to make him lose it.

William's voice brought an end to their intimacy. "Grant,
unhand her!"

Startled, Temperance broke away first. She turned to find
William glaring at Cailean. She was about to remind him
that she had been willing and was just as much to blame, but
he cut her off.

"You kiss her knowing she is to be my wife?" William
asked, his tone cutting the wind.

"Knowin'," Cailean countered calmly, "that if ye take her as yer wife, ye will sentence her to a life filled with betrayal and regret." When William began to protest, Cailean held up his palm to stop him. "I'll be leavin' right after Hogmanay to bring Marion back to ye. Ye should decide what's to be done before I return. Ye canna have them both."

William stared at him for a moment, then met Temperance's gaze. He looked away quickly and turned to stare at the house instead. Temperance knew what was going through his mind. Everyone had always assumed he and Temperance would marry. He'd live in Seth's house, the house where the leader of their small hamlet should live. It was what her father had wanted, though he had never tried to force her. It wasn't what she wanted. And now she knew it wasn't what William wanted either. At first she had been happy that William had found his true love. She'd thought for certain Will would take Marion as his wife. But he insisted on still taking *her* for his wife. She had to get to Lyon's Ridge and end this once and for all.

"There will be no reason to stay once you bring Marion back," William told Cailean woodenly. "Temperance and I will be married. I made a vow to her father to take care of her and I aim to do that."

Temperance felt like crying. Did she have no say at all in her future? She did! She would see to her own damn safety! "William, I—"

He held up his palm, cutting off Temperance's words.

"I also ask you to refrain from ever putting your mouth to my betrothed again."

No! She wanted to kiss Cailean again and again. In his arms the world was a better place—a place where she found herself and happiness again. Cailean felt it too, she could tell by his reaction to their kiss, his promise to stay a little longer. Could she get him to remain with her even longer? Mayhap for good? They stirred each other back to life and she wouldn't let anyone stop it. Not even William.

"William—and don't dare try to silence me again"— Temperance folded her arms across her chest and planted her feet firmly on the icy carpet—"I won't need to be kept safe once I kill Murdoch, his hired killer, and the bastard who gave the go-ahead to cut my father's throat. Neither you nor Cailean can stop me."

"I won't let you," William snapped at her.

"I don't need your permission," she snapped back. "And if you think for one moment that I'll let you order me about, then mayhap you should go to Perth yourself, find Marion, and then stay there with her!"

William looked so stunned that for an instant she almost regretted what she'd said.

He spoke her name, or was it the howling wind? "You don't mean that."

He was her best friend. She didn't want to hurt his feelings. But she didn't want him to give up his heart to try to keep her safe from Duncan Murdoch, who most likely wouldn't care one whit if she was married or not. She wouldn't let William do it. She couldn't marry him.

"I do mean it," she told him, doing her best to sound hard. "We will figure something out, William, but I won't marry you. We are not in love with each other, and I want that in my marriage."

Before he could argue with her, she left them both standing there in the freshly fallen snow and stormed back to the house.

"Och!" She stopped, turned, and shouted back at him, "And one more thing, William! Thank you verra much for interrupting the best kiss of my life!"

She spun on her heel to leave again. From the corner of her eye, she spotted Cailean smiling at her.

"How could ye fall in love with someone else when ye grew up with *her*?"

Deware turned to him with a knowing look in his eyes. "She is quite beautiful, I know."

"Aye." Cailean nodded, but there was more to her than her beguiling face and her shapely form. The spark of life he'd seen in her at the market, before she lost her father, had drawn him to its light. She still possessed it. He saw it in her often. He wanted to indulge in speaking with her again, kissing her again, looking at her until his last day on earth, but hell, for her sake, he should be running all the way back to Camlochlin.

"After my fifteenth year," Deware told him, "Temperance made it quite clear that she had no interest in me in any sort of romantic way. She requested that I never ask to marry her unless there was no other choice."

"So," Cailean said, "she didna want to marry ye?" Hell, what a blow that had to have been.

Deware shook his head. "She loved Archie Campbell that year. After that 'twas Will Drummond, and then Ewan Frasier. When she reached the marriageable age, though, she refused all offers."

"Why?" Cailean asked him, although he hated himself for giving a damn about the answer.

"Because she's too strong-willed for most of the men in the village and she knows it. She doesn't want to live the miserable life of a subordinate wife."

Cailean couldn't help but smile. She would never be happy obeying orders from a man. He hoped she never changed.

"What will happen when she finds out that you're a Black Rider?" Deware ruined his good mood by asking.

Cailean's smile faded. He appreciated William's candid manner. He didn't like it, but he appreciated it. "I'm...I'm not stayin' overlong. I dinna want to pursue her, Deware. I just dinna want ye to ruin her life. She's too...vibrant and alive fer that, aye?"

Finally Deware nodded in agreement and returned his gaze to the house. "I could never make her happy."

Cailean wasn't sure why Deware was confessing to him, but he didn't stop him.

"We're verra different, she and I. I want a wife who enjoys her role and performs it without quarrel or complaint," Deware admitted, then nodded when he spotted Cailean's smirk. "Aye, precisely," he agreed. "She spends her days practicing archery and hunting small game in the winter months, and in summer she rambles through the heather like she hasn't a care in the world. She has never taken the danger of Duncan Murdoch's interest in her seriously until the death of her father. Sadly, now she knows better."

Cailean wouldn't let Duncan near her. There would be nothing left of her after a year of living under his tyranny. But how much happier would she be in a passionless marriage to Deware?

Determined to rescue and restore, if he could, the carefree lass he'd seen at the market in Kenmore, he had to talk Deware out of marrying her.

It had nothing to do with his wanting her for himself. Nothing. He didn't want her, no matter how she'd managed to make him feel better about Sage, or what she'd meant when she told him that as a woman she could understand how Alison had given him her love and loyalty. Or that she'd given him a kiss that made him rethink his life, his future. None of it mattered. He'd stay here with Patrick and right his wrongs, and then he'd leave and go back to Cam- lochlin. But hell, he'd like to watch her ramble through the heather.

# Chapter Fourteen

Temperance leaned her elbows on the window in Gram's room and looked outside at the two handsome Highlanders in her yard. Patrick was chopping wood while Cailean gathered it and carried it to the door.

He moved slowly, cautious not to split open his wounds in hefting the heavy wood. Still, he looked damned appealing lifting wood to his shoulder.

Her eyes took on a dreamy look as she remembered his kiss last night. Oh, what a kiss! No one had ever seized her mouth and her heart at the same time the way Cailean had. Heaven help her, his mouth was soft and firm and...possessive. What would it be like to belong to him? The thought of it thrilled her. She imagined caring for their bairns while he was away fighting battles, falling into his strong arms when he returned to her, being carried to his bed, and watching him, heart hammering, while he climbed in beside or atop her. She was mad, but she didn't really care. Why should she? William's heart belonged to Marion. William had never made her feel like a desirable woman, because he didn't desire her. She'd never have the kind of passionate, earth-tilting love with him that her parents had shared, that her father always told her to seek.

And it was the same for Cailean. She'd seen it in his eyes when he withdrew. She'd felt it in his breath, and in his reluctance to end their kiss.

He was leaving after Hogmanay, but he'd return. She recalled his warning to William. *Ye should decide what's to be done before I return. Ye canna have them both.*

Why did he care what William decided if he wasn't interested in her? He was correct, William couldn't have both her and Marion.

She sighed with delight as the elusive sun settled on Cailean, lighting his face, his eyes, as he looked up from his work and saw her at the window.

He smiled, but looked away all too soon. Why? Why did he always look away, as if he was guilty of some terrible crime?

Or was it because of William?

Temperance slapped the deep ledge in front of her. When he'd warned Cailean to refrain from ever kissing her again, she'd been tempted to give him a slap he wouldn't soon forget.

She had to kill Duncan to save herself. She couldn't marry Will, especially not after Cailean's kiss. Why, the effects would linger for a decade, she was sure. Her mouth still tingled. Her skin went warm every time she thought of his touch, and her blood rushed to her head so quickly she felt a bit light-headed.

Patrick called to her and she waved. That one was a danger to women, always cheerful, always charming, and so damned handsome.

But Temperance had eyes for his cousin, and his cousin alone. When he looked up at her again, this time with a softer gaze, she left the window and hurried out of the room...and then the house. She didn't care if she appeared overeager for Cailean's company. She was eager. And she didn't care who knew. As far as she was concerned the wedding was off—unless it was to marry Will to Marion.

She wanted to get to know the man beneath the shield of ice. She wanted him to kiss her again, hold her, make her feel safe and truly desired.

Stepping outside, she pulled her cloak tighter around her shoulders and crunched the snow under her boots as she went to him.

"Good morning to you, Cailean, Patrick!" She greeted both men with her most radiant smile.

Cailean nearly tripped over his foot. He righted himself and the two logs on his shoulders that had come loose.

"How is your back?" Temperance asked him, hurrying closer. "You really shouldn't overdo."

"I'm fine, lass," he said, casting her a smile that proved he was the finest man she'd ever encountered. "Ye did a good job mendin' me. Worry nae more aboot it."

"Oh, but I do worry. I want you well so that—"

"I can leave?" He slanted his gaze to her.

"Nae!"

"Pay him nae heed, lass," Patrick called out to her, and brought his ax down on more wood. "He's just teasin' ye."

Cailean. Teasing?

She smiled at her Highlander and he winked at her. Her knees almost buckled beneath her.

"Why then d'ye want me well?" He stopped, letting her finish this time.

She didn't think she could. When had she become such a blathering imbecile? "Why?" She blinked and blushed like the fool she'd become.

"Aye." He stood there, looking at her with both logs resting on his wide shoulders, the wind blowing his hair across his face. "Why?"

Temperance looked around the yard, expecting to see William appear and order her back to the house. She wouldn't go. She flicked her gaze to Patrick, who'd stopped chopping and looked to be waiting for an answer as well.

All right, then: she straightened her shoulders and cleared her throat. If they wanted an answer, they'd get one.

"You're pleasant to have around."

"He is?" Patrick asked doubtfully.

"Aye." She nodded, keeping her eyes and her smile on Cailean. "He is. I like our talks."

"Now there's something every man wants to hear from a bonny lass." Patrick laughed and then began chopping again.

"I like them too," Cailean told her, ignoring his cousin.

"Perhaps we could—"

"He likely cannot," Gram's voice coming from behind her interrupted. "He and Mr. MacGregor have promised to clean out the stable after they cut and gather wood, and after that I'll need them to clear snow from the back door walkway to the front of the house. I'm afraid 'tis getting dangerously slippery fer me to walk."

"Of course, Gram," Temperance agreed. "But after all that work, they will need a hearty meal. Tomorrow is Christmas Eve and everyone in the hamlet will be here. Can we not have a quiet supper tonight? I will make arterchoak pie and quail potage."

Gram smiled. Unlike Temperance, she loved cooking and planning meals. "Ye don't like cooking, dove."

"Och, but I don't mind," she said, wide-eyed and smiling. "'Tis the least I can do for our helpful guests. I will—" she continued, but Gram was already shaking her head.

"I'll do the cooking, dear. Ye can help. Come." Gram started back to the house, reaching for Temperance's hand.

Before letting her grandmother lead her, Temperance turned again to Cailean. "I'll see you for supper, then."

He smiled and nodded and Temperance almost didn't have the strength to leave. She felt his eyes on her like turbulent twin seas. When she reached the house, she turned one last time to look at him and found him still watching her. She waved and blushed some more, or mayhap it was just the chilly air staining her cheeks. It didn't matter. He made her insides burn. She hoped he'd kiss her again tonight.

"Temperance," Gram called from inside. "Shut the door before we all freeze to death. Come inside. I wish to speak with ye."

Temperance closed her eyes and girded her loins. She knew what Gram wanted to speak to her about. Had she spoken to Will yet? She hoped William hadn't told her he'd seen her and Cailean kissing yesterday. What if he had? How would she explain it?

"Ye're fond of him?" Gram asked her while they gathered the ingredients they needed for supper.

"Aye," she admitted. She didn't want to have this conversation. What if Gram didn't think Cailean was best for her? It was almost impossible to win an argument with the wise elder. And Temperance didn't want to lose this one.

"And when he returns to his mountains, will ye be going with him?"

Temperance laughed softly, but she suddenly felt ill. Would she leave Linavar? Gram? She shook her head. "He hasn't asked, Gram."

"Let's hope he doesn't. I would miss ye terribly."

"Och, Gram, I wouldn't leave you!" Temperance was quick to tell her. But what if she lost her heart to him completely and he asked her to return to his Highland home with him? Why did her life have to be so complicated?

"He leads a dangerous life, dove. Ye said he told ye he lost his woman to a pistol ball."

"No more dangerous than Linavar is with the Murdochs ruling over us," Temperance replied quietly.

"The devil we know is better than the devil we don't know," Gram insisted just as quietly.

"But they are all equally dangerous." She understood that Gram wanted only the best for her and Temperance loved her for it, but she wanted to live. She didn't care about danger. She cared about passion, about the thousands of butterflies awakening in her belly when she saw Cailean, the fire that consumed her when she kissed him.

"I feel safe with him, Gram."

"I'm sure his Alison felt safe with him also, dove. Until she died. Hand me that pot, will ye?"

Temperance did as she was asked and then sank into the closest chair and sighed.

"I want what Mother and Father had," she confessed, planting her chin in her palm. "I will never have that with William, and it has nothing to do with Marion. It has to do with me."

"Even if it means ye dying in Mr. Grant's arms next?"

"We will all die, Gram. I would rather perish in the arms of a man who loves me fervently than in the arms of a man who would consider my death his freedom to marry another."

Finally Gram stopped chopping and nodded. "Come help me, dove," she said tenderly. "Ye promised him a hearty supper. What will he think if he comes inside to an empty plate and a lass with red, swollen eyes? 'Tis not attractive, in case ye didn't know."

Temperance let herself smile and rose from her chair. "Mayhap," she said with another long, drawn-out sigh, "my father will give us a sign that will let us know to whom I should pledge my life. 'Tis the season of miracles, after all."

They agreed and spoke of less serious things, like the lovely woolen mantles Temperance promised to help Gram sew.

Before Temperance knew it, two hours had passed, TamLin had stolen part of a quail, and the house was permeated with warmth and the succulent aromas of Gram's cooking.

She heard the men outside sharing laughter a few minutes before the door opened. She decided she loved the sound of Cailean's mirth. She wanted to hear it more often.

Patrick stepped inside first, letting in the cold that swept the rushes from the floor into a swirling eddy around her feet.

TamLin, seemingly as happy to see the next man enter as Temperance was, leaped off a chair and hurried to greet him, meowing as she went.

Even her cat fancied him, Temperance thought. Mayhap that was the sign she was looking for. She knew she was wrong when he held out a bundle of sweet-smelling winter heather. Every stem was perfectly intact, without a single tiny blossom lost.

She smiled brighter than she had since she'd lost her father. She couldn't have asked for a better sign.

"You know how to pick heather," she said, accepting his offering.

"'Tis a requirement in Camlochlin." His gaze drank her in like that of a man starving for something that had nothing to do with his belly.

With her heart thudding in her ears and her breath shaky,

she rose up on the tips of her toes and pressed her lips to his cheek, close to his ear.

"I think," she whispered so that only he could hear, "my father sent you here to me, Cailean Grant."

She stepped away, a bit embarrassed by her boldness, and didn't see his smile fade.

# Chapter Fifteen

𝒯he next morning Cailean stepped into the grand dining hall, built by a leader who had done well for his people, and decorated by a lass who loved life and the celebration of it. He smiled at the paintings hanging on the walls, obviously done by a child's hand. Temperance's. He liked it here. He could feel the warmth. He could almost envision Seth Menzie sitting at the head of one of the large rectangular tables.

But Seth Menzie hadn't sent him here, and Cailean needed to tell his daughter the truth.

He closed his eyes and heard the ghostly echoes of laughter filling the large room, cups clacking in hearty toasts to peace and prosperity. Would it ever be the same here again? He knew now that Seth Menzie had been innocent. Temperance's father wouldn't have had time to veer off and fire an arrow at men returning to Lyon's Ridge. If he had, Temperance would have known about it. She would have told him. She didn't have a reason not to tell him. She'd already voiced her hatred for the Black Riders. She thought he hated them too. No. The wrong man had died.

How could he tell her? How could he do anything more than what he'd done last night? Unable to enjoy the supper she and Gram had prepared, he'd excused himself, claiming exhaustion, and retired to bed without sharing another word with anyone. She was wrong. Her father hadn't sent him.

It was Christmas Eve, the Night of Candles, when candles were lit and placed in windows to guide the Holy Family to safety. He thought of Camlochlin Castle lighting up the vale, a refuge from the harder world around it. He imagined his kin singing and sipping warm wassail, laughing together by the hearth in the great hall. He missed them while he breathed in the sweet scents of dried pine and mountain laurel mixed with the fragrant aromas of Yule cakes and shortbread baking, along with hens and capercaillies roasting. Mince pies were also being baked and would be offered with cinnamon, cloves, and nutmeg to symbolize the gifts bestowed by the three wise men. At Gram's insistence that the Lord's birth be celebrated despite the recent death of her son, the villagers would arrive tonight with gifts and smiles.

Cailean should leave before the merriment began. But he didn't want to go. There hadn't been merriment in his life for a long time. He hadn't wanted it.

What had changed?

"Ah, there you are."

He turned at the sound of Temperance's voice and smiled at her standing under the doorframe. He spotted the mistletoe ball above her head and was tempted to follow tradition and kiss her. To refuse was bad luck. He didn't think she'd refuse, though.

He didn't do it because Deware was doing whatever was necessary to keep Temperance out of the arms of her father's executioner.

"I was explorin' the house and its many rooms," he told her. "This one is m' favorite."

"Mine too," she said softly, and stepped toward him, leaving the mistletoe and vanquishing his foolish desires. "Though I imagine it must be wonderful to live in a castle."

It was. But he had forgotten. He'd forgotten much, like what it meant to be happy, to feel fortunate that he had a family he loved and would die for. Almost losing Patrick, and finding Temperance, had helped him remember.

He ran his hand through his hair and pushed it away from his face. Why had it taken inflicting his pain on someone else to make him see how devastating it truly was?

"Camlochlin Castle is verra big and m' kin are close, but I dinna live in the castle. M' faither is a builder and he built our house and many others in the vale. He would appreciate yer faither's workmanship."

She smiled at him and moved closer.

He felt his breath stall.

"Mayhap someday I shall see your father's workmanship as you've seen mine."

"Mayhap," he agreed, watching her drift nearer. Why was he giving her any indication that he might take her home? He scowled and took a step back. She was temptation incarnate and if she found out the truth about him, she'd hate him even more for taking liberties with her.

She stopped, seeing his unease, and didn't come any closer. "You're a different kind of man, Cailean Grant," she told him, making him feel guiltier than ever. "Most men wouldn't care about William's request, especially knowing he isn't in love with me."

"He protects ye."

"Aye, I know." She didn't sound happy about it. "Tell me, am I fortunate to have such a selfless friend that he would give up his happiness fer me? Am I *selfish* because I'd rather see him happy with Marion?"

"Nae," he answered quietly when she took up her steps again. When she reached him, unable to take another step without being in his arms, he didn't move away but lowered his eyes to avoid looking at her beautiful, curious face.

"Should I bind myself to him for a chance of safety? Is that fair to either of us?"

"It doesna seem so, nae," he said in a low, thick voice, still not looking up. He could feel her breath on him, the warmth of her body so close. It didn't irritate him the way others' being too close to him had. He no longer felt raw and exposed. He could hear her heart beating...or was it his? He wanted to take her in his arms and kiss her. He knew he could love this woman and that above all else he had to guard himself against that.

Still...

He reached out to touch her, forgetting his vows to himself, forgetting Deware and everyone else. She'd nursed him back from death and continued to do so every day that he spent with her. He moved his fingers over her cheek and jaw, aching to trace the line of her mouth, to press his lips to hers. She closed her eyes and tilted her face to his touch.

"He does what's best fer ye, lass."

She opened her eyes again to look up at him. "Does he?" She kept her voice soft, like a sorceress casting a spell on him, tempting him though he was quite sure she was as pure as the freshly fallen snow.

"What if William isn't what's best for me?"

He wasn't. But was Cailean? He couldn't be. Not with all his secrets.

Looking into her eyes calmed his heart and made it beat frantically at the same time. Her full, coral lips tempted him to release every care, every concern, all his fears and misgivings, and just kiss her.

"Temperance, there is something…." He had to tell her the truth before he did anything else. Patrick had been shot. Duncan Murdoch had blamed someone in Linavar and Cailean had demanded blood. She would never forgive him. Why kiss her again and start something that would end badly? She could never love him.

"Aye?" she asked softly. "What is it, Cailean?"

He looked away. Caring for her would only lead to more heartache for him.

"Nothin'. I…I think Deware—"

"Och, please, Cailean," she whispered, and pressed her index finger to his lips to silence him. "Don't tell me William is best for me. I know he's a wonderful man. I know it better than most. But it doesn't mean he's better for me than…" She paused and looked up into his eyes.

Than he? Cailean wanted to ask her. Instead he took her hand in his and pressed a kiss to her finger. Not he. "No' me, lass."

She opened her mouth to speak, but he stopped her. "No' me. I dinna want love. 'Tis temporary and when 'tis gone, it takes some of ye with it—and I have none left to give."

"You're afraid."

"Aye, I'm afraid. I've seen what it does. I've felt the destruction. Hell, so have ye. Ye lost yer faither, Temperance."

"I did," she agreed, and let her hand fall to her side. "But I would never trade a single day I had with him for less pain at his passing."

"I would," he told her, stepping back. "I would go back and do things differently." For her. He wouldn't let Duncan Murdoch ride down the mountain to kill her father. He'd do everything to save Seth Menzie, and then he'd consider risking all to give this lass his heart.

But he couldn't go back.

"Coward," she muttered as he stepped around her and headed for the exit.

"Hell," said his cousin, entering and hearing her. "No one has ever called him that and lived." He smiled at Temperance and then reached out and snatched Cailean's arm just before he left the hall.

"Where are ye off to?"

"The kitchen."

"The kitchen, eh?" Patrick grinned at him. Cailean didn't smile back. Patrick let him go and turned to lift his auburn brow at her. "He wasn't always a broodin', stubborn pain in m' arse."

Temperance turned to Patrick and smiled. "Tell me what he used to be like, then."


"Ye look like ye just lost yer dearest friend." Gram looked up at Cailean when he entered the kitchen with TamLin hot on his heels. "Ah, Cailean, come, help me cook."

She pulled a genuine smile from him. He missed being in a kitchen. As a younger man, when he wasn't honing his fighting skills, he'd been learning how to cook in his aunt Isobel's kitchen. It soothed him. After Sage died he'd stopped. He'd just about stopped everything. He felt it was time to return.

"I have dozens of different vegetables and almost every herb ye're likely to need."

Cailean nodded and rolled up his sleeves, happy to teach her and eager to begin. "We'll start with basil salmon pâté, then to cremonese. 'Tis a spinach tart." He began moving around the kitchen, looking for his ingredients, his cautious heart forgotten. "We'll need spinach, mint, eggs." He set what he had gathered down on the chopping block, then headed out again, sometimes following her direction. "Cheese, butter, currants, cinnamon, and nutmeg. After that we'll make bouillabaisse. 'Tis a fish-and-tomato stew with fresh herbs. D'ye have almonds? Nae? I will travel to the market in Kenmore tomorrow and get some so we can make macaroons, and vanilla beans too, for the crème brûlée."

He smiled at her again when he caught her staring at him, breathless as he was.

"Ye seem happier," Gram pointed out.

He shrugged while he brought more ingredients to the table. "Mayhap I am."

She eyed him with her one eye, her expression on him going soft. "Is it the kitchen...or my granddaughter?"

"Both, I think," he confessed, trying to keep his thoughts on Temperance smiling, and not on her crying, covered in blood.

"Ye remind me of my Seth. He too enjoyed helping me cook and bake, only he never pronounced words so eloquently."

With his smile fading, he lowered his gaze and began to prepare his dishes. "I believe the French language is one of the most beautiful."

"Aye," she agreed, continuing to size him up with her shrewd eye. "Ye don't know how to treat a compliment," she said, bringing him back to the present. "I like that about ye. 'Tis refreshing. Any man who looks like ye should be used to compliments."

He lifted his gaze to hers, and, proving he could be as charming as Patrick, granted her his most guileless grin. "Unless the other men where I'm from are all more handsome than I."

She laughed and he joined her. "Ye're more clever than yer big, innocent eyes and beguiling smile imply." She grew serious again all too soon. "How are ye with fighting? How would ye ever keep my jewel safe?"

He stopped mixing and straightened his shoulders. "I was trained every single day by outlaw warriors. I can fight better than most." He noted the slight tilt of her mouth. "As far as keepin' her safe, there are two options. Stay here and kill yer enemies. Or take her home with me to the mountains."

Cailean noted her smile fading and understood that taking Gram's granddaughter away would destroy her.

"Can she farm in the mountains?" the old woman asked.

Cailean thought about it, and then shook his head. Most burghs and villages in the Highlands raised cattle, not vegetables. "No' as well as she farms here."

"The soil's in her blood, inherited from her father. She won't be happy with rocks."

Cailean set his eyes to a bowl of yeast rather than on Gram. Who'd said anything about his actually deciding to take her home? Gram had brought it up, not he.

"Ye dinna have to worry aboot me takin' her. I dinna want a woman in m' life."

"I don't blame ye," she said, swatting him with her powdered hand. "We're a troublesome bunch."

He smiled again, but not to agree with her. He simply liked how she made him feel so at home.

"Was Temperance a troublesome child?" He shouldn't let himself feel curious about her life. But he was.

"Och, she had her willful days. Still does."

He nodded with agreement this time.

"Her mother died while giving her to us," Gram told him while she kneaded a mound of dough. She smiled softly into the distant past. "I took one look at her and knew the only thing I needed in my life was to see my grandbabe happy. Many of the villagers insisted I bring in a wet nurse. They feared my little Temperance would not thrive. That she'd waste away and die without her mother's milk. Fools. I fed her easily enough with goat's milk, some hazel oil to help with stomach ailments, and a pouch with a nozzle."

Cailean listened, looking up to smile every now and then while he ground nutmeg in a small mortar.

"Not only did she thrive," Gram continued, tearing away fistfuls of dough and molding the pieces in her hands, "but she grew into a spirited child. Och, she was fearless, always getting into mischief with William. Her father spoiled her rotten."

"And ye had nothin' to do with that?" Cailean teased, and tossed a pinch of nutmeg on one of the rectangles she'd made.

"Tell the truth, Gram." Temperance's voice at the door sounded too good to his damned ears. "You tried to be stern, but you gave in more times than Papa did."

"Ye still turned out all right," Gram told her, and went back to her dough. "Most days."

They all laughed together. It felt good too, as did chopping herbs and crushing nuts. Cailean thought he might be ready to heal. Ready to return home to Camlochlin.

He'd never see Temperance again.

He put that thought away for now, and when everything was made and put away for the night's festivities, he excused himself and left the house.

He returned an hour later carrying bundles of fresh mountain laurel, boughs of evergreen, and boughs of holly. He would have replaced all the dried, dying decorations himself, but he met Temperance in the corridor, and when she offered him her most radiant, grateful smile, he wanted to drop everything and haul her into his arms. He wasn't sure what was happening to him, and he was sure it would lead to sorrow and heartbreak, but she sapped his strength to fight it.

# Chapter Sixteen

"What is this called again?" Temperance sat at one of the brightly decorated tables and lifted a second spoonful of her spinach tart to her mouth. She'd never tasted anything so delicious—save for Cailean Grant's mouth. She blinked her gaze away from it and stopped herself just in time from sighing.

"Spinach cremonese." Cailean leaned down in his chair and said it close to her ear so she could hear him over the many conversations being had in the dining hall.

The low cadence of his voice and the sensual way he spoke the foreign word sent thrilling little chills down Temperance's spine.

Since she'd found him in the kitchen with Gram, he'd seemed more receptive to her than he had last night or this morning in this same hall. She remembered how he'd kept control over himself while she tempted him. At least she'd tried to tempt him. What in blazes did she know about tempting men? She'd certainly failed with him. According to Patrick, many lasses had.

"Patrick told me"—she tipped her head a bit to look him in the eyes. She almost regretted doing it, but on the other hand she never wanted to look away—"that you and he and two other cousins found yourselves in much trouble together while growing up. But you and Patrick were the most wicked pair of lads in all the hills. You both schemed and fought your way out of more serious situations. Lasses refused you nothing. Am I leaving anything out?"

He lifted his gaze from hers to search out his cousin standing in the center of six smiling lasses from Linavar.

Dangling from Patrick's fingers was a sprig of mistletoe.

She watched his smile deepen into laughter at something Patrick had just called out to him. He'd laughed with her and Gram earlier as well. She wouldn't forget the sound of it, deep and robust, or how it scorched her nerve endings and made her want to spend the rest of her days making him do it more often. It was hard to believe this was the same somber man who'd woken up in her bed after being left for dead in her cabbage patch.

He'd stopped her breath then. Now he stopped her heart, the blood flow in her veins, and logical thought.

In fact, she could think of nothing but kissing him. His mouth drove her mad, so decadently full and inviting, with that deep dimple in his chin to accentuate his shapely lips. She liked him. She liked him more than she should.

When he returned his attention to her, his smile washed over her and made her want to weep at its arresting beauty. "He embellishes."

"And according to your cousin," she continued, emboldened by his good mood, "I am to believe you asked for nothing more than a kiss?"

"Is it more believable if I attest to it?" he asked.

"Why didn't you?" she asked him softly when he tilted his ear closer to her, brushing his hair across her cheek.

"I dinna want bairns in every glen, or a lass who only makes me feel with my flesh and no' m' heart. I'd always wanted m' life to be filled with real passion."

She blinked into his gaze, melting like the festive candles around her. "That's what I want for my life too."

"'Tis no' too late fer ye."

"Or for you," she countered, bringing her spoon back to her mouth.

"It—"

"Wait!" Temperance lifted her palm to her chest and closed her eyes while she tasted what was in her mouth. "Good Lord, what is this?"

"Basil salmon pâté," he told her, smiling at her reaction.

"Oh, my!" She looked at him and felt like kissing him because he could cook so well. "I've never tasted anything like it."

"Ye flatter me, lass."

She nodded and smiled, pulling the spoon out of her mouth. "What will it get me?"

He watched the spoon slide through her lips. His heated gaze sent tremors down her spine. "Whatever ye like."

Och, she'd like many things. What exactly was he offering? Another kiss? More? He hadn't given others more, save for Alison. He'd given himself to Alison. What if he loved Alison too much to love her?

Could *she* ever be so fortunate as to win his heart? She wanted to try.

"Will you teach me to speak French?"

She loved the way his sulky steel-blue eyes grazed over her face, her features, as if he were trying to emblazon the look of her in his mind. Mayhap to remember later, when he left Linavar.

*"Oui, mademoiselle."*

Had he just moved closer? Were those flecks of silver in his eyes? What were those expressive eyes telling her? Tonight they didn't seem haunted at all. There was humor, a playfulness in him she hadn't seen before. And desire, warm and rich. She felt it like a touch.

He took her hand and brought her knuckles to his lips. "But only if ye walk with me beneath the stars later." The slash of his grin when he looked up from his kiss set her nerves on fire.

"Cailean." Gram's voice dragged Temperance from her reverie. "Come. My—" Her grandmother paused when she reached them and narrowed her eye on them... mainly on how close Temperance was sitting to him. She was practically in his lap!

Mortified, Temperance moved away. She hadn't even realized she'd gotten that close.

Gram cleared her throat and began again. "Fergive me, Cailean. I'm afraid I must take ye from my granddaughter. Everyone wants to meet the man who made the salmon pâté. Come."

He stood and looked down at Temperance for help. She agreed with Gram on this one. His dishes were light, aromatic delights thrilling the palate. Folks wanted to thank him, and Gram wasn't going to let him out of accepting.

The problem, according to Patrick, was that Cailean had shut himself away from his kin, from the world he knew.

"Be yourself," she told him. "And they will adore you."

He looked uncomfortable but let Gram drag him away.

"Is that Patrick MacGregor?"

Temperance turned to William, who was taking Cailean's seat, and missed Cailean's slanting his gaze from flaxen-haired Flora Menzie to her.

"Aye, 'tis him." She nodded. "Where have you been

for the past two days?" Before he had time to answer, she pointed to her plate. "Will, you must taste this." She scooped up a spoonful of pâté and spread it on a diagonally cut piece of seasoned crust.

"I have something—" he began, then stopped when she shoved the toasted bread into his mouth. He chewed. His dark eyes widened. "Delicious!"

"I know! Cailean made it!"

"Hell," William breathed, turning to find him among the faces. "He's good."

Temperance nodded. "Now, what were you saying?" Her eye caught the spark of light that seemed to come from the tilt of Cailean's lips or from the depths of his eyes, half-hidden beneath his lashes. Either possibility irked Temperance equally, since that spark was being given to Miss Jane Deware, Will's niece.

"I was saying that I— Temp? Are you listening?"

Temperance blinked her gaze away from Cailean's resplendent smile, aimed at Jane.

"Of course," she assured him. "But you are taking your time about it."

He sighed and set his gaze to where she'd been looking. "You must send him away and forget him."

"Why?" she challenged. There was another way! Will didn't have to marry her! "Why must I?"

"Because he is dangerous," he told her. "He will shatter your heart to pieces."

Now she wanted answers. This went beyond Will's being overprotective. He sounded as if he knew things he wasn't telling her. She asked him. He denied it. "He isn't staying, Temp. I can tell you fancy him. What will you do when he leaves?"

She scowled, angry at him for ruining this festive night.

She didn't want to think about Cailean's leaving. But he hadn't spoken to anyone about making Linavar his home.

"He lied," he said, slowly returning his gaze to her. "He lied about Marion. I rode to Perth to find her for myself. But she wasn't there. I met Grant's brother, the Earl of Huntley. He didn't know who she was."

He'd ridden to Perth? He'd met Cailean's brother?

"What is the earl like?"

"He's a bit terrifying. Like he's killed more people than I care to know."

And William had gone to him alone? "You truly love Marion, don't you?"

He nodded, looking ill.

"And you think I would marry you when you love another so much?" She smiled at him and rested her hand on his cheek. "I cannot, dearest friend."

"But your father wanted you to be safe."

"My father wanted me to be happy too. I'm surprised he didn't tell you that when you spoke to him just hours after I did."

He looked away. "We didn't speak of you overlong."

"I thought you had. What did you speak of, then?" she asked curiously.

But he didn't answer her query.

"You won't find happiness with him." He turned again to look at Cailean, now sharing smiles with Maryanne Menzie. "He has secrets."

"It seems you do as well," she countered. "I'm sorry Marion wasn't in Perth, but that doesn't mean Cailean deceived us. Did the gel from Lyon's Ridge lie too? Perhaps Marion—"

Will shook his head, trying to stop her. "'Tis not just—"

"Cease this!" she cut him off. She didn't want to hear any

more. "Let there be no more talk of marriage between us. He will find Marion and you will wed her. That is what I want."

She got up and left the table. She wasn't angry with William. He hadn't done anything besides try to keep his promises and remain what he'd always been—her protector.

But she'd never take him as her husband. She wanted someone else.

She didn't see Cailean turning away from the beautiful Louise Wallace to watch her hurry out of the hall.

# Chapter Seventeen

Cailean stepped out of the house and swept his gaze over the moonlit braes and fields beyond. She was out here. He'd watched her leave the hall. Hell, he'd been just behind her. Where had she gone and why had she left the house alone? TamLin meowed at his ankles. "Where is she?" he asked the feline. "Where's yer mistress?" TamLin answered by rubbing her side against his calf. Cailean shook his head at her. "If ye were a dog ye'd know."

"Are you insulting my cat?" Temperance appeared beside him, a wintry dream come to life.

He smiled, looking at her with moonlight spilling down her hair and starlight in her eyes.

He remembered to breathe. Hell.

"What are ye doin' oot here alone?"

The slant of her mouth tempted him to lean down and kiss her. "Are you afraid someone might snatch me away?"

"Nae, lass." He moved closer and slipped his arm around her waist. "I'd just snatch ye right back."

Giving in to the pull she had over him, he bent to kiss her

as the wind tore at her breath. She spun out of his one-armed embrace and walked off, swinging her arms and calling over her shoulder, "Was it difficult tearing yourself away from your many admirers?"

He grinned, following her. "Nae, and I left one of them while she was still speakin'."

Temperance laughed, sending music into the air. "What was she saying?"

"I dinna know."

"What was her name?"

He caught up with her and shrugged, brushing her arm with his. "I dinna know that either." He reached for her hand, since he was so close to it, and twined his fingers through hers.

She didn't pull away but tightened her grip. Who was she? he wondered, walking with her beneath the stars. What were the things that brought her happiness, the things that used to make her hum and smile at the sun? His desire to know her and everything about her was irritating because it frightened him—and strong enough to make him forget that it did.

He smiled at the way she swung his hand between them. "I understand ye like to ramble through the heather."

She cut her gaze up to him. "You've been speaking with William."

"Aye." He had to lean down to see her gaze when she lowered it. "Does that displease ye, lass?"

"He doesn't like you. That displeases me."

Cailean knew her friend had a good enough reason. But he didn't want to think on that reason now.

She stopped walking and let their arms hang still at their sides. "He went to Perth, Cailean. Marion wasn't there."

"She had better be there. I paid Maeve silver to bring her. Deware didn't look in the right place."

"He met your brother."

Cailean smiled. "That couldna have been pleasant."

"He thinks you have secrets."

Cailean wanted to tell them to her. But not tonight. "Everyone has somethin' they keep close and dinna share with anyone else. Includin' Maeve 'twould appear."

"Do you?"

His heart thumped madly. He was one of the men she wanted to kill. "I miss m' kin. I havena missed them in a long time."

When she shivered he untied his plaid and wrapped her in it.

"You cannot wait to get home and see them again, then?"

His smile on her warmed. He knew what she wanted to hear. "I can wait."

Her sigh of relief was loud enough to make her blush. "Are they celebrating Christmas Eve tonight?" she asked, leaning her head on his shoulder as they picked up their steps again.

"Aye, they're outlaws, remember. They dinna care aboot the kirk's ban on Christmas."

"Neither did my father," she told him. "My mother fell in love with him on Christmas Eve, on a night much like this one, under these same stars. He told me the story of it every year. Would you like to hear it?"

"Aye." He did, mostly because she wanted to tell it. He put away his guilt and the burden of not telling her the truth because she needed to speak of the man she loved in order to heal from the loss of him.

"Sarah Cameron lived by the banks of Loch Eil. Her father, Alistair Cameron, was as mean as a wet cat." She paused to lift her head and look at him. "Try giving TamLin a bath and you will appreciate my father's resolve to court Alistair's daughter."

"I already do. Why d'ye think I had a dog?"

Her laughter warmed his cockles and he pulled her closer when they reached the fields.

"Alistair didn't think my father was good enough for Sarah. So my father set about to prove him wrong. He worked Alistair's fields for two full harvests, pulling in more crops than the Camerons had seen in years. More importantly, though, every morning he left a sprig of heather on my mother's windowsill. 'Twas her favorite flower."

Cailean listened, understanding now why she thought her father had sent him to Linavar—to her—when Cailean had picked heather for her.

"My father had done everything he could to court her," Temperance continued, "but it wasn't until Christmas Eve, while they walked in the fields behind her home, that she told him he had won her heart."

"She must have been an extraordinary lass fer yer faither to pursue her the way he had."

"According to my father and Gram, she was. She died bringing me into the world, so I never knew her."

A tightness settled in Cailean's chest. He tilted his head to look at her while they walked. "I'm thinkin' ye are verra much like her. M' kin would appreciate yer affinity fer heather."

Thanks to his conversation with Gram in her kitchen this morning, he hadn't stopped thinking about bringing Temperance home—and Gram too.

"But I'm a Menzie."

Was that her only concern? Nothing about leaving Linavar, her friends, or her farming?

"They have accepted Fergussons, an Englishman or two, pirates, and even the monarchy. They wouldna care who ye were once they knew who ye were to me."

She stopped walking and pulled on his hand to stop him as well. "Who am I to you?"

What? What had he said? He realized quickly enough, scowled, and then smiled, giving in to what his heart was telling him. "Ye are—" He paused, not truly sure what to say. He hadn't wanted to care for her, but he did. He'd let her in, but how could he have denied her entrance? She'd been through much, thanks to him, and yet she still smiled, she still sang, she still had compassion to help him heal.

He began again, reaching for her. He pulled her closer and wrapped his arms around her plaid-encased body, shielding her from the wind. "Ye are my candle in the dark." He stopped again to take her in. He smiled. "I'm better at puttin' a quill to m' words than I am at speakin' them."

Her wide, beautiful eyes glittered like the snow dusting the braes. He wanted to lose himself there in the expectant hope that lit her gaze.

"You're doing just fine," she assured him softly. "Continue, please."

He shoved aside everything on his mind but her. What was left scared the hell out him. "I canna—"

She waited in silence while he fought his demon for her. Her hope began to fade to disappointment.

It made him smile to think her hope was to be with him and she was waiting to hear him tell her.

"I canna take my gaze from ye, lass. No matter what I'm doin', m' eyes find their way back to yer rich dark hair fallin' over yer flawless jaw, the relaxed curl of your bottom lip that tempts my legs to bring me to wherever ye are. I lay awake at night imaginin' yer soft inhalations of breath. They fill my heart with something other than mortar and fury. I want to bring ye to me but I'm unworthy of yer dreams. Still, I want to be in them, as ye are in mine."

"You see?" she said breathlessly. "Just fine." She closed her eyes and parted her lips when he dipped his head to hers.

He moved his mouth over hers, basking in the intimacy of kissing her, capturing her short, eager breaths. His senses came alive and he used each one of them to fill himself with her. She tasted like passion and innocence. When he slipped his tongue over hers, she opened her arms and coiled them around his neck, covering them both in his plaid. He listened to her heart beating like ancient drums. Or was it his own heart he was hearing? He withdrew a hairbreadth so he could look at her again. The sight of her dreamy-eyed and wanting more nearly drove him mad. He brushed his nose across her temple to her hair, drinking in the scent of her, like the familiar fragrance of peat and pine. "Ye're bringin' me back to life, lass."

He kissed her again, barely holding back the passion raging inside him to be released.

They went back to the house when it began to snow. They were almost too cold to walk, so they ran, laughing and almost tumbling in the snow twice.

Only half the guests remained, and most of them found too much interest in their cups and in their singing to take notice of the happy pair entering the dining hall.

Gram noticed them, though, and pulled Temperance to the side. "Where have ye been, gel?"

Temperance wouldn't lie to her. Not about this. Not about her heart. "I was in the fields with Cailean, Gram."

Gram's eye narrowed on her. Temperance stood her ground but prayed that Gram would understand.

"Did he kiss ye?"

"Aye, Gram." Temperance smiled and nodded. "He did."

"Ye look happy about it." Her grandmother didn't look

happy—or surprised. Temperance's heart sank, but she wouldn't be deterred. Just like her father when he'd fought for his Sarah.

"I am happy," she said, her smile unrepentant. "He makes me happy. Och, Gram." She let her defenses fall with a breathless sigh. "You should have heard the things he said to me. He told me I was his candle in the dark. He said he wants to be in my dreams as I am in his."

Gram blinked and turned to have another look at Cailean across the hall with Patrick. "And William?"

Och, for Heaven's sake, she was tired of having this conversation! "I am not in love with William!" She realized she'd shouted when every eye in the hall turned to her, including William's.

Instantly she felt terrible. The last thing she wanted to do was mortify her friend. "And he doesn't love me," she said, more quietly, but loud enough to save him the embarrassment of appearing rejected.

Gram waited for William to speak up, perhaps to deny Temperance's charge, but he didn't. In fact, he looked quite drunk. Poor man. No doubt he was worried for Marion. Temperance would ask Cailean later to make haste and find her.

"Yer betrothal to William is over," Gram told her, turning away from the guests. "I'll not have ye marry a man who's too deep into his cups to fight fer ye. But we'll discuss Cailean Grant later."

Temperance did her best not to smile, but she was overflowing with joy. Her betrothal was truly dissolved! Without their leader, and since William was doing little to step up to the position, Gram's word was as powerful as Seth's had been.

She wasted no time in returning to Cailean's side. When she arrived there, he moved a step closer until her shoulder rested beneath his. They laughed with Patrick and wanted to cover their ears when he took up singing a Christmas ditty.

Temperance wasn't sure how she managed to keep her eyes off Cailean when some of the villagers sought his attention. She wanted him to kiss her again, move his hands over her again, as he'd done in the fields, as if knowing all her slopes and hills was vital to his existence.

She didn't want the night to end, but soon only a handful of villagers remained. Anne Gilbert and William were among them.

The first fell into a fit of crying soon after midnight. Poor Anne missed her love, the man who'd asked for her hand just hours before he was taken from her. Nothing could comfort her save Gram's gentle touch and promise to see her home.

Cailean offered to walk them to Anne's house and escort Gram back. Patrick pulled William to his feet and promised to get him home without their falling into a hole and freezing to death.

They left Temperance alone, and while she cleared up the tables, she spoke to her father. "You would like him, Papa. He can pick heather without ruining it. I think 'tis him I wish to marry. I think 'tis him who I love."

※

# Chapter Eighteen

"Where's Gram?" Temperance asked when Cailean returned with Patrick a short while later.

"Miss Gilbert wanted her to stay the night."

"And Gram agreed to leave me here alone with you?"

"Nae," he told her, removing his plaid and tossing it to a chair. "She agreed after Patrick vowed to keep me away from ye."

Patrick aimed a cheerful grin at her and snatched a tankard of whisky from the table. "Night then," he bid them. "I'll likely see ye sometime after noon tomorrow. I'm off to meet Maryanne Menzie."

"But you gave your word to Gram," Temperance called out as he opened the door. Not that she wanted him to stay.

"I willna tell her if ye dinna," Patrick called back, and left.

"He's a heedless rogue," Cailean said, coming to her side.

"'Tis Christmas," Temperance reminded him when they were alone.

"So 'tis." He smiled at her, turning her insides to liquid. "D'ye want to celebrate it with me, lass?"

"I shouldn't," she whispered honestly. But oh, how she wanted to.

"Nor should I."

They laughed together before he took her hand and pulled her closer.

She looked up at him, wanting to spread her fingers over his bristly jaw and plump, pouty lips. "Thank you for a wonderful night. I shall never forget it." Her voice went low, honest, and grateful. She smoothed her thumb over his fingers. "I...I don't want you to leave, Cailean."

He stared into her eyes, making her doubt the good of her senses, her logic. He had a home to go to, and he'd be going after Hogmanay. She was a fool to lose her heart to him, but it was already too late.

Bending to her, he kissed her remaining thoughts from her head. His lips were soft, tempered with something he leashed...something she wanted to set free.

This had to be what her father had meant about love. It hit her like lightning, buckled her knees, set her heart racing at the very thought of him. She could love Cailean Grant.

"Cailean," she whispered as he withdrew, bent to sweep her up in his arms, and carried her to her room.

Temperance should have stopped him. But she had no intention of doing any such thing. Tonight she'd realized that she was falling in love with him. She wanted to tell him, the way her mother had told her father on Christmas Eve. She remembered the way he'd kissed her while the wind howled around them. Her blood still sizzled in her veins. That had to be why she cupped Cailean's face in her hands while he carried her and drew his mouth to hers again and again.

When they reached her room, he kicked the door shut and brought home the bolt with one hand. He used the other to keep her drawn against him.

"Gram," she worried.

"She willna return alone in the dark," he assured her.

"Then"—she pulled him to her and kissed him again—"we have all night."

She hurried him to the bed and sat him down. "Wait here." She left his side and went to her chest of drawers. "I have something for you."

He waited, smiling and shaking her world at its core. "'Twas my father's," she told him, bringing a box to where he sat.

He looked down at her offering and then accepted it from her. The sight of his long fingers undraping the silk around the box scalded her blood.

"I know how you like to use the quill and ink." She waited while he opened the box to reveal a beautiful quill and a small bottle of black ink. "My father tried to learn the art of writing but never got around to it. He would have wanted you to have it."

His fingers were broad and elegant, holding the quill perfectly. His eyes moved over the sleek feather slowly, taking in the shape, the color, and the weight. His eyes flicked to hers when she began speaking again.

"Tis the first flight feather of a greylag goose. 'Twill retain its shape and requires infrequent—"

"Sharpening," he finished, proving that he was familiar with the quill's superior quality. "Temperance."

He spoke her name and her blood scalded her veins. Her mouth went utterly dry. How in blazes did her name on his lips make her feel so warm and wanton?

"Thank ye. The set is fine indeed, but…" He dipped his eyes, shielding them behind his long, sooty lashes, and clenched his jaw.

Och, why had she stopped kissing him? She wanted to leap into his lap and kiss him senseless.

"I canna accept it," he said quietly.

"Of course you can," she corrected, sitting next to him on the bed. "'Tis a gift."

"Nae." He handed it back to her. "'Tis too fine."

He had to accept it. She'd been so anxious to give it to him. Her eyes widened and she lowered them to conceal her disappointment. "You don't like it."

He reached his fingers under her chin and smiled when she met his gaze, exposing his slightly crooked front tooth. "If 'tweren't fer ye, 'twould be the most breathtakin' thing m' eyes have seen in a long time."

Her heart flipped, making her cough and then sigh. "Then please." She pushed the box back into his hands. "Take it and write something for me."

Goodness, she couldn't believe she was so bold! What had come over her? Write something for her? But wasn't that what she'd been thinking about since Patrick had told her Cailean wrote?

"Did you write poems or songs about Alison?"

He shook his head. "Nae."

"Am I too bold in asking you to pen something for me?"

He stared into her eyes and shook his head again. "Nae, lass. But 'twas yer faither's," he continued. "I canna accept it. I shall find another way to write aboot ye, Temperance."

He stood up and moved toward the door. He always tried to leave whenever they spoke about her father. This time she wouldn't let him go.

She rose to her feet and called out to him. "Please, Cailean. Don't go."

She watched his shoulders tighten as if the weight of something tremendous were settling on them, and then straighten again as if he were resigned to bearing it.

He turned to look at her from the door. His tortured eyes

called to her and she took a step nearer. " 'Tis best that I do, lass."

Best to run away from her? Why? What was so terrible about her?

No! He was afraid. Afraid of caring for her. But she couldn't let him go, for she cared for him already.

"You set my blood racing in my veins, Cailean," she confessed on short, shallow breaths. "Please, don't shut me out. I understand the fear of losing someone you love, but I…" Her voice faded as he came to her as if drawn by something stronger than chain.

He took her in his arms in a rush of breath and surrender. Arched over the crook of his arm, she gazed at him with restless anticipation as he smoothed her brow and bent his mouth to hers.

"Ye are braw, Temperance. Ye call to me and I can do nothin' but follow ye."

He quirked his mouth into a smile just before he kissed her, making her wonder if he would truly follow her to the edge.

Clutching his sinuous shoulder in the fingers of one hand and tunneling the fingers of the other in his hair, she pulled him even closer, until she almost couldn't breathe from his weight over her.

His lips did not deceive. They settled across hers, tenderly consuming her in flames that scorched below her navel. He dipped his tongue into her mouth, cautiously at first, exploring her deepest shadows.

She groaned and tried to calm her nerves. They were alone in her room behind a locked door. Her heart leaped and pounded. Was she ready to take this path with him? She had denied her best friend in search of love, the kind of love her father had told her to seek. Now, free of her betrothal, she could shape her own future. Her father would have understood, for he'd known the desires of her heart better than anyone else.

She trembled in Cailean's embrace when he laid her down on the bed. She should say something. Tell him she'd never taken a man to her bed before. But then he kissed her again and all thoughts of speaking vanished.

He felt so big poised over her, so powerful when he slipped one arm beneath her and drew her up. She held on when he dipped his mouth and raked his teeth down the column of her throat.

She liked his strength and dominance. The night she'd helplessly stood by while her father fell at her feet had stripped her of her power.

She wanted it back.

Breaking their kiss, she smiled up at him and spoke quickly, before she lost her nerve. "Come here."

She pushed him down and slipped over him. With his back pressed to the mattress and all the muscles in his hard front pressed against her, he thrilled the breath right out of her.

Emboldened when he didn't protest, she took both of his wrists and spread them over his head, loving the control he allowed her to wield over him. He was hard as a damn mountain beneath her and she wedged her hips against him a bit deeper.

He closed his eyes and tossed back his head to groan, exposing the tense muscles in his neck. Someplace between her thighs ached and made her want to bite him.

Acting purely from instinct and deep desire for him, she spread her tongue over the thick column of his throat and felt him go hard between her legs. Her own crux swelled and throbbed. When he lowered his head, she kissed his dimpled chin, and then his hungry mouth.

She let go of his wrists and he reached for her face and then cupped it in his hands. He held her away for a moment, his smile fading, the fire in his eyes growing dim.

"What?" She lifted her fingers to his mouth and traced his lips. "What is it, Cailean? Tell me."

What if he told her he had no fondness for her? She lifted herself off him when he didn't answer her. But he pulled her close again, back against him, so they lay side by side in the soft rose-gold glow of the firelight.

"I . . . ," he began, and then paused again, his eyes staring into hers. "Temperance, I . . . Och, hell." He closed his eyes and looked a little pale.

She didn't want him to leave, so she didn't push him. Instead she smiled and rubbed her thumb over his dimpled chin.

"I like your face."

It worked. His smile returned. He covered her hand with his and kissed each of her fingers.

"I like yers too."

She smiled, trying very hard not to shout in victory because he did indeed like something about her. "Would you let me cut off your whiskers tomorrow?"

"I would let ye do whatever ye wanted to me," he whispered in a rough voice. "Save if it could harm ye."

So he believed that going further with her in bed could harm her. He was correct. It could. It was honorable of him and she knew then that a part of her loved him because of it. But the other part desired him, ached for him, more and more of him.

"Tidying you up won't hurt me."

He nodded, his gaze the color of storm clouds. "Temperance?"

She blinked. "Aye?"

"I'm no' certain m' heart is open to love again."

"Is it terrible, then," she whispered, their gazes locked on each other, "that I am jealous of Alison?"

"Nae." He shook his head and then laughed a little. "Nothin' aboot ye is terrible." He leaned forward and kissed her, making her lips tingle when he withdrew.

"You can pen that to me with my gift to you."

He grinned at her and rolled his eyes heavenward. "Och, but ye're stubborn."

"Will tells me that all the time."

He leaned up on his elbow and rested his head in his hand. "Tell me who ye are, Temperance Menzie. Tell me things only Will knows. I would know them too."

She told him between kisses and amid laughter and intimate smiles. "I'm a farmer, and the daughter and granddaughter of farmers. I love the spring and dirtying my hands and growing the food that sustains us. I love the harvest in autumn and the lush carpet of flora in summer. Up until now winter was my least favorite season."

"What has changed aboot winter?" he queried, knowing full well, as his intimate kiss revealed.

"You have changed it," she told him, looking deep into his cool gaze when he withdrew. "'Tis less gloomy, less frozen and hopeless. You brought life back."

"Nae, lass," he told her quietly, meaningfully. "Ye did that."

Dear God, she wanted a life with him. She wanted to roil in his arms, stir up a storm she believed more every day was coming. She missed her father. She was angry at those responsible for his death. Her determination to kill Duncan and those responsible for killing her father hadn't changed, but Cailean made her forget. He gave her peace in a violent world. His arms were safe and she didn't want to leave them.

Boldly she moved over him. He bit her lower lip, then

dipped his tongue into her mouth and spread his hands down her back and over her buttocks.

She could feel every rock-hard inch of him, and something so deeply primitive washed over her, she hardly recognized herself. She wanted to tear away the clothes between them and do more to his thick shaft than rub herself on it.

She'd never been intimate with a man before, but she and Will, along with a few other friends of theirs, had talked about it in the summer months when they sat around fires at night. She knew how babes were conceived, and who had to put what where. Some women even liked it—with the right man, of course. Temperance was convinced Cailean was the right man. She wanted to give herself to him. She'd never felt anything like the power of it before. She wanted him inside her, filling her. Pushing her fears away, she yanked up her skirts, and before she had time to do anything else, he flipped her over on her back and pushed her skirts up over her thighs.

He didn't give her what her body instinctively wanted— his heavy cock. He spread her with his fingers and traced his deft fingers over her tight bud until she writhed and cried out his name.

Shockingly, he bent his head to her upper thigh next. He kissed her sensitive skin and then slowly, sensually licked and scraped his teeth against her until she bucked beneath him. She coiled her fingers around his locks and pulled his face closer to satisfy a need so primal she blushed at herself. Oh, what was he doing to her? His mouth burned her until she felt wholly consumed in flames. He drank from her, nibbled an excruciating path over her again and again. It didn't take much more for her to find release at the tip of his titillating tongue.

In the aftermath she lay wrapped in his arms.

She thought about how she'd found herself in bed with a man, a man who had just shared intimacies with her, who made her grunt and pant and tremble in his arms. A man like Cailean Grant. She was tempted to tell him what she thought of him, and not just how he looked, though he looked fine indeed.

"Did ye like…" He didn't finish but smiled a little shyly at her.

She remembered his telling her that Alison had been his first.

"I liked it verra much," she answered, blushing again, liking that he wasn't a master at pleasing women, even though everything he did to her felt perfect.

He kissed the top of her head and didn't say anything else for a little while. The sound of his breath lulled her to sleepiness. She felt his body shift in her bed. He was either coming closer or moving away, she was too dreamy to know which.

"My fairest," she heard him whisper, and sighed, close to slumber. "Fer months now I have felt like I died in Newcastle with Alison…after Sage…but ye've brought fire back to me, Tem."

He called her the name her father had always used. She prayed she wasn't dreaming, and if she was, then never let her wake up.

# Chapter Nineteen

Cailean sat at the small table in Temperance's room, her father's quill in his hand. He turned to look out the window he'd unbarred a few hours ago. He'd freed the shutters to let some cool air inside, but it hadn't helped, and now the sun was almost up. He felt as if he were burning from the inside—about to self-combust.

He looked over the second letter he was in the middle of penning. The first had been to his brother Malcolm at Ravenglade. The second was to Temperance. He jabbed his fingers through his hair, sweeping it out of his eyes. She'd sparked a fire in him to write again. He wanted to tell her that thoughts of her consumed him, that she had snatched his weary heart and held it renewed in her hands. But he wanted to tell her while she was awake, so he put down his quill. His gaze found her in her bed, still looking as maddeningly beautiful as she'd looked last night. He didn't wake her but slipped out of the room and into Gram, about to enter.

"I aim to have words with yer cousin," she told him sharply. "Where might he be?"

Cailean knew exactly where Patrick was, but decided it was best not to share.

"Do I need to tell ye that I'm not pleased at finding ye in her room with her in bed?" Gram told him as they entered the kitchen.

"She's asleep and fully clothed," Cailean defended himself, wearing a playful smile.

"I know. That's why ye're standing here still pretty. She's my dove, Cailean Grant. If ye hurt her…" She made a cutting motion along her throat.

He met her narrowed eye and did his best to prevent the memory of what he'd done to her granddaughter from showing in his expression. "I'd let nae harm come to her."

Her smile brightened and his went along with it.

"Let me make ye some fresh black buns fer Christmas morn. 'Twill take me but a few moments to prepare."

"Och, ye tempt me mercilessly, Gram. But I'm off to the market in Kenmore."

She raised her brow. "Fer what?"

"Gifts—something special fer yer granddaughter. I want to get an early start. I'll take one of yer horses if 'tis all right. I should be back by midday. By the way—" He reached into a fold in his plaid. "Will ye see that this letter gets to m' brother at Ravenglade in Perth. I'll pay the deliverer handsomely."

She nodded and took the missive and the coin, then steadied her soft gaze on him. "D'ye care fer her, then, Highlander?"

"I care fer all of ye, Gram." He plucked a blackberry scone from one of Gram's baskets and headed for the back door. "But I'm fallin' in love with yer granddaughter." He paused and turned back to offer her a smile. "Dinna worry. I'll no' take her from ye."

He didn't wait for her reply but left the house humming

a song he'd heard an angel singing to him once when she pulled him from the fires of hell.

Temperance opened her eyes and smiled as her dream of Cailean began to fade. Had last night been real? She smiled and stretched, then ran her palm over where Cailean had lain in her bed. 'Twas cool. She sat up.

"Cailean?" she called out softly.

She looked at the unshuttered window and the shafts of morning light that stabbed the air. Morning. Her eyes drifted to the door. Gram was likely home. If she was, she'd definitely checked on her granddaughter.

Temperance still wore her shift and kirtle from the day before, but where was Cailean? Had Gram found him in Temperance's bed?

She sat up and flung her legs over the side of the bed. Had Gram thrown him out? She left the bed and hurried to the door.

"Happy Christmas, Gram!" She hurried into the kitchen and gave her grandmother a kiss on the back of her head. "How is Anne Gilbert?"

"Not as well as ye this morn, I'm sure. Patrick Mac-Gregor is a dishonorable lout."

"Aye." Temperance blushed, then looked down at Tam-Lin mewling at her feet. "Cailean warned us the first day Patrick came here. Have you seen him?"

"Patrick?"

Temperance sighed. Gram knew perfectly well whom she meant. "Cailean."

"Och, he rode to Kenmore fer gifts."

Temperance blinked her sleepy eyes. "Gifts? For who?"

"Ye, dear. He's quite taken with ye."

Temperance smiled, thinking about lying in bed with him and all the kisses they had shared. He'd already given her everything she'd ever wanted. She wanted to twirl and sing and smile at the new day! Christmas! But Gram would no doubt catch on to her ridiculous joy and refuse to let Cailean back inside when he returned.

But oh, his mouth, and the mastery of it. She blushed and turned away before Gram saw her.

She'd wanted more of him. She wanted to lie awake with him all night and talk with him again and again...and then she wanted him to undress her and explore her. She wanted to do the same to him.

She wanted to know what it all meant. How far gone was her heart for him? Would he remain here in Linavar? If he did, he'd likely fight Murdoch next time the lord's son arrived. And Cailean would just as likely die.

Her heart sank and her smile faded. He couldn't stay here, no matter how much Temperance wished he could. Not while Duncan Murdoch was alive and there was a chance he'd come back and try to kill Cailean again. She had no doubts about Duncan's guilt in the first attempt.

She had to kill the lord's son. And soon. She'd lost her father to him. She wouldn't lose Cailean too.

She didn't want Cailean to leave. She missed him even now. She missed his increasingly warm gaze, the attention he showed her, the way he helped her get through having lost her father. Seeing him around the house. Seeing him finally give in to laughter and beautiful unpretentious smiles.

She reached for a bowl and trudged along to the pot burning over the fire.

"What are ye moping around about?" Gram asked, not letting anything escape her notice.

"I'm not moping. I just—"

She stopped at the commotion coming from outside and went to the window to investigate. What she saw stopped her heart.

"Gram," she breathed, her eyes fastened on Duncan Murdoch seated high in his saddle as he approached the house. Twelve hooded, masked riders rode behind him.

Her grandmother set down her apron and came to the window.

"Get to the back of the house, Temperance," Gram ordered, and went for the door. She stopped when she reached it and turned to her granddaughter again. "Yer father isn't here to protect ye. Stay hidden. Don't come out."

Temperance noticed Gram's hands shaking. Fury coursed through her. She hated Duncan. She hated that Linavar lived in the shadow of his tyranny. He'd taken her father's life. He should have died for it already, but Cailean had stepped into her path.

She was glad Cailean had gone to Kenmore and Duncan wouldn't discover that he hadn't killed his father's guest that day in her cabbage patch.

She would apologize to Gram later for not doing as she'd asked, but she wasn't about to leave her beloved grandmother out there alone with Duncan Murdoch.

First, though, there was something she needed.

She took off down the hall for the room she'd been sharing with Gram.

"Temperance!"

Duncan's voice shouting for her stilled her steps and her breath. He'd come for her, just as her father had feared he would. Should she have wed William sooner? No, Duncan would likely have killed him next. She didn't want anyone else to die. Just Duncan. And she wanted to do *that* herself.

With a hardened resolve to keep her vow to her father, she ran to the room, grabbed her bow and quiver from where they'd been set against the wall, and ran back out.

"Temperance," he called her again, sounding closer. Temperance squeezed her eyes shut at the sound of his loathsome voice. The one that had accused her father and then pronounced him guilty.

He was just behind the door. Where was Gram?

There was no more time to think as Duncan kicked open the door. He stopped when he saw Temperance standing on the other side, her arrow nocked and ready to fly.

"What's this?" he asked, his grin intact.

"Your last day on earth."

He laughed while Gram hurried into the house behind him. Temperance glanced at her, relieved to see her alive.

"Put down that bow, Purrance."

Temperance hated when he called her that. It was the name he used to call her when they were children and his father used to ride down from Càrn Gorm to do business with her father.

"I'm going to—"

He lifted a gloved hand and his riders rushed into the house next. One of them took hold of Gram from behind and put his gleaming dagger to her throat.

No! Temperance dropped her bow. The arrow skidded across the floor. "Duncan, please!" she begged, holding her hands up. "Please don't!" Not Gram! She would perish if she lost Gram.

One of the riders suddenly crumpled to the floor. The one next to him went down just as quickly.

Temperance saw Patrick at the same moment that he saw Gram. He stopped swinging and held up his palm to still any further movement from anyone. Coming through the doorway next, William also came to a screeching halt when he saw the scene before him.

"Patrick?" Duncan angled his head to get a better look at him. "I'd wondered where you had gone. What the hell are you doing here?"

Temperance didn't breathe. She prayed he didn't mention that Cailean was alive. Duncan would surely want to finish what he'd started with two punctures in Cailean's back.

"What d'ye think I'm doin' here?" Patrick drawled. "Her name is Maryanne." He ignored Duncan when the lord's son quirked his mouth at him.

"Even a fresh arrow wound cannot keep you down, eh?"

"What are ye doin' here, Duncan?"

"I've come for my bride."

A sound came from William, as if horror had just made its home in his guts. But when Temperance cut him a glance, she noted that it was Patrick he stared at, not her.

She slipped her gaze to her bow and then to Gram. Her blood coursed through her veins, the sound rushing through her ears. "I won't marry you, Duncan," she swore.

"Oh, but you will." He came closer. His grin deepened with naked male intent. "And since I understand that there have been no marriage vows spoken, I will keep the promise I made to you when you were but a spring maiden, to be your first. Do you remember, Purrance?"

She moved her face away from his hand when he stretched it toward her. "I remember slapping your face so hard I loosened your tooth."

He laughed, then stopped when Patrick's voice rang out. "Duncan, why don't ye leave before someone is hurt?"

"This doesn't concern you, Patrick. Go back to rutting your whore." He kept his eyes on Temperance the entire time. "If you don't leave with me, your grandmother will die. Do you want that, Temperance, so close to losing your father?"

Tears filled Temperance's eyes and she tasted blood when she bit down on her tongue. She held her hand up to Patrick, silently begging him to back down. She couldn't lose Gram.

"Let Gram go and I'll come with you."

He shook his head. "It's not your choice."

She'd go with him to save Gram. But did the fool think she'd marry him? She'd kill him first chance she got. Her bow would do no good. Crushed nightshade root would see it done. It was the most potent poison Gram allowed in the house. There was plenty of it to go around, since it flourished behind Anne Gilbert's house. "Verra well then, Duncan. Just let me get some of my things."

"Hurry along, then," Duncan allowed with a wave of his hand. "And if you return with a dagger or pistol, you will only have yourself to blame for this dear woman's death."

Temperance hurried down the hall, but turned for the kitchen rather than her room. She worked quickly, gathering what she needed. She was careful handling the dried nightshade root, since even a little in a slight flesh wound was dangerous. She also shoved some smaller vials of hemlock seeds into the hidden pockets of her skirts.

She returned with TamLin in her arms instead of a satchel of clothing.

"Saying farewell to her is more important than anything I own," she told Duncan.

She glared at the covered face of the bastard holding a blade to Gram's neck. Was he the same man who had killed her father? He had dark-brown eyes. That was all she could see, but she would remember them.

"Don't fret over me, Gram," she said, throwing her arms around her grandmother. "I will return to you." She spoke the last in a low whisper.

"She'll be coming with us." Duncan stepped forward and nodded to Gram's captor to bring her with them. "To ensure your compliance, you understand," he told Temperance.

Temperance's stomach turned as he led her and Gram out

of the house. He shouted orders to his men to help his two fallen mercenaries back to their horses. At least there was no longer a knife at Gram's throat. She didn't want Gram at Lyon's Ridge, but at least they would be together and she could keep an eye on her.

She studied the eyes of the rest of the Black Riders, searching for the one with silvery eyes, the Rider who'd nodded just before... Where was he? Who was he? No matter. She'd find him at the castle and he would suffer with the rest. She'd have to time the poisoning just right to keep herself and Gram safe. Little doses were safest. Her victims would die slowly, pointing no blame to her or Gram.

She passed Patrick with a brief glance, hoping he understood not to fight, for Gram's sake.

William stopped her as she walked by him. "There is something I must tell you."

She handed him her cat. "Watch over TamLin for me." She hugged him and whispered quickly in his ear, "Tell Cailean not to come for me." He could never fight all Murdoch's men and live. She wanted to tell him that she'd get her and Gram out with her poison, but Duncan stepped forward and pulled her away.

"Your days of speaking to him are over," Duncan told her, and shoved her along.

Temperance turned to glare at him. He wouldn't have his barbarian kill Gram as long as he could use her to control her granddaughter.

She didn't worry about never speaking to Will again. She pushed her feelings away and grasped the fury she'd leashed since her father died. Nothing had changed. She would decide her own future—even if it meant killing everyone in the castle.

She braced herself, and let the frigid cold consume her as she stepped outside.

# Chapter Twenty

Cailean reined in his horse just before he reached the house. When he saw the crowd of villagers huddled around the open doorway, and Patrick's fallen expression when he saw his cousin, Cailean's heart dropped. Something was terribly wrong. He leaped from his saddle and hurried toward them.

"What's wrong?" He went directly to Patrick. He felt sick with fear and dread. Why wasn't she out here with them? "Where's Temperance?" he demanded.

"Where the hell have ye been?" Patrick asked him with equal force.

"Patrick." He came close. The need to take hold of his cousin and shake him until he answered overwhelmed him. "Where is Temperance?"

"Duncan came—he took her, Cailean."

Cailean stepped back. His head spun. His heart pounded, making it hard to see anything but red, blind fury. "What do ye mean, he took her?"

"He means to take her as his wife. He—"

"And ye let him go?" Cailean shouted. He looked around

at the terrified faces around him, including William's. "Did anyone try to stop him?"

"He would have killed Gram." Patrick tried to calm him. "He had a dozen men and a blade at Gram's throat."

For an instant a well of emotions threatened to erupt inside Cailean. He felt the sting of moisture at the brinks of his eyes as he thought of Temperance seeing a blade at her loved one's throat again. This time her grandmother.

He wouldn't let it happen. He wouldn't let her lose Gram.

"Where is she?" he asked. "Where's Gram?"

"He took her too." This time William answered, his voice strained, his eyes and nose red.

Cailean didn't need to glance at Patrick to understand what Temperance meant to her childhood friend.

"This is all my fault," William lamented. He leaned against the doorframe for support when he seemed to fall apart before them.

Cailean didn't have time for mercy now.

Patrick did, though. "Ye would have died and gotten Gram killed along with yerself if ye had tried to fight."

Deware shook his head and ran his hands down his face and then up through his hair. "You don't understand. The arrow…" He closed his eyes and clenched his jaw, as if what he wanted to say refused to be uttered. "I…I believe 'twas mine."

"What arrow?" Patrick asked, lifting his hand to the wound in his chest. Finally the truth dawned on him. "It was ye?"

Cailean wanted to kill someone. Deware would do. He moved toward him like a deadly storm. "Her faither was killed fer shootin' a man that afternoon." He reached Deware and stood over him. "Ye didna want me with her because I was a Black Rider—when all the time, 'twas ye who started everything."

Cailean wanted to hit him, knock out a few teeth. But

wasn't he guilty of even more? He was a Black Rider and he was too cowardly to tell her. It was he who'd wanted blood for blood that night. When he leaned in closer, Deware stared him in the eye, awaiting his judgment.

"And I was the one who gave the go-ahead."

He said nothing else, but turned for his mount.

"Wait! Where are ye goin'?" Patrick called out to him.

"I'm goin' to get them back," Cailean called back as he leaped into the saddle. He paused a moment before he took off and turned back to Deware. "Where's TamLin?"

"At my house."

Cailean nodded, then turned his horse toward the hill.

"We'll speak another time about why ye shot me," Patrick told William, and then hurried after Cailean. "Cailean, wait, I'm comin' with ye."

Cailean stopped and waited for Patrick to catch up. "There will likely be killin'," Cailean warned him in a voice as cold as the open braes.

They reined in on the snow-covered crest of Càrn Gorm. Cailean looked around as the wind slapped his hair across his face and eyes. Dark clouds rolled across the pewter sky, promising more snow. It was Christmas Day and not a soul was to be caught celebrating.

The wind echoed in the silence like Temperance's laughter…like William Deware's confession. Cailean still reeled from it. Something about Seth Menzie pricked at him. He couldn't think on it now. He knew getting Temperance and Gram out of the castle wouldn't be easy, but nothing precious was ever easy to attain.

"Are ye goin' to tell me the plan?" Patrick asked from his mount beneath the tall outer wall. In their younger days they'd always had a plan.

Cailean didn't have one now. Not yet. He wanted to kill Duncan. That was as far as he'd gotten.

"They're goin' to let us in," Cailean informed him, scanning the battlements.

Patrick turned to cast him a wry grin. "That's it? We're just going to walk through the doors?"

Cailean returned the look. "D'ye have something better ye wish to discuss?"

Patrick thought about it and shrugged his shoulders. "No' off the top of m' head."

"Murdoch!" Cailean's shout pierced the night air, stirring movement and sound from above. Several guards called down, demanding to know who was there. "'Tis I, Cailean Grant. Tell yer lord I've returned from the grave!"

More shouts erupted from the wall.

"Cailean," Patrick said, stopping him before the guards gave the call to let them in. "Once ye go in, she's goin' to find oot the truth."

Aye, Cailean knew that as soon as Murdoch saw him the truth of who he was would come to light. "I should have told her from the beginnin'," he said, tightening his jaw. She was going to hate him. What would he do if he lost her? He couldn't. Somehow he would win her back. He had to. But first he would save her from marrying Duncan.

Another few moments passed before a small group of armed men appeared at the gate.

"Grant?" John Gunns called out from the other side. "But you're dead!"

"I'm verra much alive," Cailean corrected him. "Let us in."

Gunns opened the gate as Cailean and Patrick dismounted. Immediately they were met by ten of Murdoch's men, all curious about where he'd been. Where had he met up with Patrick? Cailean promised to give them answers later. Right now he needed to get inside the castle.

"Where's Duncan?" he asked them.

"He's with his father in the solar," Gunns told him. "Been locked away in there with Seth Menzie's daughter."

Cailean did his best to remain calm. "Is a priest with them?"

Gunns shook his head. "Just them and the old woman from Linavar."

They were in the solar. Cailean considered busting down the door and taking them back, but they'd never get out alive. He needed to remain rational. Only fools rushed in. They were with Edward, so they were safe for now. He would see her later, when he could tell her the truth in private. He didn't want to think about what he would say to her, or her reaction. He needed to think clearly. He had plans to make. First he had to see how many men he might be up against.

"Are you going to tell us where you've been?" Erik Mac-Cormack asked, following him.

"Aye, but first I could use a drink."

The men approved with boisterous exclamations. Patrick joined in, clapping the men on their backs as if no time had passed at all.

The castle was abuzz with whispers from the many lasses and servants watching as the two Highlanders strode through the corridors.

On the way to the great hall, Cailean pondered what he would do about Duncan. He realized that killing him right away wouldn't be in Linavar's best interest. It would only push the lord to wage war against them. He wanted to keep the hamlet safe. But Duncan had to be stopped and Cailean was going to be the one to do it.

Following the aroma of black bread and the stale odor of

ale, he stepped into the hall and looked around. He eyed a few more of the men and wondered how he would kill them if he had to. He knew he could take at least three at a time. Murdoch's mercenaries were skilled men, but none had trained with MacGregors and Grants since they were of six summers. Cailean was thankful he'd never gotten too close with the mercenaries, preferring to be alone. It would be easier to do what was necessary to save Temperance.

"Grant?" Tavish Innes stood up from his chair and squinted in the soft glow of the firelight. "Grant!" he called again when he was sure his eyes weren't deceiving him. "Where the hell—?"

"Cailean Grant!" Brodie Garrow also left his seat and hurried toward him. "We were told ye were dead!"

Aye, Duncan thought he'd killed him. But at least, Cailean concluded, these two weren't in on it.

He grinned at the men and accepted the seat they offered him. "I was attacked and left fer dead," he told them. "But I'll no' be defeated by a coward."

"Who?" Garrow asked, his dark eyes fixed on Cailean. "Who attacked ye?"

Could Cailean tell them the truth? He wanted to, but he knew some, mayhap all of the men were loyal to Duncan, so he shook his head. He wouldn't make any accusation, but lead the men to the truth and see where they stood after that. "I'm no' sure who. I was on m' way to Kenmore and someone attacked me from behind. But I'll find oot and then I'll see that they're repaid fer tryin' to kill me. As good fortune would have it, I met up with Patrick on m' way back here."

While they ate and drank, John told him about Duncan's going to fetch his long-awaited bride that morn.

Cailean leaned back in his seat and brought his cup to his lips. He slid his gaze over the men. "So the night we rode into

Linavar to avenge Patrick had nothing to do with the attack on us. Duncan had the leader killed so he could take his daughter."

"What's wrong with that?" Brodie Garrow argued. "She's a fine-looking woman. I would have done the same." He laughed and held up his cup to a few of the others who agreed Duncan had bollocks.

Cailean's gaze settled on them like the weight of the moon, cold as steel. Save for John Gunns, Garrow and these others wouldn't stand idly by if Cailean tried to kill Duncan. He glanced at his cousin. Patrick nodded slightly, reading his thoughts. Cailean was glad his cousin was here. If they had to fight to get out alive, Patrick's arm would help gain them victory.

"'Twas likely some scoundrel from Linavar who attacked ye," Garrow warned. "Just like one of them attacked Patrick. Duncan says they want us all dead and will stop at nothing to see our end."

Cailean stared at him blankly. So a town of thirty untrained farmers was planning an insurrection against their lord's most skilled assassins?

He could have laughed in the men's faces, proving what he thought of Duncan's accusations and what he thought of them for believing him. But mocking them wouldn't gain him an advantage.

"Nae," he said, shaking his head, "there was a witness." He remembered what Patrick had told him about his horse. "I was told m' attacker left me in a pool of blood and took m' horse. I went to Linavar in search of m' mount but the beast was no' there."

"Duncan brought back yer horse," John Gunns told him.

Good. Letting them come to their own conclusion would help convince them of the truth.

"Hell, I would hate it if ye're correct," Cailean told them.

"'Twould mean he has no regard fer his faither's elite and might even be capable of tryin' to kill one or two of them."

"But why would he?" Erik asked, after guzzling his brew and wiping his mouth with his sleeve. His eyes caught the gaze of one of Maeve's girls. His fingers shackled her wrist and he yanked her into his lap.

Ellie, Cailean believed was her name.

Ellie giggled and shoved her free hand down the Red's breeches.

"Duncan didn't do it," Tavish Innes told him in a low voice. "Suggesting it could cause trouble."

"Aye, drink what's in your cup." Dougal held his up. "We'll blame your mutinous talk on weariness."

Aye, now this was what Cailean needed to see. Who was most loyal to the wee twit in the solar? He looked around. What about the rest?

He set his hard gaze on Dougal first. "Do I look weary to ye?" Rather than lie straight to his face, Dougal looked at his brother, who had paused in his grunting when he heard Cailean's threatening tone.

He pushed the rest with a curl of his mouth. "I think he did it." He set his gaze on each of them, looking for anger or offense and finding it. When his eyes settled on Gunns, the mercenary gave him a subtle nod.

A few shouts erupted, which Patrick subdued with a loud request for more jugs on their table and more women in their laps.

Cailean didn't care if they went to Duncan with his accusation. He knew what he had to do next.

He rose from his place and left the dining hall alone, leaving Patrick with the lovely lass in his arms, and headed for the lists. He'd see who was there—find out whom else he might have to kill in a fight.

He stepped outside when he reached the carved doorway and spread his gaze over the faces, some—and then more—turning to gape at him. He spotted Cutty sitting on a stone bench, his eyes wide with fear as he recognized Cailean.

Stunned, he managed to rise up, produce a dagger, and fling it at Cailean.

It came close enough to Cailean's shoulder to tear his flesh.

"'Tis a phantom!" Cutty shouted, terrified and reaching behind him for one of the swords resting against the short wall.

Cailean held up his hands as he stepped out of the shadows and into the light. "Easy, Cutty," he said in a calm voice. "Do phantoms bleed?"

He unlaced his shirt and pulled it over his head and one shoulder, exposing his own fresh wound.

"I'm real," he said, walking toward him. "I was attacked on the road and left fer dead by a thief who stole m' horse. Or, as I've recently been corrected, Duncan Murdoch. D'ye know anything aboot that, Cutty?"

He watched the mercenary squirm a little, and he enjoyed it.

"I sure as hell didn't," Cutty swore. "I know him and you don't share fondness, but I'd have nothing to do with killing you."

Cailean didn't let him off so easily. "But Duncan tried, aye?"

"He might have." One edge of Cutty's mouth tilted upward. "You did threaten to beat him senseless."

Aye, Cailean agreed, he had. He wished he'd done it too. "We killed the wrong man that night in Linavar."

Cutty shrugged. "It happens."

*It happens.*

Once again Patrick's urgings to leave this life behind and return to Camlochlin seeped through Cailean's flesh, his bones. He hadn't been born to be a cold, mindless mercenary. He had been raised to fight and defend with honor. He'd trained since he was three, practicing defense two days of a sennight in the yard with his mother, and offense three and a half days with his father. When he was six, he'd begun training with his uncles. He wasn't afraid to fight anyone, anytime, but his passions ran deepest with the pen, the cooking knife, and sometimes the brush. He'd stopped using them all for a long time and chosen to exist solely on the one thing that was easiest to feel—anger.

Until the night Seth Menzie died.

"Why do you care about Menzie?" Cutty asked. "And why do you think he was the wrong man?"

Cailean wouldn't tell him what he'd learned. William had to live with the guilt of what he'd caused, just as Cailean did. "Because," he said, "the leader of the people of Linavar would never have risked the wrath of the lord. There was mutual respect between them. Menzie made certain his farmers produced a good harvest and supplied Murdoch's coffers with plenty of coin. The lord is goin' to be angry when he finds oot Menzie is dead. If he doesna already know, thanks to the two women Duncan foolishly brought back here today."

He watched Cutty's doubts and the fear that followed. Aye, Cailean had had a part in it, but *Cutty* had done the killing.

"What do you think he'll do?"

Cailean held up his hands. "We'll find oot soon enough, I imagine." He hoped Cutty would run. One fewer Black Rider to deal with.

"I'd better have one of the girls see to m' wound." Without another word Cailean left the lists.

"Oh, dear," a worried voice said behind him. "You're bleeding all over the floor."

Cailean turned, preparing to apologize. His mouth closed and he blinked as if he was hoping his eyes deceived him. "Marion?"

# Chapter Twenty-One

"Marion?" Cailean rushed closer to her and had a better look at her in the soft light. It was she! So Maeve hadn't brought her to Perth. No wonder William hadn't found her when he'd gone looking. What the hell was she doing here?

Before he had a chance to ask her, another voice made the frosty air crackle.

"Grant!" Edward Murdoch stood at the open solar door and then strode to him. "I was told you had perished." He eyed him from over the bridge of his thick nose and then broke into a wide grin. "You look well!"

Despite the terror his son had caused Linavar, Cailean liked the lord of Glen Lyon. He was a big, boisterous man who knew when to settle himself down for a quiet game of chess. He was damn good at the game too, beating Cailean half the time.

"Come." Murdoch tossed his arm over Cailean's shoulder. "Tell me what the hell happened to you."

Cailean angled his head, trying to have a look over

Murdoch's shoulder into the solar. Was Temperance still inside? He wanted to call out her name. For a moment it seemed as if his heart existed for that single purpose. But he leashed that passion the way he had done before...before Temperance Menzie had led him gently out of the dark.

He called instead upon that dark now. He needed to keep his head and not let his heart carry him into a rabid attack that would likely find him dead at the end. He and Patrick against nineteen were not good odds.

He settled his gaze on Murdoch instead. "M' lord, I understand ye have guests. Where have they been taken?"

"To the hall, why? Do they have something to do with you?"

"Aye, they do," Cailean told him truthfully.

Murdoch's smile faded into a look of concern, and then he led the way.

Cailean looked toward the hall. He wanted to find out what Edward had agreed to, but he wanted to go after her also. Patrick was there.

He followed Murdoch into the chamber and took the chair usually reserved for Duncan. The chair where he'd sat and played chess and sometimes listened to the lord's concerns about his vile offspring.

"When I first opened m' eyes," he said, watching Murdoch cut across the room to get them drinks, "I thought I was in hell. I was stabbed in the back and left fer dead."

"Where?"

"This occurred in Linavar, m' lord."

"Ah, that makes sense," Murdoch said, bringing Cailean his cup. "After my fool of a son had their cherished leader killed, they took revenge of you."

He knew, then, that Duncan had had Seth Menzie killed. Temperance and Gram had likely told him.

"No one from Linavar did this," Cailean continued, sipping his wine. It felt good and warm going down. "I suffered a number of fevers after infection had set into m' wounds. If no' fer the care I received from the people there, I would have died. They saved m' life."

"Any idea who stabbed you, then?"

"I know only that m' attacker stole m' horse."

Edward's eyes fastened on him from his heavy chair. "Duncan found your horse."

Cailean nodded. "Aye, and he had Seth Menzie killed so that he could take his daughter."

Cailean suspected this was difficult to hear about any son. Murdoch was quiet for a while, contemplating it all, no doubt.

"Duncan did in fact bring Menzie's daughter and mother here and asked me to agree to marriage between him and the girl."

"Did ye agree?" Cailean fought to remember to breathe steadily while he waited.

"Not yet," Murdoch answered. "Though it would secure my good relations with Linavar."

Cailean smirked, heart pounding. "Good relations when their dead leader's daughter is forced to wed his murderer? Ye'll be fortunate if their crops yield a single carrot."

Murdoch's eyes narrowed on him. "What do you suggest?"

Murdoch liked him. He was one of probably only a few men in the castle who did. Cailean prayed the lord would agree to his request and save the lives of most of his men. "Let me return Miss Menzie and her grandmother to Linavar so she can wed a man with whom the people will be happy."

Another thing she would hate him for, but Cailean was sure she'd rather wed Deware than Duncan. He also knew she'd never wed him once she found out he was the Black Rider who'd nodded.

"You care so much about my crops?" Murdoch asked him with a dubious quirk of his thick brow.

"Nae," Cailean replied. "Yer coffers. How will I get paid if yer coffers are empty?"

That seemed to mollify the lord for a time.

"So," he said after another moment. "You think Duncan stabbed you in Linavar."

"Aye, he'd wanted to linger after Menzie was killed and I threatened to do him harm if he did."

"Well, 'tis good that one of you had some sense," Murdoch said, and stared for a moment at the chair Cailean was sitting in. "No matter what he's done, I will handle it. Do you hear me? I like you, Grant." Murdoch leaned back in his chair and stared into the flames of the hearth. "Pour me a another drink."

Cailean did as he was asked. He knew Murdoch liked him. He'd use it to his advantage.

"I'm not a fool," the lord sighed, sounding older than Cailean had ever heard him. "I know what kind of man Duncan is. I'm aware of some of the things he's guilty of doing. He terrorizes Linavar. He killed their leader, a man I considered a friend."

Cailean nodded and handed him his drink.

Edward accepted it and smiled at him. "You're a good man, Cailean. You're more just than Duncan, and a better warrior. Sometimes I wish I could leave all this to you."

Cailean shook his head, then dipped his chin to his chest. "I dinna want it."

"Precisely why you should have it." Edward swigged his drink, then set down the cup.

"Nae," Cailean said more sternly. "I willna take a man's inheritance while he yet lives."

The lord stared at him while Cailean rose from his chair. He knew exactly what his hired Highland mercenary meant, so he gripped Cailean's wrist before he turned to leave. "Don't kill him."

Cailean swallowed, bowed his head, and stepped back. "I'd like to tend m' wound."

"Go." Edward motioned with his chin toward the door.

Cailean left the solar and then walked on toward the hall. He didn't hurry, for the time was growing nearer when the terrible truth would be revealed.

Temperance had never been in Lyon's Ridge's great hall before. Her father had visited many times in the past but he'd never taken her along. Edward Murdoch had always had Black Riders in his service. Most were not the same men who served him today, but they were still all crass and hard.

Temperance hated that Gram was here seated among them.

She was surprised and worried when she saw Patrick among the men. Was Cailean here too? William? She hoped not. The men who filled this hall looked as if they'd been killing men for years. They were rough and rowdy and a few were already throwing punches over a few of the lasses serving their brew.

"You look like a frightened bird," Duncan said, seated across from her at the table and looking quite pleased with himself. "Wide-eyed and skittish in the midst of a flock of ravens."

"I happen to like ravens," she told him, meeting his dark gaze. "These are more like vultures."

"Aye," he agreed, looking around him, "you're correct. They do look like— Is that MacGregor? What the hell is he doing back here?"

Gram, sitting beside her, hadn't said much since they'd entered the hall. Temperance guessed the poor dear was tired from filling Edward Murdoch's ears with things he hadn't known, such as how his son had killed hers.

"Mr. Murdoch?" Now she spoke up, her unpatched eye piercing both of his. "Tell me something."

He gave her his attention, his black widow's peak accentuating his high forehead and arched brow. "What is it?"

"What is it that has made ye so vile?"

Temperance looked at him, also waiting for his answer.

"Never mind." Gram held up her weathered hands and rose to her feet. "I don't truly care. I'd like a nap, and if I must remain here until ye are firmly put in yer place, please see to a room fer me."

"Old woman, you forget yourself," Duncan warned. Temperance kept her eye on him. If he made a move to hurt Gram, she'd kill him with the knife she'd taken from Gram's kitchen, now hidden in the folds of her dress. She didn't care about getting out alive if Gram perished.

" 'Tis ye who fergets, young Murdoch." Gram didn't back down. "When yer father found out who I was, he guaranteed my safety. Ye are vile, but not so big a fool. Or am I mistaken?"

Temperance fingered the handle of her kitchen knife, but Duncan's impotent glare was no threat.

"You!" he shouted to a lass somewhere over Temperance's head. "Marion! Bring this crone to a room!"

Marion? Temperance and Gram exchanged a brief look, and then Temperance joined her grandmother on her feet to greet her friend.

"William searched everywhere for you," Temperance told her close to her ear when she embraced the auburn-haired beauty.

Marion cast her a reluctant, remorseful look when they separated.

Temperance's smile remained while Gram embraced Marion next. The poor gel was ashamed for loving William. Temperance wanted to tell her not to be. She wanted to tell her how happy she was to see her alive and seemingly well, and how happy it would make her best friend.

But she turned to pin Duncan with her most scathing stare instead, hating him more than ever. "You kidnapped her from the hamlet."

He shook his head and shoved a spoonful of mutton stew into his mouth. "Not I. 'Twas the MacCormack brothers."

"Come." Marion took both their arms. "Let me find rooms for you."

"You stay." Duncan pointed his spoon at Temperance.

She opened her mouth to refuse. She wanted to stay with Gram. She wanted to speak with Marion.

"If you continue to defy me," Duncan warned, "Linavar will suffer. I'll see to it. And remember that if you try to leave Lyon's Ridge, your grandmother will be punished." He turned his flinty eyes on Marion. "What are you waiting for? Get that one out of my sight."

Temperance watched them leave the hall and then turned to sit down again. Her eye caught Duncan's glance dipping disturbingly to her hips.

She eyed the jug on the wooden table between them. Could she get some of her nightshade into it before he refilled his cup?

"Things will go much more smoothly between us now that your father is no longer here to deny my every request."

Mayhap cutting his throat would be more satisfying than poisoning him.

"You're an even bigger fool than any of us realized if you

believe that, Duncan," she replied acidly. "You went to Lina-var to kill him under the pretense that he'd shot one of your men. Do you think I ever care if you die and rot before my eyes?"

"Now, Temperance." He feigned a pout. "Your father was no saint. He did indeed shoot an arrow through a relative of one of my men earlier that day. His blood was demanded."

"He shot no one!" she insisted. "Who is the man who accused him? Point me to the one who demanded his blood."

She wanted to know. To hell with poison. She would slice him open from end to wretched end.

The doors to the hall creaked open. A few of the men gasped at who stood beneath the arched frame. One or two even crossed themselves.

Temperance turned to look over her shoulder and felt her heart rise to her throat, pulling her back to her feet. It was Cailean! Her Cailean! He'd come for her, and if she'd had any concerns about his not being able to take on all these men, she cast them away now. His murderous gaze, raking over Duncan, chilled her blood and melted her heart at the same time. Anything vulnerable about his mouth and chin was gone and had been replaced by chiseled steel.

His gaze met hers behind loose strands of his dark hair and Temperance couldn't stop the smile beginning to form on her lips.

Seeing him, Duncan too rose to his feet. His face was ashy white, his jaw slack. His spoon dropped to the floor.

"Grant, you're alive."

Cailean didn't answer, but stepped around another table and came closer.

"Miss Menzie and I were just speaking of you."

# Chapter Twenty-Two

$\mathscr{F}$or a precious three or four moments, Temperance didn't know why Duncan had lied. They hadn't been speaking of Cailean. They'd been discussing the man who had— She turned to laugh at Duncan's tactics. Imagine Cailean's being the one who'd demanded her father's blood! It was the most pathetic ploy Duncan had ever come up with.

She opened her mouth to tell him but he called out to the men spread out over various tables, "Let us welcome home our brother whom we thought dead."

The men all shouted greetings to him, holding up their drinks and calling him brother.

"Nay." She didn't realize she'd spoken out loud. She looked at Cailean. No, he wasn't one of them. He was the lord's guest. That was how the men knew him.

"And," Duncan continued, lifting his own cup, "is it not good to see Patrick almost fully recovered from being shot with an arrow and almost killed?"

Temperance's gaze shot to Patrick but quickly returned

to Cailean. It couldn't be. But it made sense. Patrick had been attacked and Cailean had sought revenge.

His gaze softened on her. But it wasn't love she saw in his eyes. It was guilt. He was stricken with it. And to all who watched him, he appeared like a deadly warrior coming undone.

"You're a Black Rider," she whispered on a breath that brought her heart shattering to her feet. She lifted her hand to her forehead and tried to think clearly. Cailean was a Black Rider. Despite her fighting them back, her eyes filled with tears. She almost choked on her next question, but she had to ask it. "Are you the one who demanded my father's blood? The one who nodded?"

He breathed and his exhalation seemed to go on forever. Finally he bent his head and clasped his hands before him. "I am."

Everything around her shook. The floor rose up on a wave to consume her. Her knees were the first to go. She reeled back and fell into her chair. Everything came flooding back to her: the care she'd taken in saving his life, the smiles she'd offered him, the kisses he'd stolen from her, and all the lies.

"Do you know him?" she heard Duncan ask her.

Aye, she knew how his mouth tasted, how his tongue moved over her, tasting her in return.

"I dreamed of him once," she said in a low, still voice that sharpened her gaze and drew blood. "A devil with moonlit eyes and no mercy in his soul."

"That sounds like Cailean Grant to me," Duncan agreed. "A devil that will not die."

Cailean's gaze flicked to Duncan like a streak of lightning from under his dark brow. Lightning that sought to kill. And finally it became easy for Temperance to see him as part of the deadly mercenaries around her.

She wanted to shut her eyes and open her mouth to scream until nothing remained of her. It was about to happen and it made her panic. God help her, she'd fallen in love with the man who'd had her father killed! She loved him. No, it couldn't be he. They were all wrong. She loved this man!

"I wish to retire," she said coolly, not lifting her gaze from the table.

"But we're all just getting reacquainted," Duncan sang.

"I'm...I'm not feeling well." She scooted around her chair and moved for the doors.

"Sit down, Temperance," Duncan commanded, all traces of mirth gone. "Before I begin to suspect another reason for your hasty departure."

"Let her go, Son," Edward Murdoch called to his son while he stepped out of her path. "I haven't yet decided if I'll let you take her as a bride. Until then, she and her grandmother may move about freely as long as they don't leave without my permission."

Before she hurried out, Temperance looked over her shoulder. "Be careful, my lord. My father tried to keep me from him and got his throat slashed for it."

She lifted her skirts without waiting for his reply and ran for the stairs. She didn't know which room Gram had been taken to. She wasn't looking for it. She needed to be alone— alone to take in all her moments spent with her father's killer.

When she reached the third landing, she turned the corner and leaned her back against the wall. She felt too ill to move. How had he fooled her so thoroughly? So thoughtlessly? Not Cailean. Anyone but Cailean. She squeezed her eyes shut and covered her mouth with her hand to stop the cries aching for release.

She didn't hear his footsteps following her, but when

he turned the same corner and spoke her name she nearly crumpled to the floor.

"Please share a word with me."

She didn't want to look at him or hear his broken voice. But she opened her eyes and faced the monster who had trampled her heart under his feet. "What do you think you can possibly say to me?"

Just as she'd suspected, he had nothing more to say. She pushed off the wall and moved away from him.

"Rot in hell, Black Rider."

"Temperance," he called again. The pain in his voice almost made her stop.

She had to get away from him, and ran for the next door she came to. Pushing it open, she hurled herself inside and apologized to the girl sitting up in her bed.

Temperance locked the door and then stared at it, not thinking or caring what the girl thought of her for breaking into her room and locking them inside.

She didn't shriek or wail the way her heart demanded. She wouldn't. Not for her father's killer.

*Nay!* She reached for the edge of the bed and sat down just as her knees quaked and her legs gave out.

"Are you unwell, lass?" the girl asked her, resting a hand on her shoulder.

"I'm a fool."

"We all are." The girl smiled. "I'm Esmé."

Temperance nodded and looked at the door. "He killed my father."

"Oh, there now. That is terrible. I'm—"

Temperance snatched a bowl from the table beside the bed and bent over. She felt sick, as if her body needed to purge itself of everything having to do with Cailean Grant. It couldn't be true! It couldn't be! She'd laughed with him and listened to his tales of heartbreak. She'd believed him about Sage and about Alison. She'd looked into his eyes between kisses, and let herself trust him. She'd let him distract her from having lost her father. She'd let him kiss her and she'd kissed him back. He'd touched her as no other man had ever touched her before, and spoken words to her last eve that still, even now, played like a melody across her heart.

But now the melody had become an ode of anguish and betrayal.

Instinctually she fought to deny the shattering of her heart. But he'd touched her soul somehow as well, and she couldn't deny them both. Her throat ached from the burden of suppressing her sobs. Dizziness and nausea overwhelmed her.

She'd let him in. She'd fallen in love with him. He might not be the same monster who'd sliced her father's throat, but he was a monster just the same. *Och, Father, forgive me!*

Why had he come to Linavar that morning when she'd run into his horse? Had he come to kidnap for Duncan?

Before she could stop it, her mouth opened and a groan so laden with sorrow escaped her that beside her Esmé wiped her eyes.

She heard the soft knock at the door, the honeyed, pleading voice behind it.

"Tem, please fergive me. I—"

She covered her ears with her hands. She would never forgive him and she never wanted to hear him call her Tem again. It was her father's name for her. If Cailean Grant ever said it again she'd cut off his lips.

"Go away!" she shouted. She wanted to open the door and bury her knife in him. He'd deceived her in the most important, the most colossal two events of her life—losing her father and falling in love.

"I hate you, Cailean!" she shrieked at the door. She swiped the tears from her cheeks and choked on the rest of her words. "Stay away from me! I hate you."

She threw herself onto Esmé's pillow and wept.

"Temperance, let me in, please," he begged stubbornly.

"I'll only kill you if I do," she promised, not lifting her head from her arm, cushioning it.

"I wanted to tell ye, but I was afraid, lass."

"Leave me alone!" she screamed again. There was no mercy in her. Instead his words, his voice, only incensed her further. Her blood boiled up in her veins. "I hope someone kills you. I hope 'tis me."

He finally left the door and let her weep in peace.

Esmé left her with a promise to fetch Marion. A few moments later Gram pushed open the door and hurried to Temperance's side.

"Och, dove, so ye discovered yer Cailean is a Black Rider."

Temperance pulled back from her arms and stared at her. "Aye, and which Black Rider in particular. Did you know that it was Cailean...Cailean who brought Duncan and the Black Riders to Linavar?"

Gram nodded. "Only after Marion told me that 'twas Patrick who'd been shot that day. I remembered they had come because someone had been shot. When Marion told me Cailean was a Black Rider, I deduced which one he was."

"I'm going to kill him, Gram."

"Nay, dove, ye're not. He's going to get us out of here."

"Why would he?" Temperance asked her. "He's the reason we're here."

"That's why he's going to save us," the elder said stubbornly. "That, and because he loves ye."

• • •

Cailean sat in the hall, staring into his cup. The others didn't bother him, familiar with the dark, quiet rider who sat among them. They thought he hadn't changed.

But he knew the truth. He was worse.

He hadn't told her who he was or what he'd done. He'd let her believe he was innocent. She had every right to hate him, but he didn't want her to. He wanted to talk to her, try to win her back. He knew he never could.

He'd never forget the pain and crushing disbelief in her eyes when she'd learned the truth. It had taken every last bit of strength she possessed to remain in the hall while he changed from a man she cared for to the man who'd had a hand in killing her father. The tears she'd shed behind that blasted locked door had nearly destroyed him completely.

There was so much he wanted to say to her. He wasn't worthy of her forgiveness, but he wanted it. He needed it to live.

"Mr. Grant?"

He looked up from his cup and managed to produce a smile when he saw Marion standing over him, her bright auburn braid swinging about her waist like a fiery sword. What the hell was she still doing here? Had any of the Black Riders, or any other men at the castle, touched her?

"You haven't seen to your wound," she noted, pointing to his bloodstained shirt.

What the hell did he care about a cut to his flesh when his heart was ripped open within? "Ye're supposed to be in Perth. Why did ye no' go?"

"After you left Lyon's Ridge, Maeve refused to take me."

He ground his teeth. He would have words with the madam.

"But one of her lasses told Deware that you had gone."

Her eyes opened wider and her breath stalled. "William was here?"

His gaze fell over her russet-colored hair and the delicate curve of her jawline. "Aye, and then he rode to Perth to find ye." When she smiled, his heart sank.

"If ye've been...defiled by anyone here, point out his face to me and I'll—"

Her smile on him deepened and then she blushed. "I haven't been defiled."

He sighed out loud with relief. "How have ye managed to decline—?"

"Everyone but Lord Murdoch believes I carry syphilis."

"Why does the lord no' believe it?"

"Because I told him the truth—that I lied to get out of bedding them. I told him I would only give up my body to the man I loved. He promised to protect me. I think he cares for me."

"Ye love Deware."

"Aye, I love him. We were going to tell Temperance. Will knew she wasn't in love with him. But she *is* in love with you."

If that was supposed to make him feel better, it didn't. In fact, it made him want to smash his cup into the hearth.

"And you love her."

Aye. Aye, he did. "She nursed m' body back to good health after she found me wounded in her garden. She nursed m' soul as well, I think. But it doesna matter. What I've done canna be fergiven."

"You cannot just give up," she insisted.

He looked at her, not caring if she saw his whole heart in his eyes. "I dinna intend to, but what can I do to win her back?"

"Fight." Marion's eyes blazed as she took his hand. "If you love her then fight for her."

Aye, he sat up straighter. That was the plan.

# *Chapter Twenty-Three*

Cailean found Patrick in the training lists later that day. His opponent was Brodie Garrow, one of Lord Murdoch's harder, more experienced mercs, and one of Duncan's most loyal men. Cailean watched the fight with a careful eye, noting Garrow's weak points as well as his strong ones.

He'd wanted to kill Duncan. He still did. But killing the lord of Glen Lyon's son would hurt the people of Linavar. He thought about killing both Duncan and his father, and before knowing Temperance he might have considered it. But despite what he wanted the other men in the castle to believe, he was not the same cool, detached beast.

He liked Edward Murdoch and didn't want to kill him.

He'd grown up in a place where honor abounded, and though it had been buried beneath the weight of grief and guilt, it was still there, embedded deep within.

He sat forward on the bench, momentarily concerned for his cousin when Garrow ducked beneath Patrick's blade and came back up behind him. He smashed his heavy blade on top of Patrick's, knocking it out of his hand. Thankfully,

Patrick's father, Tristan, had taught his son well how to fight without a sword. In fact, Patrick often fought better with just his hands and feet—as he did now. Cailean watched his cousin fell the brutish Black Rider, twice with a swipe of his booted foot across Garrow's ankles and knees, and once with a chopping blow with his forearm to Garrow's throat.

Patrick left Garrow where he'd fallen in the grass and went to sit by Cailean on the bench. "Ye should let me kill him."

"Ye were just laughlin' with him an hour ago." Cailean shook his head at him.

"What better way is there to disarm a man than with friendship?" Patrick asked without a hint of remorse. "I smile at them, but it means nothin'. They kidnap lasses and turn them into whores. I smile at them to keep from killin' them."

"MacGregor!"

Cailean and Patrick turned to see Edward Murdoch leaving the castle and making his way to the lists to join them.

"If we dinna do it"—Patrick leaned in close to Cailean and spoke quickly—"yer Temperance will. I told ye what Gram said aboot her. She is plannin' on killin' some mercenaries. Ye'll likely be the first."

Cailean remembered Temperance's promises to kill the men responsible for killing her father. He had to stop her somehow. Not for Duncan's and Cutty's sakes. Not for his own, but for Linavar's and for her sake. She had too much to lose, Gram, Deware, Anne Gilbert. He wouldn't let her put them all in danger. He wouldn't let her lose more of her kin, her friends, for revenge.

The lord of Lyon's Ridge looked toward Garrow rising to his feet, his hand clutched to his neck. Murdoch laughed and set his gaze back on Patrick. "How much do you want in your purse every month to fight like that for me?"

Patrick smiled without a trace of guile, proving again to his cousin how clever and ruthless a MacGregor could truly be.

"I've told ye, m' lord," Patrick said as Murdoch reached them. "This isna the life fer me."

It wasn't the life for Cailean either. Not anymore. He was ready to live again. But first he had to get Temperance, Gram, Marion, and likely a horde of other lasses the hell out of Glen Lyon.

Murdoch clapped Patrick on the shoulder. "Pity. I could likely take Scotland with just the both of you at my side."

He patted Cailean next, then drew him in under his arm. "'Tis good to have you back. How are you feeling? You were quite pale when I saw you last."

"I'm well," Cailean lied. He felt like hell. "And eager for a word with you."

"If it's about Miss Menzie"—Murdoch smiled and released him to take a seat on the bench—"I haven't yet decided what to do with her. It is her whom you want to have a word about, is it not?" he asked indulgently when Cailean didn't reply right away.

"Aye, 'tis," Cailean admitted.

"You had gone to Linavar to see her when Duncan stabbed you, am I correct?"

Cailean sat next to him on the bench while Patrick remained standing. He hadn't planned on confessing his heart to the lord of Glen Lyon, but if he was going to fight for her, Murdoch needed to know how serious he was. "Ye are. And after your son left me to bleed to death, she was the one who brought me back to life."

"You care for her, I understand—"

"I'm in love with her, m' lord," Cailean corrected him. Damn it, but it felt good to say it, like chains melting off his heart. He wanted to tell her. He wanted to tell all the men in the castle. He loved her and he'd kill anyone who touched her.

"Then truly we have a quandary," Murdoch said, looking him in the eyes. "Duncan wants her. He's been in love with her for years."

Cailean screwed up his face and shook his head. "Was it love when he watched her faither die? When he heard her anguish and instead of falling to his knees fer bringin' her such sorrow, he intended to take her from the rest of her kin? If Seth Menzie was your friend, then dinna sentence his daughter to a life with yer son."

Edward folded his arms across his chest and exhaled a loud breath. "What do you purpose I do, then, Cailean?"

Here was what Cailean wanted to speak with him about—his plan to get Temperance away from Duncan.

"Let me fight fer her. When I win, let me take her back to Linavar with the promise to keep Duncan oot of her life."

"Fight who? My son?" The lord threw back his head and laughed when Cailean nodded. "Duncan wouldn't last long enough for the priest to recite a prayer over him."

"Of course he wouldn't," Cailean agreed. He'd proven that enough times over the last four months. "That's why I will fight ten more before him. Five today and five tomorrow."

Patrick kicked a sword off its stand and swore under his breath. He hadn't agreed to the plan when Cailean had first presented it to him. He didn't have to agree to it. Cailean needed to do it. He hoped that fighting until he was worn down, and continuing, for her, might ease his shame.

"You wish to go up against ten of the men before you fight Duncan?"

"Aye." Cailean's grin was as guileless as his cousin's had

been. He had to do this. It was the only way. "Ye like sport, m' lord, dinna ye?"

"You know I do," Murdoch said, laughing. "I know you do as well. You have more skill than anyone here, but ten men?"

"Aye," Patrick intoned, concern still marring his brow. "'Tis madness. M' lord, ye must refuse."

Cailean frowned at him. He was beginning to feel a bit insulted. Did Patrick believe he would lose? Lose Temperance?

Murdoch studied him for a moment and then waved his hand. "I will allow it."

Cailean smiled. Patrick did not.

"If you lose—" Murdoch began.

"I will no' lose."

"But you will most definitely get your arse beaten," the lord offered. "Is she worth it?"

Cailean didn't hesitate. "Aye, she is."

Murdoch looked doubtful, but he shrugged his beefy shoulders, then patted Cailean on the shoulder again before he rose to his feet. "Very well, then. You'll fight ten of the men and then Duncan. If you win, you can take Miss Menzie back to Linavar and do what you will with her. I'll inform the men. Who did you have in mind to take on?"

"Garrow, the MacCormack brothers, Innes, MacRae, and whoever else wishes to fight me," Cailean told him, and followed him back inside the castle. Patrick followed as well, mumbling as he went.

"Those five are Duncan's most loyal men," Murdoch pointed out.

"Aye, I know."

Cailean thought he saw Murdoch smile slightly as they entered the hall.

It didn't take the men long to answer Murdoch's thunderous summons to gather in the great hall for an announcement, especially with the delicious aroma of fresh black buns, mince pie, and roasted turkey wafting through the hall.

"What is that heavenly smell?" the lord asked, looking around with delight before he took a seat at one of the tables.

"Seth Menzie's mother must have taken over yer kitchen," Patrick informed him, and sat down at the same table.

Cailean had the urge to head off to the kitchen in search of Gram. He'd been eating at Lyon's Ridge long enough to know its cook could never conjure such appetizing aromas. He smiled. It was Christmas, and by preparing traditional Christmas dishes, Gram was going to make certain Murdoch and his Black Riders knew it. Knowing her, she'd likely have the men singing outlawed hymns by the end of the night.

He looked around. Was Temperance in the kitchen with her?

"Men!" Murdoch banged his fist on a table to get his men's attention. "I have an announcement!"

The Black Riders quieted down to hear him, but Cailean had stopped listening.

Every sound faded from Cailean's ears as Temperance entered the hall with Marion.

She wore her hair swept off her neck and piled loosely atop her head. The style accentuated the soft angles of her features, gave more prominence to her sapphire eyes, softened her chin and the sweet dip of her lower lip.

Cailean couldn't keep his eyes off her. They returned with a will of their own.

He glanced at the men in their seats, all eyeing her as covetously as if she were the rarest of gems, which, of course, she was, having been kept from all of them for years.

He gritted his teeth and straightened his spine. The first to touch her would be the first to die.

"Our brother Cailean Grant has offered a challenge to ten of our best," Murdoch told them. "A two-day fight, ending with him and Duncan, in the lists. You will each fight on Duncan's side. The prize will go either to my son or to Grant."

A round of approval went up among the men. Across the table Patrick shook his head at his cousin. Temperance looked even more displeased, stopping in her place to stare at him.

"Huzzah, Grant!" Tavish Innes called out. "Will you fight us all at once, then?"

Murdoch held up his hands. "How would that be fair, Innes?" the lord asked. "He'll fight you one at a time beginning tomorrow morn." He read off the five names Cailean had requested, offering the last five slots to any of his men.

Patrick slammed his palm on the table. "His arm is wounded! He needs a day or two to heal!"

"Tomorrow morn," Murdoch insisted. "The first five who will participate should be ready."

"What is the prize?" Cutty called out while he dragged one of Maeve's lasses into his lap.

Murdoch turned to Temperance. "She is."

Cailean was certain he heard Temperance utter an oath a moment before she stormed toward him.

"Welcome, Miss Menzie," Murdoch greeted her when she stood before their table.

Cailean stood from his chair, prompting the others to do the same.

"What do you think of Grant's challenge?" Murdoch asked her, though it was clear to read in her angry expression.

She told them nonetheless. "I think you should call it off," she replied. "I'm not a prize to be—"

"Grant disagrees," Murdoch said with a smile curling his lips.

"I don't care what he thinks," she said, risking Murdoch's ire.

"I dinna want ye to be forced to marry Duncan."

She glared at Cailean when he spoke. His heart faltered a little. At least she was acknowledging him. It was a start.

"My future is not your concern, Mr. Grant. Besides"— she dipped her voice but kept it from becoming a growl—"I can think of worse men to marry."

Hell, she was fine, braw and bonny in her hatred of him. She tempted him to smile like some captivated half-wit. But he didn't. He didn't want her to hate him, and her words stung.

He'd never wanted to hurt her. But he had. He felt ill with the weight of it. She was joy, innocence, a flame in the darkness. He was the monster who had taken it all from her. How could he ever win her back? He doubted fighting a hundred men would be enough.

She went back to pretending he didn't exist, which drove Cailean closer toward the edge. But he'd expected this, hadn't he? That's why he hadn't told her the truth. He'd known she'd hate him and he'd wanted to avoid the inevitable. But the truth had caught up with him and now he had to face the ugliness of it.

He wasn't supposed to care. Not again. He'd vowed to himself that he'd never let love in again.

How easily he'd given in.

Had it been the sadness in her gaze, which came from someplace so deep it felt as if nothing could ever penetrate it? The anguish he was so familiar with, that had pulled him to her? Mayhap in the beginning, but then she'd made him smile. She'd brought laughter back to him. She'd made him feel again, whether he wanted to or not. He wasn't about to let anyone harm her... or take her from him.

When Murdoch offered her a seat, she refused. When he waved his hand to one of the servers to bring her a bowl, she shook her head.

"I'm not hungry."

The lord blinked at her, then offered Cailean a perplexed look.

Cailean realized that Murdoch had no idea how to handle a lass who defied him. He also realized Temperance was defying the lord because of him.

He rose from his seat again. He didn't want to leave. He wanted to sit with her, speak with her, look at her.

"Far be it from me to keep a lady from eating. If m' presence offends her, I shall leave." He smiled at Murdoch and then at her.

He bowed and, without another word, left the table.

Before he reached John Gunns's table, the doors opened again and Duncan Murdoch stepped inside the hall. He looked around, spotted Temperance sitting with his father, and headed over.

Cailean stepped into his path, stopping him. "Where's m' horse?"

"Dead," Duncan told him with a trace of a smile he didn't bother to conceal. "The trip and the cold were too much for the beast. He had to be put down."

Cailean moved closer to him. He'd never wanted to kill a man as badly as he wanted to kill Duncan.

"If that's the truth," he warned quietly, keeping his temper leashed—for now—"I'm goin' to tie ye to the back of *yer* horse and let him drag ye along the braes until ye're no' easily recognized. Then again, after I'm done with ye tomorrow in the lists, I willna need to involve a horse."

"The lists?" Duncan eyed him as if he'd just sprouted a pair of horns. "My father will not—"

"Yer faither has already agreed. He is goin' to watch ye fall to yer knees before me and then there will be no more doubt in his mind who among us is the better warrior."

He smiled ever so slightly and whacked the lord's son on the back. Duncan almost fell forward. Cailean caught him and leaned down to speak low in his ear.

"Ye should no' have left me alive in Linavar."

## Chapter Twenty-Four

*I* should have let you die."

Cailean looked away from Temperance's angry face; his own was lined with guilt and regret. He would have preferred death over causing her so much pain.

They were alone in the hall: Marion, Temperance's escort, had left them at Cailean's quiet request a moment after he appeared out of the shadows, blocking their path.

Temperance moved to pass him on her way to her room for the night. His fingers around her wrist stopped her. What could he say? She was correct. He deserved death as payment for the life he'd taken from her. He knew, though, that it would not be enough.

"I know the pain I caused ye," he told her as a bleak, empty hole, vaster than the one before it, consumed him. "I know it, Temperance. I dinna know how to say I'm sorry fer burdenin' ye with it."

"Don't!" She pulled away from him.

She would never forgive him. He would never forgive

himself, just as he hadn't forgiven himself for Sage's death—
or for Alison's.

"And what do you mean by fighting all the Black Riders?
Are you mad?"

Aye, he was indeed out of his mind. But it had nothing to
do with his decision to fight Murdoch's elite. "I fight fer ye,
lass. I want to prove to ye—"

"You prove nothing!" Her beautiful blue eyes sharpened
on his. "Do you think fighting a horde of beasts will put an
end to what you did? Is this your foolish way of trying to win
back my favor?"

He shook his head. He knew that winning back her favor
was impossible, but he couldn't let her go through with her
plans. "I'm goin' to get ye and Gram oot of here. I know ye
want blood fer blood, but hear me when I tell ye, no good
will come of revenge. 'Twill only change who ye are."

"I welcome that change."

She didn't mean it. She didn't know what it was to lose
her heart to such darkness. He did.

"The lord will kill ye if ye harm his son."

"And yet you came here to do just that," she threw back
at him.

He didn't care about his own life, but he wouldn't let her
ruin hers with Duncan. "Temperance, I—"

"You wanted blood," she cut him off. "You led your
friends to the hamlet that night and you let them kill my
father. He was innocent, Cailean!"

"I know," he said softly.

He saw her hand coming but he remained still and let her
palm crack across his face. The force of her strike bent his head
back, but he returned his tortured gaze to her unforgiving one.

"Which one of them killed him?" she asked, her voice
and her hand trembling. "I want his name."

He wasn't about to tell her it had been Cutty. He didn't doubt the mercenary would be dead by morning if he did. After that he doubted he would be able to talk Murdoch out of punishing her.

"Dinna go through with whatever ye mean to do, I beg ye."

"Go to hell," she replied numbly.

He was already there. He'd let himself fall in love with her and now he was losing her too.

He loved her. And it was nothing like what he'd felt for Alison. It was bigger, more powerful than anything he'd felt in the past. His body shook with the fear of it. How would he recover this time? He wouldn't. He didn't want to.

"Let me take ye back to the hamlet," he begged her. "I will take care of Duncan. Ye'll never have to worry aboot him again. Marry..." He paused, letting the thought of her with someone else sour his belly. "Marry someone ye love and live oot yer life in peace."

He thought he saw tears making her eyes sparkle in the candlelit corridor. The urge to touch her, to take her in his arms, stole over him. He didn't move. Fear of loving and losing her paralyzed him.

"I don't want peace, Cailean," she told him, coating her words with frost. "I want revenge and I'll have it with a careful dose of nightshade. Lord Murdoch will not even know his son is dying until 'tis too late."

He stepped closer to her, tilting his head to gaze at her. Every muscle, every nerve ending ached for him to take her in his arms. "Will ye poison me as well?"

She caught her breath at his nearness, then stepped back, widening the distance between them. "I cared for you and betrayed my father in doing so. Stay out of my way, Mr. Grant, or I will take joy in killing you."

He let her go and watched her leave with his heart in his eyes. He wanted to call her back, go after her—anything to keep her close.

She didn't turn back, but slammed the door after she entered her room.

With nothing more to do, he turned on his heel and walked into Maeve.

"Ye love her," said the madam, reading what was clear in his eyes.

Cailean's gaze on her hardened. "I paid ye handsomely to get Marion oot of here and bring her to Perth. Why did ye no' do it?"

Maeve shrugged her shoulders, giving bounce to her cleavage. "I sure as hell wasn't about to go to Perth alone with some pretty young gel. We would likely have been attacked on the road and either left fer dead or taken to someplace worse than Lyon's Ridge. How would ye have found her then? I did ye a favor, Mr. Grant. But I wondered why ye offered so much coin fer her protection. I feared she belonged to a powerful family, so I spread the word that she was gone. Was that not enough?"

"Nae," he growled. "'Twasn't. She's still here, and the lord has grown fond of her."

"So?" Maeve argued. "That's a good thing. She's safe from the other men. But tell me," she said, keeping her voice low. "Why do ye care about Marion when 'tis clear that yer heart belongs to Miss Menzie?"

He didn't care if Patrick made light of what his father... what all the men of Camlochlin stood for; Cailean believed in honor. He might have forgotten it these last few months, but he loved his kin for instilling the belief in him.

"Decide where ye stand, Maeve. Kidnappin' lasses and forcin' them to please men is wrong and I'm goin' to do something aboot it."

He left her in the hall without another word and strode to the barracks. He made a quick stop in the lord's solar, making certain it was empty, and collected some parchment, a quill, and a small jar of ink.

He didn't know what to say to Temperance, but mayhap writing it would be easier.

Dragging a chair to the window in his room, he tried penning words to her with the moon and the light from a single candle illuminating his parchment. Nothing came. He tugged on his hair for more hours than he cared to count, wishing he could tear the words from his soul. Finally he flung the ink and quill against the wall.

A knock came at the door. He didn't want company now, but thinking it might be Temperance, he leaped from his chair and hurried for the door.

Gram stood on the other side, waiting for him to invite her in. "We need to speak."

Her son was dead because of him. He didn't want to speak to her. He wasn't sure he could.

Nodding, he let her inside.

She eyed the ink-stained wall and then turned her gaze on him. He shrank back, too filled with guilt and regret to face her.

"Before ye left Linavar," she began quietly, "ye told me ye loved my granddaughter."

His belly sank as he awaited her just accusations.

"Gram, fergive me." It was all he could manage to utter. His heart had never felt so heavy, save for when he'd spoken to Temperance.

"Fer loving her?"

He shook his head. "Fer yer son. I—"

She held up her hand to stop him. "Marion told me of the night ye brought Patrick back to the castle. He was close to death." She drew out a long sigh and sat in the chair where he'd attempted to pen words to her granddaughter. "I know how difficult that must have been fer ye. Ye should have told us the truth, though I understand why ye didn't."

Did she? He wanted her to know how difficult it had become to tell them the truth, first because of guilt and fear that they would kill him while he was weak and then because he'd grown to care for them—for Temperance. "Every time she spoke of him…" He paused to run his hands down his face, knowing what she had lost and what he could never give back to her. It was driving him mad. "Every moment I spent with her chipped away at m' defenses and I saw with clarity the cold beast I had become, and what a coward, fer no matter how much I wanted to tell her the truth, I couldna."

Gram listened to what he had to say, shedding a tear or two while she did.

"Ye might understand, Gram, but it doesna change the fact that I am responsible fer Seth dyin'. I hope ye can some-day fergive me, but I understand if ye refuse to grant it."

"I do fergive ye, Cailean." She offered him a faint smile. "'Tis Christmas. More wondrous things have happened on this day."

Cailean looked at her, feeling some of the burden lifting from his shoulders.

"I'm thankful ye intend to save my dove from Duncan," she continued, pulling a small handkerchief from her skirts and dabbing her nose with it, "but why fight ten men? Is this some sort of self-inflicted punishment?"

He shrugged, taking a seat at the edge of his bed. "I want to free Temperance from Duncan and I thought that fightin' fer her might—"

"Prove yer love?" she finished for him, then shook her head. "She doesn't need to watch ye beat men to the ground, lad. She needs ye to fight fer her with yer words. Show her ye're no longer a Black Rider. I already know it, since I'd never let my gel marry one of those vile men, but 'tis Temp who needs convincing."

But wasn't he the most vile of all?

"Show her yer true heart," Gram advised, "or are ye still afraid to share it?"

He wasn't afraid. Not anymore. Not with Temperance. "I want a life with her," he told her, the sharp hook of regret that it was likely too late digging deep into his heart. "I dinna want to lose her."

Gram rose from the chair and headed for the door. "Then mayhap ye'd do well to tell her."

He watched Gram leave. Could it be that simple? Would pouring out his heart to Temperance be easy? It hadn't been when he'd tried to pen the words to her. What if he did and she rejected him, walked out of his life for good?

He lay back on his bed and tossed his arm over his head. Gram had forgiven him. Mayhap Temperance would too.

It was Christmas, after all.

# Chapter Twenty-Five

*I* don't care if 'tis Christmas, I won't have you decorating my castle with parts of the forest!"

Cailean walked into the great hall and smiled at Gram clutching branches of evergreen to her chest and glaring up at Edward Murdoch with one eye.

"D'ye care if ye go back to eating moldy bread and foul meat?" Gram challenged.

Cailean sniffed the air sweetened with aromas of honey cakes and orange pudding. He wasn't at all surprised when Murdoch gave him a defeated look, proving just how bad the food here had been.

"'Tis best if ye dinna fight it," Cailean told him. "Let her have her way. She willna be here after I win the competition."

"Her cooking is making me want you to lose," Murdoch confessed, then waved his hand at her to finish decorating the hall. "I'll be in trouble with the kirk if they found out."

"Pah!" Gram answered. "Like anyone from the church would come here."

Murdoch glowered at her and then turned to Cailean.

"She's been vexing me all morning about it being St. Stephen's Day and how I should leave boxes of coins at the people of Linavar's doorsteps."

"'Twould strengthen good relations," Cailean pointed out, and went to Gram to help hang a bough over the entryway.

"Are you ready for the day's events?" the lord asked him. "I must tell you that Miss Menzie doesn't seem to share your sentiments. Are you certain you want to do this?"

"Aye, I'm certain," Cailean said. "Are the men ready?"

"They are. Most are already waiting for you."

"First"—Gram pointed a bony finger at him—"ye will eat!"

Cailean nodded and looked around the hall for Temperance. He was glad when he didn't find her. He needed to stay focused on the task at hand. Hearing her hatred might distract him from staying alive—or at least from keeping his teeth.

Soon enough, though, his belly was half-full and he rose to leave the hall.

Murdoch and Gram followed him outside, with the lord leaning in to have a few more words with him. "If you still have any fight left in you when you meet Duncan, I would ask that you don't make him look the fool."

Duncan Murdoch didn't need his help to accomplish that feat. Cailean nodded his agreement but kept his opinion to himself.

Pewter clouds rolled across the pale morning sky, boding poor weather. A waiting stillness settled over the training lists where the men waited, some sharpening their swords. None of the fights were to be to the death, but these were mercenaries, and if an opportunity to gain victory presented itself, they would take it.

Cailean moved onward, undaunted by the flashing metal

and the icy chill that swept through the air and the ghoulish howl of the wind swirling around him.

He spotted Cutty, whom he had been informed would fight tomorrow. Cailean suspected Duncan had ordered the ruthless mercenary to finish Cailean when he would be most weary.

"Are ye truly goin' through with this?" Patrick asked, hurrying to stand beside him.

"Aye, and I'd appreciate yer confidence in me. Have I no' practiced every day since I was a babe?"

"Aye, every day before ye were stabbed in the back!" Patrick argued. "Ye're no' ready."

"I'll be fine. I willna lose. I've practiced with these men fer four months and have never lost to any of them."

"Aye, that's why they're so eager to kick yer arse this mornin'. They all have something to prove."

Cailean was done trying to convince him. "Have ye seen Temperance?" He searched for hers amid the faces gathering to watch, but didn't find her.

"Aye, but she will no' speak to me," Patrick replied.

Cailean needed to stop thinking about her. He looked to the men gathered around, ready to fight. None of them were distracted. When he'd trained with them in the past, he'd been a different man, colder, more ruthless, less merciful. He had to be that man today if he wanted to save Temperance.

He listened to Edward Murdoch cite the rules. No striking a fatal blow. If an opponent could no longer defend himself he would be removed from the lists and the next man would enter.

Cailean stepped into the lists, the hilt of his great claymore gripped in both hands. With a flick of his wrist the blade danced and flashed beneath a stray beam of sunlight.

Erik MacCormack came forward.

Cailean smiled.

• • •

"He's a stubborn fool," Temperance said on a shallow breath, watching Cailean from her window.

"This is my fault." Marion chewed her bottom lip. "I suggested he fight for you, but I didn't mean this!"

Temperance didn't blame her friend. What did fighting ten men have to do with her? Nothing. This was who Cailean was—a Black Rider. He enjoyed wielding his blade. Hell, it seemed to come as naturally to him as breathing. He possessed an inimitable air of confidence. Each subtle nuance of movement, even the slight curling of his mouth when he met a huge red-haired mercenary, spoke of a man at ease with his skill, certain of his devastating power. Truly, she shouldn't be worried about him. Why was she? She hated him. She didn't care if he was injured. It would save her the trouble of killing him.

"He enjoys this," she said more to herself than to Marion. "He thirsts for blood."

"You know Mr. Grant better than I," Marion said, "but he doesn't strike me as a bloodthirsty avenger."

Temperance smiled benignly at the memory of Cailean's rugged face. "Don't let those wide haunting eyes and perfectly bow-shaped mouth fool you into thinking there is innocence in him, Marion." Temperance knew what she was talking about. He'd fooled her. "'Tis the kind of beauty that has led many astray."

Marion's smile on her softened. Temperance didn't like it.

"Could it be that he is such an accomplished master of disguise?"

It was a simple question Marion put to her, but Temperance didn't know how to answer. Could it be? She remembered his emotion when he'd told her about Alison, and then again when he'd told her about Sage. Had that emotion been feigned? Had the words he'd whispered to her while she laughed with him been empty? His passionate kisses meaningless?

She turned back to the window as the red-haired brute swung his blade hard enough to push Cailean backward. She covered her eyes. He was a fool! Barely healed of two fevers that had drained his strength!

Watching through a space between her fingers, she noted him bracing his feet on the ground, ready for more.

She scowled at Gram, standing in the cold with Patrick. Why hadn't either one of them stopped him? Surely he would have listened to his cousin... and Gram! Why, no one defied her!

"Och, good Lord!" She thought she might faint when his opponent swung his blade high over his shoulder and then brought it down hard toward Cailean's shoulder.

Temperance stared, horrified that she was about to watch Cailean lose an arm. She didn't want to care. She didn't want to watch another second, but she couldn't look away. This was the man who had shared the deepest parts of his heart with her, the man who had brought back her joy while she helped him rediscover his. The man who had captured her heart and given her hope for the kind of love she'd always desired.

The man who'd helped take her father from her.

He blocked, holding his claymore sideways and letting the metal absorb most of the impact, then answered with a flurry of swings, his sword moving with incredible speed and might.

His opponent tried to parry, but Cailean changed position suddenly and his blade twisted and danced in the air before sending the red-haired man's sword across the lists. Cailean took a swift step forward and held the tip of his blade to his opponent's throat. He said something Temperance couldn't hear, then looked up at the others and called out, "Next!"

Temperance watched three more men come against Cailean. He was victorious over all, but she could tell he was growing weary. From her window she could see blood on his cheek, and his arm appeared to be growing stiff. She wasn't the only one who noticed. Two of his opponents struck him in the same spot numerous times, trying to wear him down. The Black Riders didn't hold back, but neither did Cailean. He fought as if his life depended on it.

Watching him mesmerized her, stole her breath. She didn't want to think him beautiful. She didn't want to believe he was doing this for her. She wanted to go outside and call him a fool to his face.

She decided to do just that.

Marion snatched up their cloaks and followed her when Temperance left the room.

They stepped out of the castle and into the gray late afternoon just as snow began to fall. Following the path from the back, outdoor stairway, they made their way to the western edge of the lists, a short distance away from where the rest of the men stood.

Fergus MacRae, a big burly brute who looked as if he were hiding three more men beneath his fur cloak, stepped into the lists and pointed his blade at Cailean.

Temperance's heart beat frantically when she saw that Cailean's eyes were not on his deadly-looking opponent, but on her.

Their gazes met across the snowy expanse and for a moment no one else existed but the two of them, nothing else mattered but their hearts, aching and broken.

Fergus MacRae's sword swished through the air, a mere inch from Cailean's head.

Temperance gasped, snatching Cailean back to the present. He shifted his weight instantly and blocked a series of powerful blows coming at him in rapid succession.

"MacRae is going to carve him up like that delicious turkey we ate last eve!" one of the men called out.

Temperance turned to glare at him, and then hid her satisfied grin when Patrick clubbed him in the back of his head with his fist.

"Dinna try m' temper, Cutty," Patrick warned him. "Ye have yet to see the harder side of me."

Standing with Patrick, Gram left his side and shuffled over to her granddaughter. "I didn't think you would come to watch."

"I've been watching from my window. He fights well but he appears weary."

Gram shook her head. "He is revived now that ye are here, dove."

Temperance watched him as the sun began its slow descent, casting him in an eerie silvery glow. His hair fell around his handsome face. He cleared the damp locks away with one hand and clutched the hilt of his sword with the other.

Temperance hated herself for the silent prayer she offered up for him. She hated herself for giving a damn about the man who'd lied to her, who'd let her fall in love with him knowing what he'd done. She fought her feelings harder than she'd ever fought anything else. He'd nodded and her father's life had ended. How could she ever forgive him? How could she ever shed another tear over him without betraying her father even more?

Unable to look away, she watched as he prepared for MacRae's second attack. He sidestepped what would have been a crushing blow and then parried, making his sword sing. MacRae advanced again and smashed his blade against Cailean's, causing sparks to fly.

Temperance wanted to call out for them to cease. Cailean could barely hold up his weapon against MacRae's vicious assault. He fought back with what seemed his last ounce of strength.

Spotting an opening, MacRae swung the flat of his blade hard and low across Cailean's legs. With the speed and agility of a cat, Cailean jumped up. He landed in a crouched position, and before MacRae could swing again was back on his feet holding the edge of his shiny sword against Mac-Rae's throat.

Hearty cheers rose up from at least six of the men watching, the loudest coming from Patrick. Temperance remembered to breathe, and then forgot again when Cailean sheathed his sword and strode toward her.

## Chapter Twenty-Six

*E*very part of him hurt, but Cailean could think of only one thing as he left the lists. He kept his eyes on Temperance as he tried to cut through the crowd of men and even some of Maeve's lasses swarming around him.

"Huzzah! Well done!" came the shouts, along with pats on the back.

Cailean nodded and pushed his way through, trying to reach her. She stood off to the side, her dark locks dusted with white, her sapphire eyes glistening in the early twilight.

When she turned to leave he held up his hand as if to stop her. She saw him and kept going.

"You still have the rest of us to face tomorrow, Grant!" someone called out as Temperance passed them. Her shoulders went stiff as she stormed back inside.

"Then ye should spend the night practicin'," Cailean called back, and shoved his way out of the crowd.

A man stood in his way.

"You think you're going to take her away from me, but you're wrong."

Cailean set his frosty gaze on Duncan. "Get oot of m' way before I toss ye over the wall."

The lord's son lifted his lips into a twisted smile. "My father tells me you love her. You're a Black Rider. She will never return your affections. You are wasting your time here."

Cailean barely listened. Instead he studied Duncan more closely. Was the bastard drunk? His eyes seemed unfocused, a little glassy. His words were slurred just a bit. No! Cailean's heart sank. No, she couldn't have!

"I will have her, Grant! I'll take her as my wife and then I'll fu—"

Cailean had heard enough. Grasping fistfuls of Duncan's collar, he lifted him off his feet and tossed him out of his way. The lord's son went sprawling some feet away, face-down in the dirt.

Coming toward them, Patrick chuckled at the fallen mercenary and waved at him when Duncan looked up.

"Go!" Patrick called out to his cousin. "I'll watch this one."

Cailean nodded and continued to the castle. Hell, he ached all over. His body had not fully recovered from the infection that had coursed through him, ravaging him with fevers. But it was his heart that ached the most.

He had to find Temperance and tell her…damnation, there was so much he wanted to tell her. But first he needed to know if she had poisoned Duncan.

He found her on her way to the great hall. "Temperance," he called. When she turned to look at him, he paused. He loved her, but there was so much more. Gram had told him to show her his true heart. Did he even know where to find it?

Aye, he thought when he saw her that his heart was with her.

When she began to turn away from him again, he rushed toward her and clasped her wrist. "Did ye poison Duncan?"

She didn't answer but tried to free herself from his grip. "Let go of me," she warned.

"Listen to me. If he dies, his faither will kill ye!"

"I don't care!" she threw back at him. "This is no longer your concern."

People were beginning to file into the hall. Cailean's heart raged within him. He had to talk her out of this madness before it was too late.

Lowering his voice, he pulled her closer. "There's no comin' back from this, Temperance. Once ye take a man's life, ye will be forever changed. This isn't who ye are, lass."

Her eyes bored into him. "You don't know who I am or what I'm capable of doing. I'm not a fool. I only put a little nightshade into Duncan's drink. He will die slowly. His father will not suspect any foul play."

He closed his eyes and tried to think clearly. Dear God, she had poisoned the lord's son and she had no intention of stopping.

"And what if he does?" he asked her quietly, quickly, as the hall filled with voices and laughter. "What if he discovers what ye've done and takes his revenge on the people of Linavar? What if he kills Gram... William—"

The horror in her eyes convinced him to continue. "Please, cease this madness before 'tis too late, Temperance."

"And what of you?" she asked acidly, though when her eyes fell to his swollen lip, her gaze softened. "Will you continue with this foolishness of fighting more Black Riders tomorrow?"

"In order to save ye from marryin' Duncan, aye, I will."

"I don't need you to save me. I can save myself."

Someone called his name and she broke away from him and hurried off.

Damn it! Cailean ran his palm down his face. There was only one thing left to do. He was going to have to save Duncan before Temperance killed him.

It didn't take him long to find Duncan later that night. The bastard was in his private chambers, in his bed with one of Maeve's girls.

Cailean didn't pause when he saw the two in the throes of passion. He interrupted them with a shout from the door, startling the lass, who leaped from Duncan's body and wrapped herself in his bedsheet.

"The fight tomorrow is off, Murdoch. Meet me in the lists now," Cailean demanded in a chilling tone. "Or I'll come back here and kill ye in yer bed."

He left them looking equally terrified. He didn't stop or even pause when he heard Murdoch shout for him to come back. There was no turning back.

He met his cousin on the way to the castle doors.

"Where are ye off to at this late hour?" Patrick asked him, abandoning a pretty blond lass named Bess... or Beth. Cailean hated himself for not knowing.

"I'm goin' to beat the senses oot of Duncan Murdoch," Cailean told him, ignoring the lass's gasp.

He waited a moment while Patrick told the gel to go to her room and not come out until the morning.

"Pack yer things," Cailean added, glancing at her. "Patrick's goin' to bring ye and whoever else wants to go to Skye when this is all over."

"He is?" the lass asked, shifting her worshipful gaze to his cousin. "You are?"

Instead of answering her, Patrick glared at Cailean and sent her on her way.

"What the hell d'ye mean by tellin' her that? I want to see

them oot of Lyon's Ridge. I never said a word aboot bringin' them to Camlochlin. Cailean, damn ye, she's goin' to think I care fer her!"

"I've nae doubt," Cailean retorted coolly, turning to continue toward the doors, "that ye were goin' to bed her tonight. Carin' fer her should already be the reason."

"Well, 'tis no'," his cousin argued, following him. "Ye canna bring ladies of the night to Camlochlin. We'll be tossed oot on our arses."

"I dinna care."

"I do!"

Cailean finally stopped and turned on him. "I thought ye wanted to help them."

"I do, but we can help them by bringin' them someplace else."

"Ye truly dinna possess any honor, do ye, Pat." It wasn't a question, and it was voiced with contempt.

That didn't seem to bother Patrick all that much. He hurried forward and stepped in front of Cailean, blocking his path to the door.

"Mayhap ye're correct, Cousin, but I do possess a rational mind, which is more than I can say fer ye presently. Ye're goin' to have the Black Riders oot fer blood if ye kill their leader. They'll follow us to Camlochlin—"

"I dinna intend on killin' him, though 'twouldna be difficult. I intend to save his life."

"What the hell are ye talking aboot?" Patrick asked him. "Did one of the lads hit ye in the head too hard?"

Cailean stopped and turned to him. "Temperance—" He paused to look around the halls and make certain no one was present to overhear him. He lowered his voice to a whisper. "She has poisoned him with nightshade. She plans on continuing to feed him small doses until he's dead. I dinna know what his faither will do if she succeeds. I willna wait aroond to find oot."

Patrick nodded, understanding now. "What d'ye plan to do?"

"I'm goin' to hurt him enough to put him to a sickbed so that the symptoms he's already beginnin' to experience are mistaken fer the effects of a good beatin'. I need to get her oot of here quickly, though, before she finishes what she started."

"How will ye explain to Lord Murdoch why ye took his son to the lists tonight instead of tomorrow?"

Cailean shrugged. "I'll figure that oot tomorrow."

Patrick nodded and followed him outside into the dark.

They waited in silence, lighting the lists with torches. Cailean didn't particularly need to see in order to fight. He'd trained in the dark before and done well, better than most of his cousins, as a matter of fact. It wouldn't take him long.

"Patrick!" Duncan appeared a little while later with Cutty at his side. "I hope you're here to talk some sense into your cousin."

Patrick held up his hands. "I tried."

The sound of Cailean's sword leaving its sheath stilled the air and the breath of those in attendance. With a shrug of his shoulders, his cloak fell to the ground.

"Murdoch," he said in a low, deadly voice, "quit tryin' to postpone the inevitable and ready yer blade."

"We're supposed to do this tomorrow, Grant," Murdoch pointed out nervously.

He blinked rapidly and Cailean ground his teeth. How much nightshade had Temperance fed him?

"Are you afraid of coming against Dougal MacCormack and Cutty first?" Duncan laughed and missed the sword Cutty tossed to him.

Hell, Cailean wondered if Duncan would even be able to fight him.

"You want her for yourself," the scrawny bastard said while he picked the sword up off the ground. "But I'm going to have her. You'll be gone and she'll be mine. You can't stop—"

He didn't see Cailean's blade even though it flashed before him in the torchlight. He was able to block... barely. Another strike caught him on the arm. It was a slice rather than a chopping blow. Blood flowed and Murdoch cried out, dropping his blade. He swooned on his feet and Cutty ran to his aid.

"Leave me alone!" Duncan hit his hand away. "I don't need your help!" He glared at Cailean for a moment and then charged.

Cailean smiled and tossed his blade away into the grass beside Duncan's. He couldn't kill the bastard without possibly starting a war. Beating him senseless was what he'd come to do. "Aye, come on," he growled, shoving his sleeves over his elbows. "Let's get on with it, then." He swung and his fist connected with Murdoch's jaw.

Surprisingly Murdoch fought back, sending a crushing fist of his own into Cailean's face.

Aye, now this was more like it. Cailean swiped his wrist across his nose, clearing away the blood, and then advanced like a man void of mercy. Void of everything. He'd waited to do this for months. For everything. For Seth Menzie. For Temperance and Gram.

He had to admit, though, it wasn't exactly a fair fight. Duncan's movements were slow. One could blame the nightshade, but Cailean had practiced with Duncan in the past and it hadn't been any better. Duncan's father knew it, and when Cailean was through with him tonight, Duncan would no longer be able to deny it.

Twice Duncan swung his fist and twice Cailean avoided being hit. Patrick snickered from the sideline while Cutty called out moves Duncan should make.

Duncan didn't listen and was struck with a flurry of punches that pushed him backward. Cailean thought he saw a tooth go flying to the right. A right hook to the jaw sprayed blood across Cailean's face.

"Cailean!" Patrick shouted. "He has a dagger!"

Aye, Cailean saw the small blade flash in the firelight when Duncan pulled it from his boot. He swung, aiming for Cailean's face, missed, and then swiped it across Cailean's chest.

*Bastard*, Cailean thought when he felt the blade slice through his plaid and the shirt beneath. The wound wasn't deep, just a scratch, but it ignited a fresh fire in Cailean to finish Duncan. A right hook to his jaw and another combination to the guts brought him to his knees.

Cailean lifted his fist one more time and sent it into Duncan's temple.

Cutty leaped forward as his friend crumpled in a heap at Cailean's feet. He struck Cailean with a hard fist to the chin that made Cailean sway on his feet. But he wasn't about to go down so easily. A thunderous uppercut sent Cutty reeling back. It took less than an instant for the bastard to return. Cailean caught him with a sprawling left and was hit back with a right, just as menacing.

This had to end now. Cailean was still weary from the day's competition. He didn't want to grow careless and lose. Remembering what Cutty had done to Seth Menzie gave him the spurt of anger he needed to finish.

His next blow nearly dislocated the merc's jaw.

Watching them, Patrick yawned.

# Chapter Twenty-Seven

Temperance opened her eyes to the glare of the winter sun lighting her room and Marion sitting beside her bed, wringing her hands through her skirts.

"What is it?" She sat up, her heart battering against her chest so hard she thought she should lie back down before she passed out. Was it Cailean? Gram? Will?

"Marion?" She reached out, trying to offer Marion some sort of support. The poor gel was as white as Gram's purest wool. "Has something happened? Tell me, please. Is it Cailean?"

"'Tis Duncan," Will's beloved told her, trading wringing her skirts for squeezing Temperance's hand. "Cailean trounced him last eve in the lists. Severely. Duncan suffers a broken nose, two broken ribs, and he lost a tooth. His eye looks quite bad too. I fear the socket may be broken. Cutty told Lord Murdoch that he never saw a man fight the way Cailean had. He said 'twas as if Cailean was possessed by the devil. He said while Duncan lay bleeding and broken on the ground, Cailean went after him next and nearly broke Cutty's jaw."

Temperance's face drained of color. What in blazes did Cailean think he was doing? He'd warned her not to harm the lord's son and then he'd gone and broken Duncan's bones in the lists before the day's challenge. Why?

"The lord is furious," Marion continued, "but strangely enough he's most angry with his son. I heard him shouting at Duncan that his son spent too much time rutting whores and not enough time practicing."

*Och, thank God he didn't order Cailean's death*, Temperance comforted herself. She left the bed the instant her legs felt strong enough to hold her up.

Fool! Why in blazes would he take such a chance when she had poison?

"Oh, but there's more, Temp," Marion told her in a shaky voice, holding back her tears. "Edward still wants Cailean punished for fighting his son in the dead of night."

"What? What is his punishment to be?" Temperance asked on a withered breath.

"You are to tend his son."

Temperance reached for her gown and let out a sigh of relief that Lord Murdoch hadn't hanged Cailean. She shouldn't care, but she did. She didn't want Cailean to die because of her, but an instant later her blood boiled. "How is he punishing Cailean by making me tend his son?" She felt ill. She didn't want to tend him! "I won't do it!"

"Oh, but you must," Marion insisted. "Edward has ordered it."

Temperance didn't care what the lord had ordered. Damn Cailean for doing this. She rubbed her head. She wanted to scream. She'd intended to kill Duncan quietly and now she was expected to nurse him back to health!

"Edward asked Cailean why he did it," Marion went on, watching Temperance pick up her gown and step into it.

"Cailean told him that he'd discovered who had shot Patrick on their way back from Kenmore that fateful day. He said 'twas Duncan."

Temperance thought about it while she stepped into her gown. It made sense. Duncan was clever enough to— She stopped thinking when Marion began to sob into her hands. "Is there more, then?" Temperance went to her friend's chair and knelt beside it. "What are you not telling me?"

"I don't think 'twas Duncan. I think 'twas Will who started this."

"Will?" Temperance echoed, not understanding. What the hell did William have to do with any of it?

"He always told me that if the Black Riders hurt me, he would shoot them in the heart with his arrow. I...I think 'twas Will who shot Patrick. I think he shot him. I was here that day—and so was Duncan. He never left the castle. He was here, Temperance," Marion wept, her pretty green eyes shimmering with tears. "I know your father would never have shot at any of Murdoch's men. The consequences were too great and..."

"My father was with me," Temperance said in a low, hollow whisper. William. She remembered no one had seen him that day. He'd returned later for the celebration. He hadn't told them where he'd been. Was it possible that he...? He knew her father had been killed because one of Duncan's men had been shot. He knew and he'd never said a word.

*Nay.* She shook her head but tears were already forming over the rims of her eyes. How could this be happening? How could she have been duped and lied to by the two men she loved?

"Oh, I should not have told you!" Marion cried harder seeing Temperance's tears. "Mayhap I am wrong! But...but he loves me and he is rash at times."

Aye, he was. "Why would he not have told me?" She wasn't expecting an answer from Marion, and her friend had no answer to give her.

Temperance wiped her eyes. She was good and tired of excuses. Her father was dead because of William and Cailean. She hated them all. She laughed, but the sound was void of mirth and filled with only rage.

"Oh, Temperance, what are you going to do?" Marion leaped from her chair when Temperance headed for the door.

"I'm going to tend Duncan and feed him poison slowly. Him and the others, and then I'm going to fetch my grandmother and get her the hell out of Linavar."

She didn't wait to hear Marion's opinion on the matter but snatched up her sachet of herbs and left the room, her heart pounding and her fingers clenched at her sides.

She wouldn't weep. She was done with all that. She'd also never allow herself to be deceived again by any man!

She entered Duncan Murdoch's room a few moments later with a smile on her face and a small pouch of deadly herbs in her hand.

She didn't let her smile fade when he demanded to know where she'd been all morning.

"I'm here now, Duncan," she sang, entering the room and going to his sickbed.

She gave him a quick looking-over. "My, but you look frighteningly bad. What happened?"

He glared at her through one eye. The other eye was sealed shut. The flesh around both eyes was purple and a tad blue, most likely due to his broken nose. The same unsightly color stained two places on his jaw. There were two or three gashes on his shoulder and upper arm, delivered, she guessed, by Cailean's sword. After a quick examination, she discovered that Marion was correct: his ribs were broken as well.

A swell of pride and satisfaction coursed through her that Cailean had done this to him. She did her very best not to smile.

"I had a run-in with a demon," he told her. "Cailean Grant."

"Whatever did you do to cause him to beat you so mercilessly?"

He shrugged his rather dainty shoulders and then grimaced with the pain of moving. "I'm guessing it had something to do with your father. He doesn't understand what it means to be in a position of power and to have a man like Seth Menzie defy your every command."

Temperance found the strength not to punch him in his broken nose. "My father," she said with more calmness than she felt, "did not defy you. But I don't understand why Mr. Grant would fight you over it. It was his demand for revenge that brought the Black Riders to Linavar, was it not?"

"It was, indeed," he verified. "But after it was done, he was angry. He didn't think your father was the one who shot his cousin—"

"He wasn't."

Duncan ignored her interruption. "He'd promised to fight me and last night he made good on it."

So Cailean had been angry that Duncan had had her father killed. She would think about what it meant later.

"He cares for you, Temperance."

"Don't be a fool, Duncan."

He grinned at her, though it was more like a hideous snarl she wanted to scratch off his face.

"And you care for him," he drawled. "A Black Rider. You betray your father."

She felt sick. He was correct and she hated herself for it.

"I could never care for a Black Rider."

"You could if you hadn't known he was one." He laughed,

but only for a moment before he went pale at the pain from his ribs. "You didn't know, did you? He never told you."

"I don't care for him, Duncan. I hope he rots in hell with you at his side. But tell me before I see to your wounds, why did he attack Cutty after he did this to you?" She had to know the truth, and Duncan seemed to be enjoying telling her. "Was it Cutty who slashed my father's throat?"

"You're a perceptive little wench." He smiled again. "That one enjoys his work."

Temperance would enjoy hers as well.

She let him talk, though he said nothing else about her father or that fateful night. He wasn't sorry. In fact, he'd taken pleasure in ridding himself of her father. He would pay for it. She'd make sure of it. She'd kill his father as well, and Linavar would finally be free of the tyrant Murdochs.

She didn't listen to him while she rewrapped the bandages around his waist, a bit tighter than necessary.

"It's hard to breathe," he complained.

Good. She hoped he'd suffocate before she left the room.

Paying him little heed, she applied ointment to his eye and wrapped that as well. When she was done, she mixed him a drink of her herbs, not too much. She wanted him to die slowly.

"Drink it," she commanded. "'Twill ease some of your pain."

"Is it poison, my pet?" he asked, leering at her.

She rolled her eyes and took a sip of the drink herself to prove it wasn't. A tiny amount wouldn't hurt her.

She gave him a stoic nod when he accepted her offering. He drank it and settled farther into his bed.

"I will return in an hour to see how you're doing."

He nodded and squeezed her hand. She smiled as she left the room.

# Chapter Twenty-Eight

*C*ailean entered the great hall and spotted Temperance sitting at a table with Marion, Patrick, Cutty, and John Gunns. They were all drinking. His blood went cold.

What the hell was she doing with Cutty? Did she know about him, then? Surely Patrick wouldn't have let her poison the mercenary's drink. What about Duncan? Was he already dead? He should go check on him, but he really didn't care if the bastard was cold in his bed. Let the lord blame Cailean if he was. Mayhap he would reply if charged that the dainty bastard hadn't been able to survive a beating. The lord should be grateful that Cailean had helped rid Lyon's Ridge of him.

But killing the other Black Riders would surely get Temperance killed.

He made his way toward the table, pausing when Temperance saw him and rose from her chair. He didn't stop her or speak a word to her when she left the table with Marion hot on her heels.

"Should I get ready to block another blow?" Cutty asked him as Cailean took a seat at the table.

"Only if ye come at me again fer Murdoch's sake," Cailean promised, then glanced Temperance's way and relaxed a bit when she sat at a table with some of Maeve's girls. He looked away just as she smiled at the madam. He missed the way she'd smiled at him. Would he ever see it again?

"I think you came close to breaking my jaw, you bastard."

"Ye'll live," Cailean replied benignly. It was more than he could say for Seth Menzie. Ignoring his cousin's dimpled grin beside him, he raised his hand to a server and called for a cup of ale.

"She's an interesting lass, that one."

Cailean's gaze shifted to Gunns. "Who?"

"Miss Menzie," John answered. "She has every reason to hate us, and yet she just sat here and shared a few humorous tales about her grandmother with us."

"Did she?" Cailean put to him. "Did ye all share a laugh that Cutty killed her faither?"

"Hell," Cutty murmured. "You're not still going on about him, are you?"

Cailean smiled, though it was difficult for him to keep himself from finishing what he'd started last night in the lists. "Destroyin' families irritates me, Cutty. What are ye drinkin'?

"Ale," the mercenary told him.

Cailean looked at the cup in Cutty's big hand. Had Temperance served him? He glanced at Patrick, but no help came.

The server returned with a cup for him and a wink when he met her gaze. He offered her the briefest of smiles, but it was enough to make her fall into his lap.

"Can I get you something else?" she purred, settling in.

His eyes found Temperance again in time to see her watching, her lips tight with anger.

Was she jealous? Mayhap it wasn't too late. It gave him the barest trace of hope and made his heart feel lighter than it had in days.

"Nae." He gave the server a slight push off. She fell into Patrick's waiting arms and laughed when the handsome Highlander's lips fell to her throat.

Paying them no heed, Cailean raised his cup to his lips, then paused and looked toward Temperance once again. Was all the ale poisoned? She had said she wanted to kill all the Black Riders. Would she try to kill him too?

He guzzled the drink, keeping his gaze steady on hers while the ale went down. If he was dead in the morning then he deserved it.

Hell, he was a wretched fool. How could he have let himself destroy her? If he lived to be a hundred, he'd never forget her words to him. He wanted to get up, toss his chair out of the way, and run to her. He wanted to gather her up in his arms and kiss her just one more time—and then hand her his dagger and command that she ram it into his heart. If it would have brought her father back from the dead he would have done it in an instant.

His legs ached to go to her. When she rose from her seat and left the hall, he couldn't sit another instant.

"I'm goin' to take a walk," he told the others, leaving his chair as well.

He followed her, not too close, turning corners a moment or two after her. She was heading to Duncan's chamber. He watched her, longing to sweep her up in his arms and pledge his life to her. When she disappeared into the room, he waited outside the door. He hated that she was tending the lord's son. For that too he had only himself to blame.

Had he turned Temperance into what he had been? Was she feeding poison to Duncan inside? Hell, she was going to get them all killed. He leaned his ear to the cool wood but heard nothing. If she screamed he'd kick open the door and save her and to hell with the consequences. He thought about doing it anyway. He could snatch her up and bring her to Camlochlin before she did anything she'd regret. She'd be safe on the misty isle of Skye. He'd fight to win her heart, to mend the pieces he'd broken, and promise never to hurt her again.

Twice he hid in the shadows when he heard footsteps in the hall. He knew he was risking much, constantly seeking her out, but presently he didn't give a damn.

His fingers itched to pen her words of his love, to paint her, touch her, laugh with her again. She had every right to hate him, but the thought of it made him want to fall to his knees and tear out his hair.

When the door finally opened a half hour later, he stood with his back pressed to the wall, opposite her as she stepped out into the hall.

He smiled. He couldn't help himself, she was everything he'd ever desired and he couldn't let her go.

"Does he still live?" he asked her as lightly as he could manage.

"For now." She wiped her hands on a small cloth she toted, but instead of running from him, she stared at him. Something in her gaze softened for just a moment, renewing his hope yet again.

"He told me you were angry with him that night."

"I was," he said on a suspended breath.

"You didn't want him to kill my father."

He shook his head. "I did no' want it, Temperance."

"You were the one who shouted for Cutty to wait."

Then she knew it had been Cutty. "Aye, and when yer faither fell, yer cries tore me from the darkness."

"And plunged me into them instead."

Hell, he'd never shed a tear before. He'd held back his emotions when Sage died, and again later when he lost Alison. But now his throat burned and his vision blurred.

What could he say? Could he ever make it right between them again?

"'Tis clear to me now why you always clamped up when I spoke of my father to you. How did you look at me all those moments we spent together? How could you have kissed me, touched me?"

He had been able to because he loved her. But it wasn't enough.

"I call you a fool," she continued, "but no one was a bigger fool than I."

"Nae, lass," he said in a low despondent voice, lifting his eyes.

"How could you?" she asked him, her eyes glimmering with unshed tears.

He moved closer, hovered over her, his gaze dark and anguished, his voice deep and desperate.

"Och, m' dearest Temperance, I would have ye know that I claim full responsibility fer takin' yer faither from ye. There is no way to tell ye how I regret my decisions of that night. There are no' sufficient words to tell ye how sorry I am—how sorry I've been. But please, lass, allow me to try."

She shook her head. "Nay, I—"

"Men do monstrous things because of fear," he told her quickly. He had to fight for her. He had to bare his heart to her. "I am one of them. I had forgotten who I was. M' life had become a meaningless endeavor to fill a void I had created. Nothin' I touched was dark enough. I left all that I loved and allowed a monster to take hold of me. I didna recognize him until I watched yer faither die in yer arms.

"I dinna tell ye this fer absolution. I'm fully aware that I deserve yer contempt. I would give m' life to bring yer faither back to ye. Fer ye I would give up m' last breath."

He hadn't thought he could ever feel like a worse monster than he already did, but when she began to weep and covered her face in his hands, he knew he had been wrong. He didn't care if she stabbed him or poisoned him later for it, he had to hold her.

"M' dearest beloved," he whispered close to her ear when he took her into his embrace. "I thought I was beyond repair, but ye found me, lass. Ye put me back together, mendin' me with yer smiles, yer fire, and selfishly I let ye do it. Instead of tellin' ye the truth, I took the coward's way oot because every moment I spent with ye was like bein' reborn, and I was afraid of dyin' again. Fergive me. Fergive me."

He held her close while she sobbed into his shirt and he cried with her. "I will do anything... anything to win ye back. Please, tell me I have a chance."

Finally she sniffed and moved away a bit to look up at him. "Why did you beat Duncan?"

"I couldna let him die by yer hand."

"So instead you would let him die by yours?"

"Aye, lass. I love ye. I love who ye are—I love the joy I saw in yer eyes, the way ye love yer kin, the way I believe ye loved me. I want that all back. Walk with me," he pleaded, then breathed again when she nodded.

She fell in step beside him and his heart broke at the small size of her so near. They walked in silence back to her room, and to his surprise and elation, she invited him in.

"Should I worry fer m' life?" He tried to sound lighthearted as he entered.

"I've seen what you did to five men and Duncan. You've nothing to fear from me."

Oh, but she was wrong. She, and she alone, had the power to slay him.

"Ye could poison me, lass." He moved about the room and went to stand by the window. Looking out, he could see the tiny hamlet in the distance below. A need to protect everyone in it washed over him. He wanted to go back... with her.

"I could," she agreed, sitting on the edge of her bed. "But then I would get no answers from you."

He turned to look at her. "What do ye want to know? Ask me what ye will and I'll tell ye the truth."

"Cutty killed my father, aye?"

"Aye." He'd known it would be difficult, nae, near impossible to confess to her, but it was happening now and he wasn't prepared for the pain in her gaze as she looked away, remembering.

"Why did you return to Linavar after?"

She looked at him, her eyes misty and empty. He went to her and knelt at her feet. "I wanted yer forgiveness—yers and Gram's. I watched ye bury him and I knew I'd never get it."

She blinked and a tear fell to her cheek. He ached to wipe it away. To wipe it all away.

"You were there that morning?"

"Aye, and that first night as well. I heard ye talkin' to William. I heard him tellin' ye to be strong and I knew... I understood how hard that is to do and how alone it makes ye feel."

"Aye," she whispered softly, her large, luminous eyes filling with tears again. "I didn't want to be strong." She swiped at her eyes but more tears came.

He understood. He knew what it was like to have your heart and soul wrenched out while people around you went on living, laughing, not truly understanding.

He reached up to smooth a tendril away from her face. If she rejected him, so be it. He longed to comfort her. "Ye dinna have to be strong, lass," he said tenderly. "Ye suffered a tremendous loss."

She didn't push his hand away but brought her own hands up, buried her face in them, and let her tears fall freely.

Instantly Cailean drew her into his arms, moving to sit beside her on the bed. With every shift of her delicate shoulders as she pulled in air, only to expel it again on an anguished sob, he ached to comfort her more. He let her cry, as she needed to, holding her, whispering tender promises that all would be well. When she finally looked up at him, her face wet with tears, he smiled softly and smoothed away her hair.

"I love ye. I love ye and it scares the hell oot of me. I want to live m' life with ye. I want to see ye smile, hear yer laughter, hear ye tell me ye love me. Please fergive me, lass. I'll go mad if ye refuse."

Instead of answering him, she lifted her arms and coiled them around his neck. Her mouth was so close, her breath warm on his chin. Her body trembled against him, tempting him to kill for her, to die for her.

Hell, he was lost.

Lowering his face to hers, he kissed her soft mouth and pulled her closer against him. She responded with an eagerness that made his body go hard. She was more than what he desired, more than he'd expected, or ever deserved. He wanted her, every part of her, and he couldn't wait any longer.

He deepened their kiss and groaned against her mouth. She replied with equal fervor, running her palms over the coarse hair along his jaw.

How was it that she forgave him so easily? He didn't care. His heart leaped, his blood boiled.

He drew her down on the bed and they tore at each other's clothes. His plaid and trews flew across the room, followed by his boots, until he lay naked against her. He pulled her gown up farther until they had to separate their lips to lift the dress over her head, then he lowered his mouth to hers again, heady with want for her. Temperance continued to weep, but now, as he kissed away her tears, she smiled and whispered the words that captured his heart and claimed it for all time.

"I love you, Cailean. I forgive you."

# Chapter Twenty-Nine

Temperance gazed up into Cailean's eyes, watching them darken with need, close as he kissed her mouth, her cheek, her ear, his sweet breath stirring tendrils of her hair.

Her tears had finally purged her of the terrible sorrow of losing her father. She felt as if she were dreaming the most wonderful dream. She wasn't angry with Cailean any longer. Oh, how could she be? After his declaration to her, she understood him a little better. He loved her. He'd suffered over his actions, so much that he hadn't been able to tell her. Aye, it was he who had brought the Black Riders to the hamlet that night, but he hadn't wanted her father's death. He'd tried to stop Cutty but his call to wait had been too late. She understood the monster because she'd become one. The words he'd said to her rang in her ears. He had forgotten who he was after losing Sage and Alison. He'd let darkness and fear take over. She understood. She had let hatred and rage consume her. She'd wanted to kill. She'd wanted revenge, vowing it over her father's grave.

But Cailean had saved her. If she'd known the truth earlier, she never would have let him help her smile again. She would have become that same cold beast.

He'd saved her, just as she had saved him.

But she refused to think on it now. Instead she thought only of his body, hard and lean atop hers, his warm flesh trembling beneath her fingers as she ran them over his corded arms.

His kisses fell on her throat while his broad hands sculpted her shape, learning her, knowing her in a way so intimate each touch became a declaration of possession, a love shared freely. He lifted his head and gazed down at her, lost in contemplation.

She slipped her fingers through the soft strands of hair falling over his forehead, her fingertips lingering on his strong, bristled jaw, his perfectly dimpled chin.

The need in his eyes thrilled her and frightened her at the same time. He traced the contours of her face and paused, as if what they were about to do overwhelmed him as much as it did her.

"I love ye, Temperance," he whispered on a ragged breath. He sounded frightened of his own emotions, as if he'd never expected to feel them again.

She understood his fear and what it was costing him to feel his passions again. They both needed healing, and they could attain it only from each other.

She loved him despite it all. She'd never stopped loving him. She needed to tell him. "I love you, Cailean. I love you."

With delicate mastery that ignited tiny fires below her navel, he kissed her lower lip, then dipped his tongue into her mouth, tasting her, possessing her in a way no man ever had before.

She could feel every rock-hard inch of him and something

so deeply primitive washed over her, she hardly recognized herself.

She wanted to give herself to him. She'd never felt anything like the power of it before. She loved the dominant strength that pinned her. She wanted him inside her, filling her.

With boldness born of pure desire, she lifted her legs and wrapped them around his thighs.

His slow, seductive smile nearly caused her to come undone.

Clutching him close, she rubbed her body against his and then startled at the feel of his heavy cock at her moist entrance.

He stared into her eyes. "What would I ever do withoot ye in m' life, m' beloved? I would die fer ye, kill fer ye."

Her heart answered as she arched her back and offered herself to him.

Watching her ecstasy with smoky, hooded eyes, he entered her gently, knowing she was a flower yet to fully bloom. His lips were gentle at first, his tongue stroking, teasing the inside of her mouth. His teeth traced the delicate curve of her chin, then down to her neck, and lower still, where he stopped to nibble before feverishly finding her breasts. He kissed and suckled her and made her writhe beneath him. He slid his hands under her, cupping her buttocks tightly, pushing her up closer to take her more deeply. He withdrew slowly, then sank inside her again and again, each time deeper than the one before.

She wasn't prepared for the pain of being torn in two by his substantial arousal. She pressed her palm to his chest to stop him, though she wanted more, ached for more.

He slowed and lifted her hand to kiss her fingers.

Poised above her, he shared her breath and consumed her

in his loving embrace. He moved slowly, patiently, and when she cried out, he whispered how much he loved her again and again, stroking her face with the backs of his fingers.

His touch and his words made her quiver in his arms and fueled her desire.

Soon she forgot the pain and relaxed in his strong embrace, feeling safe, knowing he would never hurt her again or allow anyone else to do so.

She watched him, staring deep into his eyes with each slow, scintillating thrust of his body.

"Ye brought me back to life, m' love," he told her quietly, his voice thick with emotion.

She smiled, her gaze never leaving his as they moved to nature's rhythm, becoming one pulsing body.

He pushed harder, sinking deeper, like the waves of a tumultuous sea rocking her back and forth, until she shuddered and clung to him.

How could she have ever thought she hated him? Why, he meant more to her than her own life. Her breath came harder as her pleasure increased. Her muscles convulsed around him, each one's heart quickening at the sight of the other coming undone.

She could hear his breath, hard and shallow, as though he were giving her everything he had, everything he was. And then he threw his marvelous head back and shut his eyes tightly as he found release inside her. He came down and gasped into her neck and Temperance smiled, closing her eyes at the power he had given her to please him.

In the flickering candlelight, he promised they weren't done.

In the aftermath they lay wrapped in each other's arms. Temperance listened to his breath, his heart beating against his chest, his soft, deep voice telling her how she made him feel.

"I didna think ye would ever fergive me," he told her, his warm breath close to her mouth.

"I didn't think so either," she admitted, looking into his fathomless blue-gray eyes. "My trust in you was shattered."

She traced her finger over the downward sweep of his thick dark lashes when he looked away.

She smiled, loving him all the more because of how he seemed to melt at the sight of her. "I didn't know how you felt. That you loved me and that you were suffering because you hurt me."

He closed his eyes as if her words pained him. "M' love seemed insignificant compared to what I'd done," he said softly, opening his eyes to gaze at her again.

"So tell me," she said softly, tracing her fingertips over his chest. "Would you truly give up your life for me?"

He ran his hands down her back, over her bare buttocks, wedging her closer. "Aye, Tem, I would."

"I don't want you to," she whispered, kissing his face. "I want to spend my nights in your arms and wake up to your smile each morning. I want..."

"Aye?" he asked, running his hand down her thigh.

His touch tickled and she buried her face in his neck and giggled.

"What else do ye want, lass?"

"I want to live a life filled with passion and laughter with you."

He dipped his mouth to her throat and began kissing her there. She could feel his renewed desire against her, huge and ready, and she gave herself over to it.

He spread her with his deft fingers and stroked her tight bud until she writhed and cried out his name.

That touch, so primal, so intoxicating, quaked her to her soul.

He moved her to lie flat on her back and then bent his body to her, kissing a scorching path over the peaks of her erect nipples, pausing there to lick and suck her until she grasped fistfuls of his hair and gasped.

He didn't stop but continued, lower. He kissed her sensitive skin and then slowly, sensually licked and scraped his teeth against her until she bucked beneath him. She dug her fingernails into his shoulders and arched her back. Oh, what was he doing to her that she would spread herself wide beneath him?

His kisses grew more passionate as he laved his tongue over her most intimate place. She tried to wiggle away, embarrassed that she took such pleasure in such a scandalous touch. He held her still with his big, capable hands and drew her into his warm mouth. His hunger burned her until she felt wholly consumed in flames. He drank from her, nibbled an excruciating path over her again and again. It didn't take much more for her to find release at the tip of his titillating tongue.

She lay spent and shaking beside him. "Cailean," she asked quietly while he slid up beside her once again, "do other men and women practice such intimacy?"

He shrugged. "So I've been told by m' brother. Before he fell in love with his bride, he was known for practicin' much and with many lasses."

"And now?"

"Now," he told her, kissing a soft tendril of her hair. "Now he practices only with her."

"Mayhap," she said shyly, "we can practice more."

He grinned, sparking her belly with a thousand embers. "We can practice as often as ye'd like."

She nodded and then laughed at the sound of her belly rumbling. "First I'd like something to eat. I'm spoiled by yours and Gram's cooking. The food here is bland."

He rose up, leaving her cold from his absence. "I'll go fetch some fruit. The cook here cannot spoil that."

She smiled and watched him dress, loving his tight belly and muscular arms and legs.

Planting another kiss on her forehead, he promised to return to her soon and left the room.

Cailean didn't make it to the kitchen before Dougal and Erik abducted him. They held him still with the edges of their daggers pressed close to his throat while the lord appeared before him, his dark eyes hard and merciless.

"What the hell is goin' on?" Cailean demanded. Had they seen him coming from Temperance's room?

"Cutty is dead. He was poisoned," Edward told him. "And I am assured that it was by your hand. Tell me it isn't true and you will have your freedom."

Cailean closed his eyes. Temperance had indeed poisoned him then.

"Aye," he said, opening his eyes to look Edward Murdoch straight in the eye. "'Tis true."

# Chapter Thirty

Temperance didn't realize she had fallen asleep until the pounding on her door woke her up later that day.

"A moment, please!" she called out, scrambling out of bed and hurrying to dress.

The knocking came again, this time followed by Patrick's impatient voice. "Temp, hurry!"

Immediately her heartbeat quickened and she ran to the door to open it. When she saw Patrick's pale expression she knew something was terribly wrong. Where was Cailean? Why hadn't he returned to her?

"What is it?" she demanded. "Where is Cailean?"

"In the dungeon." Patrick rushed into her room and shut the door. "He was taken prisoner fer the death of Cutty Ross."

"What?" All color drained from her face. No! She'd poisoned her father's killer in the great hall. She'd put enough nightshade into his cup to see the task done by nightfall. How did they know he'd been poisoned? She'd hoped he'd simply die in his sleep.

"No, Patrick, this can't be! 'Twas I who poisoned him! I must go to the lord and tell him the truth!"

She tried to push past him, but Patrick's arm holding her back was strong.

"Ye canna do that, lass."

"But I must! I won't have Cailean pay for my crime!"

"I spoke to Cailean already. That's why I'm here. He has forbidden ye to confess."

"What?" she practically shrieked at him. "I don't care what he's forbidden! I won't let him—"

"Temperance, hear me," Patrick commanded, taking her by the shoulders. "The lord is fond of Cailean and will spare him. But ye . . ." He paused and shook his head at her, telling her what he didn't want to say. He said it anyway. "If ye confess, he'll deduce that ye likely poisoned his son as well and ye'll be hanged, mayhap Gram with ye. Ye must keep silent."

Tears formed above the rims of her eyes. "Oh, Patrick, I cannot. What will be done to Cailean? Will he be released, then?"

She knew the answer before Patrick lowered his gaze from hers.

"He's confessed, lass—"

No! She backed away when he released her and fell back against the nearest wall, shaking her head. "Why? Why would he—"

"To save ye," he answered quietly. "Mayhap even to save the people of Linavar. Edward might no' believe ye were alone in this." He continued even as her tears fell freely. "Cailean is willin' to . . . he's to be whipped tomorrow at midday."

Whipped? Dear God, no! Oh, what had she done? She was the monster now and Cailean was going to pay for it! "Nay, Patrick," she cried. "I cannot let him do this for me. I will tell Murdoch that I acted alone. I will tell him—"

"Ye'll tell him nothin', lass." His green eyes fixed on her, stilling her movements to flee past him and go to the lord. "Cailean would never fergive me, and I wouldna fergive m'self. He'll take the lashes and live, and then we'll all get the hell oot of here, as I've wanted from the beginnin'."

She suddenly felt as if her body existed only to contain the rawness of her sobs. But she couldn't fall apart. She had to do something to stop this.

"I want to see him."

He shook his head. "'Tis too dangerous."

"Patrick." She pulled herself together as much as she could and glared at him with the last shred of strength she possessed. "Find a way for me to see him or I'm going to the lord."

His hesitation lasted only a moment before he nodded. "Come with me." He snatched her hand and led her out of the room.

They hurried through the corridors, avoiding curious eyes, and headed down the stairs, deeper and deeper into Lyon's Ridge's dank halls until they came to the dimly lit lower cavern.

One man stood guard before the wrought iron gate separating them from Cailean's cell. He looked intimidating enough, with a wide chest, thick arms crossed over it, and an enormous sword dangling at his side.

"I'm here to see the prisoner," Patrick told him, stepping closer.

The guard looked him over with dark, narrowed eyes and shook his head. "Lord Murdoch gave me instructions not to let you see him again."

The guard was tall, but dressed in his Highland plaid, the hem dangling around his muscular calves and an even bigger claymore swinging from his side, Patrick was a daunting force. "I dinna care what yer lord said. Not only will I see m' cousin, but ye'll leave yer post while I do or ye'll die where ye stand."

The face-off lasted only a few moments. The guard saw something in Patrick's normally friendly expression that demanded obedience. Temperance suspected it was the same thing most people saw in MacGregors and that that was why they were outlawed. He gave in, unlocked the heavy gated door, and walked away, disappearing down the dark corridor.

The instant they were alone, Patrick ushered her into the cell with her beloved.

Cailean stood illuminated by a single blazing torch, his wrists shackled to the wall behind him. He pulled on them when he saw her, wanting to go to her.

"Cailean!" she cried, rushing to him. When she reached him, she threw her arms around his neck and kissed his face. "Oh, Cailean, I'm so sorry! Have you been hurt?"

"Nae, m' love, nae. No one has hurt me." He couldn't reach his arms around her but he smiled.

Oh, he smiled! It made Temperance want to scream.

"Patrick told me what happened." She turned to Cailean's cousin and found him waiting outside the gate.

"Tem, look at me," Cailean whispered, and she obeyed. "Ye must leave. If Murdoch discovers—"

"Nay! I cannot let you do this!"

"Ye willna stop me, lass. D'ye hear? Murdoch is fond of me. He willna do more than punish me, but if he suspects ye...I willna take the chance."

"This is all my fault!" She ran her palms over his cheeks, then hugged him again. Oh, what had she done? "I never meant for you to—"

"I know, m' love." The torchlight reflected in his eyes as

he gazed at her as if nothing mattered in the world but her. "But now ye must go. Get Gram and go with Patrick. Leave Lyon's Ridge tonight and—"

"Nay! Nay, I cannot leave without you! I won't!"

"Ye must do as I say," he insisted, whispering into her neck when she clung to him again. "Please, I canna go on in this world without ye. Dinna sentence me to that."

She finally nodded, stepping away from him. She heard him call for Patrick to come take her away.

But it was too late.

They heard footfalls and turned to see Edward Murdoch and two of his men approaching. Temperance stood in front of Cailean, blocking him from his accuser. She saw Patrick cast her a look of defeat before he was hit over the head with something and crumpled to the floor.

No! She went to Cailean's fallen cousin and shook him while tears filled her eyes. This was her fault! She wanted to tell the lord, but what if Cailean and Patrick were correct? What if they tried to hurt Gram?

Cailean shouted and fought against his chains to no avail. "If Patrick is dead—"

The lord swished his hand before his face as if swatting away a fly. "He's not dead. Fortunately for him, he's well liked, and John Gunns didn't deal a lethal blow. Did you, John?"

"No, lord," Gunns confirmed. "He already stirs. He has a thick skull."

"There, you see?" Murdoch said. His gaze turned to Temperance next as she straightened to her feet again. "Step away from him, Miss Menzie."

She shook her head. "Nay!" She was done living her life in fear of these men. They had taken much from her, from Gram, and from Linavar. She wouldn't cower to the Murdochs ever again. "Cutty killed my father."

Behind her she heard Cailean mutter a tight oath, but she straightened her shoulders and continued. "At your son's command."

The lord nodded and offered her a regretful look. "I am truly sorry for his actions. Your father was a good man, Miss Menzie. But I cannot let the men think I won't protect them—even from a lass bent on revenge." He cast her a woeful look. "I suspected 'twas you who poisoned Cutty. If Cailean wanted him dead, he would have killed him with his sword. Poison is a woman's weapon."

"Murdoch, nae." Cailean fought his restraints behind her. "Ye're wrong. 'Twas I who poisoned him."

But the lord shook his head. "You take the blame because you love her. You've put me in a very tight spot, Grant. The men know you confessed. They are angry enough with me for calling off the fight you had agreed to and letting you take my son to the lists without retribution. They expect you to be punished for this. If I tell them the truth, they will turn their anger on her. I do you a favor by not telling them, because I like you."

"Then have me flogged before them," Cailean insisted. "But let me take her away when 'tis over."

"And let her go unpunished? Nay, I have decided that she will remain here and help aid good relations with the people of Linavar by marrying my son."

"I will not wed your son!" Temperance said boldly, defiantly. "He killed my father!"

The lord ignored her and turned away to leave. "Take her away," he ordered his men.

"Don't touch me!" Her command was issued with such venom that Brodie Garrow, who had reached for her, paused.

He looked over her shoulder at Cailean instead.

"Put yer hand to her," Cailean growled with murderous intent, "and I'll dismember ye the instant I'm free."

No one touched her and she turned to Cailean with a whole new strength in her eyes.

She would see him again. She'd kill Duncan and watch him fall at the priest's feet. But she wouldn't marry him. Even if it would bring her father back, she wouldn't.

"M' lord," she heard Cailean call to Murdoch before she was escorted away. "Wait, I wish to have a word with ye alone."

Later that night Temperance sat on her bed with Gram, who held her while she wept. Tomorrow twenty lashes would be delivered by the Black Rider Brodie Garrow in the sight of any who wanted to watch, excluding Temperance and Gram. They were forbidden to witness the punishment and had instead been put away in their room with two guards stationed outside the door.

"'Tis my fault, Gram. I poisoned that Black Rider. I cannot let Cailean take the blame for something he didn't do. I wasn't there to save my father. Perhaps if I hadn't stayed behind with Will—" William. "Och, dear God, Gram..." Her hands shook and her heart drummed like thunder as the obvious truth became clear. "William shot Patrick."

"So Marion believes."

"He did it, Gram, and Father knew." She remembered William's telling her that he had spoken to her father that day. "I think William told him what he'd done. I think Father took the blame rather than see the man he'd loved as a son killed. 'Twas why his last words to me were to ask for my forgiveness."

Gram was quiet for a while. When she finally spoke, her voice was gentle and laced with admiration. "My Seth was the best of men."

"Aye, and William let him die," Temperance retorted angrily.

"Nay, dove. William wasn't there to stop it, and I don't think Seth would have wanted him to. Ye mustn't be angry with him fer not telling ye the truth." She held up her hand to stop Temperance from saying anything more. "'Tis time to get on with life and not harbor ill will toward others. 'Twill only darken yer own heart."

Temperance nodded, remembering Cailean's words to her about himself and how anger had almost destroyed him.

*Nothing I touched was dark enough. I left all that I loved and allowed a monster to take hold of me.*

She would try not to let it happen to her, but she also wouldn't accept a future commanded by Edward Murdoch.

"I will not marry Duncan," Temperance swore to her grandmother. "I will not!"

"Nay, dove, ye will not," Gram promised. "Cailean will recover from his wounds and ye will take him as yer husband. 'Twill be a marvelous celebration with many delicious dishes and singing and dancing." Her voice and her words finally comforted Temperance.

Until the morning came.

# Chapter Thirty-One

*C*ailean was led outside late the next afternoon stripped of his weapons, his plaid wrapped around his bare waist and ropes around his wrists. He looked up, sensing, feeling her gaze piercing the bitter cold and warming him. He saw her in her window and decided that if his plan didn't work and he perished today, he wanted her to be the last glorious thing he saw.

She held up her hand to him and he smiled, wondering how he could be so fortunate as to have won her heart. She'd forgiven him and lifted his burden. She'd lit his way out of the deepest canyons of his heart. He wasn't about to lose her to Duncan...or even to death.

He wouldn't die. He bent his head to Brodie Garrow on his left. He'd kill if he had to, but he wouldn't die.

Patrick, on his right, remained silent as they walked toward the whipping post.

Cailean looked around at the faces in the crowd that had gathered in the courtyard beside the lists. He took note of every Black Rider and, most important, Edward Murdoch.

In just a moment his cousin would...

Patrick pulled a dagger from his belt and whacked it between Cailean's hands, freeing him with one powerful slice.

For a split second Cailean looked down, expecting to see at least one of his fingers on the ground.

They were all intact. His hands were free and he turned them on Garrow while Patrick pushed up his sleeves and readied his fists and his dagger against the rest.

A combination of right punches to the nose and jaw and Garrow went down like a tree. Cailean snatched up his sword and ran toward the others. He swung Garrow's blade against another six mercenaries, taking blows and delivering harder ones of his own while working his way toward Edward.

He reached the lord in three long strides, drawing his sword as he went. The blade sliced through a snowflake while the rest began to fall around him, and came to a stop at the edge of Murdoch's throat. Everything came to a halt. It seemed even the sun's descent paused in the sky. MacRae and Gunns stood fixed in their spots, shocked at Cailean's skill and boldness in launching such an attack on their lord.

"Settle yer hounds!" Cailean commanded, moving to stand behind the lord and pushing the blade closer to Murdoch's neck. "Or I'll toss yer head to them before I kill them and ride oot of here with m' woman."

"You've got bollocks, lad," the lord said with the slightest of smiles before he shouted for his men to end their fighting.

"How do you think you can escape?" Garrow called out. "You cannot fight against so many men."

"I'm a Grant. Ye'd be stunned to know how many I can fight against. Now back away while I lead yer lord into the castle."

Patrick held up the pistol he'd lifted from Fergus MacRae while they'd fought and cocked it at the crowd, keeping them at bay while Cailean led the lord away.

"He's coming to get us!" Temperance uttered, and backed away from the window. She met Gram's eye and smiled. "Did you see him, Gram?" She felt like spinning around in a circle. He'd been glorious to watch, taking on each man who had come against him with pulsing muscles and powerful strikes. If she'd thought he'd never tire, she would have watched him all day.

And Patrick! Why, he'd struck down hardened mercenaries with a single punch. He had a dagger but he hadn't used any other weapon until he raised a pistol in the air.

"We must get Marion!" Temperance clasped Gram's shoulders and then ran to the door.

She backed away when she heard voices on the other side. They were coming! He was coming! Her pulse raced and her legs felt like heated mud beneath her skirts.

She counted her breaths while she waited for the door to open. When it did and Cailean appeared before her, she couldn't stop herself from leaping into his arms. He'd escaped his punishment. She wanted to weep with joy.

Lifting her face from the crook of his neck, she smiled at Patrick, who was leading the lord into the room with his pistol pointed at the back of Murdoch's head.

"Were ye harmed?"

She slipped her gaze to Cailean's concerned one. "Nay, my love," she breathed, cupping his face in her palms then kissing the worry off his mouth.

But it was his tight, tender embrace that soothed her own roiling heart. Here, in his arms, was where she found her passion, her safety, that kind of love that came around only once or twice in a lifetime.

Gram cleared her throat and Temperance withdrew with a slight blush and stepped away when he let her go.

" 'Tis good to see ye again, and unharmed." Gram tossed him a fetching smile.

Her grandmother liked Cailean. It drew a small sigh of relief from Temperance's lips. Gram tolerated many people, but she liked only a few.

" 'Tis good to see ye as well, Gram." His wide, open smile beguiled the socks right off her grandmother. It remained with a hint of mischief darkening his gaze as he turned to Lord Murdoch.

They shared no words, but Temperance was suddenly convinced that what she had witnessed outside her window had not been what it looked like.

"Patrick," Cailean said, turning to him. "Go fetch Marion and set her to her task. We're leavin' soon."

*Soon?* Temperance thought. *Why not right now?* And why did Patrick shove his pistol into his belt and let Lord Murdoch roam about freely?

"We will gather in the solar," the lord said. "Who are your friends here, Grant?"

Temperance looked at Murdoch taking a seat on the edge of her bed. "Who will gather in the solar?" she asked him, then glanced at Cailean. "What's going on?"

Cailean thought about it for a moment and then answered Lord Murdoch's question. "Gunns, mayhap, though we havena shared many words. Why do ye want any of the men with us?"

Murdoch stared at him, then blinked and shook his head. "You've been at Lyon's Ridge for almost five months and you have one friend, *you think*, among twenty?"

"I didna come here to make friends," Cailean answered with a shrug.

Temperance turned to cast Gram a questioning look. When even she had no answers, Temperance took Cailean's hand.

"What's going on?" she asked again. She watched his cool-colored eyes dip to hers and go as soft as his smile.

"I'm takin' ye home, lass, and Lord Murdoch is helpin' us leave withoot eighteen men on our arses."

Which home did he mean? The question came to her suddenly and with a numbing truth. He loved his home in Skye and she loved hers in Linavar. Where would he choose to live? It didn't matter now! He was getting her and Gram out of Lyon's Ridge.

"Why would he help us?" she asked.

"He's helpin' his men more than he's helpin' us," Cailean told her. "I sent a missive to m' brother Malcolm before I returned here, tellin' him what I had done and what I had become—and how ye saved me. I told him of Duncan Murdoch. If I know him well, and I do, he should be in Linavar by mornin'. If we're no' there when he arrives, William will tell him where I am and what has happened. He'll come here and things will get ugly. We dinna want that."

"No, we don't," Murdoch agreed. "But I aid you for her sake. And—I admit I also have a selfish motive that I will discuss with you later."

Cailean appeared surprised—but not by the fact that they'd tricked everyone into believing their lord had been taken hostage. He and Lord Murdoch had devised this hoax in advance. How far in advance?

"My main reason for aiding you"—Murdoch looked at her—"is that your father was my friend for many years, Miss Menzie. He spoke of you often during our dealings. He loved Linavar, but you were always his main concern."

Temperance had never stopped to consider that her father might have spoken of her to the lord.

"He was always fair and honest with me." He glanced up at Cailean standing at her side and then returned his eyes to her. "And Cailean has those same traits. He'd make a good leader."

"Linavar already has a new leader," Cailean told him. "A man chosen and trained fer the duty by yer friend."

The lord smiled at her. "You see?" He shook his head and waved his hand across his face. "About your father, he wanted you to be happy and helping you do that is the last thing I can do for him."

Gram clasped her hands together in front of her face and smiled at the ceiling.

"Up until I last spoke to him," Murdoch told her, "he thought you would be happy with William Deware. Grant has filled me in on why that isn't so. Either way, I could not let you, in good faith to your father, marry Duncan. He's a ruthless, uncaring lad, who will eventually need to be dealt with. And if anyone can keep the hamlet safe in the meantime, 'tis Cailean—whether he leads Linavar or not."

"M' lord," Cailean said. "I told ye, I willna be here."

Temperance turned to fasten Gram with a worried look. So it was home to Camlochlin, then. Whether he took her with him or not, she would have to give up something.

The door swung open again and Patrick stood on the other side.

"Are we spendin' the night, or are we goin' through with this?" Patrick asked them when they didn't move instantly.

They left the room with Murdoch returned to his place beside Patrick's pistol, and made their way to the lord's solar, picking up John Gunns on the way.

When they came upon any group of Black Riders, Murdoch ordered his men to stand down.

When they reached their destination, Murdoch ordered

Gunns to bolt the door while he took a seat in his chair beside the roaring hearth. The rest of them followed his example, finding chairs and upholstered settees to sit upon, save for Cailean, who remained standing.

He turned to the man at the door. "Gunns, ye're wonderin' what's happenin'."

"The thought crossed my mind."

"Lord Murdoch was never in any danger," Cailean told him, and headed for the jug on one of the tables. "He's allowin' us to leave."

"Everything you saw outside between us was staged," the lord added, motioning to Cailean to pour him a drink.

Temperance watched the scene feeling as if she were in a dream. It was odd seeing Cailean so comfortable in the lord's solar. Had they shared many conversations here?

"The fighting—?" Gunns asked.

"Nae." Patrick gave his sore shoulder a rub. "That was real."

"Neither of you lack bollocks," Murdoch said, accepting the cup Cailean offered him. "Which is why I ask you both not to leave Glen Lyon but to swear fealty to me."

Patrick smiled and untied his mantle. "I've already sworn fealty to m' cousin, Rob MacGregor, laird of the Mac-Gregors of Skye."

"And you, Grant?" Murdoch settled his gaze on Cailean. "I have high aspirations for you. Stay here and serve me and—"

"Ye mean serve yer murderous son," Cailean cut him off. "I must decline."

"Duncan won't be here forever. Just stay for a year, lad," Murdoch pressed on. "My son will not rest if you take her away. I fear in his agitated state he will bring his fury down on Linavar. Men like Brodie Garrow and Tavish Innes, and many others, would help Duncan overtake the castle if and when he chooses to. I need men I can depend on."

Cailean held up his hand, stopping Murdoch from going any further.

Temperance's heart boomed through her ears. She wanted Cailean to stay for another year. But what if he refused? Would she leave with him? Leave her home? Her family and friends?

"I'll serve ye, lord," he said, pouring himself a drink and taking Duncan's seat beside the lord.

"Cailean, nae," Patrick groaned, and buried his face in his hand.

"I'll stay fer a year."

"As a Black Rider?" Murdoch asked with a hopeful grin.

Cailean turned to Temperance in a seat close to his and waited for her answer.

She wasn't surprised the lord wanted Cailean to stay. Her Highlander was not only skilled, he was clever as well. But could she love a Black Rider? Would she prefer him to remain a mercenary for another year rather than leave her home?

"Aye, as a Black Rider," he agreed when she nodded.

# Chapter Thirty-Two

*I* have a few conditions," Cailean continued from his seat in the lord's private solar.

Murdoch arched his brows. "Oh? And what are they?"

"I will no' reside here but in Linavar with the villagers. I'll work with them and yer harvest willna fail."

"Granted," Murdoch said.

Cailean smiled, and for the first time in almost a year, he was hopeful for a happily ever after. He wanted to get Temperance alone and ask her if she wanted to spend her life with him. He'd promise to keep her safe from every harm. He'd write to her every night. He'd cook her favorite meals, and when the days were done, he'd take her to his bed and satisfy her every desire.

"We want every lass under Maeve's direction to be given a choice to stay here or leave. Marion is informin' them as we speak. Any lass who wants to leave is to meet us ootside."

"But the men—" Murdoch tried to protest.

"Ye'll give the lasses up fer a full crop," Cailean told him. "What does the trade usually bring ye in value? The men," he said, without waiting for an answer, "have told me that ye added the entire western wing yerself. That's costly labor. Ye're dressed well. Ye eat well. Giving up lasses who dinna wish to be here isna too much to ask."

Murdoch slapped his thigh and leered at Cailean. "Do you fear anything? Offending me might be a good beginning. This wasn't part of the arrangement we agreed to when you were chained in my cellar."

"Neither was me stayin' here as a Black Rider," Cailean countered smoothly.

The lord glowered at him. "Very well. Is that all?"

"Nae, we want—" He stopped and addressed Gram. "What percentage of profit does he make fer our crop?"

"Sixty-three percent," Gram informed him.

Cailean's gaze darkened on the lord. "I think forty-eight is fair."

Edward sat up and flung his cup into the hearth.

"I thought negotiations were left to the leader of Linavar."

"He isna here," Cailean answered, unfazed. "Do we strike our deal?"

Murdoch grumbled in his chair and then finally nodded. "Aye, we have a deal."

"Ye've thought this through." Patrick's accusation wasn't spoken in anger. "What aboot Camlochlin?"

Cailean caught Temperance's anxious gaze and remembered Gram's words.

*The soil's in her blood, inherited from her father. She won't be happy with rocks.*

What if Temperance wouldn't be happy on Skye? What if she refused to go with him?

"Camlochlin will still be there a year from now," he said. He would discuss it further with Temperance later. "This is what's best fer all. And no one dies."

"Except Duncan," John Gunns pointed out. "Killing a man in a fight is one thing…"

Cailean turned to him and wondered if it had been wise to include him. Would he rush back to Duncan and tell him all?

"Oh, I'm not going to kill him," Murdoch assured Gunns. "He's my son, for hell's sake. I was thinking of sending him to my brother in Wales."

"And what is my role in all of this?" Gunns asked.

Aye, Cailean had wondered that as well. Why had Murdoch wanted to know who his friends were?

"You don't have a role," Murdoch told him, "you have a side to choose. Mine or my son's. I need men I can trust. I trust a man who calls Grant a friend, though I had hoped there would be more than one of you."

Gunns cast a knowing glance in Cailean's direction. When Cailean grinned at him in response, the merc stepped back, as if it was the last thing he'd expected to see.

Murdoch continued. "Are there any others among the men who would go against Duncan with me?"

Gunns thought about it and then shook his head. "They are all cut from the same cloth."

Murdoch's face grew red when he heard the news. He swigged his wine, then swiped his hand across his mouth. "Very well, then. 'Tis just you, Gunns. Fight at Grant's side for me. Or hang in the morning."

"What the hell kind of choice is that?" Cailean turned to him with a dark frown.

Murdoch blinked up at him. "What? He knows too much! He'll tell Duncan my—"

Gunns cut him off. "I'll tell him nothing. I've been waiting for the day I could make this choice."

"Then ye're with us?" Cailean asked, and clapped him on the back when the mercenary nodded.

"So." Gunns clasped his hands, eager to get on with it. "What do we do now?"

"We wait," Cailean told him.

"Until when?"

"Until the men all fall asleep, of course. There's no reason to fight if we dinna have to, aye?"

Aye, he was a different man. He hadn't become his old self again. He'd been reborn into someone better, wiser.

And it was because of her. He gazed at Temperance. All traces of joylessness were gone from him. He basked in the sight of her, hopeful and newly awakened to everything around him, mostly her.

"Are ye truly goin' to go through with this?" Patrick asked while they waited, interrupting his thoughts.

"We're gettin' them oot, aye?"

"Aye," Patrick answered. "But ye didna answer m' question. Are ye stayin' here?"

"Aye. I'm stayin' with her fer now. Go home, Cousin. Tell our kin I miss them and I will return in a year when things have settled here."

"Aye, I wish to leave this dreary place," Patrick told him. "The urge for fighting runs smoothly through m' blood, but I'd much rather live and bask in m' fertile youth, in bed and on the field. I'll help rescue any who need rescuin', and then I'm gettin' the hell out of here, with or withoot ye."

Cailean nodded and then went to kneel before Temperance's chair. He'd noticed her squirming a time or two and glancing at Gram as if there was something pressing on her mind. He had an idea what it might be.

"M' love," he said softly. "I can tell Murdoch that I've changed m' mind. I know how ye feel aboot Black Riders—"

She shook her head, taking the hand he offered. "I can

live with it, as long as he never asks you to fight anyone from Linavar."

"I would refuse if he did."

She smiled at him but then dipped her gaze to their clasped hands. "I don't want you to leave Linavar."

Did she think he would leave without her? He began to tell her that his life meant nothing without her in it, but he heard Murdoch tell Gunns to go check on the men, get them drunk if he had to, but do something to get them to sleep faster so this business could be under way.

Cailean slipped his finger under her chin and brought her attention back to him. He wanted to look into her eyes when he told her. He wanted her to see what she'd given him.

"Temperance, I love ye, lass. There are no' enough words to tell ye how much, so I'm goin' to show ye, every day, wherever ye want."

Hell, but her eyes, filled with tears, sparkled like stars guiding him home. Normally her tears wouldn't please him. But they fell onto a smile before she swiped them away.

"Would ye wed a Black Rider?" If she said no, he would tell Murdoch the deal was off.

"I would wed you," she said, lightening his heart.

She turned then to her grandmother in the chair beside hers, who was obviously listening, and said, "I would wed him."

Patrick, listening on the other side of him, clapped him on the back. "Ye're fortunate to have found her, Cousin."

"I know." He turned, still holding her hand, and smiled, catching her gaze as she rose to hug Gram. He was fortunate indeed. Would he have been so merciful toward someone who had killed his father? But it was who she had been from the beginning, resilient and filled with life, even on her darkest days. The flame that sparked his heart back to life.

For one selfish moment, he wanted to deny Gram her embrace and pull Temperance in for a kiss. Just a kiss.

Soon she would be his wife, and he would have more than that.

But still, he wanted a kiss.

On the other side of the door, which no one had bothered to check after John Gunns had left it slightly ajar, Duncan Murdoch balled his hands into fists, cursed his father to hell, and then limped back to his room to get his pistol.

An hour later they stepped around a few bodies belonging to Lord Murdoch's mercenaries. John Gunns had informed them that, growing impatient waiting for them to go to sleep on their own, he'd slipped a bit of valerian, found in the kitchen, into the wine and offered it up. It hadn't taken long after that.

They entered the courtyard and saddled their horses against the bracing wind. Gram would ride across Patrick's lap, and Temperance with Cailean. John Gunns was with them after Lord Murdoch had insisted he ride back to Linavar with them.

"Where are the gels?" Naturally it was Patrick who brought them up.

They arrived with Marion as he spoke. Temperance smiled when she saw Esmé and Beth.

"Is that all?" Cailean called out to Marion as Lord Murdoch helped her into her saddle.

"The others wish to stay," she informed him, helping Esmé up behind her.

Patrick hauled Beth up with one hand and set her down behind him. In front of him, Gram patted Beth's hand when the gel wrapped it around Patrick's waist.

Temperance watched the freed girls and vowed to God and to herself that she would love Cailean and care for him until her dying day, and likely after that. Her father would have been happy to have him love his daughter.

Cailean was willing to give up his home for her. She could be his wife and stay in Linavar! But she knew she wouldn't. She wouldn't ask him to make such a sacrifice for her.

Oh, what kind of love was this that made her want to do anything to make him happy? Wasn't that what he was doing for her? She had wanted this kind of love, but she'd had no idea how powerful it was. It made her want to surrender every part of herself to him, knowing he would cherish all of it.

"That went flawlessly."

Temperance looked down at Lord Murdoch, and so did Cailean.

"Thanks to ye, m' lord," her betrothed said, smiling.

Goodness, but Temperance could get used to seeing that smile every moment of her life.

"Go," Lord Murdoch said, "and keep your brother away from here. You did say he would be here by morning, aye?"

"If he thinks I'm in danger, aye. If he left the same day, he should be here by mornin'. Dinna fret, lord. I'll tell him we are friends."

Lord Murdoch raised his brows and then smiled. "Two friends. You're getting better."

# ✠

# *Chapter Thirty-Three*

*E*dward Murdoch watched the last of Grant's party disappear down the Munro. *Flawless*, he thought, and smiled in the cold darkness. He'd saved Grant from the whip, Seth Menzie's daughter from Duncan, and possibly himself from a revolt with his son leading the charge. There was only one more small detail to be seen to before he rendered Duncan powerless and then sent him off.

When there was nothing left to see, he pulled his cloak tighter around him and left the courtyard.

He stepped inside his castle and looked around. He shook his head at the bodies littering the hall. How easy it had been for Gunns to deceive them. How easy it would be for him.

"Wake up!" he shouted, and began kicking the bodies. "I said wake up! Every one of you, and then go wake your brothers!"

"What's going on?" Erik MacCormack stood and rubbed his head.

"I'll tell you what's going on! While you all slept, Grant

and MacGregor left! I should withhold your pay this month. All of you!"

"We'll go get them and bring them back, my lord!" another scoundrel called out. Some of his comrades agreed. There was still time to catch them.

"You expect me to send a bunch of useless men who cannot hold their cups to fight those two?" Murdoch argued. "Why, they nearly took you all down in the setting sun. You wouldn't know what hit you in the darkness. You'll go in the morning. At least then you'll have a chance."

They agreed and drifted back to their beds, gathering the rest of their number as they went.

Murdoch smiled.

Flawless.

"Father?"

Edward Murdoch's heart sank as he turned to his son.

"May I have a word?" Duncan held his wrapped ribs with one hand and lifted a pistol with the other.

The shot rang out, bringing the Black Riders running back.

Riding back to the hamlet, Cailean thought about how smoothly everything had gone. He'd been surprised yesterday in his cell when he'd asked Murdoch to let him escape and the lord had agreed. He knew Murdoch was fond of him, and Seth Menzie was a good-enough reason for him to want to aid Temperance, but Cailean was certain his brother's pending arrival had had a lot to do with Murdoch's unquestioning compliance.

No one with any sense in his head was unafraid of the MacGregors and Grants. Murdoch wasn't a fool.

They had gotten out of Lyon's Ridge and no blood had been shed. His uncle Tristan would have been proud of him.

He was on his way home with Temperance.

Home. Linavar would be Cailean's home for the next year, and all the years left to him after that if that's what she wanted. He'd see his kin again. Mayhap he'd take Temp and Gram home to Camlochlin next Christmas. But for now the hamlet was his home.

"You're smiling again."

He looked at the beautiful woman riding in his saddle in front of him. "Thanks to ye, lass," he told her. "Ye've given back to me everything my heart has ever desired."

"I hope to give you even more," Temperance told him, with a provocative smile curling her mouth and sending heat through his body. "I cannot wait to be alone with you," she continued boldly.

He couldn't wait either, but they'd need a priest. He was sure Gram wouldn't approve of their sharing a room unless he made Temperance his wife, which he planned on doing as soon as they returned.

They reached the hamlet and found it lit with torches at every door.

When Gram almost leaped out of Patrick's lap, the Highlander laughed and caught her bony body. "If ye're rushin' off to yer kitchen, I could use a cup of ginger mead."

"I'll make a batch for all of us," Gram called happily, taking off the moment her boots hit the ground.

"I'd like to see William," Marion said, turning to go.

"Stay here, lass," Patrick told her while he helped Beth dismount. "Gunns and I will fetch him."

"What a thoughtful man." Beth swooned over him. "He doesn't want Marion to walk alone in the dark."

Patrick smiled, then winked at Cailean, who knew better. His cousin had promised Deware that they would discuss the shooting. Cailean hoped William arrived with all his teeth.

"And bring my cat, please!" Temperance called out to Patrick, then smiled at Cailean as he helped her out of the saddle. "She'll want to see you and never want to let you out of her sight again."

When her feet touched the ground, he pulled her into his arms. "And what of her mistress?"

She laughed softly against his ear and pulled a slight groan from the back of his throat.

"I will see that her wish is granted."

He bent his lips to hers, hungry for her, eager to begin sharing his life—his bed—with her.

"Gels!" Gram called from inside. "Come inside before ye all catch yer death."

Cailean sank his forehead to Temperance's as Marion, Beth, and Esmé hurried inside. "'Tis goin' to be difficult to keep m' hands off ye until tomorrow."

"What's tomorrow?" she teased, wiggling out of his embrace.

"When we find the priest."

"Are you that anxious for me?"

He hauled her back and pressed her against him, letting her feel the evidence of his desire. "Aye, lass, I am. But I shall be patient fer one more day."

She ran the back of her hand across his jaw, tempting him beyond reason to kiss her. But she stepped away from him before he did. "'Twill be more days than that," she said over her shoulder. "Gram is planning for a spring wedding."

"Spring?" he nearly choked out. Och, hell, there was no way he was going to wait until spring! He'd think of something. He had to or he'd go mad.

He followed her into the house, enjoying the view before him.

He stepped inside still reeling at the thought of months

before he could take Temperance as his own. He breathed in the sweet, familiar scents of Christmas evergreen and laurel and let them soothe him. He liked this house. He had from the moment he'd stepped out of Temperance's brightly lit room and into its warm halls.

He made his way to the dining hall now and lit the hearth fire. He lit more candles and turned to look around the spacious hall. Warmth filled every hollow, seeping from dark-red wood, a child's paintings hung on the walls, and cheerful boughs of pine and holly throughout.

The home built by Seth Menzie was intimate and inviting, designed by a leader who loved the people he led.

Cailean wished he could have met him.

He would have thanked him for raising a daughter like Temperance—a name, Cailean decided, that fit her perfectly. Cailean would tell him he was sorry his freedom had cost Seth his life.

But now he had a future to see to. He realized the villagers hadn't had their Christmas Day feast.

He smiled as a new plan hatched in his mind.

The sound of Temperance's laughter interrupted his thoughts. He would endeavor to do whatever he could to make her happy every day. He followed the joyous sound to the kitchen and came up behind her, wrapping one arm around her waist.

"How is it possible," he lifted his face from Temperance's hair and asked her and Gram, "that ye've only been in here fer a few moments and it already smells so good?"

Gram smiled, standing at the oven, and stirred whatever she was brewing so late at night. "A cook must keep some of her secrets, ye know."

He smiled back, finding that opening his heart to love Temperance had opened it to love others as well. He let go of

Temperance before he found it any harder to do so, and made his way to the oven and Gram.

"There are only a few days left before Hogmanay."

"I know," Gram replied, stirring.

"We should do something grand the day before, while 'tis still Christmas."

She looked up from her broth and narrowed her eye on him. "How grand?"

He smiled at her. According to Temperance, Gram loved feasts. "As grand as ye like."

He knew he had her then. He also knew it was devious to dangle the joys of cooking for the village over a small old woman's head, but he didn't want to wait until spring!

"And what day is it we're celebrating?" she asked, forgetting her pot. "It should have a name."

"Call it Yer Dove's Weddin' Day."

His grin faded when hers did. "Ye want to marry her in two days?"

"Nae." He shook his head. "I want to marry her tomorrow."

"Ye're daft if ye think I can prepare fer that kind of celebration by tomorrow!"

Damn it, now what was he to do? Just looking at Temperance made him want to take her to bed.

"Two days, and not an hour sooner!"

Had she said two days? Cailean's smile returned. It was better than spring.

He bent to kiss her head. "Thank ye, Gram." But she wasn't listening. He could almost hear her conjuring recipes in her head.

They all heard the front door open. Cailean was the first to move. When he stepped into the hall, he sheathed his sword and smiled at Patrick, or rather at the mound of fur under his cousin's arm.

Deware followed closely behind, along with a half-dozen others who'd heard of their return and had come to welcome them home.

Hell, Cailean thought as he bent to catch a running cat in his arms, who would have ever thought that such a fickle creature would choose him to love?

Just as Sage had. He smiled and kissed the cat's head.

William hurried by him and Cailean returned to the kitchen to watch the reunion.

"Marion." When he saw her, her name left William's throat as if it pained him. Cailean knew William would never have loved Temperance the way he did Marion. "My love." He hurried to her and gathered her into his tight embrace. "I searched for you. Oh, to have you back!" After a long kiss and another moment or two spent staring into her eyes, Will turned his attention to Cailean and Patrick.

"I can never repay you." He released Marion long enough to pull Cailean into his embrace. "You brought her back to me when I feared she was lost for good."

"Aye." Cailean knew how good it felt to get your life back.

Deware turned to Temperance. "There is something I need to tell you."

"That 'twas you who shot Patrick?" she asked, letting her dear friend off tenderly. "Or that my father knew it?"

"Both." He opened his mouth to say more, but her loving smile stopped him.

"The past is over, aye? Let us make our own future now."

Cailean couldn't help but bask in the sight of her. This was the woman he loved. Their futures would be bright.

But he still hadn't kissed her.

�֎

# Chapter Thirty-Four

*W*hy don't Will and Marion say their vows with us?"
Temperance turned to Gram. "Can we?"

Gram nodded with a sigh. "I don't see why not. Save that
'twill rob us of another day's feast."

Cailean was still contemplating what they had said when
someone screamed outside. What made it all the more chilling was that they screamed Cailean's name.

"Everyone stay where ye are!" he shouted, and turned
immediately to Patrick. His cousin was already on his way
to the front door to bolt it.

He peered out the window and called back to Cailean,
"Black Riders!"

Damn it, he'd thought Gunns had sedated them. How had
they arrived here so fast? His blood boiled. If they wanted a
fight, he was going to give them one. He called out orders to
everyone present. Patrick and Gunns would stay with him
while Deware remained inside, keeping the others safe.

"You don't seem all that fazed by this." Temperance
came to him while he packed two pistols in his boots.

"What's there to be fazed aboot? I'm goin' to end this tonight."

"I'm not going to let them take anyone else," she vowed, picking her bow and arrow up off the floor, where they'd landed the day Duncan had taken her. "Even if I die, I'll go knowing I did all I could this time."

"Ye willna die," he promised while he plucked her weapon out of her hand.

Temperance tugged on his sleeve, her face a mask of dread. "Well, since you're so certain I won't, will you? Die?"

His smile was wide, boyish, with a hint of badness deep inside. "Nae, I willna die either. Have faith in me."

She nodded. "I do."

"Cailean!" Duncan Murdoch shouted from outside. "Show your face or I will burn this village to the ground!"

Temperance lifted her hands to her mouth. "Don't let him do it, Cailean!"

"No harm will come to Linavar," he vowed while she threw her arms around him and whispered that she loved him.

Invigorated by her affection, he left the house and stepped into the shadows against the wall cast by the torches lighting the outer yard. From his position he could see the riders well enough, though they couldn't see him. He curled his mouth at Fergus MacRae and the other Black Riders surrounding Duncan.

He turned when he heard Patrick leaving the house, oaths spilling from his cousin's lips. Their eyes met and Cailean nodded. They didn't want to kill these men they'd eaten and drunk with for four months, but Cailean would. If that's what it took to protect the woman he was going to marry in two days, and Gram and her guests huddled in the house, terrified.

"Step out of the darkness and let me see you," Duncan demanded from his saddle. Cailean, Patrick, and Gunns held their positions.

"Duncan, where's yer faither?" Cailean called to him.

The lord's son held his pistol aloft, trying to get a better look. "Getting cold on his castle floor. Where do you think he'd be after he betrayed me and gave everything that was mine to you?"

Cailean swore under his breath and felt his resolve falter for a moment. Edward Murdoch was dead? No, he hoped it wasn't so. Now more than ever, Duncan had to be stopped.

He stopped Gunns from cocking his pistol. Not yet.

"Ye're goin' to protect him after he killed yer lord?" he called out to the men.

"Edward Murdoch's dead. We fight for the man with the key to the coffers."

Patrick had been correct. Cailean wasn't one of them. He could never be.

"Put the pistol doun, Duncan," he warned, "before ye tempt me to kill ye."

Duncan laughed and pointed the barrel in the direction of Cailean's voice. "One of us will die tonight, Grant, and it won't be me."

Cailean didn't wait to discover if Duncan would fire or not. He reached for his dagger and with lightning speed hurled the blade at Duncan's hand.

The blade struck the pistol and propelled it into the darkness. Duncan shouted and the men around him drew their weapons.

Cailean had leaped forward, ready to drag Fergus Mac-Rae from his saddle, when another horse came barreling out of the darkness and almost crushed him underfoot.

Cailean looked up at the rider and was about to reach for

the pistol in his boot when he saw a familiar face smiling down at him.

"D'ye mind gettin' oot of the way, Cailean? I didna ride all the way here to kill m' brother."

Malcolm. His brother had arrived, and with others, Cailean realized as their horses whipped past him. And they were early!

Cailean's face broke into a grin as something flew by his ear.

Draped in his fur cloak, Malcolm Grant groaned like the dangerous wounded bear he resembled, and clutched the arrow jutting from his calf.

Cailean turned to see who had fired the arrow and found Temperance by the door, bow in hand.

What the hell was she doing out here? Cailean's heart resounded in his ears, reminding him that although he'd felt invincible earlier, they were all human.

*Get back inside. Get back inside!* He wanted to shout it at her, but Duncan hadn't seen her yet and Cailean didn't want to give away her position.

"Cailean!" Malcolm shouted to his brother as Cailean took off running. "Tell me that isna the lass ye penned me aboot."

He had to get to her and bring her back inside, but the MacCormack brothers blocking his path thought differently.

There was only one way to get by them. Cailean reached for his boot. "Let's get this over with quickly, then."

No one in Glen Lyon would deny that Duncan Murdoch was a fool. But to come at Malcolm Grant, Earl of Huntley and lord of Ravenglade, with a knife, was indeed unwise.

Wheeling on his dark stallion, Malcolm struck the first Black Rider who got in his way, knocking him out of the saddle and onto the ground. The rest all attacked at once, bringing Patrick and Gunns, as well as Edmund MacGregor and Darach Grant, into the fray.

"Stop this before ye force me to hurt ye." Patrick tried to reason with Fergus MacRae as the others fought around him.

"Apologies, Pat." Fergus drew his sword. "Duncan has a month's wage on your head, and I could use it." He swung, missed, and cried out when Patrick caught his arm, twisted it back, and broke it.

Darach Grant, a bard when he wasn't hacking into his enemies, swiped the blade of his huge claymore across the belly of Tavish Innes and then chased down another man before Tavish's body hit the ground.

Edmund MacGregor swung a set of claymores, one in each hand, and made quick work of three more men.

Temperance tried to aim her next arrow at Erik or Dougal MacCormack when they rushed at Cailean. They knocked him down while he was reaching for his boot. Almost instantly the three of them became a writhing mass on the ground. She couldn't shoot without risking hitting Cailean.

Erik landed a punch to Cailean's jaw from a vertical position. Cailean answered with an elbow to his throat. He turned on Dougal next and hammered his fist into his nose. While the brothers were down, Cailean rolled to his feet and swiped at his bloody mouth.

He was about to turn for Temperance when someone else struck him between his shoulder blades with something hard, bringing him to one knee. He heard another arrow whistle through the air and then heard his attacker fall to the ground behind him.

Temperance.

Hell.

Erik had recovered and swung his damn fist again.

Cailean took a hit to the jaw, shook his head, and then seized Erik by the throat. Dougal tried to help his brother but received a crushing fist to his nose for his effort. Cailean had to hurry. He reached for his pistol and pointed the barrel in Erik's face.

"I dinna want to kill ye." He cocked the flint in case he had to.

"Grant! Don't!" Dougal pleaded with him. "We won't fight you. Don't do it."

Temperance's scream shattered the warrior's heart and brought him to his feet, forgetting the MacCormacks. Duncan stood behind Temperance with one arm snaked about her waist, the other hand in her hair.

"Duncan, let her go!" Cailean aimed his pistol. His finger was steady against the trigger.

"Go ahead and shoot, Grant. This fever ravages me."

"'Tis the poison I fed you," Temperance told him. "Payment for my father."

Duncan pulled her back by her hair. "You bitch."

Cailean fired and the bullet found its mark. Duncan's knees hit the ground first.

Temperance followed, the glint of a hilt in her back.

For an earth-quaking moment, Cailean couldn't move.

*Not her! Nae, not her!*

He dropped his pistol and took off running.

Not her. He couldn't lose her. When he reached her, he fell to his knees to gather her in his arms.

"Temperance, m' love, please. Please, dinna go." Not her. Not like this.

Men were beginning to crowd around him but he didn't see who they were. He didn't hear what they were saying. He'd gone back somewhere in time and was holding Sage, Alison while they died. But this, this was so much worse.

This was unbearable. There was too much rage in him for him to contain it any longer. William came close and moved to take her, but then backed away when Cailean threatened to kill him.

"Cailean." It was Patrick, his voice stern but ridden with sorrow. "Let Gram have a look at her. I think she still breathes. Come, Cousin, let her have a look."

He didn't want to let her go. Not ever. But if she still lived… Did he dare to hope?

He looked up at Gram's eye saturated in sorrow and moonlight, and let her examine her granddaughter.

"Please, Gram," he begged her, begged God. "Please help her. She canna die."

Gram smiled at him and it was the most glorious thing he'd ever seen. "'Tis not a serious wound, son. Look, she opens her eyes to see ye."

He looked down, though it was hard to see through the tears that blurred his vision.

"Tem…," he choked out. Unable to say anything else, he pulled her back against his chest.

"You aren't getting rid of me that easily, Cailean Grant," she told him a bit weakly. "We have a wedding day feast to attend."

He smiled at her, then laughed. She was here. She was his. They had a future together.

A future he trusted.

Finally.

# Chapter Thirty-Five

*E*arly the next morning, Temperance looked up from her bed at the faces staring down at her. Goodness, one was more handsome than the others. Of course no one came close to Cailean, although presently he looked like hell.

She remembered how he'd fought the Black Riders. She'd never seen a man fight with such determination to win. He was a warrior indeed. And yet now he held her cat tenderly to his chest.

She reached for his free hand, which rested beside her, and squeezed. He leaned down and kissed her head.

"Never frighten me again like that, Tem." His tone was light, but she knew what the thought of losing her had done to him.

"That's the first time I've ever heard Cailean say he was afraid."

She cut her gaze to a man with lovely green eyes filled with more mischief than TamLin on the prowl for a mouse.

"That's what lasses do to ye, Cailean. I sometimes wonder if 'tis worth all the worry," he went on, despite the smack to the back of his head given by the man she'd shot with her arrow.

"Darach," the bigger one with blood soaking his calf said. "When we get home, I'll ask Janet if she thinks ye're worth the worry ye cause her."

"Certainly not as much as ye cause Emma."

Temperance glanced at Cailean and smiled when he rolled his eyes heavenward. This was his brother, the lord of Ravenglade, and his cousin, whom he'd told her about.

They'd come to Linavar, and just in time. She wasn't sure if Cailean, in his current condition, and Patrick, who liked the mercenaries too much to kill them, could have triumphed over all.

"He knew you would come," Temperance told Cailean's brother. She smiled. It was difficult not to. Goodness, but he was handsome, with beguiling dimples and cerulean eyes eclipsed by bolts of chestnut hair shot through with sheets of gold. "Thank you," she told him softly as he limped forward. "And forgive me for shooting you."

He smiled and shrugged his wide shoulders. "'Tis nothin'."

"He'd likely say the same if ye shot him in the heart."

Darach winked at her when Malcolm tossed him a dark look.

The door opened and another Highlander entered the room with Gram. This one was as glorious to behold as the rest, with soft golden curls falling over his gentle gaze.

"I've just come from Lyon's Ridge. The lord of Glen Lyon lives. He was shot, it seems by a shaky hand. He will recover. Patrick and one named John Gunns are with him."

He found Temperance staring at him and came to the edge of the bed. "Edmund MacGregor at your service, lady."

She blushed, then stopped when she met Cailean's gaze.

"Glen Lyon should have a new lord." Malcolm poked his brother in the shoulder. "Take the castle. I'll speak to the queen aboot it and gain her support."

"You know the queen?" Temperance asked him, wide-eyed.

"She's kin on our grandmother's side," Darach told her.

Temperance's head was spinning. They . . . Cailean was kin to the queen? She closed her eyes to take it all in.

"All right, everyone oot!" Cailean rose from the edge of the bed and pushed them toward the door. "We can discuss the future of Lyon's Ridge later."

When they were alone, he returned to the bed and lay in it beside her. He released TamLin and gathered Temperance carefully in his arms. She could feel his heart racing. She swore she could hear his blood rushing through his veins. She knew what it must have been like for him to hold her in his arms and fear she was dying there. Her heart broke for him.

"Gram says the dagger just broke through my skin. I'm well, my love," she said, trying to make him feel better.

It didn't help. He looked more pained than the night he'd first opened his eyes in her bed. "Temperance, fergive me fer lettin' harm come to ye last night."

"Don't you dare say that, Cailean Grant!" She pinched him on the arm hard enough to widen his stare. "Not when I was just remembering how completely valiant you looked to me. Your determination to win was fierce. You did not fight for my sake alone, but for the entire village. You are courageous and heroic in my eyes, a breed of man all your own, and you are mine."

He dipped his head to kiss her but she pushed him away. If he started kissing her she would never let him stop. "Go. Go see to Lord Murdoch. I am fine. And will rest, I promise. I have plans to discuss with Gram and Marion about the celebration tomorrow." She sat up to show him she was well, then pushed him away when he tried to kiss her again.

"Cailean?" she called to him before he left. "Will you do it? Will you take on the role of lord of Glen Lyon?"

He shook his head. "Nae, love. I dinna want to be lord. I want to learn how to farm."

Cailean woke up the next day facedown in a tangle of sheets and with a cat purring close to his face. Opening his eyes had been a mistake. The bright sunlight pouring forth from four open shutters in Temperance's room stung. He remembered when the sun had been the thing he hated about her room. He'd wanted only darkness but she'd set him in the light, like a wilting plant.

"Good morn, Temperance!" someone called from outside. "Are you ready for your vows today?"

"I am eager to make them, Anne."

Cailean pushed himself up on his palms and turned to smile at her while she continued to fold fresh bed linens beside the window.

"How is yer back, love? Are ye up to foldin'?"

She smiled at him, but he knew she was trying her best to be patient. Since Duncan Murdoch had put his blade to her back Cailean had doted on her, mayhap overdoing it a bit.

"If I'm up to marrying you today then I can fold fresh bedsheets."

She was going to marry him today. She'd agreed to be bound to him in the sight of God and their kin. How could one man be so fortunate?

"How is Mr. Grant?" Anne Gilbert called out.

Temperance looked at him and glanced heavenward while he sat up and swung his legs, encased in his knee-length trews, over the bed.

"He just came awake and already he's trying my patience, Anne."

He looked up at her and filled the room with his laughter. "She's fortunate I'm not carryin' her around, Miss Gilbert," he called toward the window. "She's stubborn, ye know."

A few of Miss Gilbert's companions giggled something that made Temperance scowl.

"What's wrong?" he asked from the bed, where he stretched his sinewy arms and long tight torso.

Her gaze spread over him, warm, but still a bit brooding. "I think they've been watching you for a while now."

He looked at the stream of sunlight bathing the bed from the second window from the right. She could have been correct. He slipped his gaze to hers and smiled. "Are ye jealous?"

She opened her mouth to protest but then with a sigh gave up trying to fold the linen. "I don't want to begin the day of our vows by being untruthful. You are pleasing to the eye, my love. If women stare at you overlong, I understand what they see. But I don't like them seeing you in bed all stretched out like a languid prince. That is a sight for my eyes alone."

He leaned forward and snatched the linen from her hands. "So what ye're tryin' to say is, ye're jealous." He pulled her between his thighs and smiled.

"And you're not?" she asked, trying to save her dignity.

"Who do I have to be jealous of? No one stares at ye but me. No if they want to keep their eyes."

She laughed, setting his nerve endings aflame, then let out a little moan when he kissed her neck. He was a man of many passions. Was her joy becoming one of them?

"We'll have to nail the shutters closed tonight after we're wed."

"I'll build a second floor," he promised, muffled in her hair.

She withdrew long enough to look into his eyes. "You can do that?"

"Of course. Remember I told ye m' faither is a builder. M' brother Malcolm is better at it than I, but I know what I'm doin'."

"More rooms would be ideal after we have our bairns."

"Oh?" He pulled her back and dipped his head to nibble on her ear. "How many are we havin'?"

"I would like five or six. I don't want them to be lonely growing up."

"They'll never be lonely," he promised. "M' kin will visit often."

"So I am to wed a Black Rider."

"Ye canna back out now. Gram cooked enough food to last a fortnight."

"I suppose I must if she cooked so much food." She bit her lip, dragging his gaze there. "You don't have to look like one, do you?"

He smiled, a bit confused by her query, and shook his head.

"Good, because I've been sharpening my father's straight razor this morning."

His smile deepened. He closed his hands more securely on her hips. "That sounds rather ominous."

She ran the backs of her hands over his cheeks and jaw. "Your face is too beautiful to keep covered by this bristle. Your eyes too expressive to hide behind long hair."

What did he care about hair? He would get rid of it all if it pleased her.

When she broke away, he reached out to catch her again. She laughed and hurried to the small table at the other end of the room, where she prepared a small array of blades, soap, a bowl of water, and some rags. He watched her backside, not that he could see much of it beneath all the layers of her skirts. The soft bump swaying ever so slightly while she worked was enough to make his muscles taut.

When she turned on her heel, a large tray in her hands, dark hair tumbling around her intimate smile, he pushed his palms into the bed, ready to leap to his feet and meet her halfway.

The bedroom door opened, keeping him still where he sat.

"Breakfast is ready."

"Gram." Temperance greeted her grandmother with a much brighter smile. "I was just about to give him a shave."

Gram looked them both over with a half-stern leer, and then nodded. "All right, then. I'll leave ye to it." She left, closing the door behind her, without another word.

"Don't question it." Temperance laughed at his stunned disbelief when he stood to take the tray from her hands. "I've told her," she said while he set the tray on the bed, "that you are the one my father *and* my mother would be happy I chose. As for Gram"—she pressed her hands to his chest when he faced her again, and then pushed him back down on his arse—"she has been waiting for you longer than I have. She's happy for me and will not disturb us again."

He didn't know what to say after such grand compliments. He lowered his gaze and felt his face grow a shade warmer. He didn't like them. Compliments. Her mother. How was one supposed to respond to that?

Except by asking her why they'd waited two days if Gram was so happy for them. He ached for her and it was driving him mad.

She stepped between his thighs and leaned over to reach for the rag and the bowl.

He closed his eyes and dipped his nose to inhale the scent

of lemons and ginger. He wanted to eat her alive. He opened them again in time to look down the back of her and let his gaze settle on her rump. He didn't reach for her the way his mind was shouting for him to do, but kept his hands on the bed. The sooner they got the cutting done with, the sooner they could wed, and she would be his.

She straightened and handed him the bowl. She took the rag next and wrapped it around his neck, answering his warm smile so close to her own.

How long would a kiss take?

She dipped her hand in the bowl and wet his face with the water warmed by the sun, scattering his intimate thoughts of her.

She did it again. This time she let her fingers linger over the line of his jaw, and her eyes fasten on his until he could count the different shades of blue he saw. There were four.

Finally she blinked. "Hand me the soap, please."

He leaned back and took the soap and the straight razor too.

She took the blade and held it up to the sunlight.

"Are you afraid that I might cut out your heart?"

"That is entirely unnecessary," he told her, lifting his chin to her and exposing his neck. "Ye need only ask fer m' life, and it is yers."

Her eyes lit on him and then she smiled. "I don't want your life, only your heart."

"That is yers already."

She swept her finger over his lips and then teased him some more with the briefest of kisses.

"Trust me, aye?"

"I do, lass."

She held the sharpened blade to his cheek, in front of his ear. She used one hand to pull his skin taut and the other to begin shaving. Using very little pressure, she brought it down at an angle that cut his bristles and not his flesh. She knew what she was doing.

He watched her coming close, her gaze intent on what she was doing. He studied the thickness of her lashes, the soft contours of her face. He relished in her sweet breath falling on his face. It took every ounce of strength he possessed not to close his arms around her and pull her in. But after the second pass over his chin, he lost the battle.

He touched her slowly. After all, it was his face under the blade. She closed her eyes at the feel of his fingers along her thigh.

When she opened them again, he was smiling at her. "Lass, ye're goin' to kill me yet."

He took the opportunity when she removed the blade to rinse it, and closed his hands over her buttocks and squeezed. He gritted his teeth and shook his head at himself because he couldn't keep his hands off her.

"Almost done."

Her whisper sounded like a purr in his ear.

Almost done, and then what? His hair, bath, breakfast, dressing... all while the priest waited.

He sat quiet, but his heart betrayed him while she went over him a third time, changing direction for a closer cut.

"Temperance, ye're so bonny, m' love," he told her softly while she moved in close to his chin. "I canna look at ye withoot wantin' ye, every part of ye. I canna wait to have ye in m' arms, m' bed, to be inside ye."

She stopped shaving and gazed into his eyes. "I feel the same way."

"Then let me cut m' own hair and meet ye in the hall in an hour. Aye?"

# Chapter Thirty-Six

The double ceremony went quite smoothly, though it took a bit longer than Cailean would have liked. His marriage to Temperance and Will's to Marion ushered in Hogmanay. With its many traditions, the night was going to be a long one. He knew he couldn't take his wife to bed while the celebration was going on, so he drank and sang songs and built bonfires in the fields with the villagers. They dined on venison pie, shortbread, clootie dumplings, and beef and haggis with whisky sauce, and washed it all down with Athole brose, a drink made from oats, honey, water, and whisky.

Sometime before midnight the villagers returned to their homes, but only to await their firstfoots. Traditionally it boded good fortune if a tall, dark man was the first to cross one's threshold after midnight.

Cailean gathered gifts of black buns, salt, and coal and set out with Temperance to knock on doors and share goodwill as the midnight bells were rung throughout the hamlet.

Later the villagers lit torches and marched back to the house singing old songs for a prosperous new year.

Temperance followed him back to the dining hall, where he stopped at the entrance, beneath the drying mistletoe, and finally kissed her.

Ah, he could live and die just like this, kissing her, tasting her warm, sweet breath, feeling her glorious curves against him.

Hell. He'd had enough celebrating. He didn't care if the merriment was over.

He wanted to celebrate his wife.

He carried her to the bed, their bed, and laid her down tenderly in it. He ignored the sounds of the last of the holiday revelers in the hall. Doors and shutters were shut and bolted. They were alone. Finally.

"How is it," Cailean asked, looking astounded for a moment before he ran his hand through his shortened locks, "that a simple man like me has wed the bravest, loveliest maiden in the kingdom?"

"My darling," she said, letting her gaze take in every taut inch of him, "there is nothing simple about you." Her breaths were short and shallow while he unwrapped his plaid above her. His shirt came away next, billowing to the floor.

"It leads me to consider"—her breath stole over his bare shoulder when he bent his body to hers—"how such a magnificent man is now my husband."

He kissed her throat and tugged at the neckline of the glorious cornflower-blue woolen gown Gram had given her. Another thing to love about him was that he didn't know how to get a woman out of her dress.

"The laces are in the back," she offered.

He flipped her over on her belly, surprising and thrilling

her at the same time. She giggled at the thousands of emotions he awakened within her and lay still while he pulled on her laces, setting her free from the confines of her gown.

He worked slowly, taking his time to press a kiss to every inch of her spine that he exposed. She shuddered at his tongue, at his teeth scraping tenderly over her. She imagined how his succulent lips looked pursing to devour her.

When he reached the rise of her rump, he traced his fingers over her lower back.

"Ye are sublime," he told her in a low throaty whisper that set her nerve endings on fire. "The sight of ye enraptures me."

He tugged on another string and she gasped as he pulled her gown free and tossed it in a pile on the floor.

"The sound of ye gives m' heart flight, and it soars because of ye, Temperance." He moved over her and leaned down to run his tongue over her quivering flesh. "The taste of ye, so sweetly wanton, drives me mad with desire."

When he kissed her derriere, she held her breath. Was he going to kiss her *there* again? She hoped so. It was wicked and it made her feel wild.

But not yet.

She liked what he was doing to her right now. His palms were rough with calluses that felt particularly delightful while he ran a hand over her rump. When he moved to straddle her, she turned to look at him over her shoulder.

His smile, so decadently masculine and hungry for her, made her turn beneath him, wet and ready for whatever he meant to do.

He drew his lower lip between his teeth and then dipped his mouth to the tight buds of her nipples.

She arched her back and raked her fingers through his hair. Her body ached for him. Her muscles tightened and then relaxed again as she cupped his face and drew his kisses to her mouth. He moved his plump mouth over hers, consuming her. She opened to his plunging tongue as fire coursed through her.

"I love ye," he whispered, leaving her mouth and blazing a hot trail down her throat, over her breasts, her quivering belly, to her hips.

She closed her eyes, her body awash with sensations, knowing what was coming and aching for it.

When his mouth found her, instinct made her try to close her legs. He held them apart and licked her, once, twice, and again, until she spread herself wider, inviting him to take his fill.

And he did.

He sucked softly, teasing her with his tongue, his teeth, his firm, unyielding lips. She writhed beneath him, groaning, wanting something more. She wanted him, full and heavy, atop her, inside her.

She couldn't tell him. It was bad enough that she was panting. Her boldness mortified her, so she wiggled away from him.

He rose up on his knees again and gazed down at her with worry marring his brow. "What is it?"

"Take off your breeches." Heavens, was that her own voice she heard leaving her lips? "I mean..."

His slight frown curled upward into a slow, sensual smile that promised wicked pleasures. He knelt over her, untying the strings at his abdomen, his eyes hungry and hooded on her. She watched just as hungrily while he pushed his breeches down over his hips. Her eyes widened and her heart accelerated when his cock sprang free, large and ready.

He kicked off his breeches and they fell in a heap beside the bed. He leaned down to kiss her, his body heavy and dominant on hers. He stroked her face with the backs of his fingers, smoothed her hair off her cheek, all while looking deep into her eyes, as if she were the most precious thing he'd ever possessed.

She loved the feel of him, the breadth of him. She bit her lip, a bit nervous, for she remembered the pain, but also the pleasure, of his thrusts.

He spoke to her while he spread her legs. He told her of his heart and how she had set it to beating again. He entered her slowly, methodically, careful with her.

She felt drunk with desire, hesitant, but then eager again, and lifted her legs to fit them snugly around his waist.

The room began to move as his thrusts deepened. He withdrew almost to the tip and sank deep inside her again and again, to the rhythm of her heart. She was careful not to claw at his back, and ran her palms down his bandaged sides to his buttocks. She held him, powerful and taut in her hands, while he moved. Pain and pleasure ebbed and flowed, tossing her to and fro. She pushed back, grinding her hips, pulling moans from his throat—and from her own.

"Cailean . . . I . . . I—"

Before she could finish, he sank to the bed and rolled her over. She looked down, surprised and delighted, at his smiling face and the feel of him under her.

She felt powerful and in control over every movement. Uncertain as to what she should do at first, she wriggled atop him. He groaned, lifting his head to kiss her breasts. With him still deep inside her, she began a dance that set his body to trembling. She rose up over the length of him and then down again, harder, faster, until the world turned red and orange and burst into flames.

She moved over him as if she were made of liquid, finding all the right angles to take him deepest, to make herself cry out in ecstasy.

When he cupped her bottom and arched to take her more

fully, she almost wept with pleasure. She felt her muscles constricting, felt the rush of pure bliss washing over her. She looked at him and found his gleaming gaze on her, watching her. She forgot her name, but not his, and spoke it on a ragged series of breaths while they moved faster and found release in each other.

Later she lay coiled in his arms, held in his safe embrace. She kissed his chest and pressed her ear to it to hear the music of his uneven breath.

"Cailean?"

"Aye, love?"

"Do you think I'll be a good mother?"

"Ye'll be fearless, lass—exactly what our bairns need to grow strong and face whatever the world throws at them."

"Our bairns," she echoed dreamily. "What an adventure our lives are going to be."

He stared into her eyes as if he meant to pour every bit of himself into her. The guileless quirk of his smile wrapped itself tight around her heart. When he spoke, every word was uttered with meaning, filling her with joy that she had him for another day.

"I intend to fill m' days with ye, lass," he promised on a whisper. "Ye will remain m' first passion, but I warn ye, I have many." He rose up on one elbow over her. "I think I shall write aboot ye. I will begin with yer lips."

He stared at them and she laughed.

After that day laughter often filled the braes around Linavar.

Aye, laughter was what Cailean Grant had been missing in his life all along, that and Temperance in his arms, in his bed, and in his life forever.

And a cat. The hounds of Camlochlin might not have liked TamLin, but Cailean loved her well enough.

Patrick MacGregor's content
to fight his way through Scotland,
spending his earnings on whisky
and women. But when he stumbles
upon a beautiful nymph bathing
in the woods, he's utterly captivated
by her. Could this unrepentant rake
finally be falling in love?

Please see the next page for
a preview of the new book in Paula
Quinn's sinfully sexy MacGregors:
Highland Heirs featuring Patrick
MacGregor!

❖❖❖

# Chapter One

*Y*e're undressing me with yer eyes, rogue."

Patrick MacGregor slanted his mouth into an unrepentant, dimpled grin that made the serving wench's hands tremble and the jug of ale she carried slosh and spill onto the floor. He reached out to capture her wrist in his fingers. She'd been teasing him all night with her swaying hips and veiled come-hither glances. He'd rather get himself a room and sleep for the next two days, but he wasn't one to turn down a willing maiden.

Up for the game, he pulled her into his lap and plucked the jug from her hand without spilling a drop.

"Ye're a wee bit behind, lass," he told her, dipping his mouth to the jug and then her neck. "Ye're already bare in m' arms and I'm aboot to fill m'self with the sweet taste of ye."

She giggled and nestled her rump deeper into his thighs. "I should slap ye fer yer boldness, stranger."

"Aye." He lifted his face from the folds of her hair and flicked his emerald gaze to hers. "Ye should."

He liked the full dip of her lower lip and the promise of pleasure in her bonny blue eyes.

"What are we doing still sitting here, then?" she asked.

Hell, he didn't have to be asked twice. He swigged his ale, wiped his mouth, and called to the tavern owner for a room.

"This isn't a brothel," the taverner blustered beneath his bushy brown mustache. "I run a respectable establishment."

"Good thing." Patrick rose from his chair with the lass in his arm and gave the taverner a pat on the shoulder with his free hand. "I'm certain this lovely lass would cost more coin than I carry."

She lifted herself on the tips of her toes and whispered to Patrick that she had a room abovestairs and he should follow her.

He did, tossing the taverner a wink as he went.

On the way up the stairs, Patrick set his gaze on the wench's well-rounded rump and thought of all the things he'd like to do with it. It didn't startle him when he could think of only two. He'd fought twelve fights today. His muscles still ached with tension. He smiled at her when she turned, catching the direction of his gaze. Mayhap she'd understand if he changed his mind.

When they reached the second landing, she stopped, looped her arm through his, and leaned in close. "I've been thinking about how ye taste as well."

He felt his cock stir to life. He'd been a fool to reconsider. "Lead the way."

Inside her room he watched her run to her moldy-feathered bed and slip off her shoes. Hell, he wanted to sleep on something soft. Sleeping on his plaid in the grass stopped being pleasant after three hours with pebbles in his back. He undraped his plaid, discarded his coat, and pulled his léine over his head, groaning a little as he stretched and then tossed the shirt to the floor.

He heard a little sound escape her lips. He looked at her from beneath the inky sweeps of his lashes and found her gaze fastened to the thick muscles in his arms, his taut, rippling abdomen. He wondered if he could convince her to rub down his sore muscles with some oil.

"Don't ye want to know my name?" she asked, tugging at the laces of her stays. She pulled them loose and her breasts spilled out.

"Nae," he said, giving her a slow half smile while he moved toward her, unbuckling his belt. "'Tis less to ferget."

She giggled and it struck him, as it always had, how most lasses didn't mind his detachment—until after, which was why he tried not to remain in one place too long.

He pulled one leg out of his leather breeches and then stopped to think about what he was doing here.

He wanted sleep. He'd left Camlochlin with enough coin to last long until after he arrived at his uncle Cameron Fergusson's Tarrick Hall. But women and whisky didn't come cheap, and he'd stopped in almost every town for both while he traveled to Craigneil, using up his supply.

To earn coin to eat, drink, and be merry, he'd fought for the past sennight in competitions using his fists, and in tournaments with swords. He fought better than most, with or without a sword, well enough to earn enough tender to eat and sleep in the best inns. Usually he liked to enjoy the delicacy of a lass's sheath tight around his shaft, her arms and legs coiled around him as if his body possessed the solution to all her cares. But it didn't. It sure as hell didn't help him with his. Lately he'd been less inclined to prove it to any of them.

He didn't really want to be here. All his bravado belowstairs had just been his usual play of getting the gel. He was getting a bit tired of always being victorious. Hell, even fighting would soon grow dull if he won every match.

"Lass, I—"

She looked him over like a hungry cat and leaped at him. He laughed, catching her in his arms, and bent his head to brush his mouth over hers. If she wanted him this badly...

The tight little groan he pulled from her made his blood rush to his loins like liquid fire. He hauled her into his embrace, parting his lips and molding his hungry mouth to hers to devour her with leisurely demand.

She pushed him down on the bed and he smiled on the way, liking her boldness and her eagerness for him.

But hell, the bed felt good under him.

A knock came at the door. Patrick ignored it and continued kissing her. As he'd suspected, her lips were soft, yielding to his masterful tongue. Aye, he knew how to kiss a lass. He'd been doing it since he was a lad of thirteen summers, practicing the art almost as often as he practiced fighting.

The knock came again, harder than before. Patrick leaped from the bed and yanked his bare leg back into his breeches.

A kick followed, tearing the meager bolt away. The lass screamed at the giant figure of a man standing in the doorway.

"Unhand her before I rip the head from your shoulders."

Patrick cast the wench a sour glance. The intruder was either her husband or her brother or some other damned guardian she'd failed to mention. He held up his palms to ward the brute off. He didn't want to fight. He wasn't sure if his strength would hold up.

"I'm certain we can—"

The brute didn't care about talking and came at him swinging, giving Patrick no choice but to fight back.

Patrick ducked with ease and struck the first blow, and then the second. He quirked his mouth in a feral smile when he felt the ogre's nose crack against his knuckles. All right, so he fought even better than he kissed.

Shaking off the pain of his broken nose, the man threw another punch, bringing a slight breeze close to Patrick's face as he ducked again.

Coming back up, Patrick delivered a left to the beast's guts and a right hooking strike to the jaw, and ended the combination with another fist to the belly.

Pain seemed only to enrage the brute further.

Patrick took a fist to the jaw that snapped his head back and loosened a tooth.

As he rolled the tip of his tongue over his teeth, Patrick's eyes widened and turned a darker shade of green. This wouldn't do. A broken, slightly crooked nose was one thing. A missing tooth would ruin his smile.

"Let's talk aboot this." He held his hands up again, but his opponent showed no mercy and rammed his fist into Patrick's side.

Hell, he thought as he hunched over trying to catch his breath, the blow might have been a little low.

"Hamish, enough!" the lass cried out.

Paying her no heed, Hamish yanked him up by the collarbone.

Patrick had a dagger in his boot, but why kill a man when it was unnecessary? Instead he took the opportunity to land his left fist in the man's face, followed by his right. Another man would have succumbed to Patrick's onslaught, but not this bastard.

He answered Patrick with an uppercut to the chin that pulled the tips of Patrick's boots off the ground and landed him on his arse.

Momentarily dazed, Patrick shook his head to clear it. Hamish was almost upon him. He rolled away and leaped back to his feet in time to see the lass lift a wooden jug over her head. Patrick grinned. It was just what he needed. He swiped it from her hands and, ignoring her cry of surprise, smashed the jug over Hamish's head.

The ungainly oaf hit the floor with a crash that shook the walls. The lass hurried to him while Patrick watched. He knew the jug had been meant for *his* head. Thankfully, his reflexes were quick. He didn't ask her who the man was or why he'd kicked the door in to get to her. Patrick didn't care. He'd almost had a tooth knocked out and he hadn't earned a shilling for it.

Women were trouble.

He stepped around the wench and her fallen hero and left the room to seek out one of his own, preferably with a clean bed.

The next day he traveled south toward the coastal town of Girvan. At night he drank and pulled laughing wenches into his lap. But what left Patrick with a heart that palpitated was the fact that he didn't partake in the pleasures they offered. A month ago he would have enjoyed a different lass in every village. He would have stumbled with a pounding skull into the light each new morn. What had changed? Normally he wouldn't have given it a second thought. Change was good. It helped one grow. But not this time.

Two villages behind he had tried to fight against his growing disinterest in bonny lasses by taking a lovely tavern wench with long fiery locks spilling around her freckled face to his newly rented room. He'd undressed her and then backed up to soak in the vision of her. Shockingly he'd felt very little, and had decided against bedding her at the last moment. He could no longer blame his sore body for his wilted condition. His wild, wanton ways had pricked his kin, and lately they'd been pricking him too. He didn't know why. He didn't want the kind of life most of his kin had chosen, with a wife, a few bairns, and a dog—or cat.

His lack of interest in marriage was something he'd often had to explain to his kin—his father most recently. He knew what was expected of him, but he liked his life the way it was, with no one to answer to, no one to be responsible for but himself. He didn't want it to change.

At night, alone in the beds he'd paid for, he'd been examining his life more thoroughly. Being an outlawed MacGregor, he didn't fear much. But love, ah, now there was a power he would confess scared the hell out of him. Love sought to change a man . . . and a woman. It snapped at freedom like the jaws of a determined viper. It expected much and demanded even more. If he were to fall in love, he'd have to be prepared to give up not only his heart but his soul as well. He'd seen its terrible power at work, stripping battle-hardened warriors of their convictions and their strength. Two of his cousins, Malcolm and Cailean, had recently given their lives over to love. Were they with him now on this grand adventure? *Nae.* They were concerned with their women and little else. He didn't want to be accountable for someone else's happiness. His own was enough.

But with each new day, the emptiness in his adventures, in his belly, grew like a hunger that wouldn't be satisfied, making him begin to doubt his convictions.

But no more! Today, Patrick promised himself as he set his gaze on a flock of sheep scampering over the rolling hills, things would go back to the way they had been. He'd bed a bonny wench, drink too much whisky, and wake up his old self.

He reached the River Stinchar a short while later, when the afternoon sun formed golden flashes of light on the rippling surface—and on a goddess wetting her toes in the water, her skirts hiked up to her thighs.

Patrick wasn't sure she was a mere lass. Playing in the glistening rivulets, she looked more like a self-indulgent forest fairy lit up by the sun. She didn't wear layers of heavy wool, or even a jacket or arisaid, but a gown of billowing blue linen with threads of silver sewn in around the neck and sleeves. She spun in a circle with joy in the day, her skirts flaring slightly at her hips, the fabric thin enough to expose the silhouette of her long, shapely legs. He watched, forgetting to breathe, as her raven locks fanned out around her, a crown of daisies upon her brow.

Had he happened upon something otherworldly, sent to seduce men to sin with her large, dark, feline eyes and dainty ankles?

He watched her skipping over the water as if it were a veil in the summer breeze. His heart leaped at the sight of her lost in her own reverie, freedom personified.

His sister would have scolded him for spying on the nymph unseen. He almost laughed, giving away his position. She was made of mystery and whimsy, of daisies and darkness. How could he *not* stare at her? A tiny, nagging voice—likely from one of Kate MacGregor's books on knightly behavior—compelled him to make his presence known, but Patrick decided against it. He'd left Camlochlin to escape those notions his kin, his father especially, lived by so steadfastly. The lass stirred his blood and made his muscles tighten. Honor would deny his desire, rebuke it. He didn't want to live a life dictated by commitments and duty. That's why he'd never let himself fall in love.

He never would.

# Fall in Love with Forever Romance

## MERRY CHRISTMAS COWBOY
### By Carolyn Brown

No one tells a cowboy story like *New York Times* bestselling author Carolyn Brown. So grab your hot chocolate and settle in because this Christmas, Santa's wearing a Stetson. Fiona Logan is everything Jud Dawson thought he'd never find. But with wild weather, nosy neighbors, and a new baby in the family, getting her to admit that she's falling in love might just take a Christmas miracle.

### A CHRISTMAS BRIDE
### By Hope Ramsay

*USA Today* bestselling author Hope Ramsay's new contemporary romance series is perfect for fans of Debbie Macomber, Robyn Carr, and Sherryl Woods. Haunted by regrets and grief, widower David Lyndon has a bah-humbug approach to the holidays—until he's shown the spirit of the season by his daughter and her godmother Willow. Paired up to plan a Christmas wedding for friends, David and Willow will discover that the best gift is the promise of a future spent together...

**CHRISTMAS COMES TO MAIN STREET**
**By Olivia Miles**

It's beginning to taste a lot like Christmas...or so Kara Hasting hopes. Her new cookie business is off to a promising start, until a sexy stranger makes her doubt herself. Fans of Jill Shalvis, RaeAnne Thayne, and Susan Mallery will love this sweet holiday read.

## A HIGHLANDER'S CHRISTMAS KISS
### By Paula Quinn

In the tradition of Karen Hawkins and Monica McCarty comes the next in Paula Quinn's sinfully sexy MacGregor family series. Temperance Menzie is starting to fall for the mysterious, wounded highlander she's been nursing back to health. But Cailean Grant has a dark secret, and only a Christmas miracle can keep them together.